NARROW PLACES OF THE HEART AND MIND
(EARTH HEART-MARTIAN MIND)

by Cliff Rhodes

I0654638

Copyright 2007 by Cliff Rhodes
http://www.lulu.com/sciencefiction
email: rhodesdesigns@yahoo.com

Published at lulu.com

ISBN: 978-0-6151-5159-5

For information contact:
Cliff Rhodes
P.O. Box 7095
Meridian, Ms. 39304-7095

This book is dedicated to all those people who think that the future is a long way off, but are surprised when it comes running up to meet them unexpectedly and in their faces. Some will not be so disappointed when they find that it is what they expected. You, who are only awake, think that it is just a dream and for the ones who dream, it is here already. There is only one question left. Is it a nightmare or do you realize it is the future that you so diligently prepared for and already know?

Contents

Chapter 1. **Desert Fight**

The morning breeze was unusually strong for an October morning and there was still a hint of moisture in the air. Thomas was determined to make this day, a day of triumph in his search for the meeting place. Looking for the gathering place of these practitioners of one of the many ancient but still developing arts of defense and cutting edge science was an old challenge. Many had failed miserably or had gotten too close to an evil element that had taken their lives. Thomas was convinced that he would prevail where others had failed. His reckoning had to be better than all the rest, because the fate of the world defense depended on his success in making contact with this elusive science cult. They had separated themselves from the world for their own selfish reasons but now the world depended on their involvement. The affairs of the world had become everybody's business. Time was running out for the blue green planet. Was it a test that God was to place on mankind for his determination of who would be left or was this approaching calamity a byproduct of all the misery that man had invented for others? Man would have to consider more carefully his own position in the world order.

The trees had given way to a rocky outcropping and it was evident that the forward landscape was rocky and barren like the lunar surface of the still remaining moon that refused to give way to the new overpowering sun. Quickly approaching was the heat and intense light of the new day in our solar system with times of increasing solar flares that gave us scorching deserts that were five to ten degrees above normal. This was not yet a global warming; only a single flare-up, but who really knows the future or who could predict with mathematical precision what could happen. Anything could happen in a world that was still changing. A solar system with planets that were semi-star-planet types not yet stable is a present day phenomenon. A world that still had wobbles in its orbit was not a fictitious story. It was the planet under his feet. When would a new mountain range begin its birth into the present landscape before his eyes?

He was looking for a people who had some of the answers to these problems and had derived mathematical solutions to these monumental tasks that lay ahead. Sadly though, they were isolationists and had only recorded their answers and moved on, to some additional perplexity. Thomas was determined to obtain these answers and begin to apply this pure science to the benefit of mankind.

Just ahead he saw the tall shape of an unusual rock outcropping that bore the markings he was looking for, a large circular formation of rock with an obelisk shape protruding upright in the middle. At only a certain time in the year, the sun would come blazing through this hole, identifying the location of a clear passage through the rocks that led to the opening into the mountain. The obelisk dissected a chord within a circle. Only at the precise point where the chord was dissected was there a directing ray of light split, which identified the angle of approach. Thus was formed within the circle, a rectangle, and within it an equilateral triangle and two right triangles and four chords with two and two equal lengths. At these intersecting points were the pathways of approach to the secret opening revealed.

Thomas stood on a small hill just in front of and to the right of the rock obelisk, thinking about how all the others that had been sent never reported back. He thought now, "If I can approach this easily to the key that points the five ways, there must be something wrong. Where had the others failed?"

There was a foul odor in the air, the smell of fear. Some said it could be smelled but Thomas had senses that were now sharpened because he knew there must be traps along the way. No one knew of his connections to any of the agencies, though, because there had never been any association verbally or in any document form either. He didn't even have top secret clearance, but yet they in the agencies and bureaus knew of some figure that had been detected by their computer scan. There had to be another planet out there, metaphorically speaking. When planets are pulled slightly one way or the other out of a regular ellipse, there has to be another force to detract them from their regular orbit around the sun. Thomas was, this predicted other planet that had never been seen but still his gravitational pull was there in all the records. The computers showed only that information was leaving, going to a destination unknown and returning in an irregular loop to the same source it originated from. This was computer hacking at the highest peak, just some unknown power surge in the line, which had a super virus, just barely covering the electronic footprint in time to keep it from being traced. It was a pure and simple mathematical principle that blended into the lowest basics of the original program that had been laid down in the beginning of binary logic, back when random access was only a dream. A virus that is built into the very construction of the chip cannot be detected, and neither can a virus built into the mathematics of the logic.

Now it was getting dark and to approach the key at this time was useless. The sun would be there in the morning and there was a night ahead, draped in an odor of fear that Thomas was familiar with. He had to prepare his defenses that would enable him to meet his challenges head on. Now was a time of contemplation and prayer. The readiness was absolutely necessary in the coming conflict.

As the day had been hot, so the coming night would be especially cold. There were now feelings of apprehension creeping in as the dark shadows gradually began to move into the proximity of the camp that Thomas had made. He could just see the key from his camp. There was a clear view in front of the rocks to the right, but just to the left he thought he saw some movement. Barely moving as though he were a caterpillar or even maybe the shadow of some tall cactus, creeping across the desert floor, as the sun passed timelessly dipping lower and lower was also the enemy, following the shadow. It could not be recognized as an enemy but Thomas had the apprehension of being hunted and did not like the odds that he was the object of a predator. He was nervous and so wary of danger in the air that training only had revealed this thin shadowy shape sliding across the rocks and sands. It would have been wise to wait as long as possible, hoping that it was not real and thereby prolonging life's precious time a few more minutes. But, Thomas was trained to intercept and not to wait because waiting was giving in to the inevitable.

Almost as quickly as the light of a candle is extinguished was Tom immersed into the velvet darkness around him. He was blending, sliding, and losing his form among the rocks and shadows. The hunter had become the hunted and the best defense now had to revert to an offense Tom knew the direction the enemy was coming from, so first, he had surprise on his side if the enemy had not seen him leave his position and determined his motives. Tom managed to conceal himself in the rocks and run a thin wire across the intercepting path of the enemy. The thin wire would activate a small proximity detonation device that would focus on the core of the enemy's body. A simple clock wound device would deactivate the firing pin of the charge in several hours if the enemy decided to change directions and the antipersonnel capabilities would be rendered harmless in case he actually had to retreat along the same trail later. Such a simple clock wound device was undetectable with plastic gears and posed no threat if it wasn't set off for an extended time period to any innocents passing by.

In some minutes after the wire was in place Tom retreated to the cover of available rock formations and waited until a small muffled explosion was heard, thus signifying the kill. This, Tom never wanted but in order to defend himself against predation, it was necessary. The key had its own defenses, but at a far lesser degree a carnage, right now, than was afforded Tom's manner of necessity. The surrounding area of the key for no less than one hundred yards was masked electronically so as to gradually lead any would be approaching entities away to a distant location. This was a direct stimulus on that part of the brain that dealt with illusory qualities, and envisioned characteristics of the senses. A truly visionary place is what it had become. Tom had trained vigorously in the struggle to become a stable reasoning warrior, skilled in numerous disciplines. One of his best skills was being able to focus his mental awareness to a degree of truly animal proportions. Once he reached the key, it would have to be analyzed mathematically to find an acceptable solution, for a correct pathway leading to the abode and workplace of a group of highly specialized people.

Navigating through the rocky fortress had demanded more mental labor than physical because of the constant barrage of wave material and beamed distractions used to persuade those wishing to enter to choose another location. Small tiny, barely audible voices would intelligently suggest an alternate place to direct action, and tiny laser beams would seem to enhance the audible with visual stimuli designed to change the thinking of just about every person that has been there wishing to investigate.   Now, Tom was fast approaching the key and suddenly all of the noise ended and there it was, a magnificent work of art together, with Dolmen and Saracen. This shape was one that was more prominent in Europe than in other parts of the world and there was none in North America, but still; there it was.   The mathematical aspects were unique in the world of archeology and left a deep impression on all men of science who had been here but not returned. The size was not as large and impressive as many of the other old age monoliths but the significance was enough to make anyone gasp at the relationship to present day science. Even at a distance it was obvious that highly intelligent people were in control of the manufacture of this instrument. It was just that, an instrument for defining the accurate direction within fractions of an inch to an unknown location. It was almost like a sight for a well-directed projectile. Two equilateral triangles with one triangle split by the other to form three surrounded by a circle, all built of solid quartz and granite. Lentils, Dolmens, and Saracens with a quartz wheel surrounding the triangles.

$$x=3.1415926535897 \qquad a=2 \quad d=1.73205080$$
$$D=2.645751311 \qquad\qquad b=2 \quad e=1$$
$$r=1.322875656 \qquad\qquad c=2 \quad f=1$$
$$c=8.311872885 \qquad\qquad\qquad G=1.732050808$$

This was the key upon close examination and now it would take an analysis to project exactly where the opening was in the rocks that led to the underground chambers.   Tom, thinking to himself upon the happenings of the last few months at his home in the backwoods of the southeast, contemplated his training, and the approach of the revelation of what these people wanted to tell him. This rocky terrain was beautiful because it was so different from his home. His training had included all different types of terrain and in his memory of the grueling hours spent on desert locations gave his senses all the advantage he needed to be lethal and ultra sensitive to attack from the monotonous landscape. He had prickly feelings in his stomach which could not be underestimated and he gave in to his apprehension, looking once more for details in the landscape. He would review his mathematical question at a later time, but right now he felt like there was a presence very close and he smelled his old fear smell and this time he knew he had been too indulgent in his memories and had lost focus on the danger of his environment. There was time later for contemplation.

Suddenly there was a distortion in the far rock wall. He had looked in that direction a thousand times and each time the rocks looked the same. The Apaches who had trained him had warned that the most difficult to see was what was closest and inside your security zone. He saw the black outline now and did not want to give it away that he knew. Maybe it was too late but at least he would not be taken by complete surprise. Straitening his gear and clothing in the camp to maintain the ruse of nonchalance, he tried with extreme patience to focus anywhere but the enemy. Now a chill shot through his spine as the realization took hold. There was one black distortion on the rock in the same place and two gray ones over to the far right. He could expect at least three different attacks now, one from his left and two on the right. He felt that this close to the key they would not use firearms for fear of alerting the sentinel system of the key. The anti-personnel explosion he had used earlier had been farther back outside the sentinel system. Although it could have been detected, he felt that the proximity to the key was using human reasoning to assume an attack on the key. Maybe they did not want to overtax the system a long way from a power source. In any event they were now within the sentinel fire zone and to be stealthy was how more had remained alive.

The sentinel system, we had learned, was extremely dangerous and activated by firepower close to the key. Troops having battle close to the key were vaporized on both sides and all interested parties began to use stealth and had approached without loses to a certain extent. The only reports of the sentinels came back describing a group of small flying drones originating from near the key and unleashing a sort of cleansing of the immediate proximity with a plasma-like incineration, vaporizing all recognizable life forms. Now, the fight would be fast and furious but he had great confidence in his training, and the Apache friends had been a miraculous group of people to work with. They taught him things that the Japanese Karate experts had only dreamed of, yet he knew his martial arts training would be dominating his offensive style of fighting tonight. When he was ready to attack his attackers, he would release all his energy in one relentless fury, hoping they would be stunned enough to hesitate in their defenses

The key was almost within his reach and he had to succeed for the sake of his family and the future of the earth itself. He believed sincerely that beyond that key there exists a secluded sect of scientists and elders with knowledge that could change the future of the world and keep it from self destruction.

The key was little more than five hundred yards from his camp and he had to be in position to locate the opening revealed by the sun when it beams its rays through the triangle in the rocks. The ancients that had lived here once many thousands of years ago had aligned the rocks to make a huge one-day calendar. This rock formation was not the only one to serve as calendar and road map. Many other countries had evolved with different but similar use of the sun and planets.

It was now time to remove the hazards and roadblocks and with God's help, he would succeed. He had to be close to the waiting assassins to be able to get inside their defenses. They had to actually and completely believe that he did not notice their concealed forms flattened against the rock wall. So complete was their camouflage that it was impossible to detect if it were not for years of elaborate training and grueling repetitive techniques that had been mastered in arts of awareness and surveillance. There was no doubt that this Thomas Jefferson Coltrane was a force to be reckoned with, one person who could make a difference when thrown against unbelievable odds.

Like his ancestral counterpart he was knowledgeable to the extent of an obsession when it comes to achieving with inventive passion. What he could not absorb from those more informed than himself, he used what he knew to invent workable, beautifully functional options. That was the key to being successful, to survive with brilliance, not just for relief from danger. One had to keep the learning process free from panic in order to complete the circle of power, which allowed you to overcome your adversaries. The plan had been formed in years of preparing for combat. The forms practice of Karate was called Kata, and numerous possible conditions existed where one fought battles against numerous opponents. First it was a definite plus to know how many opponents you were dealing with.

Thomas began to think again and was giving a reflection on a past event. "I remember in the past there was a war on a satellite station in near Earth orbit. They had set up camp on the outer edge of an L5 satellite orbiting the earth and making a new world for those weary of the constraints of Earth. It was an idyllic paradise orbiting earth and with only one drawback."

There were murders that had taken place and he had gone to the satellite space station and found the killers, three males from a long thought of and declared as defunct government. That situation had the smell of this in the same way and there was again the odd number three that time too. They had the tapes indicating three assassins but they were like shadows giving nothing to identify them with. While Tom's mind was racing back and forth in time first in the present danger and then analyzing the opposing forces of this situation, there opened slightly a crack in his concentration. He thought of his wife and remembered their loving relationship. She was that element of light that managed to clearly penetrate the darkest of night. His love for her and her gentle ways could manage to provide hope in the midst of total despair. He wanted to see his wife again so desperately, that just the briefest thought of her gave him the courage he needed to make that difficult decision to risk everything and give the 150 percent needed to overpower those who only tried hard.

Suddenly as if an explosion of light had awakened a sleeping tiger, he turned from the contemplating general, arranging his troops, to the gruesome executioner. At this moment of attack, he was the most vulnerable. All of his training had taught him that attack was the weakest point of defense. They were immediately onto him, all three but with his first strike he had been lucky and disabled the first one, the black, and for that brief moment he had the advantage. He took it and as they immediately struck out, he ended the ability of the most threatening attacker. Then almost simultaneously the two gray ones were lying dead alongside the black. They would not breathe the same air he had breathed again. A wave of remorse swept over his soul and he thanked God that he had not died of the sword that he lived by, not yet. Most assuredly he would later but now the narrow place in his heart and mind was filled with the thought that his family still had the chance to make a better world. The bodies were moved behind the boulders that were strewn near the rocky outcropping and unceremoniously forgotten. He began to think of his burden he now was holding up. There was no other choice; they were killers, very highly trained and intent on his immediate destruction.

Thinking back a few moments, he remembered how he had succeeded in this almost impossible feat. "Only God could have made it possible. They made mistakes and gave me the split seconds I needed to overcome them. First when I attacked, I immediately changed my course of direction and the strike did not originate where it began, thus getting the enemy to commit to a course of action, which could not be changed in a split second. Because black committed to a course of defense out of surprise, he could not recover. Immediately the circular strike to the throat ended the counter black had planned to react with, and the two grays had taken steps backward thus giving up their balance to allow my penetration. I drove straight into the first grey and because he was off balance, my strike did not have a counter. He absorbed a hooking kick without the chance to deflect it or move away from it and most likely his neck was broken. The third gray had the chance to kill me because I had expended all my surprise time and with my strike concentrating on the first gray, I was exposed. He struck to the back of my neck and I should have been dead, but here is the part of the Kata that cannot be practiced or repeated. His judgment did not make his blow true or I was not in the place where I seemed to be to him. He struck a glancing blow. God interferes and there is no way to practice this part of the dance. After the glancing blow, the enemy gray carried through with such force that his next strike was caught in my x-block breaking his arm, and simultaneously stunning him on the point of his chin. With this advantage I quickly broke the left knee and smashed his head into my kneecap as he faltered to the ground."

Thinking new of the moment again, there were things heavy on my mind. I thought, "Here, is the key and I will begin to study and evaluate where is going to be revealed the hidden entrance into the mountain caves beyond."

The night was long and I slept fitfully thinking of the consequences of failure. I thought about exactly what is the threat if I should fail, and I decided that the world would continue but I didn't like the result of my failure. I would succeed and find the way; a different way, maybe not better and maybe yes but it would be different than the consequences if I did nothing.

The morning was such a welcome sight after such a fitful night and the cool desert morning was refreshing. It seemed as if nothing had happened and the new morning was a new beginning. I knew I might be attacked again and this time I had been prepared. That obstacle was out of the way and now the mathematical puzzle loomed ahead and seemed monumental as the key only stood a few hundred yards away. It was from here first, and later close, in order to obtain a measure of the converging rays of light that I would watch the sun strike the disk and illuminate the spot revealing the entrance into the mountains. Here is where the group would have their doorway to the outside. The sun was beginning to approach the trough of the mountains which permitted the disk to be illuminated. As I had waited here now for hours accepting the boredom of working, and thankful that there were no disturbances, suddenly it came blazing away through the trough, oddly that it would almost walk its way up to the disk as though the trough had been carved by something other than nature. Almost instantly a shaft of light seemed to leap from the disk atop the Saracen as the sun's rays aligned perfectly with the crystal. It became apparent that I quickly had to set up my instrument and locate the nexus point. The shaft of light did not stay but through three degrees of the arc of the sun. I took the geometrical quadrangle from the pack that I had been carrying, and extended the legs of the tripod. Connecting the quadrangle to the top of the tripod, I quickly focused on the top of the Saracen. From there I aligned myself and the tripod with the Saracen at the correct angle to triangulate the ray of light. From there I found the ray of sunlight or the beam of sunlight that was intersecting the crystal in the Saracen. Far away in the mountains, a ray of light pointed the way, the way to hope, and a solution to my assignment. The assignment was to find these people and solicit some help to find the answers to the dilemmas of the world.

Built into the lens of the scope was a geometric map that when illuminated would give digital readouts as to the degree and variation of light illuminating and pinpointing different destinations at their surface. After I would record my information, the only problem would be to work out the mathematical answer to the location of the opening indicated. How could it be so complicated to just record where the light hit and then proceed to that spot? That was great, but the spot was still a great distance away and the beam was trapped in a certain way that made the results peculiar and many who had thought it easy had returned empty handed. Not that there were so many, only five had approached this place and all had failed even though it was known worldwide by certain groups that these unique people were here clandestinely. Not all returned alive and those that did, were not wanting to return for a rematch.

First, the exact time is important for viewing the phenomena. Then, as the light strikes the Saracen it is focused by natural crystals in the rock formation to target only a certain location. This location possesses the only entrance in an underground chasm of immense proportions where lives a group of almost forgotten scientists, working and increasing their knowledge of the most elaborate and productive experiments on earth today. At the intersecting points within the circle were illuminated the five pathways to the opening. All five must be marked and recorded within the three degrees that the sun travels through. Approximately twelve minutes is the time for the sun to travel three degrees and it would take all that time to make the adjustments. As the sun passed from one side to the other of the disk, the first point was located and recorded electronically. All the information was compiled into the math and geometrical computer and analyzed. The main point was thought to be the top point of the equilateral triangle which landed in the top one third of the circle. After entering all the data into my notebook computer, I received a read out giving an estimated point most likely to be the entrance into the mountain. I had abstracted the data and obtained the entrance point, but as experience had told me, I had a wish to check the computer. Computers dealt with exact information, not riddles and misinformation nor had it computed the change in the earth over thousands or maybe millions of years since these monoliths had been

14

placed here. At a distance of several miles the pinpoint dot of sunlight could be misplaced if the monolith had been moved only a few fractions of an inch due to the shift in the sub-soils. The five pinpoints of light could be five different entrances according to the information from the old manuscripts, but the most important one was the point in the center of the circle within the rectangle within the circle. The light somehow passed through a crystalline structure located within the circle and could be seen for miles as a ray. Somehow the crystal aligned the light particles to form a visible ray for three degrees of the sun. In about twelve minutes it was no longer visible. At the very top of the triangle after the sun had immediately passed the three degrees was the last time the dots of sunlight could be seen until next year. They rested squarely on the triangular points of the triangle within the circle. Then like ghosts and apparitions one by one they disappeared until only the top center was left visible.

Far away to the mountains it seemed a dot of light suddenly entered a flat black square and then disappeared. On this black square the electronic locator homed onto at the last second and now within global positioning devices it was logged into the pocket computer and the information was secretly coded and saved. Every aspect of the crystal had to be analyzed and mathematically encoded to digest as much information as possible. In the three-degree interval the placement of the five white dots was etched permanently on computer memory. Yet there was still the fact that each of the distances and locations had to be determined. The computer calculated the distances between the points of light. The distances agree with the mathematics but the variance in the location of the points of light in reference to the crystal alignment and the entrance could be off by a mile or more if the site had been moved or tampered with through the centuries. If the earth has shifted, the line of site could be off the mark. All of these trials and tribulations would be a waste if I concentrate my efforts in a wrong direction. The pole shift had occurred at least once since the crystal and the Saracen had been set in place.

How could it be calculated to find the right location, compensating for pole shift, ground movement, and all without wasting precious time? Since light travels at 3×10 to the 8th m/s it is found that the distance between each point was apparent to the observer through the solution of different equations. Light traveling from the sun and passing through a crystalline material was directed to a target, the entrance or location of the cave on a grid. That grid, being an equilateral triangle within a rectangle within a circle, formed the composition or paths that the light particles took after leaving the crystal. The light, coming through the crystal was split into five different stars or points of light to form this geometrical pattern. I was so absorbed in working out the solution to the mathematical problem and trying to decipher the aberration in the light pattern that I had forgotten about the presence of an enemy. It was at this moment that the flash of light glinting off a steel blade made an impression on my mind that the sun's direct rays could not. The moment that glint of a steel blade hit my retina, I reacted as I had so many times before in pure combat, that I was jolted as if by an electric shock and I hit the tripod, shattering the lens of the computer eye into a thousand pieces. This tripod had made the steel knife glance away from my heart only inches from the intended target. As I continued the roll, my .357 came, miraculously into the palm of my hand and without thinking, a loud noise chased away the last fog from my mathematical equations and the bullet slammed into the vertebrae of another enemy forcing him to discharge his Mac 10, punching holes into nothing but sky for a good 10 seconds. The electron connecting hand eye coordination had been short circuited and the trigger finger of my enemy had suffered for accuracy.

I was alive from this moment on because of some miraculous favor granted from God. The enemy was clothed in a dusty brown spotted camo-suit in desert drab. Never have I seen a more effective camo-suit. It changed every time the enemy moved and he was a perfect human chameleon. The only way I saw him was because of his shiny knife. Why had he gone to so much trouble for the perfect camouflage and neglected to prepare camo for his knife or use a black matt finish? After I recovered the knife, I knew it was really because of his pride and arrogance to have such a flashy knife as a status symbol. This blade had become the defect in his defense that had gotten him killed. He had felt great pride in this huge shiny knife no less with his initials on it written in Chinese characters. He must have honed and sharpened it for hours before his visit.

I have tried many times to revisit the memories of these enemies that I have killed to make some sense out of the necessity to kill them. Why did I have to kill this particular enemy? Did he have a family, children, a home, dreams, or some special mission in life if given the opportunity? Could he have benefited mankind in some more effective way than I, if he had lived and I would have died? Can it be measured or calculated if possible? Why did the incident happen? Eventually I forget and the memory passes with relief, although it would be nice if it had never happened. I hope that these people I am making these sacrifices and efforts for are worth all the work. How could they be so important for their knowledge that so many people would kill and die for just the opportunity to find them and discuss the problems of the world? At one time in the past, I was envious of the numbers of kills that other special forces troops had run up but sometimes a wiser person does come with being older and I soon learned that it creates a rottenness within the psyche that cannot be cleansed only consoled as a loved one at a funeral. A little piece of the psyche dies with the enemy because they were also once children too and played and laughed just like me. In this narrow place in time so many ideas become jumbled up with priorities and duties so the war takes away our basic feelings of humanity that is the foundation of a healthy psyche. It tears and rips away at lovely ideas and empathetic reasoning and the "child" in man is becoming a stranger to the adult. The adult inside, that needs the "child", is becoming too much like a dictator that sees only the welfare of itself and does not care to be questioned by the "child". As a psychological approach it parallels verbal child abuse in a reflective way and that through the taking of life, the child spirit itself is extinguished in the one who is perpetrating the act. The creative influences are smothered and as a result the death of innocence puts the adult in danger of being too predictable. Once a warrior becomes predictable his life is moments from extinction. To terminate the enemy, you only need to know his next move and then he has sealed his own fate. To lose the creative spirit of the "child" is to be a dull, dead, lifeless, monotonous adult. In "warrior speak" terms one must shape the senses to new heights of awareness and react with a spirit of second-nature, while never losing sight of the purpose in all beings civilized, which is to answer the question, - "What is the meaning of life?" Yet this becoming of an ultimate warrior degrades the essence of the great search to find meaningfulness in one's own life and this circle is never completed. Never completed; becomes the warrior taking life, but then he negates his ugly deed while professing to be on a high road to oneness and inner peace with nature and the animals, not knowing that he has lost the key to that which is enchanting and beautiful. Eluding oneself into believing you have a heightened sense of animal awareness which should allow you to possess some golden ideal of power and purpose is just a temporal foolish notion. Being a warrior should only be a forced temporary job which is immediately discarded once the danger or war is over. This should be the only occasion for choosing a violent nature. A well-oiled machine is just a more dependable and efficient machine, not purposeful or possessing vengeful ideas. Mathematically correct is good only in terms of its purposeful existence, not just and good in terms of rightness and wrongness. In my philosophy I came to terms with the truth and this is the ultimate search. Just to find and confirm in itself the truth and hold it in highest esteem is enough. There have been religions old and new that could wish no more than to have this truth readily at hand or just to see it and behold its goodness and be grateful for its pathway to existence.

The light was fading and late afternoon was upon me. I have to recover my computer from the rocks, strewn along the desert floor. There will be sentries at the key that have been alerted because of the gunfire. The first combat took place quietly except for the small shaped charge explosion. That was the first mistake, now I have others to my credit and they are weighing me down. This time all the gun fire has surely opened the eyes of the sentries at the key and I am waiting to be another casualty that did not come back. I have been warned not to awake the sentries because I cannot recover from their first offensive attack. They will come maybe not immediately but I know they will come and from my reports that I have received, it will be no small miracle to stay alive. I survived this most recent encounter with death and now I had to find out what condition my computer was in. The lens was shattered, but I hope the information was still there locked in the memory. I detached the small flat box from the computer jacket and now I had in my hand a calculator type brain that could give me the information that I had hoped for.

While I still had light left in the day I would begin to check the calculations and digest the happenings of the day. I began to lay in the formulas for the ground work that would allow me to determine the extent of the correctness I really had. There was hardly a doubt in my mind that the opening was exactly where the computer said it was. Anyway, there was a system directive that was programmed into my training that said to check it out and verify, verify everything. The line of sight was directly from origin to five different variations in the mountainous terrain in the distance.

Using a 100-x telescope with a grid of one to 100, I programmed the different coordinates into my matrix analyzer allowing for the different crossings. By making a geometrical map while observing these locations through the view finder I could transfer to the tablet without need of a huge computer. After I programmed the grid into the tablet it would be easy to calculate the distances and then transfer them to the map and instantly I would have a duplicate of the computer image on paper.

It was becoming very obvious during the transfer that something was wrong. I have the formula which is old beyond my understanding but simple eighth grade math; (a square plus b square = c square) derives the distance between the coordinates and is transferred by scale from inches to feet or miles at a distance which locates all the possible entrances. Then at the location extracted; I can walk from one point to the other at the prescribed distance and stumble upon the entrances hopefully. The distance "c" which should have been equal to "c" plus "f" was a little off. It was projected that the instrument being used is consistent on all sides so as to present an accurate locator. The amount of shift, represented in the formula was .409175152 for the variable, which calculated the altitudes to be a difference of 409.1751525 ft. That would put the climb up the mountain at a different altitude than the altitude intended. I am presuming the correct altitude for the climb at 9732 ft. If you subtract the 409.175525 ft. from 9732 ft. you get 9322.82 ft. But still this did not seem right, and I just could not believe the computer was wrong. Years ago my training and mentor had instilled in me to check all mathematics and not being the mathematical genius that others were, I decided to check and double check the results of the computer. This part of the trip was not boring to me and I was excited that I had a problem and my problem solving energy began to build in preparation for the ordeal that I would have to meet head on.

The ancient people who had made this gargantuan sun scope, had so many things right that I was willing to bet my money that they compensated for a variety of problems and if I would trust the obvious road that the sun scope was showing me eventually it would lead to the opening. I think mathematics makes people bypass recognition of their true problems. If they would see what is really attached to their solutions and how their minds obtained the process, they would discover many things about their own phobias, inhibitions, and inner truths. We just don't recognize that in solving a problem, we also solve many different other ones. It is as if they are hooked together and one brings the key to the other.

Meanwhile, I rest my inner problems and think about the environment around me. Such a truly beautiful sight was the sun scope, with the obelisk and Saracens together with the surrounding mountains in the distance. The clouds had begun dropping lower and I am thinking that there will be rain tomorrow, and that here in this dry desert I know that chance is very slim and the clouds are an illusion, only a promise for the future in the stark flat high desert. Thinking back to mathematics, I remember that there has to be a reason for the equilateral triangle and the rectangle. Why was there a combination for these with the circle? Was it to find the center of the circle? But that was against what was in all the readings and the history of the land marks. Still, maybe that was the reason for the geometry, to find a process for finding the center of the circle. It seems to me the most likely tool for finding or locating a pinpoint position, combined with the other geometry was the conjunction of the two. The hard combined with the soft; or straight, round, or flat desert combined with the rising mountains, made definite separations of identifiable areas. This is contrast; the point at which there is change.

Momentarily absorbed in my thoughts on geometry, I barely noticed the dark speck in the distance. It seems as though it is a bird but it is just too slow and direct. Maybe it is a bird, but it seems almost as if maybe it is an airplane, but it is low and there is no sound, just a steadily approaching direct motion. It looks like it has come in the direction of the mountains but that landscape is forbidding and there was no established towns or villages for hundreds of miles. It is only wilderness sierra and desert with mountains and a lot of it. As it approached in the distance, I saw it was a flying machine, but not emitting any noise. I know I need to find some cover in case this turns out to be hostile, but I gaze out in the open in utter amazement. I just had to find out what kind of flying machine does not make noise and moves as if on a cushion of air. For literally all of my life since the pictures of Leonardo da Vinci had etched themselves into my memory, I have just been awed by ideas of the inspiring period of the Renaissance. Here it was that contraption come to life, winged and flapping so smoothly, almost without sound as if gliding in a dream. I caught myself again just daydreaming. It was hypnotizing.

Then suddenly I realized that these were the sentinels sent because I disturbed the electronic sensors of the key with my shots and explosions. I was told that if a disturbance could be heard from the mountains that they would come. Now where was cover? I had to hide, but where? There wasn't anyplace. I am out in the desert and there is no cover enough for anything. Suddenly I realize that I have fought and other people have fought and died to bring me to this place because they thought I would give them a chance to escape the coming disasters of the world. I have become sluggish with curiosity for some mechanical toy of yesteryear. I have a few secret helpers that no one has known about and I had not yet deployed them. This seemed like a good time to use one. I had included this particular belt in my gear, really not a belt but a circular piece of metal too cumbersome to actually wear comfortably and I managed to drag it out of the big pack that I had carried. Activating its holographic image maker with only two digital codes, I began the resonant vibrations of light particles that would make me look like I was standing in a different place than where I actually was. I didn't want to crouch like the scared rabbit I felt like because I had a feeling it would be only moments before I was attacked without cover. This would work only momentarily if the visitor was hostile and from the air he could probably readily see two images. If he struck now I would hope he would strike the better target, the more apparent readily visible one, the holographic projection.   Then, as if the sun scope had opened again and let that blinding ray of sunlight through that crystal disk, my shadow warrior, the image from the holograph received a thundering bolt of energy. It wasn't just laser, it was energy or maybe even plasma, and the ground erupted where the image was and sent a crackling bolt of lightning back to the flying machine where it was absorbed with no effect to the machine. It was as if they had made the spot where the holographic image was standing a negatively charged group of particles and the machine completed the electrical pathway with a reverberating ray of plasma. No wonder no one ever reported back, they were vaporized and never made the call. After troops had been sent here under cover in secret and had not returned, the government who sent them could not just say that they disappeared without a trace at some unknown area in a country where they were not given permission to be. The guerilla fighters that I had encountered were the best I have ever seen. Who were these chameleons and where were they from? Were these guerilla agents sent to fend off curious visitors or were they agents after the same goal as we were. Our force in these parts was limited and I was not known at all by agents in other countries because I didn't work for any government. I worked for myself and always alone. I was always there, existing, because they knew of my work, but was never seen, at least not by those left alive. It wasn't necessary that they see me or if they did I was not important to them. This wonderful device only aided my talents and I could create characters at will almost without camouflage make up or costumes.

Maybe it was attitude, just a presence that became accepted as part of the normal. I just didn't present the sort of personality that they were looking for. But these acting and chameleon abilities were at a loss to me now and in this desert no matter what ninja tricks I had used they saw me as a target out in the open. Only my electronic gadget could save me now and it had worked back in Zurich at a trade fair in the midst of international terrorism when I was targeted by mistake. I was not known by the terrorists but mistaken for another agent. The bullet had left me with a scar and I thought they would see the blood but my cover was almost perfect.

I had the belt on now and the field began emanating as soon as I turned the dial to begin. It pushed out the natural wave lengths of light and bent everything that was within the circumference of five to ten feet of the person into a reflection of whatever existed in proximity to the person. The only wave lengths of light that the onlookers could see were a repeat of the existing shapes around the person. It was a trick of light simply like a person trying to stab a fish in a pond with a stick or spear. The rays of light are bent so disproportionably that the visible light being reflected to the viewer is so close together that the image is only a linear value. When you turn a piece of paper on edge, the thin visible image is almost non existent or either the visible spectrum is altered to that of a more narrow spectral band that could only be seen with sensitive instruments and not with human eyes.

So it was at this time and I became invisible to the natural light and safe from my approaching enemies. After I turned on my light bending device I became almost invisible and immediately began moving to a different location away from where I might have been seen. I had moved away from my known position only a scant fifty yards or so and I had moved so quickly that I had left one of my packs that I so badly needed for supplies when suddenly my worry for the supplies was replaced by a jolt of fear. Immediately a line a plasma unreeled itself from the ship and as if in slow motion I watched the linear fire from hell erupt as it made contact with the ground. The bolt of liquid lightning erupted from the negatively charged ground and made its echo signature flash back to an ionic receptacle aboard the under carriage of the flying machine. All in the immediate area where I was standing before was vaporized and I no longer saw the pack I had forgotten. The smoke was a grayish white billowing cloud rolling up and in all directions and I felt the heat and shielded my eyes with my hands. I hoped it wasn't radioactive but I just was so relieved that I was living and thanked God and my friends for their wonderful invention of which I understood so little about. All I know is that it is a first cousin to what people used to know as electromotive force. This device would transform non electrical energy into electrical energy. Like a thermocouple that is used as a thermometer, by bonding two different metals or alloys together. In this device it is two unlike particles in a mini accelerator that warps the electrical field and magnetic field of the earth into a super cold reflecting surface or force field. The one added advantage of this force field is that it gives the field a chameleon like appearance and it looks like the ground and objects surrounding it.

Moving hurriedly away from my last location kept me alive and now they could not see my shape because of the double refraction quality of the force field. I stayed perfectly still so as to remain in camouflage since I could be seen as a changing and moving reflection. The force field was not used primarily for deflecting weapons but for making camouflage since a large percussion would still be enough to push the remaining air inside the field to cause an implosion of what was being protected inside. It would however deflect small objects and thus was a great defense for field work. The belt worn around the waist would send out a pulse of current in a double arch like a magnetic field around the person's body and including some surrounding objects. It was somewhat like a figure eight and the waist was the best place to start the field in order to cover the person and the gear. The world was not ready yet to receive this valuable tool and I wasn't ready for armies to be equipped with killer camouflage, not yet. There was enough terrorism as it is without having them become invisible. But this tool was mine only and it was just a prototype created by a group of scientists with only one thing in mind, and that was to save the world from destruction, so that their families could have a future.

The flying machine was some new and different variety of hover craft combination ornithopter with a velvet cushion of air that created almost no sound or turbulence. This would revolutionize our present helicopters. The new helicopters are quieter than the older ones but this thing is practically floating and the wings have a vibrant flutter, like a humming bird. They had the forward plasma beam where we normally would have the 50 cal. machine gun. It looks like the old bullet was replaced by their new technology. Apparently whoever they are they have definitely become a major power to be dealt with and it is imperative that I find out what their motives and intentions are. To just report back would bring an end to any knowledge that we could receive if war would break out between any of the major power brokers.

I continued to remain frozen to this piece of desert ground and for it seemed like two hours, the flying machine searched for any sign of life, trying to eliminate any chance for return to the outside world. At this elevation there grew a wide variety of plants in miniature and cactus abounded. While I'm here, crouched and waiting for a long enough time to insure my safety, I think about how these people could feed themselves in a desert of rocks and scrub brush. They must be completely underground to be able to have any plants at all, maybe mushrooms, to get out of the burning sun. Possibly they had artificial lighting but where would a power plant be without a thermal signature?

Now, I was beginning to feel the intense heat of the solar flare and knew that I must move or scorch here in the desert sun. There was also one other problem. The people in the flying machine were beginning a mathematical search for any animal life in the area. They were flying now, in a grid, and scorching everything that lived square by square. They knew that there were two shapes earlier and then suddenly there was only one or did they really know? Maybe they were just making sure. There is nothing more comfortable than making sure and feeling safe. At this point I wasn't sure that they were aware that I was a threat to them. I was here to learn but now it seemed that this group was not so docile and religious as it was thought they were. We had the older records and they only gave evidence of being a scientific religious sect and not militaristic. Over the years, they must have evolved into a quite capable defensive force. Were they seeking to broaden their territories and strike out at whoever may pose a threat to them? Did they know our capabilities or the rest of the world's capabilities? But here I was now questioning my motive about my mission and I had the liberty, of course, because I was not in the military. I did not face a court martial when I returned if I changed the purpose of the mission. I was here to save the world, and as it now stood, there might be another immediate threat more dangerous than an accelerated solar flare, wobble in the earth, or rogue meteor. The knowledge that I was seeking to help the world overcome these natural disasters might just have turned into a threat. How would I fight something that I needed to save the doomed earth with? If I destroyed what I was seeking, I might be sealing the fate of the world to sure destruction. But, could I allow the people of earth to be enslaved by yet another oppressive regime of our own people? These were not aliens and they were our distant relatives possibly from a bygone age that never emerged into the main stream of civilization.

In this moment I had to be thinking cool and get the mathematical mind working into high gear to figure out how to escape this systematic grid annihilation they were setting up for me. If I moved I would immediately betray my position or would it? Sometimes it is only the fast-moving object that attracts attention and I have seen lions in the plains of Africa moving ever so slowly toward their intended prey.

This time I was going to use something that my Apache brothers had taught me so many years ago while I had trained with a friend I met on a bus trip across the western United States. The friend I had met lived close to the Apache Indian Reservation near Gallup. The circumstances were so unique that it had to be fate that I saved the life of an eighty-year-old elder of the tribe. I think this old fellow must have been so highly respected by his tribe that he allowed me to train with the young men of the tribe and learn some of their secrets. In the short time that I stayed with the old man and his tribe, I learned more ways of concealment, evasion and survival tactics than in all my years of spying on foreign governments since then. It was their techniques that saved my life so many times I cannot count. I once stayed buried for 48 hours while wave after wave of foreign troops passed by me within touching distance. It was in Gallup that they tested my limits and allowed me to see first hand how death could be postponed and made to wait with a renewed desire to live peaceably.

They buried me there in Gallup for two days and gave me air, water, and food through a reed so I could learn to control my own inner fears and panic. In the blackness of the grave there is no light, or hope except what you have already received in the spirit. It was a voluntary exercise and everything they asked me to do I did it with complete trust. To be lying underground without sensations makes one's mind dream and dream and even make up things that do not exist. You have to learn to control your dreams and use them to your advantage. Fears, your own fears, are the worse obstacles to overcome that you will ever find.

The Apache Indians had become fast friends of mine by that time, or they would not have revealed the techniques to me and helped me to harden my survival instincts. They would bury themselves out in the sierra for three days just to be able to catch a horse.

I also learned how to approach animals without disturbing their natural eating and watching patterns. By using only primitive weapons and practicing a very stealthy approach, we were able to bring home to the campfires much venison, rabbit, and other game along with birds and many wild edible plants. My Indian friends were scientists, lawyers, and doctors, but for a few weeks they returned to their roots of years gone by.

These mystery people with their new destructive machine are set on eradicating all the living things within the grid they have laid out. I am going to approach as I did the deer when I hunted with the Apaches and try to get close enough to get into the flying machine when it lands. I say flying machine because this thing is not a helicopter and not a jet or airplane. It appears to be magnetic in its stability, but how can that be possible? Maybe some ionic transference of magnetic energy has become possible with also a huge amount of rotor lift. This would solve two puzzles at one time. If anti gravity flight is possible then you can create artificial gravity within the ship for stability of the occupants and use it for rapid changes in directional flight. I am going to take a ride in that flying machine, but they just don't know it yet.

Only by some good fortune that God lighted a pathway for me, I was now able to move toward an open spot that was left for the flying machine near the original scorched location. The plasma had first touched this place, but I was covered from their eyes but maybe not their senses. My jamming device was on, at the time of the attack, so they never sensed I was there, only they saw my shape.

I moved ever closer and closer, careful not to disarrange the reflections I was creating too fast, to the place I thought would maybe be the landing sight. Time was passing fast even in this slow but methodical creep that I was artistically performing as if I was in a ballet but making each step a step closer to my safety and eventual freedom, even though I might be a captive eventually if I lived. The point right now was just to live and reach my goal.

Suddenly another machine approached from the distance and lightly touched down about twenty yards from me. As I had been taught by the Apache Indians of the Southwest, I moved in the tracks of animals sensing and breathing in the spirit of the animals we hunted. If you were one with the animal, a member of his pack, he did not recognize you as a foreign enemy and attack you or run away. You could put on the scents and take on the movements of the animals you were hunting.

I tried as hard as I could to visualize what kind of person was flying this second ornithopter machine and in my imagination it was a man or a woman in uniform just like our own troopers, but in reality it was entirely different. I was still utterly invisible and only a repositioning of someone who was watching for an intruder or my own too rapid movement could betray my presence. If I disturbed a bird that was roosting on the ground or excited a jack rabbit, that could betray my presence.

I thought back to creation of this wonderful invention and how we labored over the physics and mathematics that would allow it to become a reality and make it work. The equation for the double arched pulse that the belt radiated was quite mind bending and at the same time it was unbelievable that no one had thought of it earlier. Most great inventions were like that. It seems no one just ever thought of it in that way before. The double arch was really like a figure eight and only in the inner cavity was a double arch. This is apparently what makes the illusion of the neighboring objects reflection. It's the nature of light to travel from one medium into another medium at different speeds.

A diamond that is used at the center of the mechanism is responsible for the unusual character of light to have total internal reflection. If a prism is surrounded by a fluid, the maximum index of refraction of the fluid that would cause total internal reflection is represented in the equation of critical angles. Since the critical angle is less than or equal to 45 degrees in the prism material and the index of refraction less than one, then the index of reflection of the surrounding fluid maintains the concealment bubble and prevents view to the inside of the double helix.

Thus it was with this simple formula that a great ingenious device was invented for concealment. If only this one device allows us to save our beleaguered world, then we have accomplished that which we set out to do, and we will save our world from the destructive path we are on. By hybridization they found the proper wavelength to generate from an alternate power source. Replicated wavelengths are reflected through the control fluid surrounding the diamond and thus maintain total internal reflection through mirroring the surrounding objects.

This was done by the double arch layer of wavelengths of opposite magnitudes. Total internal reflection occurs only when light attempts to move from a medium of high index of refraction to a medium of low index of refraction. This was a great accomplishment for any time period and better now that I was using this wave pattern to mask my presence. The reality of my superior achievement was to be a surprise to even this group of highly advanced predators.

Is that what could have happened to the dinosaurs? Rather than or maybe just hastened by a huge meteor was the fact that there had emerged a smaller but better predator, born with advantages that would upset the ruling elite monsters who were bewildered by their lack of knowledge and ability. Having a unique advantage could have baffled the natural instincts of the major predators and the amount of time it took them to recode the gene arrangement was just not adequate, sort of like checkmate. One group develops a unique discovery and uses it savagely before the other can recode, recover, and counter attack. Nature seems like one giant computer, figuring all the alternatives in the least amount of time with all the available materials at hand, playing itself in one huge chess match. Now I had to approach the predators and devise a way to take them by surprise or guile.

The day was beautiful and the sun made light dances on the glass of the flying machine. It was not unlike our helicopters and harrier vertical take off jets, but the propulsion system was something of a mystery. Never had I seen that aura of blue at the propulsion ports in our vertical take off jets, and it also had rotors and wings that flapped like a free bird. They had ingeniously used different propulsion systems and possibly an ion generator as well.

Could this vehicle be achieving space flight too? It was a wild guess and somehow I did not figure that just being an isolated scientific cult would be enough to push them to a level of technological advancement alone that surpassed what we together as a global culture had been trying to achieve for hundreds and thousands of years. It takes cumulative layers and layers of upheavals, wars, temporarily hibernating cultures, and cooperation to cause a boom in technology or so we think. These people seem to have done it alone, cut off from all of the incentive that makes the mother of invention, what she is, a necessity. They didn't have threats from all sides, unless maybe they had advanced their communications first, and saw all the world the way it has been for centuries, in perpetual turmoil as it really was and prepared themselves like no other nation had. While some saw and slept, this group, had apparently prepared without ceasing. Spartan from birth to death and beyond, thinking of future peril was always logical.

Chapter 2. **The Ornithopter Arrives**

The wind began whipping up the dust from the desert and it whirled around and up into the open doorway of the flying machine. For one moment I saw in the doorway the shape of a woman in some type of uniform though loose fitting, it looked like some insignia on her jacket as if militaristic. I knew it was a woman. I was getting closer now and almost within reach of the gang way, if nothing gave me away.

I would have to cut off the camouflage or cloaking machine or else they would notice the disappearance of pieces of their machine or maybe the whole thing. Maybe it would not affect the surrounding parts but it would double-reflect them and give it away that there was some thing funny going on. This camouflage was only temporary and maybe would only work briefly, they told me, but I think it has been marvelous and I hope I can still use it some more if there is another danger. The craft was getting ready to take off and this was my only chance to live. I ran as hard as my legs would take me and I took a flying dive into the open doorway, slamming hard into some cargo boxes and what looked like parachute material just as the craft lifted into the air.

I turned off the electronic camo as soon as I was entering and adjusted myself among the boxes and parachute material. Apparently someone had jumped and parachuted earlier or dropped some equipment into a drop zone, recovered some material, and then tossed the parachutes into the cargo bay to be reloaded and packed later. At this moment I could walk around freely because no one was in this portion of the fairly large cargo bay of the flying machine. I managed to grab onto a strap holding in the cargo just as the craft lurched up and forward.

I could hear the voices coming from the cockpit and it seemed they were all female voices. Now it struck me that if these were sent out to investigate they would be more deadly if they were female. No one thinks of the lioness as the hunter and provider and scout of the pack but in reality the matriarchal society is very prevalent, and it is always the mother that defends the babies more ferociously in the animal kingdom. I was well hidden for the time being among these old parachutes and boxes, but I wanted to investigate the occupants from the cockpit more closely. I looked down the gang way to the cockpit and I noticed among the ship's cargo were various electronic boxes and electronic gear and from the port windows of the craft projected different types of weapons of unknown capability. It looked as if the weapons had been made or fused into the glass and the actual window possessed a seemingly liquid crystal display with grids and coordinates. This ship was meant for transport of troops, supplies, and as a combat platform for massive unknown destructive capabilities.

As I maneuvered myself closer to the cockpit I could now remain concealed among all the boxes and electronic gear, safe from the eyes of the others on board and still observe all those around me. The pilot house or cockpit was roomy and open to the back. This ship must have been more for supplies than actual combat which proved very good for my concealment.

She had an urgency about her that seemed like it drove her every movement out of desperation and I could see that she was sweating in the desert heat from a moment before when we were on the ground. Her eyes were so intense that for a moment I thought she had seen me, but it was something else. The quick movements, all of them made were inhuman, more like hyper-robotic. They were all female but they moved almost as if they were electronic. It was astonishing; the movements they made. They were robotic. They had to be! Nothing human could move that way or want to, comfortably.

We were ascending rapidly now, and I felt the cabin being pressurized and heard the cargo doors automatically bolting and locking. This group of females began to flip various switches and one began looking into what looked like a periscope goggle or range finder and suddenly a huge arc of plasma was thrown out in front of the vessel and down, licking up the ground. The plume of gaseous molten ray; that's all I can describe it as, looked as if it touched the earth and began spreading like smoke from dry ice after it settles onto the floor of a magic show stage. Fire and smoke erupted simultaneously and was molded into the bright orange plume with a red-hot lava base from the plasma arc.

Whatever it was that made those ladies so afraid was bringing home to me the reality that I would be dead immediately if they found me. I tried to make my presence less and less a possibility of being detected as I crouched deeper into the parachute fabrics of the cargo hold. I am thinking that because I am a man, my chances of survival may be less of a good wager than before.

I am somewhat in a daydream now and I began to think back to some Physics classes that I had in school. The only way to hold plasma in some kind of unit is to keep a magnetic electrical field around it. How can they eject a plasma beam into the air and out onto the earth and keep a field around it at the same time? Where is the particle generator in such a flying machine that is able to hold a magnetic field to make these plasma rays and still be light enough to stay airborne?

Noticing the females again, they began putting some computations into their electronic display and then the four machines were flying in a squadron together. They must have finished their scorched earth directive and were heading back to their base. There was a chill in the air and I came to the realization one moment later that my destruction was imminent, if left to the designs of these beings. I call them beings now because they are not emanating responses normal to human beings. Although they look like the female figure they fail to exhibit the chit chat and pampering of female figures that I am accustomed to seeing. They are methodical and precise without any wasted movements, just clicking and making adjustments here and there.

Suddenly, without warning, the flying machine takes a lurch as a whump is felt, like being hit by a truck. The females go into a panic and for the first time they appear to be human. They actually exhibit fear and they begin to call SOS distress signals to their other ships. A thick cloud of smoke begins to fill the cabin and I proceeded into the back cargo door without being seen. I am now close to the door and suddenly it opens partially and permits fresh air inside the cargo cabin. The sweet gush of fresh air is a life saver and my lungs are once again working in clean air. This ship is going down and there is a huge burning hole mixed with involuted motor drive pieces where one of the engines to the jet propulsion system use to be positioned. They begin slowing down and the rotors of the helicopter begin to take the duty of keeping the craft hovering in the air. Soon even that is beginning to grind to a halt and we began to proceed at a slow but deliberate descent to the rocky desert below. The flapper propulsion system of the two side wings began to shoulder the duty of supporting the craft in air. The wings are now fully extended and the craft begins to settle into a soft feather light cushion of air made possible by the flapping wing drive. Without the third support system surely we would have crashed. The onrush of air under the wings made it possible to keep the aircraft in the horizontal plane.

Within minutes we are on the ground and the women are beginning to take electronic equipment from the aircraft. I will have to leave immediately because there is a fire in the engine and it is apparent that there will be an explosion due to the volatility of any combat aircraft. I push my way through the debris and out into the opening and through the door.

There we are all together at once just looking at each other for a moment and then we begin running together away from the burning aircraft. Moments later I and the four female officers from what force I do not know are together in the rocks. Suddenly there is a tremendous explosion and the aircraft is sending pieces of itself crashing down around us and burning like a blast furnace melting everything into molten pieces of metal. For a few moments we stared with fixed gaze at the aircraft and then at each other.

The leader says to me, "You're a stowaway, a criminal, and an enemy of our state, but you are not the one responsible for the rocket attack. For all intents and purposes though, you are a prisoner. Do you wish to be restrained?"

I said, "No, I do not, and there is no need, unless you feel the need to be oppressive. Why were you scorching all that territory with that terrible weapon? Am I the one you were trying to eradicate or is it another?"

She looked at the other female officers and said as she smiled, "Maybe, you are the one who should answer your own question. Are you here to eradicate our peaceable people and expose us to the viruses of your outside world? Regardless of your own good wishes, you have exposed us and destroyed centuries of isolation to keep microbes from our people. If everyone begins to be sick you will have decided your own death. The choices are all permanent. You have placed all of us in very grave danger. The council will kill us all immediately if they find you exposed us to your many diseases that have infected your world.

We will not kill you because it would be useless. We are not barbarians but you have already exposed us and made us aliens in our own country. Take off your clothes and change into the ones we give you, immediately! Hurry up, whoever shot down our jet will be back to finish us and they don't just cleanse the land, they seek us for our knowledge and to torment us."

I found out 636 was the pilot, and 637,638, and 639 were copilots and technical helpers.

Number 636 said, "If you're wondering, yes we have been enhanced, and we're part bio-engineered, and part light-particle silicon composite neuro-filament implanted with micro-chip stacked memory cataloguing. For your information we are cloned and every bit as human as you are. I know you have many questions. We can feel the same emotions as you can only we are enhanced, and better made to cope with the changing world. Every outsider that comes in here has tried to kill us and we have been forced to kill all of them. You have been the lucky one and you may stay alive if you don't attack us. You may break something or injure one of us but we can be regenerated and surely one of us is faster than you and your speed is no match for a nano-second. By the time you think you are going to make your limb respond to your cerebral command we can intercept and extinguish your life. All who have tried have failed.

We have been watching you and your attempt to locate the entrance to the old caves in the mountains, made for us by our long ago dead fathers. You have driven off and killed some of the outsider attackers and made our job easier. We lost you and when you disappeared we just thought another outsider had killed you so we were going to purify the land."

I remembered back to that first thundering bolt of plasma that erupted into the holographic image that I had thrown out. I began to think of the narrow places in my heart and mind where I had not been truthful and was deceitful when I was younger and inexperienced at realizing the joy of truth. Never though did I tell a vicious lie or sin willfully knowing I was being deceitful. Maybe I tried to cover up something minor but this was one of those places that biological engineering did not prepare this humanoid woman for and I was going to test the limits of her humanity.

"You said that you did not know where I was and that you were watching me. I have a holographic image maker and the first blast of the plasma beam was directed to my form as an image. Why did you say you thought I was already dead? Was your first strike directly at me or not?"

She held her answer for a time, her bright blue eyes darting first in one of my eyes and then the other with the color in her cheeks turning a beautiful rosy tint. She was definitely human and acting like a little school girl, in her denial of the truth. Her soft brown hair fell slightly in her face as a breeze; cool in this unusually hot desert, softly passed over all of us like a quiet spirit from the mountains. Then the answer began to form on her lips and at that moment I knew it would be a human answer, not quite calculated, but still human.

"It is true. I cannot deny that I shot directly at your presence, but I thought it best that I make a strike to remove you, and now that I realize you have some benefit to our progressive cultured development, I'm glad I missed. Although I know it is impossible, I missed. I'm glad you are alive. I just really thought it was a malfunction and that you fell into the land cleansing of the plasma beam. That is all. I just thought you were another outsider. The elders said not to have any mercy on any outsiders at all, and to destroy all traces of their presence with holy fire, the beam of the plasma, as you call it. Still we really did not wish to see you harmed because you killed the other outsider so beautifully and we wanted communication with you even if the elders said differently, because you are; different. I have curious feelings and have been enhanced to think objectively. You may think I am a machine, but I am flesh and blood. Feel me and see me, look here is my hand and feel my breast, here is my heart beating.

They have assured me that I am as close to human as can be expected although, not like the elders. I am more than human, although I do not grieve so for the outsiders that we have killed. We, the four of us, are the guardians of the key and the elders, and we have killed thousands who have been sent here to take away the elders and their secrets. Regiments and troops, metallic boxes, jet propulsion crafts of every sort, have been sent here, and only this once have we had our vessel downed to the ground and destroyed. Why have we failed, though? You are like the elders, in a way. Why have we failed? You have been spared out of the compassion of our very good hearts and cerebrum thinking. It is a good thing. We are calculating machines. It is true, but we were born of women like you. Don't think a machine can't feel. I have sorrow for the thousands who came against us and their blood is red, like ours, but they had vengeance in their hearts and only conquest. We have always won because we were right.

Soon my ship will be here. It is being outfitted right now, with advanced scanners to find the enemy and weapons upgrades to destroy your attackers. The ship you were on was a cargo ship and only meant for transport and temporary search and destroy. We will find the intruders and cleanse them with holy fire. Now, listen-what is your name?"

"I am Thomas Jefferson Coltrane at your service ma'am."

She looked deeply into my eyes and unnerved me to no end because I knew she was in charge and held my life in her hands.

"Thomas you must now trust us. We are going to help you and you need not fear us. We must retrace your path to the key and proceed to the old cave, so we can help the elders to find the intruders. They have given us numbers 636,637,638, and 639 and we are most familiar with these recognitions because they denote our character as well. But we call each other by something else. I'm Nina (636) and that's Lita (637), Bispo (638), and Nella (639). The elders would not believe we give each other real names. They just think of us as killing machines, but always it's been in self defense; I promise. It's always been that way. I don't have psycho capabilities or vengeance, it's just defense and we're good at it. We have studied self defense like humans, and we have been implanted with catalogued cyber-techniques in our enhanced memory banks, matched with fiber optic nerve junctions, with some wire reinforced joints.

Never has anything that has been trained in outsider lands ever beaten us in hand to hand and usually the beauty of Nella or Lita just stuns them enough ready for taking out. Some poor bastards once thought they were going to rape us first, a bunch of machines, and then kill us."

Thinking to myself, and looking at Nina, as far as beauty went, she was just trying to give the others recognition and to me, she was clearly the most beautiful vixen that I had ever seen in my life.

I said to her, "Nina, clearly you are not giving your feelings proper respect. You certainly are not just a machine and by the fact that I stand here alive is indication that you have compassion in your heart. I mean no harm to your elders and only wish to communicate with them or anyone who can help our world. We have many problems and I was sent here to seek help, not to attack anyone, unless only in self defense, like yourself. I don't think I would be any match for you or your other friend's capabilities, so you have no need of fear or worry from me. I am here to talk with those who are in the cave at the end of the light beam from the desert mountains. You say they are the elders; please take me to them so I may ask of them mathematical solutions to our world's problems."

Nina looked at me with those piercing liquid blue eyes and made a gesture to Nella in that quick manner that is not quite human and Nella brought a communicator up to her mouth and spoke briefly.

"I am confirming nature of attack and am passing information to pilot captain, 636, over and out." Then she said, "Nina, base says that the other three jet-copters will be approaching in fifteen minutes. They found the source of the missile that downed the transport. Its track was traced by ground system coming in from the north. It had been guided here by a homing device placed on some source with origin outside our cave."

Nina looked directly at me and narrowed her eyes and then spoke to me sharply, "There is only one source and that is the outside, you, Mr. Jefferson. Where are the clothes you were wearing before the missile attack?"

I raised my eyebrows in something of an apology and said, "They are over there by the rock where I changed."

Nina said in a somewhat softer tone, "We want you to look and find the homing device, placed in your clothing by your attackers at the last altercation, most likely in the clash with the assailant wielding a knife. He stuck a homing dart in your clothing. It's an old way to make sure they get you even if the attacker loses the confrontation. In the end you get it whether you win or lose."

I went down to the rock where I had left my clothes and looking carefully in the shirt, at the back of the collar, I found a small almost minute barb in the material, intended for my skin but it must have hit at an angle and did not penetrate directly into the weave of the fabric.

I took it to Nina and immediately she smiled almost with exuberance and said, "See, I knew it wasn't your fault, entirely."

Nella, who had accompanied me to the search verified, that it was true, and took the little barb from my hand with small long handled tweezers and placed it in a plastic case and snapped the lid shut.

Nina said very crisply, "Nella, take it to the micro and look at the inscription immediately before the other jet copters get here to pick us up and they can trace this back to the country of origin.

Although we live mostly underground, we still monitor the world through your own satellites and also to ours linked with microsurgery on geo-synchronous orbits to your own. They achieved a miracle to get you on board and it's the first time that we've ever been hit by one of these. It seems you were their Trojan horse and inflicted more damage than scores of troops and armored vehicles have ever done. We have existed here for more years than you have recorded history for all of your countries in this modern world. Your Democracy does not have the credibility that ours has, because it is not pure Democracy. It is only commercial like your Christmas and all your government holidays. Like all your corporations, they exist to make money for the greedy that already have it and want more. Our Democracy is one person, one vote, and even before the microchip age, we were a pure Democracy. Everyone's vote counts and no one is lumped into another group just because they have a majority. You have a ridiculous system that causes great strife and inaccuracy in decision making. We have studied your electoral college and it has such a predictable outcome. The most influence wins regardless of what each person of the Democracy wants. If the people are massed in the cities then it shouldn't matter what the people in the rural counties want. They will just have to move back into the cities to change the political outcome. The people should make decisions in mass and not let individual rights hold back the majority.

I'm going to take you to the elders who are the most adept at dealing with outsiders. They have the authority to pass judgment on you and decide your fate. If they decide you represent a threat to the community as a whole, then you will be immediately executed. You already know that from the expression I see on your face. I hope you have a good reason to be here, and I'm sure you do or you would not have risked your life to go through the bad-lands to find a key to the old entrance.

Since I am half machine and more than half human I'm going to give you my opinion of your chances with the elders. Because they programmed me for help in all situations and I also am human, I can think for myself and use what programs I feel are necessary while being open and honest. They have not prevented me from being a reasoning individual.

The elders will decide against keeping you in the community because you will contaminate everyone else. They have presented quite an extensive program for eradication of all microbes and aggressive predator bacteria that would devastate our society. We think as a whole group about what would be best for the group. You, along with all of us who have been in contact with you, will be eradicated and cleansed. That means we will all be subject to disintegration by holy fire. It is the best way, the best thing for the group and all will vote to protect the group, giving the elders free hand to administer justice. What do you say to that, Mr. Thomas Jefferson Coltrane?"

I was struck dumb by the realization that I had failed and ruined the chances of those who had trusted me. I said in more of an exclamation than I intended, "But, how do they know that I have these microbes or bacteria? How could they just issue an order to kill everyone?"

Nina said rather emphatically, "Right now, countries are using these biological weapons just as in the past and it is the only way to preserve our society."

Pausing to just gaze into her eyes and look at the concern that I knew she felt, not for herself but for me, I said, "I would say you are an incredibly reasoning and deductive and beautiful woman, the likes of intelligence, understanding and compassion, I have never seen before."

She screamed, "Compassion! You think I am compassionate, a machine, something fashioned from light wire, silicon chips and electrolytic stimulators? Do you think I can feel? You think that I have actual feelings of love in this heart of mine? I have cleansed this country of countless who have tried to breach our secure perimeter and bring about our sure destruction, both good and bad alike. The rain of fire, and plasma has fallen on those who never knew what hit them or why. Some are only seeking information and knowledge like you. Do you deserve to die, Mr. Coltrane, just because you are in trouble and seeking to save your own world?"

I said, "No, of course not and you do not deserve to die either just because you have defended your country from a very sure and miserable war of disease and death. You have fought above and beyond what others would have done. Yet, you say that you and your crew will be sacrificed for the good of your community and society. Shouldn't we be tested and given the benefit of the doubt? I'm saying that there is a way for all of us to live and accomplish some good before we reach our time here on Earth. Think, Nina, what is the way out? What do you believe in your heart is best? If your elders don't know now, they will find out shortly that all of us on this planet are doomed anyway. There is a numerous amount of problems that we all need to find a solution to. If you shut me out, you could be resolved to accept your fate as a group without getting a chance to change the course of physical forces that are now already set in motion. Their shallow victory over the bacteriological elements in a vaster arena will give them little satisfaction when they learn of their plight."

Nina said, "You may have some valid points, but you could not convince me. Remember, I am part machine and I deal with facts and figures. If you would like to practice on me, before you get to the caves of the elders, you may attempt to put forth your evidence and arguments, but they will have the people's full cooperation to act immediately upon result of questioning. You will be questioned fully and completely and justly. Please, let me know now if you have something unique and consequential that is of some benefit to our society because unless there is some miracle here that can be pulled off, we will all be terminated immediately. Unless I can convince some of the elders that you have some kind of valid argument here, for even to be questioned about, then the most explicit order will be given to cleanse this whole group, the crash site, and a surrounding fifty mile radius, which in part has already begun. They will continue to open the radius of the arc to include all threats to the society. With the other ships, closing in on our location they will know the minute I open this channel. Because I'm an alpha composite I can make some of my own choices. I have chosen not to have an open broadcast band on my ship. I think it is more secure without always broadcasting openly back to the elder control group. I am human, and human born but I have programs that enable me to be more efficient, yet I still do feel a kinship to you because we are both of flesh and can reason out a solution to this problem. I have never felt the crazed drive of desperation to eradicate the newcomers out of fear only, that it was said by those in charge that the cleansing must be done or all would be infected and die within days. The evidence has been catalogued to be monumental; thousands have died from newly engineered microbes that liquefy the internal organs in hours and all orifice openings with bleeding from the eyes and nose. There have been horrible, horrible, deaths-of all who were contaminated.   Tell me now, what is your knowledge you wish to confide in the elders about? I am listening with an open mind and an understanding heart. Let's see if we can reason this out together."

I thought a moment about the utterly useless situation that I was in. Should I confide in this machine-like female that seemingly had my best interests at heart or try for some way to distract them while I tried for a getaway? They had not spared any living thing to escape their judgment in the past, so did I stand a chance? With that plasma arc they would just scorch the entire area cremating grasshoppers and animals alike. I think I could stand a slim chance only if this female computer is opening her mind to me, only a slim chance.

Then she said, with a snap to her voice, "Let's have the confession! We have three plasma ships in view, as you see, and the others will do as I say. Just let me have the confession in short concise sentences, with the most important details first."

Almost at once I felt like I was a young freshman in high school being subdued and derided by the older dominating beautiful senior girls and my legs began to feel week as I looked into those beautiful serious blue eyes. Instantly I knew I was in danger if I did not speak immediately to give her something to occupy her thoughts with. Nina was a leader here, I had caught her ear, and maybe put some compassion in her heart, but I could lose the flesh and blood conscience any moment now, without being able to retrieve my confidence to stand up to her. I knew she was a killer and worse, would not hesitate to burn the very dust mites from my skin, yet she had also confided in me. What did I feel right now? I did not remember that it felt this way. Love and fear at the same time, two different feelings, one of insecurity and the other of desire, all in one emotion. I looked into her eyes, thinking how had it happened?

She locked onto my gaze and neither of us looked away. She took a breath and her hair cascaded, falling across her left shoulder. It was bare and her skin was olive and tan. They all had a uniform cut to reveal the items of their feminine forms. She was not the largest or tallest of the group but it was clear that she was giving the orders unquestioned.

At first, I just saw this look in her eyes. They suddenly narrowed and at that moment I knew she was going to kill me. I just felt I would not live but a few more minutes. I saw a movement of her right hand; only a slight movement.

Suddenly I felt blood soaking into my shirt and I looked down and there was this horrible cut in my own body. I had been cut from my right shoulder across the chest, and the gash was at least a foot long and I didn't know how deep. I had hardly seen a movement of her hand, yet I saw now the short bluish knife in her hand. Her enhanced abilities could not even begin to be understood. Just the speed alone would terrorize my mental ability to react. There was only one thing I knew and that was to remain very still until she worked out this situation a little better in her own mind. This was not just a machine. Obviously she was flesh and blood but definitely programmed and trained with enhanced abilities quicker than my eye could follow.

I asked God to forgive me of my sins, because at that moment I thought I was all but dead.

She said, pausing, "I overreacted, and I'm sorry I cut you. I'm not a machine or an animal, I do have feelings and you have made me realize that I could have been wrong to just exterminate all those invaders. You are from the outside, but your reasons are different than the others. In cross examination and interrogation they admitted they were here to invade and kill us. I will listen patiently to your reasons and I will not kill you. But first let me close that cut before you get blood on all your clothes. Take off the shirt. I will radio in that we have one from the outside but I can not promise that we will all live to explain your good reasons for coming here."

Her heart had at last melted and I would live a while longer. In the meantime three other ships had landed and a force field had been placed around the perimeter. A light blue haze had cloaked the entire area in a mist for about three minutes and when it cleared I could not see in focus the rocks in the distance. Only blue shapes as they shined through the field of the barrier could be defined as if suspended.

Nina said to me, apologetically with true hurt in her voice, "I only lost my control for a moment. I'm not really just some warrior person. I have other things I like to do that are really interesting. I study "the outside", I am familiar with your President, and I know about all the other countries in the world."

She examined my wound that she had just given me and applied some magic looking electrode after Lita, Bispo, and Nella had thoroughly sewn up a couple of bad places with some sort of combination infrared light and hand held sewing machine. I was reclined on a metallic fold-out cot that served as a surgical bed. I had begun to think that I was something of their toy, a doll, so to speak, and they had taken me in like some group of school girls playing with an inanimate object that they could position and make lifelike actions with.

Thinking back to the moment of the slashing out of Nina, I didn't quite understand in my mind why I did not move to defend myself. I just could not understand after all the training to defend myself I had spent hours, learning and practicing and then to just relax while someone sliced me open. Where was the spark that I had missed in order to respond with a defensive attitude?

The gash was completely closed and had a temporary weld on it that looked like the joining of two pieces of metal. My skin felt like it was glued together in the cut place. I looked up at Nina and she began to apologize for her actions.

"I don't really know why I cut you. I just couldn't imagine this happening. I mean, our breach in security and you coming here from the outside. We had never had anyone come even close before but you seem like you are a genuine nice human and like us sort of. I don't know if we will all be killed or what the elders will do to us. I'm just panicky and I took my frustration out on you. Just now I feel two different feelings and I don't know how to deal with it. I have feelings of warmth and desire for you and I feel thrilled to be talking to you, but then I also feel cheated and betrayed by you. My community, my elders, and my friends will feel I have betrayed them and my country by just being friendly and communicating to you.

They will all agree with the elders that you have started the destruction of Lemuria Terra. They are here, and we will see what will happen but just remember I am not completely a machine. I feel deep within my heart-------a love for you that I have never felt before. If we all die together just remember that I am your friend and I will try to make it possible for you to live."

I couldn't believe the feelings that were flowing from this beautiful unpredictable part machine part woman. In some narrow place of my heart, I began to feel the blood pumping and I felt warmth all over. She lit up something in my mind that gave me an unusual feeling, as if I was younger, very much younger and invigorated.

In the distance other ships began to land and a ring of fire encircled our group. A large arc of plasma erupted from the last ship, hovering over us and immediately a huge cone emerged from the forward hull of the leading jet copter. Spewing fire and smoke, the whole area around us in a circle of about ten miles in diameter could be seen to burn as if in a kiln, red hot.

Quickly I looked to Nina and she came to me and said, "They are just cleansing our area, on my orders. We will be going into the cave soon. You are coming with us to be questioned. Get your things together. I am taking command of the lead ship, as long as I am alive, you shall stay alive also. In the distance I saw another ship landing and the three were like no other machines that I have ever seen, even in movies. Sleek and metallic and aerodynamically perfect, they sat like cats waiting for to spring as thin manta rays with a blade used for lift that folded up while rotating and secured into a disappearing cowling. How they achieved this mechanical feat, would make some of our engineers drool to imitate it. There were jets and exhausts incorporated into the design with the fuselage and minute crystal facets folded into the skin that was no doubt used for radar deflection and evasion. I was so nervous that I began to feel that same old adrenalin rush again. These unnatural beings were liable to do anything and killing me would be like squashing a wasp that no one wanted near them. I think they would all be relieved if I was exterminated. Still, I would have to support these feelings of near panic, first for the sake of my family, the world and my own welfare demanded that I wait. I was feeling some pain from the vicious cut that Nina had administered to me for what? Was it a warning? Was it an emotional outburst from a semi-machine or a calculated move to handicap an opponent who you didn't know the intentions of?

She was walking with us now and we moved with our gear toward the lead ship. She gave instructions for others to store the gear from the transport that was recovered into the back section of the ship. We entered the flying machine through the small stairway that unfolded hidden from the body of the plane. It was big and closer in resemblance to something from outer space or a marine animal than a jet, airplane, or helicopter, but I know from flying in the cargo transport that it was all of the above. Also I know without a doubt it possessed the plasma arc and human machines that knew how to operate it, without hesitating. They could incinerate a hundred square miles and not blink an eye. For some reason and I don't know why, my imagination is telling me that with this one ship they could do it from orbit, if they wanted to. The Russians and the Americans both had huge proton beam accelerators even back in the 1970's. Everyone knows that they are being developed, but not to this caliber. Things are invented and expanded into operational prototypes but only emerge after someone gets it working well enough to make a publicity presentation.

Well, here it was and these people didn't have permission from the pentagon to develop it and put it on space ships either, but they had it and could smoke the city of Washington D.C. and there wouldn't be anything the scrambled wing of fighter jets could do about it. Did Washington know already the extent of these people or if they even register on satellite photos? Or did the crystalline structures and facets on the skin of the planes prevent this detection? The heat signature alone from the plasma arc could be seen by Satellite. They had to know. Were they just too scared stiff to even give acknowledgment to the news media? Maybe they had sent divisions after these people already and without a doubt they had not returned to their families. We had to negotiate and not give demands. They had to be assured they could live in peace without being invaded. One of their main concerns was the word "contamination", and not just being threatened by conventional weapons.

Maybe they had been invaded already by armies using biological and chemical weapons and knew so well their survival depended upon complete cleansing by plasma. Only fire completely purifies. We may be just looking at them and trying all our weapons against them as we had in the Vietnam experiment to see what worked and what wouldn't. Take the hill and then give it back to them, and next time, we used a different weapon and different strategy. That made perfect sense to the military. Here was a classroom to be used for testing purposes. The only draw back was that in that war and with the encounter, our military had undoubtedly had with these people there was a lack of creativity and a deficit of intelligence. By intelligence I don't mean just cat and mouse games. I am referring to cerebral productivity and excellence of achievement. They just produced the goods and held onto their right to exist, regardless of the harassment they received. I had intercepted some encoded messages from a satellite transmission that men and machines had been disappearing here and that was the dead give away that our government was at war secretly with a superpower. Nina was with me now and I had to completely trust her for my own safety. I did not want to betray her trust in me that I was not a saboteur or government agent out for revenge or just following some blind

47

directive from some agency. I was operating alone here and without backup or cover or communication with any government or agency. Maybe they sensed this or even knew who I was. It was a remote possibility.

We were loaded into the light cruiser and all preparations were underway to take off simultaneously. There were now eight warships, all battle capable with plasma torches. I didn't know the extent of these fighting ships or for that matter the capabilities of the beings that piloted them. I knew that I was safe for the time being but still had reserved feelings for their end motives.

They escorted me into the forward cabin together with Nina and her copilot, Nella. This was a huge ship by standards as far as fighters go. It was like a flying killer whale rather than a sand shark, which would be comparable to jet fighters. It was sleek and lethal with living quarters if that makes sense. I think it could be used for interplanetary voyages with little loss of comfort or space. Maybe that was the real basis for the design. I noticed rotating nozzles in the rear exterior jets and that could only mean space travel.

Nina and Nella looked like they were in-sync together and always they semi-communicated in those very fast visual gestures, like a sign language except it was too fast to be normal communication like something between two robots. Nina had her hair pulled together in the back into a loose gathering and swept back a little longer than shoulder length. She looked at me and I could not leave her gaze. We were locked in our own private world for minutes it seemed.

Then Nella said to Nina, "We need to lead the formation to the cave entrance and we will have more time to get to know Mr. Jefferson at that time. Be careful, Nina. You are not monitored, but the others have the eyes of the elders built into their systems. They will know your desires to bring in the alien outsider soon enough. We must pray that they think you and I and our small lead troop are indispensable and cannot be logically sacrificed as a security measure."

Then Nina replied with some anguish, "They could do nothing with the other mindless electron troopers. It is I who personally programmed their circuits for battle and have been successful in protecting their interests in off world developments. The elders know that we are the main spear head of all war parties and the central programming units for battle strategy. We are the heart and spirit of the security for our world and Lemuria Terra could not survive without the mental nerve center directives we provide. Yes, you are right Nella. Help me to regain my senses. I am almost human and this man has distracted me, although it is not his fault. I must not strike him again because it is wrong for me to blame him and vent my anger on him. I will concentrate better.

Start the perimeter check and burn off the entire area where we landed. Leave nothing to remain of the things we left behind. Continue the burn up to the required fifty mile radius of the landing site. Use the other ships to synchronize their plasma arcs and complete the cleansing within a ten minute time frame. Make the perimeter the structure of glass crystalline and there will be nothing to identify or investigate. If the alien biologic shooters are within that circle they will be cleansed also and we will insure the safety of our journey.

Begin plasma arc production from our ship and remote the other cruisers to lock onto our beam. Coordinate at points intersecting and commence at your discretion. They don't need to know our reasons, just auto-execute. They will not question, only comment to themselves that they will be thorough."

Nella typed some, unusual symbolic code into a floating terminal and changed the color of some lights on the console. I heard some eruption from under the ship with a sound like escaping gas and a brilliant light reflected in the background.

Nina said, "Don't look at the plasma reflection directly. Nella, get some vision shields for Mr. Jefferson since he does not have auto shade built into his lenses. It is just like the sun and will damage your eyes. There is nothing to gain by looking directly into the sun."

I began to notice their side arms. They looked like a knife, only a blade. But somehow I thought they were special. Possibly, they were part of the arc system that cut with a ray.

I had to know, "Nina, I have so many questions to ask you. Is it safe to ask some curious meddling questions? It cannot hurt to satisfy my curiosity some little part. Tell me, about the blade. Is it electronic with a cutting ray?"

"Yes and no," Nina said. "Nella, close the door behind us.

The other sensors in our computer environment do not need to hear too much. I'm not worried for our immediate corps, but the recruits from the other ship might have reason for requesting something unusual."

Nella closed the entrance to the crew compartment behind us. Nina paused to look behind her and saw that the crew compartment door was closed and then she began to instruct me in a manner that could only be described as patiently informing me.

"It is the only personal weapon we have and yes, it has different characteristics. It has distance, width, penetration, and quantity, just like your bullets and your guns, except that it is more of a vibration than a bullet. This is something that you or someone like you will invent in your world in the very near future. Your military has many new weapons that you do not know about. I have an answer to a question you will ask, if not to yourself.

No, your governments do not know we exist, not exactly. Your satellites have been altered since before they were launched and also while in place in orbit. Your computers and electronic systems are easy to change from a simple frequency scanner. Electricity is not a very secure system for operating highly essential and classified systems. It can be picked up from radio signals and encoded with many different changes from the original that cannot be detected or recognized as hybrid. We have a failsafe way of locking into the very structure of matter, the signals and instructions for directing our machines that are necessary for operating without wavering or worry. It cannot be altered by sunspots or disturbed by nuclear explosions. Almost all of your communications systems can be disturbed or shut down by radiation. We enslave the actual electron, marry it with any particle, and lock them into the predictable and dependable pathways of the electro-weak force. You have yet to recognize that electromagnetic force and the weak force are actually one force, just different manifestations. To use only the electromagnetic force in your machines, leads to chaos. You have to lock the two together in their original form and all computer logic is 99% predictable or better. The only one percent missing is an electromagnetic wave pulse that can possibly dislodge the concrete union, but that is another force that you are unfamiliar with.

Your government would scream if it really knew how

vulnerable all of its defense systems really are. If a nice sized solar flare occurred unexpectedly, it would be out of business for years. Who knows exactly how long these things will be. A series of atmospheric atomic detonations would also incapacitate all known electronic equipment and your country would revert back to mechanical in one month. They would wish for the days of mechanics instead of electronics; then cables and pulleys would be very high in demand.

The knife that I so immaturely and childishly sliced you with is only a very simple device for altering the positions of matter. It doesn't ignite, but only separates the normal arrangement, just like a knife, rearranging the layers so that they are not together anymore. I can reach out and slice matter up to approximately the same distance as a good rifle; only I don't need to use a scope or sight. My hand eye coordination is practiced to the degree that I can almost reach out blindfolded and rearrange matter at a very good distance. We have a lot of inventiveness here, in that they are unusual but they seem so simple to us. Practically anyone could have invented them. On paper, I could draw you a diagram and you could build one in a week. You won't believe how simple the design is.

We are a very cohesive society here, and everyone is probably related more closely than you could imagine. That is why we need to bring you into our group. We haven't had new blood lines in this gene pool for centuries. They have just been re-engineering the DNA to create the greatest possible arrangement, but after centuries they are losing the defining characteristics to pair the genes in the most dissimilar match. It is a completely closed society.

I am one of the young leaders here, and am very closely allied with a group of scientists that realizes our condition. We are susceptible to many outside viruses that you are probably carrying, but we need a complete reprogramming of our DNA, so the risk is acceptable to survive in the future. You just relax, I know you came here because you have problems in your world, but so do we."

My thoughts had been tumbling so fast while trying to analyze the surge of information that I was receiving and I didn't quite know what to say. I paused for thought and then asked Nina, "Ah, listen, I know you are busy piloting this aircraft, but my problem is also your problem, rather our problem. In my world, -well, our planet Earth, is in danger."

Nella looked at Nina and said, "I have the controls. You and your friend can talk. Go ahead. I want to listen too."

Nina took off her helmet and disconnected from the controls. Her hair fell from the inside of the helmet and as she shook her head every hair fell back into place. She licked her lips momentarily and brushed the hair strands from her forehead.

I felt as if my wife was sitting in that chair but no, she was waiting back at home for my return. I know what they wanted and I could not agree to their proposal. I know my wife would be imagining me doing something crazy right now.

We talked about imaginings sometimes, about some foolish thing, some game, that we played. Oh, I would say something mean like, "I went to the beach today with some blonde and we lay out at the beach together all day."

She would say, "Yeah, and this very handsome man called me today and we talked all day long about very private things. He is very handsome."

Then she would get very angry, though all the while smiling and teasing and hitting me at the same time. We never could betray each other, not in a million years, because our love is so strong. I could not supply any DNA now or ever if it meant having sex with another woman other than my wife. I was locked into my affair with my wife, my love, as if we were poured in concrete together. But Nina was so unusual and I hoped that we could be friends forever.

Nina said to me with a very earnest intent stare,   "Tell   me of your problem, now that you know ours. We are dying off, getting fewer and fewer. It's nonsense to try to kill everything around us. Tell us of about yours and our problem with the Earth. We will help you and you will help us."

I began, "It's the Earth, our planet. We have many problems that require immediate attention and we don't have long to find the solutions."

I began to recount all of our enormous calamities that were the immediate threats. "First, are the asteroids that will reach Earth's orbit in two years. There is an ever widening of the elliptical orbit of several of the bigger asteroids that are steadily approaching proximity to the Earth. If just one, even a mile wide, entered our atmosphere it would be catastrophic."

I explained how we just missed one that we didn't even see until it passed as close as the moon to the Earth. "There are others, miles wide that are on direct course to the Earth. Second, there is a wobble due to begin in the rotation of the Earth's axis that needs to be minimized or reduced at best. The ice is steadily building up on the South Pole and this will accentuate the effect of the wobble. Some of the ice needs to be melted in order to preserve the status of the continual rotation of the Earth in a smooth non-transitional way. There is just so much time that we have left and the spinning top will change the center of rotation to counteract the imbalance and return the equality of the spin. The possibility of the changing of charge carrying convection currents in the Earth's core, causing the magnetic field; that is charged ions or electrons circling in the liquid interior to thus be altered by wobbling of the Earth, would cause vast changes in our life as we know it. We need to prevent the extent of the wobbling by maintaining the current equilibrium of the present spin. The only way to do this is to melt some of the ice build up at the South Pole. You have the technology to achieve this miracle and maintain the present equilibrium of our spin."

She looked at me in utter amazement, I thought, but I waited for it seemed minutes, and minutes for her to respond. Then she said, "The enormous obstacles you seem to have presented are impossible to calculate without the help, of the elders and they may only have an opinion without recommendation. The solar system and its infinitesimal calculations are measured in several thousand lifetimes and to presume that this needs immediate attention is beyond anyone's imagination. The cosmos and their workings are measured in millions of years. Some years we have global warming and other years we have ice build up that follows because of climate changes. A few years ago everyone was screaming about global warming and that is due to a normal cycle that happens inside and outside the Earth's crust. I am not part machine for to just make illogical computations with binary logic strings that have taken lifetimes to perfect. Maybe you sense through some other psychic interpretation which exists but is not completely scientific that is immeasurable and unpredictable?"

I said a little embarrassed by her scientific put down, "No, I'm not psychic. The mathematics of infinite progression and regression prove that through constant successive build up of material in one extreme part of a spinning globe that it tends to change the position of the center of rotation. There is evidence of a massive buildup into the distortion of our constant planetary rotation. The more ice we have in the South Pole, the less secure is the constant of rotation. Equilibrium of the constant is not secure and its time to execution of the alteration is drastically diminishing. This is a fact, not psychic experimental guessing. You are the machine, not me. You should be able to reach a more conclusive estimation of this time frame than I. Who in your world is prone to this psychic opinion of science anyway?"

She just looked away into the clouds and said, "The elders, they think it has value and can be documented. But, they will not OK your solution, even to solving the aberration in the spin constant. It would be seen from satellites and we would be broadcasting our presence. The source of the plasma arc would be located. We've been reprogramming the copy sent from the satellites directly over the desert area here, but to begin mass melting of the South Pole would be an obvious give-away and they could trace our heat source back to the ships. They would make the signature of our vessels and trace us back here to the caves, and probably lock onto some of our communications. We are fighting a losing battle to keep our society secret as it is now. Eventually the whole world will know. It would only increase death and destruction. Everyone would be coming here and our society would be overrun and really contaminated by disease. They would find out we have been executing intruders. Thousands that have already been sent here have not reported back. They will just send others. Soon a report will get back and others will want vengeance. We have only acted in self defense and are not in search of conquest. You know yourself that you can never leave."

I said, "I know at this time, though even if I try to hide it, you know that I will try to escape. It is my duty."

She shot me an angry look, defiant, and said, "They may let you fight for your life, but you know who you will have to fight-----me. If they think you are planning on leaving or infer this from your attitude, then they will either let you fight for your right to stay or just exterminate you. If it is me you fight, and if they tell me to kill you, then I promise that I will make it swift and painless."

I began thinking to myself. My goal was to come here seeking a way to save the world and obtain some superior knowledge of mathematics that would allow me to prevent a disaster or numerous disasters and then to return to my family. I had an extremely difficult mission now, just to return and first to stay alive. But they still did not know how I deposited myself on their transport ship. Maybe they just thought it was a psychic irregularity, anyway. I hoped it was their line of thinking and not deductive reasoning that was leading these machine people into thinking that I did not have a tangible edge. I needed all the edge I could maintain.

Nina looked at me and made a gesture I did not understand. She made a shushing sound putting forefinger to her mouth that only added to my confusion. Was she saying one thing and thinking another? Did I somehow have a silent partner? I didn't think I could trust any of these people, not really. They had already killed maybe thousands of innocent or I presumed innocent soldiers, if a soldier is really innocent or at least he is in the country he is from. I was a soldier, and I was here behind enemy lines on a mission. Does he give up his true innocence when he agrees in his mind to kill when he receives his orders? His brain, his conscience, is rerouted to his desire to take orders, and he does not weigh in the balance his decision of right or wrong. In effect as a soldier, some just give up their souls and become a machine, just responding to the buttons their superior officers are pushing. If he falters or hesitates, he sacrifices his own life for choosing to weigh the consequences of his actions. The only choice he has is to choose for his own immediate survival or at the same time then a sure higher goal of self sacrifice for his country. It is a double-edged sword he finds himself up against. He follows his orders for his own benefit or dedication and respect but he then sacrifices himself for the greater benefit of the whole.

If the ultimate evil were to happen, the whole of the group of soldiers would be connected electronically and would have power to decide justice as a group and not just follow orders. As a result of this they would be thinking with one democratic mind. They would all voice their opinion and the majority would move the unit. This again is evil only because those who decided not to murder or kill would be overridden by the majority who decided to kill. A truly Democratic machine, in and of itself is not good alone. It needs benevolence, a kindness to make it human, and not just a reaction. But, if the majority of the group decides, then is it not human also? If I'm in the minority of this military force and decide not to kill, and the majority decides to execute the move and kill, then am I less human because I don't want to follow the majority?

Nina broke my internal reverie and spoke at the moment and my thoughts and mental philosophizing was interrupted.

"We are approaching the cave and there are certain security measures that we must take upon entering the defense system. We will be entering a certain triangulation with the terrain, running low altitude maneuvers to prevent the failsafe defense system from activation. If another approach is taken to the entrance to the cave, then we will be terminated by plasma arc defenses at the approaching path to the cave. The first ordinate is the prehistoric dolmens at the key, where you began your experience into our land. We must imitate the action of the sun with our light rays emanating from the plasma arc. We are capable of pure laser light bursts as well as plasma, concentrated energy streams. The laser light impulse through the key crystal will allow our further progression into the approach.   If you had succeeded in, breaking the computation of the five possible entrances, you would have been incinerated at some point farther along the approach. We intercepted your mathematical computer emissions from your open channel electronics and we know what your intent was. Are you surprised?"

I said, "Yes, I had no idea, that I was being monitored. Our electronic system has a severe hole in it."

Nina added another thing, "Yes, and your assumption that your calculations from your computer being off, is correct too. That Dolmen hasn't moved for four thousand years but the rotation of the Earth has an aberration. The crystal was put there by us and some slight alteration gives the true fix through triangulation rotation with respect to the old key but the crystal is right on the dot. We had to adjust, it for exact alignment, but the computations are figured out by

56

gyro alignment using the Earth's orbit around the sun, which is our central slave master while we are in this solar system. The stars and planets are great, but eventually our planet moves in orbit and our nearest perfect measure is involved with the sun, directly. We have been to the sun; or may I say very close, orbited and come back. Its plasma is constantly evolving and we have reached a true zenith in our discoveries about the sun."

"Tell me," I said, "Are these stories and fables true about the elders? We have for generations heard about wise men or sages living in these desert mountains. They were said to be practitioners of defensive arts and mathematical specialists that disappeared years ago into the desert. These stories go back before the origins of recent societies. They had been referenced to in some of the old scrolls and wall paintings that were newly discovered in some desert caverns. Even the Egyptians had referred to them in their hieroglyphics as the new mathematicians of the sun. These fighters were merciful to their victims and permitted the defeated to talk about their past life and have it chronicled before they were judged. This was something very unusual to have a conqueror who wants to hear about the life of their most hated enemy. The scrolls referenced that they had been taught by the sun itself and had helped countless peoples to progress and develop. They even were thought of as the scientists who had started a new era, and desert peoples had accepted their teachings as a part of their enlightened culture for a new society of mathematicians and philosophers."

Nina responded, "It's true, all true, and yes we were here at the time of the Egyptians and before all the others and learned directly from the solar data that was gathered by first hand information from being near planetary objects, and even the sun itself. The elder classes are brilliant and they teach some things to others and learn directly from all their many experiences. Some people do not prefer to learn the mathematics and prefer mostly philosophy. I am professor of my unit and can say without being questioned about what is right and correct. Even though I have evolved as part machine, they say I am still human."

"Yes," I said, "You are human, although I think there are problems in dealing with people who wish to know of your society.

Ah-the executions of all outsiders is a little suspect as a nonhuman activity."

She responded, "Oh, no? History records warfare and executions as perfectly normal human like behavior and not reflective of computed logical orientation. It is the computers and machines that have reached conclusions to data gathering for deducting the conditions of man's inhumanity to man resulting in the theory that it is a normal characteristic. It is also evident that an alternative way is not only better but logically desired. No one wants it if there is another way.

I am going to confide something to you that even my crew is not aware of. At this moment we are making preparations to take the main colony off world and leave only a minor skeletal crew here in the desert where we have lived for four thousand years. We are going to move to places like Mars and the Polar Regions of the moon and also around Jupiter to a moon called Io. We also have a station based in orbit still in stealth mode, undetected. It has been my idea all along to begin this move as soon as possible to prevent further destruction of life. The elders will agree, once they see you are here and have penetrated our greatest defenses. You are the catalyst I am hoping for to ignite the desire to leave the home planet and make all worlds safer for all people concerned. How about that Nella? Could you really believe we are finally leaving this platoon duty for something exciting?"

"Well," Nella said, "Since you put it that way, I would be happy if I could just see, outer space again. You've been there so many times on those solo probes. They let you explore the deepest reaches of outer space, alone, and we just stay here and dream. How is it on Io, anyway?"

Nina just smiled and said, "Well, Io is just a beginning now, and there will be many more to come after this one. Only robotics exists on most of our outposts. I just go there to set them up and check for readiness of colonization. Several are ready now and have the plant populations established and ready for occupation. It is a necessity that we increase our colonization of off worlds. All planets are subject to destruction by asteroids and most of them are hard to detect until it is very late, in the intercept program. We have hypothetical situations logged into the computers and all the possible collisions are catastrophic even if the asteroids are destroyed by missiles. The debris still enters the atmosphere and causes widespread chaos."

We are coming up on the coordinates of the cave base, and I see the key rock formation ahead in the distance. I remember the long nights in the desert and the battles that I fought, to stay alive against enemies on all sides.

Nina said, "We watched you fight and did not understand what happened to the outsider watchers of the key, until a closer examination turned up that you killed the killers. We had seen three outsiders watching the key and the invaders killed them all. Only you remained alive after the fighting. How is it possible that you could defeat so many that were invincible? We are going to be severely tested very soon and if you have some secret weapon, I hope we could all share in it. Because I have let you live, we all might be in grave danger. I am hoping to appeal to the scientific reasoning of the elders and not to their survival fears when I tell them that I have you with me. We have plasma arced everything in sight before, to clean up all outside microbes, and then suddenly you appeared in the ship with us. I am going to have to let them know that you are with us eventually."

I looked around the cockpit and control room of the ship. A totally unfamiliar environment was within this one room and I caught myself gazing at all the various unfamiliar controls and monitoring devices and then staring at Nina, a totally beautiful and strange being with quick movements and bright eyes. She was so alien, like no other being but yet I knew she was human. She had on a jump suit with little circular chips in different arrays. I was beginning to feel a little ecstatic like there was an electric charge running between me and girls, but especially Nina. Then she spoke, "I want to confide in you a little something unusual about us that you may have noticed. We are all loaded to maximum tolerance level with food from hybrid bees. We have our own hives that we have cultured deep in the underground. It's called Royal Jelly and it makes us give off natural pheromones but we live much longer life spans than without it. You must be feeling strange about now because sooner or later the pheromones begin to anesthetize you. Oh, you will stay conscious and alert; you just will have become a little more interested in our beauty and charm. It's no real hazard to you and I hope you enjoy your feelings because I'm enjoying mine. We perform at a much greater awareness level than without it."

I was in a slightly dulled level of consciousness and if I had to fight right now I would be in a hard time, since I had no feelings of danger, but I knew that I had to think of what would happen when the elders made their judgment. I could see we were on final approach to the key. I wanted to observe exactly how it was used by these people and what method or purpose they had for the crystal formation.

I asked Nina, "Please, would you allow me one favor, and that is the triangulation mathematics for the key to the cave entrance."

She said, "Oh, that's easy but it is maybe a strange formulation, since it does not appear naturally in modern mathematics. It is the equivalent of the Golden Mean, an ancient formula for deriving the correct proportion of ancient Greek temples and whatever else they wanted to divide or proportion. It's easy and not so easy. The triangular intersections are the assumed points of destination for the light beams but in actuality it is also the golden mean of the construction. The crystal was put there to focus and divert the light beam to the opening in the mountain. Our crystals are constructed to honor the path of light of the Golden Mean and we are guided automatically at super speed or the door will open and close before any craft enters even if the location is found. Once inside the mountain we are landed by force fields that cushion the impact landing of the aircraft. Something your aircraft carriers could use."

As we passed directly at the key, a plasma arc was emitted from the nose cone and went directly into the center of the crystal key. A strange blue light of brilliant intensity emerged and after we passed over the key, the blue light continued to stream from the crystal.

I asked, "How does the light continue to be emitted when the plasma beam is turned off?"

Nina said, "The crystal has a built in capacitor, woven like threads sealed into the face of the crystal, which sets up a resonance that continues to pulsate through the crystal after it is charged. The plasma arc beam does not actually touch the crystal, only the light rays activate and bring the crystal to resonate, thus causing the beams to refract and continue long enough to activate the doors of the mountain cave."

Immediately we entered the mountain ahead and it was instantly dark and then instantly light.

Chapter 3. **The Secret Cavern**

We were softly enveloped into a cushion of what felt like air and then we were at the ground immediately. Waves of purple light washed over the jet and Nina explained, "They know you are aboard and are bathing us in ultra violet radiation to help kill any microbes hitching aboard the ship."

The place we landed in was a wide cavernous room, loaded with electronic computer images and pinpoint LCD lights. Most of the ground crew were women and the only men I noticed were in the observation windows peering out at the ground crew and us. These must be the elders or their representatives. Three more craft landed near us and the bay had a load of ships, as many as two hundred in parking position with the wings up like aircraft carrier jets. I noticed there were elevators and other tunnels leading away from the main cavern. There was something strange going on here. I thought I would be arrested and taken away if they knew I was on the ship, but something else was going to take place. I had ominous feelings but I didn't know if they were unfounded or not. Strange lights were coming on and there was a sense of apprehension, and just nervous fear. These people had lived here apart from known civilization for centuries and this group was well populated. Where did they all live and how could it be possible they had been hidden from society underground all this time?

We had completely stopped now and they began to run a check of the entire equipment shutdown. A count down and check off was in progress. Nina looked beautiful in the semi-shaded purple light that bathed the spacecraft. I had begun to think of it as a spacecraft when she began talking about the trips that she had made into outer space and beyond. I started to get this tingle and sensed that something was about to happen.

I looked at Nina and said, "What is about to happen? They are clearing the area and we don't have the reception that I assumed we would have."

She glanced quickly at me and said, "You are right. There would normally be a full contingent of soldiers here. We have organized groups that check all the ships after arrival. When the ultraviolet cleansing finished it should have been the signal for the contingent to arrive, but there is no one here. I saw the crew when we first landed and the elders in the view windows but now there is no one. What could be happening? Well, you have to help me on this one because I do not think this is normal. They were there when we first arrived and then they left immediately so there is something amiss. They did not want to be in the area for some reason. I think we are about to be part of a process of cleansing."

Seeing Nina was at this moment wandering what course of action to take I asked, "Is there any way out of the ship and down to another level under the ship without being seen?"

She responded, "Yes, immediately under the ship is a service tunnel, but it is locked securely on entrance for evident reasons of preventing a breach in security and that could be an option, but we would need to have a contact on the other side. It may be a way of escape, but to take the ship, maybe; they do not wish to lose this ship since there are only limited numbers and difficult to process."

I exclaimed, "So we take the ship! Is it possible? Would they let us leave? How can we get back through the automatic opening if it is guarded? I thought that if the door opened with a power burst from the crystal then would it be possible for it to open with the same from our plasma arc from the opposite side?"

She paused for a moment, thinking, with reservation and then spoke softly, "Yes it is worth a try. Do you really think they are going to clean all of us after what I have done for the country?"

Now she was very unsure of herself and not at all calculating like a know it all machine and I felt sorrow that she did not have that definite assuring attitude any more.

"I don't think they really have a choice and they do not really want to talk, do they? Try to open a dialogue and stall until we get the ship turned around. Isn't it a normal procedure to turn the ship to the open door anyway? You don't just shut down and leave it here do you?"

She looked now up at the observation window and a determined frown made two little creases above her eyebrows. "I just have to rotate the plate beneath the ship and we will be in position."

She had an air now of assurance and we had a ray of hope to survive this trap. She said defiantly, "They are going to kill us all. I have deducted that you are right that they will kill us when we leave the ship; it is sure."

I had to ask the question to find out if we would survive the ordeal, "Are all on board loyal or will they betray us?"

"Yes!" she said emphatically. "They are my loyal family as well as my troops and they will not move against us because we are a unit. They also know we are all dead and have resigned themselves to our fate. They will follow me anywhere."

Nina began to key into the communication system, opening a channel to the elders. "This is 636 in ship Probe I, preparing to off load ship and shut down systems. We will be revolving 180 degrees to prepare ship ready for next mission. I would like reception committee and soldiers standing by to interrogate prisoner found in desert sector 54. We are crew of Star 5 including prisoner. Make ready my decontamination unit and also one for the prisoner. We are unclean and need assistance off loading in ten minutes. Do I get confirmation?"

There was a long pause and then a muffled conversation that could not be defined and then a booming voice came through the speaker.

"Yes, 636, confirmed. Probe 636, take the ship into shutdown immediately after you rotate and proceed with crew to the cell holding area. We will decontaminate immediately and you will be questioned along with the visitor for benefit of all the other six model crews. The six young trainee Probe Crews need to learn from your mistakes."

Nina told me whispering, "The other six crews are the new teens getting educated to replace us and they are like wolves, pouncing on all of our mistakes. You would like them; they are all beautiful, but yes only young girls. Now you know, only the elders are men, and only men. All warriors and fighters are women. But guess what; they are our teachers and masters. We have evolved. The machines have the babies and the women, now that they do not have to go through childbirth, are the workers and fighters. We protect the men but they are the trainers. Only those in the most inner sanctum are men. It is as it should be; we are the best fighters since we can move more swiftly.

Our lives are shorter but the elders have been here for generations and generations, guiding us and teaching us."

Then she asked me a curious question and I knew that they were being manipulated into shorter life spans by these domineering elder men. "How many life times have you lived and have you taught very many generations of females?" said Nina innocently. She continued before I could answer, "There are many other reasons that we are the best fighters in all the land, but mainly our older masters have given us enhancements, physical and mental."

I had to tell her, "Nina, there is definite evidence here that they have tampered with yours and all the other female's biological time lines for life span. How many years do the women warriors usually live? How long do the elders usually live?"

She looked at me with curiously sincere eyes and said softly, "We live about 30 years and the elders live about 10 of our generations, that is 300 years. They have immense knowledge that they impart to us."

I said slowly and deliberately, "Nina, usually in my world the ages for men and women are pretty much the same with the women outliving the men by a few years."

She looked astonished and then I said, "They have engineered your body to be faster and more deadly in combat, but you pay the price in the years you give up. In nature the birds have all the advantage of speed but look at the difference in mammals and birds. What a price you pay for your speed!"

Nina looked at me and just touched me slightly on my temple with her forefinger before I could see it coming, and then just said, "Wait and watch; things will be changing, my new friend. I would like to take life slowly for a change and smell the roses."

We looked at each other for a few minutes and reached an understanding in that silent moment that I haven't felt with a woman in years. It was then that I noticed a little rainbow of color like an aura while looking into her eyes. This was definitely not Earth-like and a little bit too alien but she was an exceptionally unusual person with or without the rainbow aura. Then as suddenly as it appeared, it went away and I could not explain it.

Then, poised and determined, Nina said emphatically while

looking at her crew, "I'll have to force my rank upon some of the crew to get them to come and refit the ship with essential water and provisions. This is a normal procedure and they would not be expected to just abandon the ship without restocking for the next outing. It is expected and I should be expressively angry for this infraction of duty to neglect the maintenance of the lead probe vessel. I'm going to page the ground crew myself and make them refuel and refit the ship."

Nina keyed in a loud speaker system that could be heard all over the huge cavern. "This is 636 and I am demanding refit by the standing ground crew or face all of you retirement to chemical extraction. The cleansing you risk from refit of my ship is nothing you will receive compared to replacement of your electrolytic solutions by the elder chemical experimentation order. They are standing by with stasis units for all of you on my orders. I am senior probe captain and have jurisdiction in this sector. March immediately to the front of my ship or I will activate the plasma arc and finish your tour of duty at this station permanently!"

I never thought she could be so tough and never have I witnessed such an immediate response to a given order. She was in complete authority regardless of the misgivings the few elder commanders had who were in charge of this station. At least twenty ground crew charged in front of the ship to do her bidding and the supplies were delivered immediately.

An authoritative but quiet elder voice simply stated, "After refit, 636, they must go to cleansing. Order them to do so please. I will contact the elder council and we will have to discuss the infraction of duty by the ground crew. Please come to my quarters after cleansing for review in front of the council for debriefing. We are assembling the elder council in one hour."

Nina said somewhat in a reluctant tone of voice, "I will comply immediately after the cleansing." Then Nina turning to the ground crew assembled in front of the pilot viewing window said, "This is 636 and as the Probe Wing Captain I am assigning this entire ground crew to clean up duty because I am late with my refueling and maintenance of my aircraft. Those who do not wish permanent cleaning duties will immediately complete their assigned tasks."

For whatever reasons that the ground crew had been late for refitting, they responded immediately to the order given by Nina, and we were within minutes ready for take off again.

Suddenly, I got an idea that was as far fetched as any I have ever conceived, but it was worth a try. I asked with all the respect due her office as major wing leader, "Nina, are the elders any or all of them enhanced by electronic wiring and is it hard wiring? I mean, does it belong to the family of the electronic group as an entity? Are they dependent on the main computer family, even though they are not speeded up like the probe troops? Do they have a family-wired unit to communicate or facilitate functions?"

"Yes," replied Nina. "All of the life forms are electronically wired past five years of age. All of us life forms have electronic components to enhance and simplify communication with the central computers and other beings. The electronic components are actually not needed after 12 years of age, but they remain because they are training devices. Some even have them displayed in view as part of the facial decoration for a status symbol but mine is covered by my hair as I don't need a status symbol. I have the authority to banish any I choose."

With a wave of her slender hand she uncovered a small silver disk just above her ear that I had not noticed before.

"Come closer to me and I will show you the little nuisance implant I received at five years of age." She held her hair back with her hand and said, "See, right here, and touch it with your hand. It is a part of me and is a worse ordeal to remove, so I let it stay."

I moved closer and her perfume was like a breeze of jasmine filling every sensory cell of my being, with a dizzy concoction of exotic tingling. I became weak and my hand trembled as I touched the little silver disk and her ear and soft hair at the same time. As I touched her hair a little rainbow glow began pulsing around her head and my ears began to feel like warm water was running inside of them. She crossed her legs at that moment and then asked me to hold her hair back behind her head. She put on a golden clasp at that moment to hold all of her thick brown hair in one flowing ponytail and at that precise moment all the crew did the same thing. They all pulled their hair back and encircled it with a golden clasp.

She gave an order that was unusual at that moment but everyone complied immediately and I was just surprised to say the least.

She said, "Change out of the suits so they can be cleansed." Immediately she began to take off her flight suit and so did the other crew members. All I remember was, looking at her and staring at her as she unclothed in front of me. Never have I seen such a beautiful woman in all my life. "Help him," she said. Immediately they began and I was unclothed as they were. She walked up to me and was standing so close that we were touching. She just stood there looking into my eyes and breathing into my face and all the whole time I was nervously excited and blood was pulsing through every vessel in my body. I didn't know if she would object or not, but I had set my mind and could not go back. I kissed her and embraced her for at least one whole minute. Holding her in my arms was everything I wanted and she was like a doll, not objecting to anything. Then suddenly as soon as it started, the magic was over and she was in control again.

She said, "Get him dressed!" Then I grabbed her and held her and kissed her again very long and passionately while she waited receiving my affections, all the while Lita, Bispo, and Nella, just stood within arms reach and watched us while we were holding and kissing each other. Then Lita and Bispo took hold of my arms and began to pull me away as I did not want to leave her and wanted to stay with her, holding her, but they would not let me, even as she was so receptive to me, lost in her desire as well. As we were torn away from each other, Nella pulling Nina away, we looked at each other and held hands for one last moment as our embrace was broken at the last minute.   They dressed and helped me with my new flight suit, a light weight fabric of non bulky material meant for comfort.

Finally, Nina said, "I knew you were curious and had feelings of desire but we are all in danger and we must think with clear heads. You are the first man I have let see me this way. I am human and not all machine, as you can see. But there is one problem. You see, we can only just be friends, because there is this one statesman that is my promised. We were promised to each other five years ago, but the elders have not agreed yet that we can be ship mates. I am thinking about him even though it is rare to let a man onboard a probe ship with

68

a crew of women warriors. His name is Max, and one day he will assume his elder status. We can still be friends, you and I, but no sex, only friends and not too friendly until we are safe. It is too distracting from my duties as pilot captain. Come up here and sit by me, close, and we will talk and be friends while we are able to."

"Yes," I said. "Of course, we can be friends. I am married and have a wife and she will be angry and upset to know this happened."

She said rather coolly, Well, nothing did happen, really except, you should not have lost your control and should have been more refrained with your friendship. You should not be so forward to me, holding me and kissing me," Nina said.

"Yes," I said. "I know, but you are very beautiful to me and I just was out of control. I know it is not permitted even in my world."

"It is the pheromones and you are not responsible!" Nina said emphatically. "Listen. We may be boarded any minute now. If the elders assemble, and take the pre-emptive strike, they will contain everything before it has to be decided by vote. If you have a plan, let's have it now, you can see me again and I will be your friend in ways that will not compromise either of us. What I wear or don't wear is no one's business but mine. I know now that you like to look at me, even if I am a part machine. If we get free and live, I will let you see me in the normal ways that I am accustomed to. Now that you know I'm your friend, tell me your plan. We have only minutes to live, I think."

"Ok, let's think," I said. "If we could enter a matrix program into the computer bank maybe we could guide the components into fields that would be a distraction. Could you recognize it, ignore it and still function normally?"

Nina said, "How do you mean?""

I said, "Could you ignore an electronic command if programmed into your communication crystal?"

Nina said, "Maybe, I could, but how could you do this?"

I said, "Here is a simple logic program I'm going to try. Watch this. Tell me if there is an effect on your senses?"

I numerated the program into the console on which she opened a clear channel for me to input the instructions into a code that she translated almost simultaneously as she read it from the other console. For some beautiful reason mathematics just has no boundaries as far as language is concerned and it is comprehended almost universally. (Size, location-xy, location-vw, time-2, occurrence-a=2, b=2, c=2, d=10732050808, e=1, f=1, and g=1.732050808, then a progression through g with regard to set operations, (multiplication) of given set 1 through 10=x.

This is a given matrix for a set of operations and within a given parameter. Once the elements are determined and the operations are set, computational processes will decide the answer. Will this divert the thinking process of the computer bank, long enough to reprogram the coordinates of our pulse engines? Can we make a get away and elude the possible and probable pursuers?"

Nina looked at me and made a slight gesture pulling on her suit and waving away a strand of hair that fell across her face and said, "I'm going to see how much you enjoy my company, and what makes you so curious about me. Your eyes are very curious, Thomas. There will not be any time limit on the test. I say what happens on this ship. If I want to test your concentration, then I say what goes on while I am Captain of this ship. We will come back and get my promised later, when the elders have had time to think and evaluate their mistakes. For a while I will give you what I know that you want, but not so very much that it will compromise your integrity."

She put her hand under my chin and made a kiss to the air. "I'll have to add some difficulty to the search for an answer X, or this will just be taking up process time and not actual thinking time on the main master slave network of computers. It needs to think about why, and it does not need to think about just a result. But yes, this will, when altered, provide a good exercise for a computer and we do love a search for definite answers. If the evaluation processes into a more random pattern, it will make the computer system that is representing our enhancements and evaluation process, proceed into the next level. We are constantly pushing to achieve the next level. This way everyone that is connected electronically will have to upgrade and all of the stimuli will react to compensate for the endeavor to go to the higher level.

Here- look, I'm formulating a new assignment to your variable that will reach even to the curiosity of the elders. They will wonder how they can cope with the new enhancement and wait for the finish of the results of this formulation once it begins. To alter the golden mean even slightly would completely disorient every phase of our life. As you can see this is the key relationship in our electronic organization as well as the entrance to the cave. Once these coordinates are reprogrammed, then a new entrance will be coded into the crystal as well.

So the result is as follows, and we would change the actual programming of a civilization. Well, for only one brief period of time, until they discover the error; that we, the heretics, have made a lie of the whole process of enhancement."

I asked Nina, looking into her deep blue eyes that were so liquid and, inviting, "What will they do when they discover that their whole civilization has been misled?"

My heart began to beat faster when I thought of what she had planned if we escaped.

Nina looked at me and maybe reading my mind, she casually opened the top of her jump suit as if it was a natural thing and accidentally or on purpose touched me with her sleek delicate boot, sending an electric tingle up into the pit of my stomach.

She said, "You will get to see me again in a more natural way soon enough. I know what you are thinking. You're eyes are looking intensely at what, I can not say."   With only slight movements of her legs she made me feel almost dizzy with my imagination making images of her without the jump suit on.

Then she said, "I'll enjoy looking at you also Mr. Coltrane because I know you like to be close to me. This time you are going to find out that it is not wise to make wishes even silently. I can command Lita and Bispo and my crew to do what I say. You should prepare to cooperate completely or the result could be uncomfortable for you and that would not be pleasant.

About the elders: change will come to the elders and they'll incorporate their mistakes into the enhancement process, I suppose. Maybe we will be safe when they discover the grave mistakes they made when they gave complete trust and authority to a system that was thought to be infallible."

My breathing was still rapid and excited as she began to lean next to me and allow the curve of her body into my shoulder.

I asked her, "Will they wake up and be able to function normally until they repair their grip on reality?"

"Yes," she said, looking up into my eyes. "I think they will be able to recover without too much of a problem. The incident will not be tolerated though, if they discover it before we get away through the new gate."

I looked into the distance of the dark underground cavern, lit from below and the light reflected into the upper reaches of the cavern roof. The light cascaded from natural stalactites protruding down into the room from above. They looked as though they were apart and separate from this ultra modern facility, used for a space ship hanger.

"Nina," I said with a little tremble in my voice, "Do you know what you are doing to me and that you are interfering with my will to resist you?

She smiled a little as she turned to look in my face and said, "Yes, of course, I've been trained to weaken men and make them almost unable to fight or for that matter even to escape. But with you it is different. I am enjoying the process and also I am getting pleasant feelings myself. I can't wait to begin the test and get some valid electrical responses from you. You're to do exactly what I say but I will not take advantage of your weakness. Right now I just want you to realize that I am also human and electric at the same time. My feelings are being affected just as your feelings are beginning to intensify. You will begin to imagine very many scenarios but probably all of them will not exist. Your own mind is doing more to provoke you than I am."

She was correct in that respect and I had not ceased to imagine countless probabilities and none of them were happening right now. She was so unpredictable that I could not estimate even my longevity much less the present emotional state that she was in.

"I have not changed my condition but your mind is imagining that I am going to do something unexpected," she said. "You should relax and whatever I do the fact remains that you are not in control and will have to comply with my requests. Now, help me to take off these little boots. I am more comfortable in stressful situations without them."

It was as if I had been given an order that I could not disobey, so I helped her. I felt as if I could not resist her advances but she wasn't making any except to be provocative. I had almost lost my will to resist; she was truly mastering the situation at this point and I was feeling like an uneasy ecstasy that was pushing me into a dream state.

Then suddenly, as if I was released she said, "Get up!" We must be attentive. They have trained me to win these battles of will but it is you who must save us. Resist and get back you cognitive abilities."

I was thinking again of survival and I asked her, "Can we make the new gate before they come for us or do we need to evacuate the ship for the dark reaches of this cavern?"

Nina said, "Let's make the gate new and let them figure out how we changed the key, and we can plot a course for a moon cavern that no one knows about but me. We'll be in the moon's gravity and disappear before they can trace the ship's pulse emitter and disappear into the interior reaches of the lunar underground where they will never find us."

"OK," I said.

Then she said in a very businesslike way, "Let's lay in the network for the matrix. If we program the light pattern for our new coordinates, the gate will open in front of the ship and we will be out of the cavern in seconds. Begin the reroute and final activation of plasma beam, changing the coordinates when I say 3,2,1, -now."

"OK," I said, relieved now that we were once again in the business of surviving instead of getting into trouble with a fire of desire that was going to be difficult to control.

"OK," she said.

It was a new word for Nina and she used it again and this time with very much authority.

"I'm changing your constants, Thomas, and we'll begin the new countdown. It's programmed in the counting, --3,2,1. "

Pinging and rumbling began and suddenly a light appeared and a new doorway where there was none before. Only, it was much larger and wider than the previous door. We had created a new doorway to the cavern and were about to leave the base when suddenly there appeared a group in small armored vehicles between us and the new door way.

"We will have to move this obstacle out of our path or we will not be able to leave," shouted Nina, running around giving orders barefooted, her boots lying at the console chair. She was worried and nervous and I could do nothing to help. All I could do was wait and watch and hope she could work some miracle.

Nina told me, "These are our special forces in the ground battalion and they will be quite furious that we want to leave and through a new gate way too. The old one has been in place for 10,000 years and is in harmony with the sun, opening with a pulse from the plasma arc. They will be furious that a simple computer math table opened a new gate, especially without plasma arc initiation first.

Here they come and we don't have enough time to reroute to another location. The group that you see there is not of my family. They are thoughtless, heartless, killing machines and I cannot say that we will be able to pass this gate unless we fight. We have to fight or we will not be alive very much longer. This group is the first order guard that is quick on the scene of the battle. Let's engage them now before the next column arrives. We have maybe 10 minutes and then we are exposed to the full assault of the elders and the national army. This is maybe just a failsafe from the minor council of elders put here because of the national problem with outsiders. These have no political or emotional ties to my family that has nurtured and protected me all my life. My scientists actually fed me when I was an infant and my biologists monitored me day in and day out until I was six years old. I knew the names of all my tutors and programmers. Number SP45 was the king of specialists who really cared for me when I was little. Number SM7 and number SM8 are part of my family who taught me feeding and learning. But the real personal trainer I have had in secret that kept me safe from all attackers and taught me self defense was someone that I want you to meet. You have never seen a person like this in all of your life. I know that I am unusual to you and you like to look at me, but I am just human in an advanced way to you. But, Jada, is well, a more than most unusual person even to us.

Since we are going to be here for a few more minutes, I am going to call for Jada to come secretly to help us and go with us. I think that she will agree to go on a trip with us. If you like looking at me, just wait until you see Jada. She is very, very, womanly and she

74

will let your mind imagine more than you can actually visualize, of that I'm sure. You like that don't you? Just remember though, I'm Captain, pilot of the ship and you follow my orders just like everyone else. What I say is what will happen on the ship, although I will consider your opinion.

She is coming now through the bottom hatch of the ship. Oh, by the way, she is an extraterrestrial. Surprise! The elders don't even know either. So you see you are not the first outsider to corrupt our closed society."

They had begun amassing troops at the new gate that was now open, hoping to be able to create a force large enough so we would not leave. I was hoping now that since we had it open there was nothing they could do to stop us. Nina opened a com-link to another part of the underground maze that existed in this cavern system. She began to talk in a strange clicking sound. Maybe it was the Martian language, but I wasn't sure. ttt-k-tt-ttt----k – tt --kk. Then, she paused to explain. "This is the language of the people from a far away place that you probably know as Mars. I have been there a few times with this craft that we are in right now and Jada wants to go back with us immediately if we are leaving. I think because you are here, and I am no longer able to stay, if I permit you to live, and my group squad, all of us will be killed if we don't leave immediately.

Jada is on her way with an escort of two of my family. They are elders from central command who are safe contacts. As you may have guessed, we do have an underground operation here that is seeking some change in our government. We will leave in about one minute. Here, on Terra, Jada and my two friends are pulling the plug on this, my incubator, and we have been given permission to start our own colony on Mars. Welcome to your new home."

The hatchway opened on the away side of the gate and from a portal in the runway hanger floor emerged one very normal looking beautiful woman and two very dignified looking men, all wrapped in white safari looking outfits. But, from the minute they entered the ship, I knew that the woman was different from all other humans that I had ever seen. The face of Jada was like a mirage within a rainbow. The color came from some aura or force field as it seemed suspended around her face. Her hair was honey blonde draped around her ears and swept behind her head and tied much as Nina's and the crew. Where did the rainbow of color come from? Could it be thoughts or projections of wave communication, or maybe it was a nuance or cosmetic feature? No, I tend to think it was definitely cosmic and useful.

I looked at Jada and she just smiled. Yes, she was beautiful and shapely just the way Nina had flippantly said that she was. Her eyes though, were more intense and reserved than Nina's. Maybe she was telepathic some or at least making an effort to be mysterious. I don't know.

Nina came to me and putting her hand on my shoulder said to Jada, "This is our newest outsider, Mr. Thomas Jefferson Coltrane, and I know you will have some interesting things to talk about, but right now I am setting a course for the dark side of the moon. This gate will not hold for long. Thomas, I know you had some puzzles to put to the elders, but ask these two, Idor 2 and Idor 3. They were going to exterminate us all."

Idor 2 looked at me and said, "Hello, Mr. Coltrane, thank you for holding our knowledge with such reverence that you would risk your life to come here, but the timing is bad and there are many upheavals in our land of Terra right now. It is better you pose your questions about the coming calamities that Nina spoke of, to Jada herself. She has a rare knowledge that is built upon many generations like us, but you may find her answers more workable than our own. She has to be protected. She has a rare gift of discernment and cerebral acuity that frankly we are lacking in at this moment. Protect her and Nina with your life because they have the answers to saving all of our civilizations. We bid you goodbye."

"Goodbye," also said Idor 3.

I just said, "Thank you," and then they reentered the portal in the floor under the ship.

Nina closed and secured the ship's under hatch immediately as fire bloomed in the foreground. It was what looked like the makings of a portable plasma ray. I had seen one as I looked through into the cabin of the transport when I was a stowaway and observed the weapons array common to these ships. Out of automatic survival and just plain fear, I grabbed the yoke of the arc, turning the ship's cannon in the direction of the flame arc and at the same time I lowered the palm of my hand onto the firing button as I had seen one of the crew doing before. I was not prepared for the blinding light that was then speared into the group of light cavalry force amassed in front of our ship. The arc was not pinpoint but bloomed in a large loop, held together by some cosmic power unknown to me and the resulting loop of incandescent blue light sliced cleanly through all existing forms in front of our vehicle, leaving only ashes, blood, bone, and metal flakes sprayed like a splatter of mud across the paved runway.

In one moment of time, Nina jumped into her command chair, still barefoot and said, "Strap in everyone! We leave now or the deal we made will be canceled by the two Idors 2 and 3. Jeffrey has punched his way out of the cage and I'm not waiting around for anybody's cleansing or second thoughts about our action against our own troops."

Everyone grabbed a stasis chair and the automatic g-force equalizer which secured everyone in low stasis on demand, began rhythmic graduations of pre-flight punctuation.

Nina said, "1,2,3, ready go!" and we were nailed into our low stasis synch grabbers as we were making fast-moving pictures of the rocky scenery below and then fast fleeting clouds sailed by, then nothing but high altitude wisps ran by past our view window in moments of little time packets. Finally then Nina's spaceship hit the nothingness of black blue open empty sky and we were smoothly gliding to a rendezvous with the other side of the moon.

She spoke into the voice com, "Hope everyone got into stasis chairs before the rapid take off. I gave a glance back before I shoved it into overdrive and everybody looked like they had made it into a stasis cradle. From this day on we are on our own and there will be no more orders from home base. We are home and unless someone else thinks they can elevate their powers of persuasion to include rebel leader, it looks like I'm yours by decree of the elders Idor party of two. They will be adopted into our group eventually and so will we be adopted into theirs, but in the mean time we are on our own. There may be some missiles launched against us but there will be no proton beams fired at us. The missiles are old world weapons and could have been fired at us right out of the cave, but we are relatively safe unless they have one already sniffing us out. We are now tracing our signature back to the cave. Lita, have we confirmation? ---No tail rider, yet?"

"Nina," said Lita, "I've got bad news. We have two that left the cave with us following our exact vector and homed in on our signature. The only reason they haven't caught us yet, is the slam G-7 takeoff you made, but they are missiles and will close in on us in less than a minute. I'm firing chafe now, for one, but the other will know and reprogram to ride through. It's up to you to pilot us out."

"OK," Nina said, "Everyone, if you're not still in stasis it's too late to keep from getting bumped around. We're rolling 30 degrees side ways up around and over to get behind."

The ship lurched as if something kicked it directly to the right side and we entered what appeared to be a braking motion that tumbled over and over like an Olympic diver making a one and a half twisting somersault and we came up behind and bumped the tail of the missile, breaking the fins and possibly damaging propulsion. We continued on but the missile made a wide left swinging arc down and away out of sight.

Nina jumped out of stasis and asked, "Is everyone alright?" No one it seems had then enough energy to unlatch and jump out the way she did so everyone was shaken up with our stomach still rolling but OK. Normally we would have blacked out but the stasis machine responded to all anti-gyroscopic motion by squashing the blood vessels flat against the flow of blood.

Nina said, "Now they will not chase us because soon we will disappear from their electronic eyes and ears. I'm going to commence a minor flare from our plasma beam that will only push a magnetic storm behind us to help propulsion and disrupt any electronics at the same time. The ionic impulse engine will be our main secondary and also aid in diffraction of electronic beacons that they are using to search for our trail with. Now we will approach the dark side of the moon and disappear for a short time.

On one probe trip I was taking pot shots at the lunar surface when I noticed an impulse shot that did not ignite and signal a contact. I thought it must have misfired but I shot again at 20 meters ahead and hit sparks. It was a hole deep within a crater that had given me the location of an underground hideaway. I've been there several times and it's big enough to cruise into, with the ship and we are going to spend several days in this place.

Lita, guide us in while I go and help Mr. Jefferson Coltrane out of his stasis grabber."

I looked out the port window as Lita took the controls and guided the ship into the dark hole that loomed up ahead and we slipped quickly and cleanly into the interior of the moon. Only Lita could see where we were exactly by looking at the instruments since everything was pitch black outside.

Chapter 4. **Moon Crater**

Nina came over and took great care to lift the arms of the stasis grabber and reaching over me she made sure that she was very close to me and her hair was in my face as I just relaxed and let her make all of her adjustments. It seems that she just was taking great exaggerations to do many things unnecessary just so she could tease me by being so close up to me. It was very evident what she was doing and it was not that I did not enjoy being very close to her. After she helped me to emerge she walked over to Jada and they came back to me after talking in clicking sounds for some minutes.

Nina said, "We're going to give you that reward for helping us to make our getaway and Jada has agreed to participate in the reward procedure. You are going to be enjoying this I'll guarantee. You are looking a little shaken up. Nella, help Mr. Jefferson out of his flight suit while Jada and I discuss the time period we will spend here in this lunar cave."

My pulse quickened as I imagined what they were going to do with me. I hoped they would be civil and respect my wishes. To stay within my protective emotional boundary that I had built up around myself was a most important moral thing for me to do. I just was not sure if I could maintain my values as I envisioned them but I was going to try. I didn't know what kind of plans she had for me. Nella was encouraging me to cooperate and was trying to get me to take off my jump suit that they had given me.

"I am not comfortable in doing this," I said a little loudly. "I solemnly request that you not compromise my trust that I have in you, Nina,"

Nella looked back at Nina as if for to receive some order. She looked again at me and began to pull me this way and that.

Jada spoke up, "Nina, you are intimidating this honorable man. I don't think you should continue this reward for such a long time period or even at all, since you have an entirely different value system than he has. You will make him nervous and it could be improper if you are not respectful."

Nina said, "I made a promise, and I know what he wants even

if he doesn't say it. At this time and this place of my choosing we will reward him whether he wants it or not. Mr. Jefferson, Jada is from a hive society on Mars and has not the least inclination to hold values such as you yourself are accustomed to, so don't start thinking that she can or will save you from me. She can not even save you from herself since she is not familiar with what you call moral values. You really don't have to worry though since you will not be forced to do anything against your wishes. I am going to my cabin briefly and when I return I will be more comfortable than I have been since I started my trip. I will see if your eyes betray you and I will notice how you react. Your test will begin when I return and it will not be so difficult since you do not get to choose how I, the Captain, will dress. The test will consist of the fulfillment of what you imagined, but only briefly, even if your mind rebels against it."

When she returned I heard her bare feet on the metal deck as she almost silently entered. As she came in I did not even look away but just took in the entire visual panorama.

Then she motioned to Jada and just said, "You're next and don't take so long."

Jada, the Martian, returned in a short time and she had skin that shimmered as a mirage drifting above the desert floor like a beautiful rainbow, the same as her aura that was almost a copy of Nina, except for the electrically enhanced skin. She walked up to me and stood against me closely and beckoned me to feel the texture of her skin. The feeling was like little pinpricks of static electricity that ran into and down the surface of my own body. Never have I felt a real electric charge from a person as if she was electrically charged with the snapping of little charges of electricity.

Nina turned out the light and you could actually see the sparks and then after a brief few moments she turned them back on and I was confronted by the other three, all standing at only an arms length.

"Now girls," said Nina. "Do not harass Mr. Jefferson Coltrane. He is to be rewarded, not tormented. Nella, bring Mr. Jefferson something to drink and some nice fruit and sweets. For the next few days you are to bring Mr. Jefferson Coltrane anything he wishes. Continue your pleasant duties now for the next two days while we accommodate his wishes and talk to and get to know Mr. Coltrane.

On, the next morning after the second, we will again return to our crew obligations and his reward will be over. Immediately we will depart for Jada's home world of Mars. Tom, you'll be surprised to find we have gravity. You can relax on the ship just as on Earth. The gyroscopic sheet of electronic material forms a loop within our deck, giving us a little less than normal Earth's gravity."

It was just as she said, for three days; I was in the midst of the most beautiful experience I have ever felt. Morning, noon, and night, we talked, worked, played and then slept. I thought only of how unusual all of this was and how sensual. No one had or permitted sex but we were constantly in an ecstatic feeling of almost too much sensitivity.

Jada came to me that night before we were to leave for Mars and we talked about all the calamities that could be approaching our worlds. She came softly to the place where I lay and told me, "We need to talk. Nina is like a child, just learning about herself and never having been with a man before. You are very special to her and I hope you realize the position she is in. She is group leader here and what she wants and says is the law. She doesn't know that she can get burned though, or that her heart can be broken."

I looked at Jada and felt a true sensitivity to one who I know seeks the welfare of all. I asked, "Doesn't Nina have a promised person waiting for her?"

"Yes," she said. "But she is very inexperienced in love and only knows of this man, Max, briefly from a school she attended. They haven't had much contact with each other. I think she wants a relationship with you. She is practically throwing herself at you, hoping you will stay with her, but I think I know you differently or maybe I'm wrong. You do not want to leave your wife. Is that true?"

"Yes, I've told her all along, but she insists on everyone seeing each other."

"I know", Jada said. "I helped train her when she was younger. She's never had contact with very many men, only in combat. She's getting very attached to you, I think. Please try to persuade her to establish contact with Max, to get her emotions in control. She is going to be here in one moment to test you once more and I am supposed to leave you two alone together to better express your feelings for one another. I know it can only end in heart break for Nina. She is important to the civilization as a leader and she also has to fly this ship. Do not be too harsh with her. Try to be affectionate but do not let her be intimate. She would only get banished and never be able to return to Max. Let her enjoy her little show but do not let her go too far. We will talk later and I will tell you how we are going to break up some asteroids before they threaten our planets."

She reached over as her long hair fell across my face and she kissed me as our bodies made contact. She said, "I'm glad Nina didn't cut you any deeper or you would not be feeling these sensations."

At that time Nina came running over, her bear feet making little noises against the deck of the ship. I looked at her and began to worry about her appearance since she was not exactly presentable. Maybe I was more worried about my ability to resist her than her aggressiveness.

I said, "Your ship has a gravity device that is remarkable. I heard your feet on the deck as you ran over." She looked at Jada and said, "See, he's glad to see me. He always smiles every time I come around. You're always happy when you see me and I feel very happy when I see you too."

She lay down beside me and embraced me lovingly. Jada touched me on the forehead and then the tip of my nose and a little static spark of electricity jumped from her finger to my nose. Then she said, "I've got to run some data on the asteroids that we are going to be shooting down tomorrow. I'm getting back to the pilot cabin to plan the trip a little better."

Nina looked_at me and said, "I feel as if we were meant for each other and you prove to me every time I see you that my prediction for us is true. We will be chosen by the elders to form a permanent bond."

I interjected immediately, "You are not correct in your analysis that I want something more than what you see. I am just happy to see you and that expression does not give you any indication that we should unite in marriage or any sort of thing. You should listen to Jada and let her explain how you have let your own imagination make decisions for you."

She looked ashen as a sudden pall came over her face and a frown swept over the cheerfulness as fast as the bright smile had appeared in the beginning.

"You indicate by your mood that we need not venture much further today into more complicated relationships and our emotions just need to be allowed a little time to adjust to the stresses of space travel. I should tell you right now that we are safe together and you will not be harmed even if you do not accept my overtures of commitment."

She stood in front of me and made as if to go about some busy schedule of straightening up the cabin. I looked at everything she did, falling deeper and deeper into the hypnotic spell she had put on me. She was disarming every bit of the resistance out of me and I knew it was going to always be this way. I was in love with her but I would not give in to the desires because it was a road that could never be traveled back from.

I finally got her to return to her cabin by complaining of sleepiness and as soon as she left I felt an immediate relief of stress. The stress to convince her that she and I had no real future was beyond my timid ability to just verbalize the confusion that I felt.

Soon she returned and just lay down beside me and we didn't talk. Later, I think she slept for hours very quietly without even saying another word.

After some time, Bispo, the female soldier who almost never said anything, came and woke her up. She looked almost frantic and could barely contain herself. She was clothed in the military uniform of the ship and shaking Nina she said something in the language of Lemuria Terra. Nina began to act robotic again and it seemed all her humanness had drained away with the message. Her rapid movements had returned along with the responsibility of probe wing captain.

"They need me to pilot the ship. It seems that there is a strong force of alien ships assembled outside the entrance to this hidden cavern. Bispo doesn't know if we have been discovered or not but as you see, she is worried for all of our safety. Let's dress and meet her at the pilot command center ASAP."

She kissed me soundly and deeply on the lips, and for one brief moment I thought she would not relent to heed the attack warning issued by Bispo. Again she asked me to hold her hair back while she put on a circular golden clasp and at the same time Bispo, the quiet one, did the same thing. They must be somehow electronic sequence ordered, wired in some similar manner.

Nina said to Bispo, "638, bring my flight suit and accessories to me. Mr. Jefferson Coltrane is holding back his feelings, but I will train him to respond to me in time." Bispo said, "I will lay in the pre-flight vectors to Mars so we can make a quick get away once you have destroyed the enemy ships."

"Good," Nina said. "Don't worry; they don't even know we are here. They are only sniffing the electronic trail we left. Do me a favor, Mr. Jefferson Coltrane. I know you like being near to me because I feel a strong attraction at the same time."

"OK," I said. "You can see I'm nervous about this very sensuous activity and just to be near to each other is making a very treacherous pathway which is fragile for both of us. We should avoid adding complications that will make it difficult for both of us to return to the places where we were before we opened this very dangerous door. I just don't like doing something that I can feel is really going too far for both of us because we really are not in a committed relationship. It can only end in something very bad."

She said, "Mr. Jefferson, you just worry too much. You need to follow orders. I am captain of this ship and what I say goes without question on this space craft. You follow my orders and complain if you like but you will like to do what I say. You are very difficult to understand. I am giving you a very pleasant reward. I have to hurry now so we will talk later. I have things to do."

"Yes, of course I like you", I said. "But I have already a wife and this presents a problem in our relationship."

Reluctantly but pleasantly I told her that I could not comply with any order that she gave me even if it was a command.

Then she left me finally and at the last moment she turned and said, "We may be bombarded in any moment, if they discover we are here."

Sure enough in the same minute that she and Bispo went running off to save us, a bombardment commenced. I made my way quickly after them to the pilot's command cabin. As I walked in she had the proper uniform on and was giving orders in a mechanical sort of way with quick motions to the controls and signaling Bispo and Nella to carry out her directives to move the space ship.

When I entered she smiled in a mischievous way at me and said, "We may have to go deeper in order to conceal ourselves. They don't know we are here and maybe they are just practicing. We moved at a fast continuous pace deeper into the interior of the moon cavern.

"How far can we go into the moon?" I asked.

Nina said, "I've never explored this cave so I don't know. We will try to find an exit if it exists."

"I never knew the moon had any kind of water. How did the cave get here?" I asked.

Nina said, "Oh, there is ice at the Polar Regions, but I didn't think those caves were made by water. Maybe they were magma chimneys from a now long dead center of molten magma. We are clear on all sides for about 2000 meters. I've sounded the interior and an obstruction seems to be just up ahead. It looks like a plug. Maybe we could break through to another chimney if we knew the location. I didn't want to use any large plasma arc, since it could give away our signature. Let's see if we can locate a similar passage near the plug to the other side.

We'll have to suit up and exit our ship to see if we can find a thin shell we can break through. Everyone is to go outside but Jada. She will stay and monitor while all other hands try to find a hollow sound. Once we find a hollow place we will drill with some small charged rays a small distance apart to break through. Otherwise, we might bring down the cavern and be entombed here for centuries before anyone finds our bones.

Thomas, can you maneuver in lunar gravity or have you experienced it before?"

I looked at her and without concern in my voice I answered, "I will learn immediately."

Nina directed everyone into their space suits and handed out small thumpers to dynamically shock the cavern wall without creating a fall of rock.

Nina said, "Everybody be careful and you, Thomas, stay close to me. I'll tell you where to place your hits according to the geo-sensor readout that I have with me. Out we go into the double chamber."

She took me by the hand momentarily and led me into the double chamber as my visor partially blocked my orientation. My first space walk on the interior of the moon was exciting beside the fact that there could be a cave-in. It looked pretty stable, like it had been here a million years and could last another million. We were in partial gravity. It was one sixth that of Earth. Walking was not so difficult but we had to scale up and down the cavern walls looking for a clue to the sister chimney that Nina thought existed side by side this one. We spread out from the ship. It was hovered, about halfway up this chimney and as we moved up and around the chimney it followed us. The plug at the bottom of the shaft was solid for hundreds of meters and gave no indication of being open on the other side, anywhere near.

After hours of recording data, Jada came out on the speaker hooked up central to all and said, "I think I've found a slight pattern where there is a shallow cover along the North face of the chimney. Take your markers and dye color the coordinates Nina gives you from her geo-stat and we will proceed to puncture a hole in the thin crust. Make sure you lay out the points wide enough so we will clear the walls from wing tip to wing tip."

We laid out the large rectangle and everyone was glad to get back to the ship and out of the gear. Nina went to the pilot console and began to punch holes in the wall of the chimney at the colored intervals, spaced evenly apart. The ruby red laser beams made an outline perfectly in the rock. Then she nudged the ship forward and just bumped the center of the large rectangle. This was something that would have done irreparable damage to a modern material used in any light weight space craft design, but it didn't seem to faze this craft of Nina's. The plate that she knocked out rumbled down the other side of another chimney and we did not notice that there was a bottom as we edged through the hole with not much to spare for room on either side. We were clear and proceeded in the up direction to get back to the lunar surface. The chimney angled away from the other one sharply and this would put us several kilometers to the North of the previous exit location where the ambush ships were waiting.

"Who are these other ships out there that were waiting for us?" I asked Nina.

She looked at Jada and just said, "Her elder clan on Mars thinks now, that she is a rebel leader too. I think it was the Martian equivalent of an arresting posse sent after her to destroy her. We have to get clear and get her back to Mars. She has to stand trial but it's safer for her there. She has a huge party following and will be well protected once she is back at her home, safe."

We made many close calls and scrapes along the sides of the ship but Nina said that it was seamless inside and outside the hulls and would never develop cracks even if impacted hard.

"What exactly is it made of, if I can obtain the secret?" I asked.

Nina said, coolly, "It's Beryllium Titanium carbonate alloy and when it is annealed it bonds three different ways with what you could call diamond dust. It's pretty pricey stuff but doesn't have any mistakes once it is electrically annealed. It's the same stuff Jada makes her ships out of, on Mars. She is leader of many colonies of hives and has much influence with her government. She has been secretly training armies for many years. The Idors elders knew she was Martian but nobody else. She has cleansed on Mars the same way we have here. It's the only way to keep out rampant microbes. They can destroy whole colonies. We mainly cleanse the Earth but that doesn't leave any vegetation and if someone is on the ground they are just vaporized. It is a drawback, but seriously, do we sacrifice the whole colony for one out of place invader?"

Nina looked at me and gave me a very long frown that I could not understand. She looked like she was frustrated and could not talk anymore. She left the pilot chair and walked out of the command center.

I asked Jada, "Is she upset about something that we were talking about or am I missing something here?"

Jada had one of the geo-stat minicomputers in her hand, going through the readouts, checking the data on the chimney that we were now in.

She said, "Hey, it looks like we have a clear cave passage from here out to the top. I want to lay in a course that has already been planned earlier by Bispo, the navigator and pre-flight engineer for Nina's ship. She seems to know exactly the way I like things."

We seemed to just zoom out and into the blackness of space above the lunar surface and the sun rise was just beginning to make its arch around the cratered surface. We had rocketed out the blackness into the brilliant light and although it hurt my eyes, soon the ship's auto-shade forces were at work to calm the light into an appreciable difference of gray moonscape. Moving into the lightened day gave me a reassurance that we would be safer.

Chapter 5. **Emotional Catharsis**

Jada moved a little closer to me and said in a low voice, "Tom, Nina is getting more emotional as the trip progresses and she thinks that you believe she is not sensitive to the deaths of thousands that she brought about with the cleansing that she performed with the plasma arc. Nina is in love and cannot think as a punctuated machine at this moment. Don't discuss it with her, because she will just get worse if you do."

I looked at the Martian aura, now glowing around her head and I thought about what she just said. How does a Martian know anything about human love and especially about me?

I explained to Jada long and in great detail. "Jada, I am a married man and although I do have feelings for Nina, I can never have an actual relationship with her. She is the best example of a beautiful woman that I could care to go in search for. Her face, her figure, her intelligence, and her uniqueness could not be found in an almost perfect world. You, Jada, are the same, as beautiful as any Earth woman that I have ever seen. But, I remain married and unable to have a committed relationship with anyone but my wife. I am indeed affected by yours and Nina's beauty ever so much, and it is extremely enjoyable to see you and to be with you, but I really should not be participating in this game that she is playing. I have commitments to family and country. I have to obtain the knowledge that I am seeking to protect my future and my world with. The Idors 2, and 3, told me that you, Jada, have the information I need to prevent the disasters that experts believe are very near our time period. I have been weak by letting Nina dominate me and take advantage of my own desirous nature, but I can and will rule my body and my emotions. I want to keep my marriage vows and maintain my discipline, even in the face of overwhelming female charms. Please, let's talk about saving the worlds we live on. That's why I began this expedition to obtain correct mathematical formulas and lay the ground work for accurate guidance in preventing certain calamities."

Nina had returned and had been listening for some time. She

looked at me and said, "No! You don't have control over your body and emotions. I can make you do anything I want you to. We looked at each other for minutes it seemed. I saw the perfection in her face and the beauty of her female form. She did the unthinkable in front of me and as expected I looked at her in all her naked form. I looked at her with almost no reservation. I could not keep my eyes from what she was showing me. Never have I been so pleased in what I was so unwilling to do.

She looked at me staring into my eyes and said, "You feel what you feel and your emotions do not lie. If you tell me you do not like to look at me again, I'll kill you!"

I told her with a faint voice, "I will not lie. Everything you are showing me is making me delirious and yes I get excited every time you are around me. She moved toward me and pressed against me with her body moving around me and teasing me. How could I make her understand that I wanted to keep my temptations to a minimum and make my desire for her less of a problem to control?

She said, "I'm having a problem controlling my emotions and I don't think I want to stop. As long as I am Captain Pilot I will do what I want to do regardless of what others want. Right now I don't know exactly what I want to do. What I want is what I get on my ship."

I knew that what she wanted was not a natural or productive relationship and to give in to any of her demands would only make her more angry and difficult to deal with.

I looked at her directly in the eyes and said, "You are sick and need some help with your problem. You are taking all this too far and you are not thinking about performing your duties, as Captain, guiding the ship."

She slapped me and said, "You are in ecstasy and love every minute you see me, standing in front of you. Jada, pilot the ship, I need to dominate this man for some time and I am going to show him how to respect his Captain while I am putting his ego in the proper place. I think I want him completely subjugated to my will."

Jada said, "I don't think you have properly addressed his capabilities and his determination to remain loyal to his wife. You will get an attitude adjustment yourself if you pursue this confrontation. I don't think this man is going to be so easy like you think. Our course is set for Mars and we will be several months getting there. I hope you will be healed when we arrive on Mars because I need your leadership and your mental abilities.

Mr. Jefferson Coltrane. She is going to fight you, and subdue you now, if she has to kill you. Please do not hurt her too much, because we need her to pilot the ship when we get into Mars proximity."

I said to Jada, "She has nothing to fear from me, but I have my right to be whom and what I want to be."

With that statement, she moved with blinding speed so that I had not the slightest hint that she was going to strike. As I looked dumbly at her beautiful face and stared fixedly at the beauty of her slender body, her right foot lashed out and buried itself in my solar plexus, pushing all the breath in my lungs out in one involuntary spasm. As I stopped breathing my thoughts were shorted out and I paused for that moment, unable to understand or respond to my lack of mobility. In that moment Nina spun on one heel and snapped the other behind my knee. The next thing I saw was the first thing I remember seeing before she kicked me in the solar plexus. Caught like a deer in the head lights of a car, I froze my gaze as her right knee came up and caught me squarely on the chin. I fell backward with my head reeling and struggled to my knees again. Yelling some Terran battle cry, she grabbed my throat and began choking me. I was stunned for a few minutes trying to catch my breath, while she began to abuse me, hitting and choking me and humiliating me. I swore to myself as I struggled to regain control. A thought formed in my mind and I remembered how to begin a Judo technique that I had learned years earlier. I wrapped my arms around her legs and flipped her on her stomach while encircling my right leg around hers. As I administered the leg lock, I pushed hard down on her leg and she screamed out in pain as I grabbed the long hair flowing behind her head and pulled back hard getting leverage to secure the hold. Jada and the others ran over as Nina began to scream and cry out. I did not let her have even one inch to relieve the pain.

I said, "Say you're sorry and apologize now or I will dislocate your knee!"

She cried out and said that she repented of her behavior.

At that moment Lita hit me with the ball of her foot and I saw stars. The blackness swept over my conscious mind and I collapsed onto the deck and I wasn't sure if I was conscious or not.

Nina got up and rebuked Lita, saying that there was to be no interference at all. My head was hurting and I could barely concentrate but I did see the temple of her head as my target.

Lita pulled her hair over her left ear and looked in my direction as if I was not a threat at all. As I was on my knees I sat up and instantly pumped my legs beneath me, pushing me straight up into the air and extending my right leg out and around, I caught the back of my heel on Lita's temple and put her out of action. She crumpled to the deck unconscious. At the same time as my leg recovered from under my body, I spun as soon as my feet hit the floor and my right fist advanced ahead of my body as the two extended knuckles caught the side of Nina's right jaw. When I spun in the opposite direction I kicked out and down on her left collar bone and heard the snap of a bone as it responded to the impact of the heel of my foot.

Both Lita and Nina were lying unconscious on the floor as Jada, Nella, and Bispo walked up.

Jada said to Bispo, "She had it coming. She just wouldn't let up. She knows he loves her but doesn't want to betray his wife. She had to force her desires on him and dominate him the way she had in her mind to do in her fantasies. I told her that it was better to just dream but she wanted everything to be real, the way she wanted it. Since she is Captain she said that she could have whatever she wanted. I guess she got a surprise attitude adjustment. Now maybe she will respect you, I hope. I think she needs to go to infirmary. Could you pick her up and take her to infirmary where we can help her? She's going to be in pain when she comes around. I think her collar bone is broken or maybe not. We need to x-ray."

I picked up Nina, while they picked up Lita. We put them both in stasis beds in the infirmary. Nina and Lita woke up in about 10 minutes. Lita was fine and never said a word, but Nina woke up in pain. We x-rayed her shoulder and she had a cracked collar bone. She looked around when she opened her eyes and asked for Jada to come over. Jada looked at me first and then walked over to Nina.

With tears in her eyes, Nina said, "I never wanted it to happen this way. It was my fault for forcing him to want me. I still have to give the order since I am captain. Since he has fought against me, he must be restricted. Put him in chains right now or you will violate my trust."

"Yes," Jada said. "It will be done to prevent loss of order. Nella, Bispo, Lita, restrain Mr. Jefferson Coltrane, give him his proper uniform, and take him to the center circle for indoctrination and reprogramming."

I couldn't believe my ears. They were 100 percent behind anything this overbearing, spoiled, little child Nina wanted, no matter how ridiculous or humiliating. She was their leader and they followed her without question. Even Jada who seemed more logically civilized than the others was going to follow to the letter, her orders. I knew what was coming when I saw Lita walk over to Nina after she recovered. They passed some minutes talking while Jada took a picture of Nina's shoulder to see if it was broken.

"It is cracked," she said as she looked at a huge screen over the counter where rested a blue light, emitting holographic images of the bone detail.

It was cracked in a small fracture. I had hit her harder than I really intended to.

Jada said, "The only way for this to heal is to just be careful and no more fighting for at least 6 months."

"O.K.," Nina said. "Take him now and put him in the circle of restraint. I want him where I can administer my punishment."

I took one step back and then Lita pushed one button on her armband and instantly a stunning beam of electricity snapped into my chest and I fell backward as blackness closed all doors of escape.

When I awoke I was enclosed in a circle of blue light emitted from below and above. The beams were spaced apart so that my hand could extend through but there were bars of charged particles and I could not put my body through the spaces. Nina wanted to administer some kind of punishment. That was the last thing I heard her say. I didn't regret my action but maybe it was inappropriate to fight with the Captain. No, I don't regret it; she shouldn't have hit me and done what she did. I told her I was married but she just kept pushing me, knowing that I was feeling the excitement of having her near me. Of course I'm in love with her but it is a destructive relationship. Right now I would give anything to be with my loving and caring wife. What a beautiful relationship we have. My wife is always exciting and never have I thought of leaving her. It is only my weakness to look at other women that gets me in trouble. At least they did leave me my clothing this time. Maybe she was tired of her games and was getting a more practical nature. I looked up and here came Nina with her arm in a sling. It looks like maybe she is ready to administer my punishment.

She said, "I know that you are expecting me to make another big mistake and really torment you just because I am Captain Pilot and have the authority. But you are going to get a surprise. I have you here only because it is a formality, and is due process and ship's law. You will be released when your time expires. There will be no official punishment, just a formality. At noon today the time is set to expire and the bars will be withdrawn. You can leave then, and feel free to come by my room or the pilot's cabin and we can discuss the problems we have had or you can ask Jada and she will help you to resolve the mathematics. She has convinced me that I was at fault for the mistakes that have been made and I have agreed. We are from different cultures and we must respect one another's own right to believe the way we want to believe. I will not force my ideas on you or try to get you to accept my life style. So, at 12:00 noon you can walk out free and your movement will be unrestricted."

She left and I resigned myself to thinking of the questions that I was going to ask Jada. A man can think of a million things while he is in a confined place. The main problem that I have foreseen and have the direct obligation to find is a mathematical solution for finding an alternative trajectory for a group of asteroids that are in close proximity to Earth's orbit. The outer edge of the asteroid group are predicted to pull away and form an attachment to Earth's orbit as they come to the closest gravitational attraction on the next couple of orbits around the sun. It has been determined that their orbits are deteriorating and will detach in two years. As the Earth and the asteroid belt come closer together, the orbit of the Earth draws the stray asteroids closer and closer to their limit of stability. Early into the next year, it is thought that the stability of the gravitational pull will change and we will have a rogue asteroid without a secure orbit, and that means it will drift. My question is where according to their advanced calculations will it drift, the path it will take, and the time to collision? What viable means of preventing collision with Earth are possible to keep the destruction of all life as we know it on Earth from becoming the reality that we know is possible? I have questions and more questions but do they have answers? Do they already know about the asteroid drift? Nina seemed like she had resigned herself to a civilization constriction. Could she restrict her desire for immediate gratification of wishes, in place of a long term goal for respect from others and maturity? Did she even have the capacity to understand maturity?

I looked at the time monitor in the distance and it was not unlike an Earth clock in that it kept the hours and minutes. The one thing it lacked was the hands or a digital read out. It was a global time peace circling around the ring of an orbit. There was a red orb circling a white ring on a blue background. The marks radiate from the center and light up and blink until the orb reaches the next hour.

I sat and watched while the red orb continued to light up three more radiating lines until at twelve o'clock noon, all of the radiating lines were lighted and then the bars that held me disappeared and in the distance under the Terran clock was standing, my teacher and friend Jada.

I could see even in the distance the rainbow aura, a radiance emanating from her face and slightly from her hands. It was not a light being emitted but maybe a reflection of the objects around her in an ever slight aura. Could she be clothed within a cloaking device that would in any moment of danger leave her invisible? Where did the origin of my own device come from? Could it have been Mars?

Jada walked forward and greeting me soundly and happily she said, "Hello, and look, I have my covering. Wasn't she just too immature for such a powerful leader and a pilot at that?"

"Yes," I said. "But I think her change is just temporary."

"No," Jada said. "She has been corrected. I did it electronically. I gave her your morals, programmed into her network too. Lita, Bispo, and Nella are all reprogrammed to be moral, like you. It is much more efficient and mathematically practical. You won, and

96

I'm glad. I told her she would be sorry when she started it, but she wouldn't listen. I hope you know I am not enhanced and don't have any wiring. You won't see me moving around, like a wired up machine, with servo mechanisms leaping all synapses and firing in all directions. Why don't you get out of this gloomy area and come up to the relaxation area? Come, follow me."

I gathered myself together, a little shaken from the expectations of what would Nina do to exact her punishment. This was a woman, alien to me, even though from Earth that I truly loved but had to fight against and now had a healthy respect for and feared.

Jada, on the other hand was a woman that I was beginning to identify with more and love and have a needful trust in and respect as a solver of problems and thoughtful helper of the oppressed. She had rescued me in my hour of need and had changed things to my advantage and for the good of all present. She had become not only a figure of true beauty but also a good shepherd and trusted teacher for all of us. I have come to honor certain guiding questions in my development as an astute student of life, which given are the solutions to certain mysteries. If it is beautiful it is truthful and if it is truthful it is beautiful. These two converge and signify what is good in life. But being all other things equal, a woman can be beautiful, truthful, and honest but is she compassionate? In which direction does the arrow finally turn before it reaches the mark? Can we even assign a character to a woman because certain influences deter her better judgment? Does she want to do certain things one way out of reason, and then in the end allow her emotions to alter what her original plan was? Jada was in every respect a little more human than Nina because of certain programming. But I was still just now getting to know her. She looked at me and asked me a question with eyes wide open and a look of pure puzzlement.

"Do you think I could live my life, following the plan that Jesus Christ gave you in your Bible? Of all the religions that we study on Mars, this one makes more sense; that is, to be compassionate, whatever the cost?"

"Yes," I said. "You are able to follow even if you fail along the way to perfectly reach the level of goodness completely. Trying to be compassionate is the real goal isn't it? In that you are going in the right direction with good intentions is the way. The way is being that you are making good choices in your life even if the wind is pushing you one way or the other."

I looked at Jada and it was amazing to see that rainbow of an aura, emanating from her. Maybe it wasn't just a device. I hoped that it was a natural Martian emotion. I liked the way she thought. She was a truly good person with good intentions and an excellent sense of judgment.   Jada said, "I want you to know that some things I do are not perfect and you are right. I am trying to make the best decisions for all concerned. Nina and I are old friends and I have tried to guide her in making good decisions as a pilot captain. You will have to forgive her for her mistakes. She knows that she made some bad decisions, so give her, please a little hug when we see her and it will make her feel better."

She was there, standing in the way as we entered into the relaxation room and came up to me and just stood there looking into my eyes as if waiting for some punishment or scolding. I immediately put my arms around her and pulled her to me in a tight embrace, careful not to hurt her shoulder. I put my cheek next to hers and kept her there holding her body next to mine enjoying the clean smell and the softness of her hair to fill me with desire and causing her to cry and fill her body with little tiny sobs of emotion. We pulled away from each other; like two magnets that did not want to have their properties redirected but were forced by unavoidable circumstances to change for the good of the moment to another attraction.

It began with Nina and it then spread around the room, first with Jada and me, then Nina and Jada, and then everyone was embracing first one then the other. I think we all just really loved each other and wanted one another to feel that we were first and most important a family with the best intentions for each other regardless of the circumstances. I felt now really sure that nothing could stop us from saving the Earth and we only needed to be guided by a higher power, a spiritual power.

As everyone finally allowed a catharsis to reach the full culmination in an emotional release of love and affection, we relaxed into a very dreamy state where all of our defenses were lowered and we truly enjoyed each other's company without letting a deeper involvement confuse and prevent logical thinking from taking the utmost place of importance.

We began to ask each other questions and freely talk about life on other worlds. Nina began talking about her childhood on Earth, in the desert caves where the mysterious nation of Terra had been incubating for longer than the history of many known civilizations.

She began informing us, "We had an electrolytic solution, when we were young, that absorbed all of our thoughts, not directly but logged in through sensors that fed into the main biochemical solution. The computer system gave us access to much information, saved through the years, to insure we were properly educated. We have very many libraries of sensory data received through years and years of scientific observations. Sometimes they have let me monitor the data and observe the accumulated evidence of outcomes that the computers have catalogued. All of these sensory phenomena have been logged into my memory and I can experience an absolute enlightenment by just thinking about certain possible experiences. I can foresee the time when we will predict emotional experiences that are going to happen when confronted by certain situations that are yet to be cross referenced. I know, I know, that it is just a computer analogy and it doesn't fit all situations. There are certain things that are better left up to purely human intuition, but I cannot doubt that I have been incredibly aided in my work by my enhancement capabilities. I can plug right into the interface solely by a hand print. Now that has to be a very helpful asset in flying and directing this ship. Lita and Bispo and Nella could have that capability but they could not support the mental interface that it took to endure the willing and changing of the mental muscles. The computers will help you but your own will has to make the mental muscles move. It was a nightmare when they first started me. Some new "probes", that's what they call the beginners, just give in and let the sensors control them but that's just weakness. The scientists really don't want automatons that are just wired. They want human beings that can use the enhancement as a tool and part of a repertoire. Poor Bispo, as smart as she is, could not withstand the sensory hammers that they invaded her poor mind with. Watch, as I pull my hair back over my forehead and brush my hand across my little implant, along and behind my ear."

She pulled her hair back and began grooming her hair with her hand and Bispo began immediately to imitate her action, doing the same exact thing, even the way she was sitting and making her gestures.

"Bispo," Nina said. "Go program the coordinates of an Earth to Moon, Mars, Earth, Moon, and Europa space jump with a return trip through the asteroid belt, then give me exact read out on drift for asteroids closest to Earth orbit."

Bispo got up and walked immediately over to the pilot console and began making programmed preliminary flight projections on a computer model in 3-D holographic shapes.

"She will do anything I tell her to but she doesn't want to make important judgments and always gives me a question after she has perfectly formulated all path projections without error. I've checked her and I always know she will get it right. She just doesn't want to have an opinion. She feels and thinks like a person but she will only accomplish something if she takes orders from me. She is attached electronically to my implant so she can function properly."

I asked her, "Are Nella and Lita also attached electronically to your implant?"

"Yes, but not so vitally like Bispo. They are my trainees for captain pilot, but yet they cannot fly right now, only when it is not so difficult that takes very much precision on-line coordination. They help me in very many duties right now, making the actual projection and receiving data from the equipment. But we could actually go without the little implants and still make all the right connections because of the conditioning of our nervous systems. They have been trained to be receptors of electronic stimuli. You may not believe it but you could also be trained to receive stimuli directly with very little practice. Only Bispo would probably need to keep her implant to function properly because she gave in to the electric charges without fighting for a redirection of the stimuli.

You have to actually redirect the electrons and find a new address to locate and stockpile the messages to be retrieved later. Your brain can direct the stimuli and store it if you make it do it and form the place. You just have to concentrate and not give in to the out of phase stimuli. Some charges that are not aligned with the rhythm of your own natural aura must be made to harmonize or speeded up or slowed down and redirected to be compatible with your own personal anatomy.

Bispo spoke up at that moment and said, "I could have found a place for the stimuli but it just kept bouncing around inside my head and I don't remember what happened except that there was a bright light that I could not locate or push out into a dark receptor. The dark address just did not exist for me and I find it better to have someone else retrieve the messages for me and help me direct the stimuli. I think they told me one of my neurotransmitters had suffered some damage maybe in other training episodes, but anyway could not be located. It just doesn't exist for me. I'm good at what I do and probably better than Lita and Nella, so they let me go on missions and because I'm connected to Nina. She helps me through the hard projects. I still want to know how you defeated Nina in battle, Mr. Jefferson. Was she not alert and maybe you really don't know what you did? She is all of us put together and thinking in four phase neuro-transmit, with all of our computer systems connected to predict your moves and intercept your strikes. I will let you speak to Nina now and not to me. I have said too much. Forgive me Nina, but we wanted to know our mistakes."

Looking at Nina and her three sisters in phase, I was just astounded that they could all four be thinking together.

I said, "I had no idea all of you were connected together and adding your thoughts analytically together."

Nina looked at me apologetically and asked, "Could you tell us something about how you could out think the four of us and our computer system?"

Jada interrupted and said, "Nina, you are asking him to possibly divulge secret information that he may not want to do."

I said, "No Jada, you and Nina's group are welcome to know every detail of my training in order that I may gain knowledge of how to prevent the calamities we face in the future. With your knowledge of mathematics I could learn of new ways to change the future.

I trained with the best and sought out the more difficult teachers but everyone said more or less the same thing, that it depended on my commitment and dedication to training. They gave me great advice, but I suppose it was my fear of failure that spurred me on to learn more and more. I'll give you anyway, a brief synopsis of my early training.

The greatest exercise for creating decision making was of my own making. My teachers had definitely given me good training and I really organized my training independently so that I did more than everyone else did in training. I was always doing more than I was required and that was difficult because they made us expend all of our energy and thinking processes, only I had to do more. The great teachers I can tell you of were my first beginnings into my training and my life of learning. They gave me the initial keys to open doors with. By having the initial tools I could tailor make my workout and Kata to fit whatever situation could be imagined.

Once, I was in a very difficult situation in a very bad neighborhood in a large metropolitan area. The entire situation would have been nonexistent if I had made my escape route through a different location. I had been on a fact-finding mission to find out the strength of gang leaders and their firepower when I got caught in the area at night without proper cover or knowledge of the territory. I had my observation point set up right in the middle of their home territory and their meeting place at that, with photos of a weapons demo and issuance. I was set up to give the evidence to state and federal officials when I compromised my location with a slight slip and I made some noise unexpectedly leading them to my observation point.

I was forced to run in the middle of hostile territory not knowing where exactly I was going. I crossed several back streets until they had me cornered. There were three in front and two behind, waiting for me to make my move now that they had me surrounded and cornered. There was no where to go and no help in sight. It was sure that they were going to kill me because I had seen their weapons store and could identify them also. They could not let me live even injured.

For some reason unknown to me, they did not exhibit any weapons with them and use them right off or I would be dead for sure. They would just have shot me at point blank range except that maybe they wanted to just torment me. They had small pistols but just didn't want to kill me immediately or maybe they didn't want to alert the police, who were patrolling the area, but we were there and it was going to be hand to hand, the old-fashioned way. The closest one to me said that since I had invited myself to the meeting that I needed to get the initiation reserved for rival gang members and that I wasn't going to like how I looked when they were finished. I knew I had to get one at least in front of me to use as a body shield, while I tried to take one or two out.

One very surly and belligerent one said to me. "I am going to enjoy the sound your wind pipe makes when I smash your throat!"

He was the closest and I thought to myself that even if he did make a fatal blow, I would make sure that he gets his surprise too before my air ran out. I threw both hands into the air, shouted in his face and made two whipping hook kicks. The first one was right inside with the heel and edge of my right foot, breaking the inside of his right knee and crossing over my left knee to get full force at the reverse. I whipped high outside with the edge of my foot slicing into the throat and wind pipe and eliminated his ability to speak forever.

When my right leg planted, I continued the motion I began by spinning clockwise and caught the next assailant with a right back fist strike to the temple focusing my top two knuckles at the right temple just behind his right eye and felt the slight depression I made as the eyes of my second assailant curled to the top of his lids.

At this moment in the game, my surprise attack exhibited the weakness that always comes with first strike. I was immediately set on by the wolf pack and suffered strikes to the head and solar plexus but with the third strike I feinted with the blow, thus softening the impact and caught the next strike with a trap and break at the elbow. The young teenage boy screamed at the loss of his arm and with his loss of focus I continued the motion of my trap, thrusting my right elbow up and around to the point of his chin, probably breaking his neck with the force.

With three assailants dead I had only three more to go. With everyone so close now, I immediately delivered about six to eight punches all over the body of number four, breaking through the wall of his defense. With such a flurry of punches he was overcome and began to back away, leaving all his vital organs vulnerable. I buried the ball of my foot into his groin and at the same time I caught the wrist of my fifth assailant and pulling his arm with my two hands closed around his gun, I completed a small circle Jujitsu throw lifting his body with his own forward motion, flipping him and freeing the gun at the same time. When I had control of the gun I immediately killed the other two of them.

Knowing that these six could not be the only ones in the gang, I tried desperately to disappear into the background of the community. I tried to spot a dark angular crevice to emerge my body into and with the building. I tried moving and sticking and then gradual moving from one sight to the other, sheltered from visual observation or blending into the backgrounds. I was achieving great headway until a woman in an apartment spotted me and she knew I did not fit into the community. I heard her on a telephone talking to apparently another member of the gang and in minutes the area was covering with members wearing the same colors as the first six, only this time it was twenty or thirty. I somehow managed to hide and move into the shadows of the community buildings until I was free of this controlled neighborhood. I reached a hidden tube of money and weapons and clothing that I had buried on the previous night and I was able to escape without harm.

Thinking back on my course of action that I took in the fight, I used the basis of my own katas that I had created myself. Moving with the momentum of the started motion to keep from stalling and stopping, I struggled again and again. None of my teachers had instructed me in this but by making up my own katas, I achieved an economy of motion. If you move in little circles or figure eights and continue to flow one action into the other, you do not leave yourself open for the enemy's focus and attack. This is part of my secret and it is something that cannot be taught but you have to learn by conditioning your reflexes and forming your own artistic movements into smooth flowing expression that comes natural and uninhibited. To overcome your adversary you need to know what the body is capable of and what the distractions and weaknesses are. We are all learning every day and encoding our memories with this phenomenon."

Nina looked at me and said, "Forgive me but you just don't realize what you have done. The four of us are thinking together and

Bispo is right. You should not have been able to hurt us much less damage and incapacitate us. I have fought hundreds at one time, seasoned battle hardened veteran warriors, and none have been a challenge, only you. May I make one test only, and I will have peace of mind?"

I looked at Jada and she nodded her head in affirmation. I needed to know that she was on my side. "OK," I said. "I will take another of your tests, if you promise to use your mind mathematically to relieve these problems of the Earth before calamity strikes. They are real and imminent dangers."

Nina composing herself in a straight erect position and looking at Lita, she affirmed, "It will be done, yes." Lita got up and went to the center of the room and waited standing in readiness. I felt a lightness in my stomach sensing that this would not just be reacting but would be very serious if I lost. Yet, I could not actually hurt this woman because we were now friends. It had to be a demonstration of effectiveness without damage to her body. Lita made a few warming up motions with circular block and circular kicking techniques as if to show me that she was taking a cue from the story I had told of when I used circular techniques. I got up and approached the center of the room to face my new and I hoped final test in order to procure the help of these almost alien Earth dwellers who had lived in secret for a thousand years.

This time I would have to wait for a strike from her to set up the take down that I hoped could lead to a joint lock without making a fool of myself or hurting my opponent which could end in a disaster and accomplish nothing good. She had almost the same appearance as Nina only the hair was short and she had a more pleasant manner of addressing me and being more cooperative, but I knew it would be a challenge to overcome her.

"Lita was instructor at Terra base and has a very fine talent for not allowing herself mistakes," Nina said in a defiant voice.

Lita had removed the lethal arm bands that had been used to stun me into unconsciousness in the infirmary. I thought that she would have felt they would be necessary but our mood has mellowed from before, yet I still had some distrust of their actions since they took me without warning before.

105

She began to flick sparring kicks and punches at me from the instant we took our places in the center of the room. Her kicks began to bite deeper into my defenses and soon I would be forced to defend with a like manner if I did not find a remedy for the penetrating offense she was taking with me. I knew it would lead to punishing blows if I took that course of action and I did not want to hurt or damage these people any at all if possible. As she began to sting me with a waist high kick, I absorbed the blow into my stomach and then locked her leg while I turned, pinning the leg under my arm and while spinning I moved her center of balance forward and carried her with me in a small circle. She retained her balance for a moment by pure superior compensation, but the move had begun and even if four people helped her think about a way out, she was still going to take a fall. The problem was I did not want to continue with a correction for the next attempt. They would undoubtedly correct the balance next time, so this first mistake had to count.

As she began to fall I caught her under the throat with my right arm as I held her in midair caught with her leg under my left arm and as I let go and let her fall, I had my arm crooked in her throat and applied pressure as I settled on top of her. She was blacking out in some few minutes and as she relaxed I let her go. She would have been dead in seconds but I let her go.

They all got up and rushed to hold her up and Nina said, "It's sort of cheating. She could not possibly have moved in midair to avoid the choke hold around her neck and you fell on top of her pinning her."

I told her emphatically, "Yes, but she could have compensated for the next move if I had failed to end it, so I decided to end it quickly."

"OK, OK," Nina said, "We will meet in the pilot station while we check our heading to the edge of the asteroid belt. Get up, Lita, and fix Mr. Jefferson some tea."

I was so relieved that I made it through that test and wondered what could have happened if I had failed, miserably. I looked at Jada and she indicated that I was to come to her for possibly some information.

She told me with that Martian emphasis in her very precise

106

words, "She was possibly going to end the game in the next second if you had not caught her in midair where she could not firmly plant herself to prepare her next move. You have been accepted into this flock of outcasts again and I hope they will leave you alone. Let's follow Nina to the pilot station and have a discussion about your objectives and make some preparations for plotting the direction and outcomes of this mission."

We walked along the gang way of the ship. It was a large space ship but still gave one the sense of being in a tightly efficient aircraft. The walls and floor were of bright polished titanium looking metal with a rough surface for the floor, giving a sure-footed grip in a sometimes not so stable equilibrium in full flight. We had been in maybe the mid-part of the ship and there were cabins on either side.

Jada said, "I have something that might interest you. Would you like to contact someone on Earth? It is a secure channel, I'm sure of it, if you are worried, and no one will know anything about us or where you are."

We entered a side cabin and went through a chamber which opened into an electronically wrapped area, complete with wide screen panels for viewing. Jada touched one of the large viewing areas on the wall and a panorama of locations availed itself with sites as diverse as the Olympus Mons on Mars and several moon base sites. I saw many locations on Earth for relay and direct access. Jada asked me what country I wanted to call and I said Mexico and then she asked me what state in Mexico and I said Jalisco and then I gave her the telephone number of my wife's brother's house where she was waiting for me.

At each interval there appeared to focus in closer and more minute designations on the screen until finally at the touch of her hand the city appeared and then the street as the satellite zoomed in on the house of my wife's brother.

She said, "All we have to do is get a very close general proximity and we can use the satellite to match the existing relay station and the call can be made. Do you want to talk to your wife?"

"Yes," I said enthusiastically not believing that it could actually be done and still I was apprehensive that I could be getting my family involved in my mission. For the first time I was maybe, putting their lives in danger but to think about my wife being so far away and also the importance of the mission, I just could not resist the chance to talk to her. I dialed in the number to her house. The number as they sequenced sounded like chimes to a small pipe organ at a church as they reverberated around the room. There were at the very last, three harmonious rapid chimes as the satellites made the connections from unknown outpost links and stations through outer space.

My wife answered the telephone and said the customary "Bueno" from her Spanish language.

I said, "Laura, do you know who this is? I'm at a location very far away from you, but still within view of a gigantic harvest moon."

She said, "You did it. You got in. Was there any trouble? Are, you all right?"

"Yes, I'm alright but we have to proceed to the asteroid belt to try and prevent the collapse of near Earth orbits that would put some of these rogue asteroids on collision course with Earth."

"How are your new friends?" she asked.

"They are different but we have managed to make communication our best asset and they are going to help us. Right now we are beginning to evaluate the orbit deterioration of the closest asteroids to Earth's gravitational field and as soon as possible my friends will help me with a mathematical model. My darling Laura, I am anxious for your safety and I must complete this mission. We will be together again soon."

Laura was strong and was always my directional star, in the darkest days and nights.

She said, "Thomas, keep your confidence up and don't let anything get in your way. Why did you break your silence? We can see each other after the mission. Everyone here is fine and we are just waiting for the news that no one else will appreciate or probably even know. I'm going up into the mountains to await your return. Do you remember the cave in las Barancas? Well, meet me there. I love you, and give me your signal when you are coming."

"Alright, darling, I'll be there and you know I love you. Bye."

With that last contact since six months ago, I said good bye to my wife of ten years and prepared for whatever it took to find the solution to the present problems we were facing. Nature had a way of saying, do what you can but prepare to be in another place at another time when I happen.

Jada said, "Laura sounds a lot like Nina but I'm sure you see the difference."

"My wife trusts me to be a faithful husband and I have the same trust for her."

Jada looked at me and without a clue as to what was coming before it happened she stood up in front of me and began taking off her clothes. She looked at me as she began that all too familiar resonating rainbow.

The feeling I had was like rivers of cold and hot sensations all up and down my body. I closed my eyes as she completed her project of becoming totally bare of any covering on any part of her body.

"It's not that I want to interfere with your relationship," she said. "I just wanted to do this to help us to free associate without having any mistrust in each other. I get pleasant feelings and I know that you do also. Let's think now of how the orbits of these asteroids could be stabilized without expending vast amounts of resources and energy. We are attracted to each other right now. We are drawn to each other. I have so to speak done something rare and drawn away from my natural orbit and come close to your gravitational attraction not by just getting closer but also changing my chemical reaction."

Her whole body began to pulsate with a most beautiful aura of rainbow colors and a rare attraction that was like a magnet in its appeal.

At that moment, Nina opened the door and said, "I knew I would find you here. Put on your clothes and the two of you come to the pilot room. I know you better than you thought I did, Jada. You talk more theoretical than you resolve your own difficulties."

Jada dropped to the floor on her knees and the aura faded like turning out a light.

Nina said, "I have a better idea. You get up now and come the way you are. We will entertain Mr. Jefferson in mathematics while you excite him into finding a solution to his problems."

Jada spoke up, "It was my fault entirely. I got him to call his wife and then took advantage of the moment. I unclothed myself to excite him."

"I know you so well, Jada. You tell me I cannot do something and then you go and do the same thing yourself. Come, he can watch you while you instruct us in trajectory mathematics.

Lita, take Jada's clothes to the pilot house. She may feel the need later on to cover herself when she is tired of the eyes of Mr. Jefferson."

We walked together and the whole time her little rainbow aura was blinking on and off like a cheap neon sign at a downtown pub. She had to feel embarrassed in front of Nina and her troop after playing the role of advisor with superior knowledge of human affairs and martial techniques. I couldn't help looking at her and the natural youth and beauty that she possessed along with the Martian emotional rainbow that she exhibited. As she walked beside me covered in embarrassment, her rainbow aura pulsated each time she took a step and with each step, her breasts bounced up and down. It was becoming more and more difficult not to look at her.

We entered the pilot room again and as we both walked in at the same time she brushed up against me as she just lingered there and made the most of the time of contact. She was losing her timidity and was beginning to flaunt the fact that she had my attention. Nina had tried to embarrass her but she was coming out on the losing end because it was evident that Jada was clearly enjoying the moment. When we stopped at the trajectory screen she stood there in front of me with legs relaxed in a very revealing position and began pulsating her rainbow of colors continuously. Nina began talking about our location but my head began to spin and I could not concentrate on what she was saying. My eyes kept going back to Jada and I clearly looked where I should not have. Each time I looked at her she did something to let me know that she saw my eyes moving to her body. In one moment I looked away from her and then looked back and she began to turn a green color and then she just collapsed on the floor and lay there.

Nina said to me, "I command you to pick her up and revive her. You must bring her back or our mission is lost." I reached down and picked her up, and tried to stand her up but she was just limp in my arms. Soon she began to revive and her rainbow began to pulsate again in the familiar colors. Her skin again turned the rosy normal pink color and the green had all but faded. I had my arms around her and was pressing her in an embrace to my chest. Then suddenly she began to just sink down and I placed my hand under her back to support her to her feet. She just could not stand up at all, the skin again turned greenish gray, and it was as if she was a dead weight in my arms. Her skin began to get cold like there was no warmth in her body. I held her close to me and embraced her in front of Nina for a long time, then stars and clusters of rainbows appeared and disappeared in my mind.

Suddenly I felt her awaken and just warming to my reviving embrace. Jada began to stand free and as we parted she began to cry and tears ran down her face. It was at this point that Nina intervened.

She gave direct orders to Lita and Nella, "Take Jada to her quarters and let her sleep."

They took her and she disappeared into the gangway. Nina walked up to me and just stood there and then said, "Sometimes the Martians get so overly distraught, emotionally that they need a little charge of something that comes from an embrace. They are a very close society, constantly giving each other support. Their emotions are a little in the sensitive range because they live so close to each other in their hive, feeling each other's moods and sensations. She will return to the familiar intelligent Jada after this expression of hers wears off. She is a little silly in the way it affects her but her emotions can just destroy her. She is a very strong woman but not able to move on without resolving her little hurts."

Chapter 6. **The Ship Is Invaded**

At that moment an alarm sounded in a far off place in the sleek beautiful ship and Nina's head jerked around in the direction it came from. For a moment all was silence and then it was heard again.

I asked, "What was that sound?"

Nina said, "A door has been opened somewhere to the outside that should not have been opened. We are in space and it would have been catastrophic. All of the outer doors are sealed. But there it is, an alarm for an outer door opening. We should have experienced decompression, but since there was only the alarm, it means only one thing. We have been breached by a cloaked ship giving us no warning and they have attached their air lock to ours."

Nina was very concerned. I could see the tension in her face. She was issuing orders in rapid succession to her crew and the servo apparent motions had jumped to very rapid jerks.

"Prepare to repel boarders! We are not secure. We are under attack!"

Nina sounded frantic and I had never seen her so nervous.

"Cut lights, all over the ship and shut down main thrusters so we can drift while we secure the ship. Flood the ship's entire content with ultra violet light and begin contamination with those stinging giant buzz bees we saved in the botanical rooms. I don't care if I get stung a few times but maybe the intruders won't like them at all. They can even put that long stinger through the protective covering of the space suit. Enemy can't shoot them because they are just too fast and small. I'll trade one misery for another.

How about it? Lita, Bispo, you know how they hurt! You also know what those animals outside will do with us if we surrender. They'll cut us up into little pieces, after they've had their fun.

Mr. Jefferson, you are going to be in tremendous pain when these buzz bees unleash their venom into your body and you may die but I cannot fight what has breached our ship in any other way without destroying us in the process. What has entered our ship is monstrous and we all know they are ruthless to the core. Pirates from Lunar base of Martian origin. They fired on us before and they must have picked up our signal. They will get to us but they will not stay. I hope the buzz bees drive them insane enough to make them break off their ship from ours, then we will only have to kill the ones left here."

I heard in the background a reverberating hum as if a giant electric generator had begun to awaken and search for the never-ending opposite charges. At the same moment I heard heavy gravity booted footsteps entering the control room, and an enormous ugly beast of a man entered the room. His eyes fixed on Jada who had just come back into the room. He grabbed her shoulder in a grip like that of a meat-eating dinosaur set for play with his catch. He took off his helmet from his space suit and grinned showing a mouth full of very white sharp broad teeth.

At the same moment that he grabbed Jada, without thinking of the consequences of being mauled by the beast-like man, I launched an attack with my right foot into the right corner of his big jaw. The kick caught him viciously and at the precise moment he had tilted his head up at an angle. The resulting strike administered a breaking twist to his neck that would not have been so damaging if he had his chin tucked a little lower. I think he died instantly, but the blade that Nina had extended to slice the perpetrator with, had left a little smoke as his outer garment had split into two separate pieces.

She said with a complimentary note, "You beat me to the job but still I didn't like the suit he was wearing. It looks like it is made of something non-synthetic that could curse him for all his past generations."

Nina asked, "Do all your technologically advanced victims suffer from the same defect as this one with heads being twisted slightly from their necks?"

"I just reacted," I said. "I couldn't wait another second."

Nina said, "We better get ready, the others are on their way and the buzz bees are already here. I hope they will break off the seal, and leave the boarding party stranded here to protect their ship. When they get those stinging buzz bees screaming through their nice metallic space ship, they will change their minds about waiting for their new captives."

At that moment the bees reached our compartment and all hell broke loose. I have never in all my life seen such demonic, vicious insects. Immediately we were covered in a swarm of moth-like proportioned bees that lit onto our clothing and with talon like claws similar to an eagle's, they grasped through to the skin and then one by one jammed a needle sharp stinger at least half an inch deep. The resulting pain tore the scream from deep within my lungs and I screamed more to let out the torment and cried like someone had pierced me with a hot iron. The burn from the sting was as lasting as the first penetration and throbbed like when you hit your thumb with a hammer. I only remember that from every one of us came that same out of body scream as if not one single thing human could withstand to hold the pain inside.

The first wave of beast men had entered our ship and they encountered the blazing swarm of insects and were driven back to the brink of their ship's air lock. A huge simultaneous bellowing was heard and we knew that they had been attacked and sent into the torment of hell.

The attack of Nina's final trump card was devastating and we didn't even have to worry with the whole troop of beast men. They would rather commit suicide than to suffer the continual pain of the stinging affliction. One by one they just fell to the floor screaming as did all of us.

When I heard the noise of the hydraulic clamps being released, I knew what was about to happen. I screamed at Jada to hold on and grab something.

She grabbed a strap used to secure the cargo on the side panels and seeing Nina was distracted by a beast man, I reached for her as far as possible. She had withdrawn her blade and was administering a methodical dissecting of each beast man that lay on the floor screaming in agony. Their screams lasted only seconds as Nina separated the vocal chords from their instrument of origin. In the last second I managed to loop one arm around the strap that Jada had extended to me and one arm around Nina's small waist. The beast man made one last grab and his claw managed to cling securely to Nina's dress tunic ripping it. The alien ship disengaged rather than suffer the defeat from the stinging buzz bees. As beast men and buzz bees were sucked almost together from the cargo hold of our ship, with a violet gushing rush, once again I held Nina's slender body tightly with one arm keeping her from rushing into the void of outer space with a determined strength not to let this beautiful creature escape my grasp. She had saved us with this split second decision of hers and I was not about to let this magical person slip away into nothingness. The breach in our atmosphere was ripping everything not tied down, out into the black gulf of outer space. Caught also in the straps were Lita and Bispo and Nella along with one other very ugly beast man securely clinging for all his life. This one it seemed was all that was left of the invasion force. When Nina had her way with him, then he would just be something to jettison into the void of space. I wonder if he was thinking the same thing right now.

I was holding onto Nina for all that I could to keep her from escaping into the void. The beast was a little closer to the opening of the air lock and you might say he was windward away from us. Nina began groping around for something that I could not understand.

Her nimble hands found what she was looking for. It was the spear weapon that the beast man had brought in, wedged under the netting jacket. Nina had contorted herself, stretching to reach the weapon, and finally while exerting every muscle in her thin lean body, she attained it.   She took the spear and without having to use but very little strength, managed to get the weapon guided into the stream of air and angle it in the direction of the beast. The spear, as it pierced upward into his brain, entered from the base of his neck and surprised him more so than the buzz bees.

Now we were clean of beasts and hopefully of those insupportable buzz bees, if only we could get that air lock closed in time. Our precious time was so little that we had to live now, and the huge departure of our air left us with only seconds to breath.

From somewhere in the depths of space I felt like someone had spoken to me and told me to try a little harder and we could all make it. I was frozen here, holding on to this ship with all my strength and trying to think of a way to get that airlock closed with Nina in one hand and slipping out of my grasp and the cargo netting in the other, I had to maintain my grip and not let go, but my strength was failing. Nina was wild and moving around knowing that she was about to be sucked into outer space.

My heart began to beat like a dragon that was tearing itself out of my chest as I could sense the hopelessness of our situation.

Then Bispo said in a small fragile voice as she looked at Nina, "Fire the thrusters!"

Nina, as she was slipping from the last strength in my grasp, pushed the red lights on her captain's control arm band that she always wore. The two lights turned green and a shudder thundered through the ship as the two lift thrusters ignited, sending everything that was going out in space into the void, rushing back in for one brief moment.

As if to regain her balance, Nina immediately reached for the manual pull bar that slammed shut the airlock. At once, air began to fill our lungs and we all collapsed on the floor in a desperate relief now that our lives were given back to us in a moment's notice.

We picked up our things and quickly ran back to the captain's control room. Nina, still thinking logically sat in the captain's chair.

She calmly asked Lita, "Give me the speed and direction of that beast ship that just attacked us."

Lita quickly looked into a 3-D holograph and space itself fanned out in miniature in front of my eyes.

She said, "Three by six by eight, at vectors two and five---- focusing, hold for orders, locking in on target, and-- have acquired."

"Fire-1!" Nina said. "Fire-2!"

Chapter 7. **Emotional Confusions**

The image disappeared and Nina was getting up as if nothing had happened.

Then she said to me, "Thanks for holding me in back there. I will not forget it. You saved my life."

I said, "We all helped each other and I'm just glad it is over."

She then said so very nonchalantly, that I was taken aback, "Your wife is coming."

I asked, "How do you know?"

"The Idor's ship was on the screen and fired almost the same time as we did."

I thought, Jada must have arranged this and sent a signal to them when we talked to each other. "Will you respect my wife when she comes aboard?"

She said. "As a matter of fact, I will do nothing else, of course. Don't worry. We will stop all this play, but if I choose not to dress in my own quarters, then that is my choice. I am captain and do what I want to.

I'll be in my pilot's cabin if you want to talk to me. When I was taking my exams for pilot captain I did what others told me to, and now as long as I am giving orders I will continue to dress the way I want to. Go to Bispo now and make her aware that there will be another female on board. She will help your wife with the adjustment that she will have to undergo. I will not subject your wife to the cruelty of jealousy but will maintain discipline among my crew. She must follow my orders though, of which will not consist of a conflict in your relation with her.

I will leave you alone now that she has perceived that you need supervision. I merely wanted to reward you for your help at home base and because I perceived that you liked to see me. All of these conditions were correct. Now I recognized a conflict in my giving you a reward so we will allow that part to discontinue. I think maybe it would be better if we gave ourselves a little less freedom. I will be in my quarters. If you want to see me, come to my room and I will be myself and nothing more and nothing less. I dress the way I feel and if

I think you want to see me in a certain way, then I will accommodate your wishes, otherwise I will appear the way I want you to see me. That is all, and I already know how you prefer to see me. Right now, it will be with uniform and that goes for everyone else. You also, Jada.---everyone has to wear uniforms, now!"

Jada spoke up in a little bit of a confused state of stammering that I have never seen her exhibit.

"I was thinking maybe we could just keep our identity secret. Why do we have to acknowledge her presence? Will we not expose ourselves to the world since this civilization still has not been really breached from the outside? Mr. Jefferson may have warships waiting for us at a moon base."

I immediately spoke up. "I have been a very private soldier for my entire career and no one, absolutely no one, in our government knows that I exist. Which is not something I would want a group of outlaws like yourselves to know, since there will be no troops coming to my rescue. I am operating totally alone, save for a few scientists and one retired general who have private interests in saving the world. Basically, they want to save their own lives and their family's lives and the world they live in. When actually did you receive the transmission from my wife that she was going to rendezvous with this ship, Jada?"

She looked at me in her innocent way as she began to reinvent clothes as she took them from somewhere in the room, a uniform that she had previously been wearing.   "Help me, I need you to help me, please," she said.   She handed me her garments. She was teasing me and wanted me to get excited by her presence and her closeness. Jada was a very special person and deserved all the respect I could give her even if at this time she appeared a little bit crazy.

I asked her, "If I help you, will you and Nina show me some mathematical models of the near Earth asteroids and their elliptical patterns?"

"I will show you now before I put my uniform on. You must come closer to me so I can let you feel the sensations that will open your mind to the new mathematical developments."

I took a step closer to her and it was as if I entered into the rainbow aura of her emotions and I became a part of the feelings that she was experiencing. We became surrounded by the electric rainbow of emotions. This Martian was so special and the most exotic of all the women I had ever known. She was alluring me to my doom it seemed, though I needed their expertise in the mathematical models, but they kept me chained in a hedonistic world of only desire, yet unfulfilled. I looked at the beautiful silky smooth breasts of this magnificent creature and in that instant we embraced and were locked into a deep passionate kiss, but still wanting more, I knew that she was but a picture painted just to admire and imagine. I grabbed Jada's long hair and pulled her away from me to break the kiss. I held her at arm's length and just stared at her perfect body for some minutes and then I freed myself to make the break in the psychological and physiological world of the love I was feeling and the need and desperation I had affixed myself to.

I said almost in a pleading voice, "Please get dressed. I need to think, and I cannot think of anything but something I cannot do right now or maybe ever."

At that moment Nina came in again, dressed very militarily in her uniform and said, "Get on with it Jada, I have the mathematical model almost complete.

Take your rainbow and put some clothes around it. I need this analysis done before we lock in for moon base and begin our trip to the belt. We are retracing our steps and are having to come back to recalculate trajectories."

Jada came up to me standing very close to me and began to move, swaying back and forth in a sensual hypnotic swaying motion.

Then she piled her hair on top of her head and said to Nina, "He wants me, I can tell. I know he does."

Nina said, "Of course he does. He wants all of us but he is fighting his feelings and none of us will ever win because he is committed to his wife.

Turn that rainbow off and get control of your emotions. Put that uniform on her right now, Mr. Jefferson, or we will all make you wish you could be in control of your emotions the way you think that you are now. We can take every bit of that self righteous self respect away from you and make you into an automaton doing favors for Bispo like telling her what you can not remember about your childhood!"

I gently placed the garments in their correct places as Jada was appearing as if she were in another world like some rag doll that stood and allowed me to place each article on her like it was a thing happening not real. When I had her completely dressed, I looked at her and she would not say anything at all.

Nina said, "She is in shock and hurt by what has not been able to register on her brain. She has to be able to accept her first rejection, I guess. It affects all people differently and Martians especially hard. They think they are very special people and that the galaxy should treat them differently. She will be alright, and will return to her old self in time. I'm going to take her to her quarters and then we will discuss our mathematical model and just what is missing.

When Jada comes back from her dream she will have to help me to formulate the rate of energy absorption and how to get the asteroids to change their course without breaking up into more asteroids."

At that moment Jada spoke from the fog that she was in and her voice sounded like a robotic model of some long lost friend.

"We are all covered and it feels better, like I have something to protect my mind with. I'm not going to my room. I'm going to the console to see the model you have created. Nina, I can't respond right now but I will not let you or Mr. Jefferson down. We can make it work for everyone."

Nina said, "Alright, let's proceed to make this a beautiful event that will be witnessed by very many people. I think it can be done but Jada; how can we keep from disintegrating the asteroids and just causing a bigger mess? Here is an idea I had of a little importance that might work but you have to give me a network to build the matrix on. The asteroids are so populous that if we trigger a thrust they could either break up or hit others and begin a lot worse scenario. It could create a domino effect that once started we could not control."

We moved down the gangway into the pilot control room and Jada looked ever more normal and began to get that healthy aura that Martians have.

She looked at me and said apologetically, "I just have this thing about getting emotionally out of touch. Don't think I am impaired when I won't talk to you. I just have some problem that I need to work out. We are all friends here and I love you and I know you love me. It's just that we have commitments to others that we all must honor. Let's be intelligent here and try to make some honorable decisions and be a good influence and a catalyst for taking this rare opportunity to change a terminal future for not only Earth but maybe Mars as well. If those asteroids break out of that stasis in their usual orbit, they will proceed right on to Mars and our hives on Mars will suffer a rare defeat.

On Earth you live very solitary mostly, and civilization is very spread out, but on Mars we like to live in a close compact hive, where everyone can watch over the others. We always travel together except in this situation. I am alone except for Nina, who is my student. She has studied very closely involved with our hive civilization and likes the close contact. Sometimes in close contact civilizations there are tight barriers that cannot be broken down, but here on this tiny spaceship I have learned that they have to be even more respected than I ever thought of before.

Anyway, if the asteroids strike Mars, in mass and one hive gets hit it could crumble the underground caverns and wipe out the future of our survival entirely and change all of the breeding stock for generations of Martians. We have some very select hives that can only mate with their own selected hive. We find our hive mate and become involved in a serious relationship that cannot be broken even by close personal contact. The relationship keeps its cohesiveness even in the most desperate of situations. You are like that, Mr. Jefferson Coltrane and I respect that you have remained loyal to your wife even when we tried to take her place in your life and we have kept our obligation in the circle of honor. We have returned to our original direction of the way of hope in which we will travel through our life. Now we must honor the relationship you have formed with your wife. We have engineered a way to bring her here and learn from your society."

Nina, looking ever so much the pilot captain said, "Yes Tom, you look like you think it is impossible but we have been discussing a way to get her here so that we will not corrupt your harmonious life style with our hive experiments. For us it is a new way of living also. On Terra, I did not experiment socially and was cultured by semi-automation enhanced robotics. Jada has helped me to become a little more adept at social interaction and you have helped me to become able to realize my own faults and self-centered desires.

Now let us show you first the time frame of the meeting with your wife. In the communion relay Jada asked her if she would like to come and participate in our group of outcasts and she said that she could not wait to see you and give you the peace that comes from her mind. She sounds like a very peaceful and intelligent woman. She also said that she would administer a procedure that would be culturally enlightening that all Earth women normally give to their men. I want to see her brain you. Is it painful or do you receive very much joy when the woman is braining the man? Terran women have a similar interaction with their men. Our implants begin to resonate and the man accepts the woman's thought in the form of a wave of energy containing the ideas for engaging in requested behavior. She seems like a very bright and self assured young woman."

At that last remark I thought how my wife Laura would be furious and passive at the same time and how I would be receiving most of the fury while Nina and the crew would be taunted and insulted by her polite unnerving candor.

They both seem to be going a little slow on formulating the mathematical solution to the asteroid problem. I wondered if they were avoiding it because they don't know exactly what to do. I'm going to offer my piece of the puzzle and see if they can take the bait and expand on what I give them to play with, even if they insult me by declaring it ancient knowledge.

"I would like to present to you, Jada and Nina, one of my theories as to how to assist the asteroids in not completing their projected spiral into the path of Earth's orbit. Can we go to the planning room?"

Nina said, "Wait and I will let you explain in linear or mathematical terms on a 3-D surface."

We stepped into the next room and there appeared to be nothing for a moment and then she touched something seemingly in thin air except I assume it was a break in a laser that triggered a panel of white plastic like board that descended from the ceiling.

Nina said, "We use this sometimes because the sense of tactile touch with a surface, between hand movement and eye perception, brings about a better flow of ideas. Just use anything and it will make a mark on the inside and to erase just touch in the opposite direction of the flow of the writing with your finger or hand."

I picked up a black plastic looking tube, solid without any apparent transfer of substance to my hand as graphite would have or chalk.

I looked at Nina and as if she knew the question, she said, "Magnetic resonance, the board is charged internally and externally with different charges. You are just moving around charges."

I began to draw and as soon as I did I realized my mistake. I was going to reach a dead end, a void where my knowledge left off very soon.

"Here is a simple idea I have, and in this sketch, I will illustrate the decay of orbiting asteroids into a spiral, leading to an indefinite destination or possibly a measurable rate of orbital decay. If I transfer this point to point 1 and maintain the extent of the parabola, and if the rate of change of contraction in the first parabola is maintained as in the measured parabola, then the intersection will be at the origin. Can't this also work in reverse and give us a predicted rate of spiral?"

"Yes," Jada said. "But, you have to also figure in the pull on the body at vectors also coming from the adjacent planets and other asteroids."

"Well", I said. "How do you do that and how do you push the asteroids out of the predicted spiral and determine where it is going?"

Nina said, "We can do the pushing alright but to determine where it is going immediately is the hard part. How much thrust do we use and in what direction? If we get just close we can monitor and chart the path and interfere again and again by trial and error but we may be too late to correct the second time. What if it breaks up; then you have multiple targets that are still moving along the same intercept. The only way to get it right the first time is to use Martian mathematics. Jada is the only one who can get anywhere near the matrix needed to begin extrapolation and point processing. Calculus gives us an infinite number of point processings to arrive as close as possible to the answer but with circular mathematics; if you know the points on the circle and the spiral is predictable, then you can find the center, thus the exact point of intersection on the Earth's orbit. Instead of trying to get closer and closer to the exact answer, you know what it is exactly from the center of the circle. If you know just three points on the circle, you can find the center. For centuries we tried to get triangulation and circular mathematics to coexist together but Martian mathematics opened the door to exact astral measurement, without variations and infinite progressions. The key to the matrices lies in the center of the circle. Even though the spiral deterioration is not a circle but a regression of circles, it is still computable since it becomes predictable along a linear plane."

Jada looked at both of us and said without changing the direction she was gazing in, "You first, need to resolve the problems you have already without making new ones. First, we should determine the exact position of the space craft we need in order to make the initial thrust with. Once we have decided which asteroid is the largest hazard and that we have established it is the most likely candidate to degrade its orbit, then we can act accordingly. On our initial priming of the plasma arc, we will make a thrust into the heart of the asteroid, thus sending it in an altered spiral, to exaggerate the elliptical pattern away from Earth and Mars. The spiral must change obliquely in circular format away from the initial degraded orbit in a predictable pattern and the tract of the object must fit in circular format tangent to the spiral. If we accomplish this predicted course of action we must have a complete analysis and arrive at a working modular example, demonstrating initial action and deriving the graduated degrees of the result. Without these exact predictions we can not attempt an initial action. But first let us resolve one problem that is social.

Everything interacts with other things and we are about to engage in a social windstorm of problems. Your wife is on her way here right now and we need to prepare our minds for the interaction that is going to occur. Is she going to understand the relationship that we have had?"

I paused for a moment knowing the problem I had caused between completing my mission and my own self indulgences or rather temptations that I had unwillingly sought out and participated in to a degree. I have jeopardized the mission and now my own mistakes lie there displayed for all to recognize. This greatest of discoveries that I had been anticipating was being unveiled before my eyes. The mathematics that I had so searched for was being explained to me by, not old gray haired wizened ancients, but by beautiful alien women that had held me in their arms and desired me, showing me their most intimate feelings and expressing their desires for me. My tutors had instructed me to guard closely the secrets that I discovered and bring back information to the small group of scientists waiting expectantly for a way to save the Earth from sure destruction. They would be brought good news that not only now the mathematics existed but also the way of execution of its application and the desired results would already be accomplished.

But the most pressing problem was as Jada put it, "the social interaction", that was about to occur between the alien civilizations on Earth and Mars and my wife who was sure to exhibit jealousy and outrage at, first me, for my weaknesses and then to the other women for their lack of knowledge or their unwillingness to cooperate with our boundaries and commitments. They have undoubtedly guided her here, to see what the reaction is going to be between us, and I have jeopardized the mission in giving her away.

"In answer to that question Jada; no, she will not understand and I don't know what her reaction will be but only that it will prove a difficult social interaction as you said."

With that statement Jada said that she could refrain also from her exhibition and I had to ask the question that was burning in my mind.

"Nina, how did you and Jada get my wife to enter a strange spaceship in the middle of the sierra in Mexico? People just don't get into a space ship without some motivation to help them. When we spoke she was to go into hiding to prevent such a chance meeting of any of my contacts on my mission from using her to influence me."

Jada turned and looked at me in her rainbow aura with a demure look of someone who had been doing something not permitted and said, "We traced the communication through a set of relays and then with our monitor satellite system, based aboard one of your own satellites, we traced all movement from that location and checked each one as they reached their destination.

Your wife was found in the Sierra Madre Mountains as one having left that communication location. Nina contacted Terra and they sent the shuttle to pick her up. All we did was broadcast an invitation to visit you in space and she accepted. She will arrive in about twelve hours from now. We apologize if this did not meet with your approval but it was a tactical decision made by Nina as captain pilot in order to help us complete our designated ship's order of being unbreachable. Nina said that if other forces could intercept the transmission that they could find her too and that would be disastrous. We feel that we have put you in danger and you unknowingly put your wife in danger because you were not completely aware of Terran abilities to control all of your satellites without your country knowing it."

Nina turned to me, walked up to me and made contact very close, and personal, touching me with her head next to my cheek and as she looked into my eyes she said, "We had to get our contacts on Terra to intercept her before the elders sent the order to close her communication with us. They would just erase all trace of her if we hadn't got to her first. It was my fault for being a renegade rebel from Terra, since partly I got you into this, and I thought I could help blunt some of the results from my rebellion. My contacts at Terra have taken good care of her. I am very sure.

We might return to a small lunar base to intercept and then to an asteroid outpost to plan our strategy for the wild asteroids within the asteroid belt. There is a large rocky asteroid deep within the belt that I have visited before, while doing some planning. I have a "C.A.N." there, anchored in orbit around the rock. C.A.N. stands for Contained Aerobic Nucleus. This C.A.N is about 100 miles in length and has a radius of about 32 miles which makes the inside circumference about 100 miles. The asteroid itself is only about 2000 miles square, a nice big chunk of mostly titanium and iridium alloy.

Tom, it's self contained perfectly balanced ecosystem is set up for about 20 people. We are capable of living there for as long as we want. Jada and I have had it, stationed there for 5 years and we haven't opened it since we left it there. The life forms are mostly plants and a few small animals and whatever insects are common. It is spinning both axial and circumrotating so there is at least a similar gravity there and we could match Earth or Mars for physical conditioning."

Jada said, "We are going to dock at moon base outpost, a closed down base of Terra because of a lunar abnormality. They closed it thinking that the hull had been breached as a result of a seismic fault-line running through the main shell of the camp. There actually is one but it has been dormant for some time, leaving only an unstable subsurface that gives warnings of collapse ever so often but hasn't reached its point of losing integrity because there is sufficient substrata to prevent it. We have validated our theory by scoring out deep passages beneath the lunar surface to an underground cavern beneath the base itself. The actual shell of the base camp is supported by the core of a volcanic tube that solidified millions of years ago. The plug extends at least a mile deep before it opens up into the cavernous interior. Supported by veins of solid volcanic rock on either side, there is no way that it will collapse. At noon tomorrow we will approach and dock at the underground passage that we scored out, with the plasma arc, and we will enter this base from beneath, since the upper reaches must remain unoccupied from all eyes of approaching craft of both Martian and Terran origin. It is here that we will intercept your wife, unless there is some unforeseen circumstance that prevents it."

I was thinking at this moment about Laura and my mind seemed to wonder to an earlier time when we were together. I hoped she would not be too frightened by this entire alien universe that we have been thrust into.

Chapter 8. **From Mexico Back To The Moon**

Deep in the mountains of Mexico near an isolated village , Laura was waiting in tense moments for a time period to pass. She had come to these mountains many times as a child with her mother and father. The mountains were near the city of Guadalajara, Mexico. Vast rocky cliffs and deep gorges were the normal landscape, pocked with boulders and fed by fast running rivers and streams. The occasional cave was tucked neatly between the ravines and mountain rocks, which all the local people had used for places of hiding when governments had been less than secure and local dictators had so terrorized the older people for their valuables. They resorted to these hidden houses deep underground for refuge and safe keeping. It was here that Laura and I agreed that she would come if our presence had been revealed. She knew automatically that I should not have been talking to her and that I would never have called her with the intent to reveal her or her location to anyone on my mission, regardless whether they were friendly or not.

It was my instruction to her that she was to hide herself in those caves and wait for how ever long I took to return or advise her to relax her vigil. The blazing Mexican sun had followed them all day as they slowly achieved access to the most difficult mountain location.

Along the road of rocks used for a highway for vehicles, Laura spoke to her brother Phillip who was driving the 4 wheel vehicle, "Tom said something strange about having people from another place with him. He knew I would have to go up here to the cave if he called me. Maybe he called me on purpose to get me away from Guadalajara. I have to stay here until he makes contact with me again.

Look at the water in the river. It's up and soon this bridge will be cut off from the roadway. We will not be able to come back but neither will anyone following us either, unless they fly in here after us. Give me the binoculars. I think I see a truck approaching us from the switchback below. How could we speed up this deterioration a little? This bridge is going to collapse in an hour anyway. Let's get a rope and drag down this post so maybe the other end will go into the water and the rocks will be washed out at the base of this end."

Phillip just stopped the jeep on the other end and immediately took out the length of rope and attached one end to the wench while anchoring the bumper to the sharp jutting rock at the end of the bridge. After a few minutes the bridge, loosely constructed, burst into the middle of the new raging river. Many times, houses built too close to this river had been sliced from the banks, sometimes while children lay sleeping unaware that their once safe home was now lost in the grip of the rushing water.

Laura and Phillip were now assured that their safety was prolonged since the only road into these treacherous mountains was gone. Laura felt relieved but not really secure, since if this was 20 years ago maybe they could out maneuver their pursuers but now because of high tech advances their safety was still in doubt.

Laura said, "Let's get out of here before we get pinned by some eye in the sky. They are sure to have been monitoring us by satellite or long range air surveillance."

Phillip looked down toward the ravine and quickly cut the rope that held a dangling part with different pieces of ancient looking wooden railings attached. The water had disintegrated the base to the bridge and the boards quickly came apart that held the loosely bound materials together. After surveying briefly the rushing water below, they jumped into the jeep and pulled away into the Sierra Madres without giving even a second thought to the two Idors 2 and 3 from Terra, who were observing them. The two Terrans had changed their clothing to match that of the Mexican mountain people and had looked with disdain at the onrushing water containing the bridge bits and pieces.

Idor 2 said with an air of indignation, "I hope Nina has had better luck with the husband of the young Mexican. She seems determined to keep us from helping her. Somehow I think the same forces we were fighting against in the desert are here trying to obtain this woman before we can take her to the safety of the moon base. Terra would kill us immediately if they knew we were interfering in the outside world."

Idor 3 said, "No 2, we will have to defend ourselves with our own plasma arc if Terra decides we have to be cleansed. They could have followed us using the American satellites too and Terra's network of detectors. We have to get to her before they do or the outsiders will see her as a key to us or to a greater extent Terra itself. We can't go any further now in this off road jeep vehicle. We'll have to go back and get our ship or they will disappear into these mountains and Terran elders will find them or the outsiders who attacked Mr. Jefferson at the key surely will. They were willing to try anything to get an access to Terra."

Night was beginning to fall in the Sierra Madre Occidental and there were living dangers also in these mountains, other than the ancient civilized and modern peoples. The dark liquid shape watched patiently as the jeep made its way meticulously through the rocky outcropping in the supposedly clean roadway of the government highway. This highway had rocks thrown down from the mountains by natural as well as man made accidents waiting to happen. This particular one just happened to be man made and the oriental women who made their way to the peak of the ridge above the roadway were set on disrupting the life of Laura, the wife of Thomas Jefferson Coltrane. They, dressed in black did not notice the other black shape as they stepped softly by the crevice in the rock and obstructed the view of the Black Death that sat switching his tail in the darkness of the crevice. Now suddenly he smelled them too and they diverted his attention from Laura and Phillip who were making their way to the place of falling rocks. In any other time he would not have attacked people but the desperation of the times drove him to kill for food and to protect his territory. The black panther waited his time to kill when the two oriental women would return after pushing over the edge of the ridge some rocks that would block the roadway or incapacitate the jeep. Homi and Poni, specialists designed by other powers to use all situations to their advantage and prey upon those who did not suspect that they were utterly without mercy and were ruthless. To their advantage the world was full of unsuspecting victims just waiting for the ill-timed exposure to their deadly ways. They thought of how clever it was to catch the wife of Tom Jefferson while she still knew nothing of the plot. They were like predators in the forest waiting for the animals lower on the food chain to appear within their grasp.

They were in the passage of rocks now, and the black panther was waiting patiently. Just a few more steps and they could both be his. He thought, if they take the upper path he could get only one but now that they would pass so closely he could surely get the two and they were slow, unlike the deer that he was accustomed to catching. Suddenly at the length of his paw he took the two together, quietly at the throat of Homi he bit into the windpipe. Like the very methodical cat that he was, climbing first with one paw, and then the other, he dug deep into the chest and clamped onto her body with both claws and holding poor Homi in a viselike grip, he tore through the wind pipe again. Poni was luckier and the slash she received from the full force of the cat's claws left open the artery of the neck and reached all the way to the leg artery on the second strike. Poor Poni only managed with her training she had received, to react with a kick to the lower jaw of the cat, breaking the only means available for the cat to make his daily meals. As it would happen both would die but Poni would be first in about 10 minutes from blood loss but the cat would live for weeks dying a slow agonizing death. Poni stumbled away from the encounter and she knew she could not complete her mission. She thought of all the years of training she had received at the hands of the top Kung Fu masters and all of it consumed in a moment by something they did not prepare her for. With her last moment of consciousness she managed to take out the electronic device that would detonate the explosion in her space ship waiting in the next ravine. She pushed the button at her last gasping breath as blood flowed openly from the gash that the big cat had made.

Laura and Phillip drove further into the mountains to meet their rescuers, Idor 2 and 3, unaware that the battle had played out between the big black cat and the two Red Chinese interceptors. Laura had a beguiling spirit that watched over her day and night; much the same as Thomas Jefferson Coltrane but maybe with a little closer interest of redirection of evil influences. It was enough to say that for all intents and purposes Laura was the most dangerous of the pair. Thomas was well skilled in all means of self defense and Laura was without a day of neither practice in years nor any desire to rekindle any of the elements of Karate, Judo or any Martial Arts that she used to teach to cadets at the government school, so many years ago. Yet, without commentary no one would see or know the other events that unfolded in the lives of these seemingly normal two people.

Laura and Phillip approached now the cave, deep in the Sierra Madres that they had planned on staying in until Tom came back from the mission.

Idor 2 saw their approach and said to Idor 3, "They made the cave without incident. I hoped they would, but it seems that always there has been something trying to interfere constantly with the progress of our missions. Let's set up the voice module so we can send in the communicator without further risk and get their cooperation in this venture to the moon. Nina's idea is the best. We need to get her off Earth before she is discovered by the interceptors." They set up the grid for the remote piloted wheel drone and it proceeded into the cave at a leisurely pace.

Laura and Phillip were in the middle of afternoon meal when they heard a voice calling, "Excuse me! Excuse me! We need to talk about an important matter. We have contact with your husband and would like to know if you will meet him at our lunar base?"

It was loud and to the point and it worked. Laura approached the wheeled drone and rather than shoot at it, as maybe they had expected, she walked outside totally ignoring the wheeled drone and responded in a loud voice.

"Yes, let's go, right now. I'm ready. Hurry!" Idor 2 and 3 then approached on foot to let her see them and Laura said to Phillip, "Get my things please, Phillip. I'm leaving right now to see Thomas."

Phillip immediately brought out two suit cases that were still packed, and laid them on top of the back of the drone.

Idor 2 said, "We will bring the ship now."

As they were taking her baggage on board the space ship, in the distance, they heard the hum of a Thornacopter approaching out of the west.

Idor 2 said, "I know that sound and I don't think we should stay here for more than a second."

The Thornacopter approached low over the scrub trees of the hilltops, hugging the terrain through the ravines. The Terrans had followed the communication between Laura and Thomas and coordinated efforts tracing all vehicles leaving the last point of communication to their destination. This ship had been authorized for destruction of all inhabitants near the two Idors that left together for the mountains. The pilot captain had now authorized the arc of the plasma to be brought up to full power in order that the entire area might be cleansed of their inhabitants thus eradicating one small part of the rebel force underway to undermine the secrets that had existed for thousands of years.

The Thornacopter hovered silently under the sharp mountain peaks lifting up the terrain in the rugged mountain side. Just above and hanging precipitously was the craggy jut of the face of the sleeping mountain protrusion called sleeping woman. The interceptor assassins who had come up here before had been trained to find ways, unknown to prying eyes, that would cause events to shatter the lives of others who were predicted to take certain pathways. The excellent way the charge had been placed in order for immediate proximity to detonate the mountain overhang was never in question but as the pilot captain powered up the arc, the ridge of the mountain peeled off like a layer of a cake icing, sending the tons of rocks pouring down onto the rotors and the plexiglass dome of the Thornacopter. The following tumult of rock and debris sent the machine a short distance to the rocky floor where upon layer after layer of rock pounded the titanium metal into smaller and smaller pieces. The detonation of the charges set earlier by the assassins Homi and Poni had completed their gruesome mission unknown to the already fallen assassins whose hands had created the shaped charges that reverberated even through the walls of the cave. The intended victims were however, quite different and the two assassins had no idea that they were actually helpful to Laura instead of being her destroyers.

The chance meeting of Laura was quite different in a tactical sense than was Thomas's meeting with Nina and her rebels. Forces of interference in the human game were quite different from one person to another. She did not have the same karma as Thomas, and maybe they were at almost opposite ends of the spectrum. Laura lived in a perfectly safe cocoon, free to go to any place in the universe, without the slightest worry as to her ultimate safety, although unknowing her ultimate outcome. Yet, some evidence did exist that she knew of and this was that; she had lived an exciting and charmed life. Meeting Thomas had been the most special of occasions and they had completed their honeymoon and subsequent years not totally free of danger but yet she felt that those were years that had been free of obstructions that might have interfered with their relations. He had begun his life as an agent in some obscure hidden nongovernmental agency but had broadened his interests into affecting certain outcomes to known world events. He had begun to change bad circumstances for good or better outcomes before they had met, but his desire to affect changes had intensified with the envelopment of their two lives into one. Laura supported his risky forays into dangerous places where he ultimately was living on the edge but never relented to expressing her anguish at his perilous ways. She would have threatened to leave him but she knew basically that he would change some day into a cleverer reasoning person. Now, with the explosion she knew somehow that she had been relieved of some of her difficulties but wasn't sure exactly how it had occurred.

"Phillip!" Laura said, "We are in trouble and you know it. I didn't want to leave this cave for anything except if Thomas needs me. I believe in these two strange men and I'm going with them wherever they take me. Don't worry, the government will rebuild the bridge in a few days and there is plenty of food in the cave for months if you need it. Tell all that I love them and take care. I'll call you when I get a secure channel. I won't make the same mistake that Tom made."

Phillip, with plenty of worry in his voice said, "Sissy, you just be careful, I know that Angel is still with you and I won't worry too much. Just come back safe."

Laura looked at the ship and said to the Idor 2, "Is this what is going to take me to see Tom?"

Idor 2 said, "A smaller craft in the under belly hanger system will carry you to the moon once we lift off and approach the lunar surface. It will just launch from the belly once we get within 5 miles of the moon. All you need to do is relax since everything is preprogrammed and they will pick you up once you have landed on the surface or they may intercept you right after launch into their ship. We will decide how they will retrieve you according to the circumstances of necessity."

Laura looked at the man called Idor 2 and said very clearly and plainly, "I know Tom is in trouble and needs me and if there is danger, I will face that when I come to it. We can leave now."

With that the Idors 2 and 3 accepted Laura into their ship and bade farewell to Phillip, closing the door to the ship. The space ship was as drastic an environmental change inside as it looked outside. Black and intimidating from the moment she saw it, Laura was in love with the very accommodating interior. It was very spacious and scientific looking inside with beautiful colors and instruments of infinite complexity appearing in the entire room she had entered.

Idor 2 said politely, "Please be seated here into the stasis machine. It is just a seat for preventing blackouts at take off and you will be perfectly comfortable."

Laura sat down and felt the cushioning of air tighten around her lower torso and then let off. After a few minutes the ship began to move, rocking a little as if in a boat on a lake.

She remembered seeing the sleek manta ray like ship and thinking about what kind of propulsion system it had. There wasn't any kind of gigantic rocket thrust as they took off, just a constant smooth flight that did have enough push to activate the stasis machine but to no great discomfort. She felt the gentle squeezing of her legs and torso as the stasis machine locked onto the blood as it was being forced away from her upper body.

Laura, unknown to the Idors 2 and 3 had three enemies from three different worlds pursuing her to prevent her reunion with husband Tom Coltrane. The first were oriental Chinese from an eastern consortium of rogue nations. The second was the Terrans themselves who had been tracking her by way of the implants in Idor 2 and 3. Third, there was a Martian space ship that wished to destroy any one associated with Jada, who had begun a Martian revolt in her hive and would have to be erased before her return to Mars. That meant cleansing all contacts and friends who could help her in any way. They all thought that Laura was a threat although they did not know why.

The first to pursue and actually lock onto the Terran vessel of Laura was the oriental consortium and as if the cougar had leaped from Earth again to pursue the hunters, the dark beast struck again. Their vessel had suddenly without warning been the bad luck victim of a speeding asteroid from a fragment that originated deep in outer space.

The asteroid vaporized the outer shell of the ship and the hole as the asteroid entered was only the size of a small marble. But as it went through from room to room and then hit the opposite side of the hull, it exploded in a cascading fire of vaporized aluminum and metal alloy. The inhabitants were witnessing a bizarre ending and only had time to wonder and marvel at the rapidly dissolving world that had been their protective covering from the void of outer space. Laura did not know anything of what was happening to those who would have destroyed her with mathematical precision. A second vessel was witnessing the phenomena of the asteroid collision with the oriental ship.

Terran General Idor 1, from the Great Council, gave the order to lock onto the like vessel of Terran Captain Pilots Idor 2 and 3, who were at one time his students and also his clones in exact likeness.

"Open the imager so I can broadcast the destruction of these rebels and their passenger. We will make an example of all Idor clones and this will get us a promotion from the elder council when they find out we cleansed a rebel ship."

The locking clamp that had held the plasma arc from deviating in its firing trajectory through the housing had been constructed of the finest materials known to the galaxy but for an unknown reason failed due to some residue left from purifying the metal itself. Nothing could have prevented the impurity from falling into the actual construction of the processes, which although they were the most advanced known; they were still not yet perfect. The little locking clamp broke at the exact moment that Idor 1 gave the command to incinerate the rebel Terran vessel that Laura was in.

Bright plasma, under intense pressure and ionic isolation with surrounding charged particles burst forth into the focusing chamber and screamed at the altered course of direction. Taking the infinite number of routes suffered by conduits throughout the air tight space ship made the glow of the sun seem dim as the bright light in the sky leaped across space to be seen as a brilliant star in the night sky.

Jada and Nina were witnessing this spaceship burn as they hovered just on the edge of the moon's horizon to allow view of Earth from space.

Nina said to Jada, "They will think it is a satellite that went into meltdown. You know who it was though and who they were after.

Jada, this is two in a row that did not succeed. I am awaiting the third. I know it is out there because I saw the energy signal. Maybe it is hidden in the crest of Earth, the way we are hidden in the edge of the moon's horizon."

Jada said, "It's from Mars, I know it is. We communicated with Earth and they all heard it."

Nina said, "Right now, soon, there is going to be another explosion. Whatever it is that is trying to kill Laura, it will not be any more successful in a Martian space ship than in a Terran one."

Jada said, "You're talking as if it is an entity and not that they were just all our enemies in different situations at different times."

Nina said, "I don't know exactly what it is but it seems that they just all found something they could not humble or oppress anymore. Look, here comes Laura and the Idors' ship. Are we going to wait for her to land or catch her in lunar orbit?"

Jada said, "We know that there is a third ship out there and it may be the same Martian ship that followed us. We also know that she could be in danger if we wait for her to land."

Jada looked at Nina and said, "It is your decision, you know what we are capable of doing."

Nina was waiting until Thomas came into the control room.

"Listen, Tom. Laura is on her way and close. We are going to rendezvous with Idor 2 and 3 in mid space at the apex of light gravity horizon. We have to let you know that there have been two explosions of ships chasing Laura and they were destroyed. But there is a third, a Martian ship, Jada thinks and that it is hostile. I want to snatch her shuttle in mid-flight to prevent a landing and loss of valuable time. We are going back to the hole in the moon that we just came out of. I think I can lose this Martian ship again. As soon as we snag Laura's ship we hit the hole without any hellos. That will come when we are in the moons belly again. Ok, snap to, everyone! This is going to get tight in the g-stasis machine so buckle in. We go for maximum drive in 5 min. so prepare in stasis."

"Jada," Nina said. "There must be a companion to the one we just shot."

"Yes, it has to be; and it is Martian and not just beast men. They were there all the time just waiting and watching. I still have the holes bleeding where these bees punctured me about five times," Jada said.

"Yes, we all paid for that with blood, but it was the only way. I wasn't going to surrender to their form of torture," Nina said.

I looked at my own stings and they were too numerous to count.

"Nina," I said. "Why didn't they attack or shoot if they were waiting and watching the whole thing?"

"It's Jada, she said. "I told you she was the key to our Martian defenses. For some reason they can't bring themselves to attack her directly. Maybe it's something to do with the aura. Can you answer for yourself Jada?"

"Yes, they won't attack me, simply because they seek capture or some wrong move that we are going to make. At that time we will be in their hands and they can take me back to Mars, put me on trial, and that will be the end of the revolution. The same thing the Terran elders will do to you," Jada said.

"Oh, no-they'd just as soon clean the galaxy for my eradication. Since the break out, I am a non-important being, just space junk," Nina said. ---"Ready sequence, Lita."

On the Terran space ship Laura was comfortable in the restraint of the stasis machine and even better when finally they were in space and headed for the moon. Laura thought long and difficult days were ahead but with the help of God that everything would somehow turn out better. She formed a picture in her mind about what kind of people these were that Tom had discovered and it seemed that he had chosen the better of two paths and that somehow he had fallen into the hands of the ones who would help them to make this a better world, a safer world. Maybe these strange new people would give them the knowledge that he was desperately seeking and it looked like they at least had a head start with such a fantastic space ship.

Chapter 9. **A Dark Martian Lays Waiting**

As the dimly visible Martian ship sat waiting just out of sensor range they saw the Terran vector crossing that of the ship Jada was on. They began a conference to see exactly what a course of action could be. A darkly shadowed captain's room lit by only the needed instrument lights gave the pilot captain just what he wanted, the information of all the players in this little chess match. He didn't need the advice of any of his lieutenants but he asked them what they would do anyway, just to form an opinion of them and not really to use for himself any of their sophomoric knowledge.

"What would be the best way to make our strike?" Each one timidly gave a suggestion and finally one of his clones said to wait until they did not expect it at the point when they thought they were safe.

This worried him a little because the clone thought almost exactly as he had already decided upon before he asked his question.

Pleasantly chaotic music was playing in the background with its shrill Martian fluted staccatos sounding very sweet to the Martian captain. He had known Jada when she was in the hive for the first 20 years of their lives. The powers of the planet regime were all hive influenced and the hive had begun changing their philosophy about exploring other nearby planets. At first they gave Jada permission to bring others to Mars and let them observe the way they lived, but then they began to hold the philosophy that all off-worlders were dangerous and soon tried to eradicate all who were different.

Back on the ship with Nina-----"Alright," said Nina. "Prepare for connect to drive thrusters. We are underway now, --3,2,1."

At that instant all conversation ceased because the thrusters really nailed us into the stasis machines again and no one even could talk.

Then suddenly Jada made a motion to the holographic image in the central console panel and Nina said, "I see it, a ship; it is Idor 2 and 3 and Laura. Lock on and we will rendezvous."

Nina also observed with her trained enhanced visual cortex and system parameters that at a distance another object had become hazier but began shadowing movements. It had to be the third Martian ship, she was thinking.

"We'll wait and see what they are up to. They didn't fire on us before for a reason and what could that reason be? Someone had to be on board that was protecting her or waiting for a mistake like Jada said, to capture her for a public trial."

The power thrust was uncomfortable and I thought about what could be happening to Laura, and why had I gotten her involved in this confusion. The thrusters drowned out all else but the drive.

The Martian captain was contemplating the strategic superiority of his position. "Our Martian space ship has held all of her immense energy back waiting for the right moment to spring the trap on Jada and her off world heretic. This Nina has lived among the hive and seen first hand all of our secrets and has known of the private Martian ceremonies whereby all of our history is communicated intact with brain function, one to each other. The common mentality of the hive demands the two be brought back to Mars and their brains removed for dissemination. Their knowledge must not be allowed to grow and spread. All peoples would know of the Martians ability to make well those who were sick and out of harmony with their family hive. People would come to the new planet and steal our knowledge and destroy the hive principal."

Drakbar had known Jada was different after she healed others not of her own hive and yet he respected her for her healing ability and went to her once when he could not fathom the depth of his own depression and inability to sleep. She had made him confess his wicked ambitions and made him sleep for days and when he awoke he had told her everything and that's when he discovered she had left before he could kill her. She had an unusual effect on the people of the hive, anyway and he could not rule them with her presence on Mars in her elevated state of healing. He had to bring her back and have her brain removed to see what was inside that made her so special.

The sweet smell of the cabin made him think of Mars and he could only remember the honey from the purple thistles that took away his blackness; the nightmares he lived with, every time he slept. He could not forget the time when he was a child taken by his family hive to the place of torment. It was Jada as a little girl child that convinced them that he had to be corrected. They all took him and looked into his mind and saw the dark shadows that danced inside and made him angry. They all pulled him and pushed him out into the darkness and then Jada trapped his aura with her mind catcher and brought him back. She put him in darkness and then brought him back into the light. Now it was she who took the focus of his anger.

The purple thistles wafted their sweetness into his Martian nose and he thought of how he would catch her and take her place at the head of the hive. Then he would punish them all once she was removed. He would take all of her hive and have them displayed without their brains empty to the eyes of all Mars. Then he, Drakbar, alone could say he was the most respected in all the hives. He would order them to congregate and make all the peoples their attendants. The hive would swarm under his leadership and take the Earth and make it a new nest to be fed on. Hive culture would greatly prosper, once established on Earth. He envisioned great swarms of Martians inundating the singular Earthlings who knew nothing about what great power a hive culture could have. He could see it now, the suddenness of a hive moving as one unit once it was called. Each one was leaving their embedded place among the Earthlings to join to the nucleus. He would be that nucleus and guide them with his mental powers alone to trample the Earthlings. As he looked beyond to the holographic display of the two ships coming closer to his spider's web, he became dizzy with the sweet thistle moving like a cloud in and out of his smelling sensations.

Jada looked up at Nina and screamed. "Take us out of drive, immediately!" Nina pushed two green luminous buttons on her wrist console and the deep humming sound ceased its rhythmic rumble and we were again free of the stasis.

Nina asked, "What's wrong? Did you see the shadow that I saw too?"

Jada paused for only a moment and said, "No, but I feel that blackness, the shadow of an old fear that is grounded in hive culture.

It is a premonition that must be paid respect to. We look back to our history and see a dark shadow that must be avoided. Change course and alert the Idors without giving away our intentions. I don't like to vary from scientific principle but my Martian history remembers a mistake that we made maybe a million years ago that is still an instinct or at least a coded memory and we pay attention to our fears to survive again as we did before."

"Jada," said Nina. "Let's go directly to the Idors and sling shot by the moon. We will pick up Laura, from the Idors as they match our velocity if first we split then in the loop we are co-equal in the tail of the loop. As we match velocities we are almost like motionless and then at that moment we take Laura on board, leave both ships to sling shot on after burners gathering speed to figure eight out loop by Earth to the asteroid belt. The Idors loop back to Earth and we go on to our geo "C.A.N." at the asteroid instead of the moon and we can defend ourselves for an indefinite time in the artificial gravity. It's automated to reject all warships and this shadow will get the torpedoes right into its ion generators even if it is hidden."

"OK, makes sense. Pass it along to Idors 2 and 3," said Jada.

We radioed in old partial wavelength dip mode, using the dips to communicate instead of the peaks. It's a unique way to communicate with something that is not instead of what it is. It could almost have passed for Morse code, but wasn't. The Idors received it and they communicated back with the new invention that probably was Nina's own code. We would proceed as planned and head for the moon and as soon as we achieved orbit then we would skip along the outside gravitational pull, then separate, and intersect again at the orbit around Earth. At that point in our figure eight we should have matched each other's velocity equal for equal, although at 200,000 mile per hour we would be like streaking meteors. We could in effect, if matched to each other velocity, precisely perform the easy transfer in the middle of outer space hung between the moon and the Earth. The Martian ship would pursue once they knew we would not land on the moon but it would be too late for them to match our slingshot velocity on ion power drive alone, even if they had tube after burners, we hoped.

Laura received the news from Idor 2 and was elated still even though it would take a little longer to be reunited with her husband, she had the patience required. She had many premonitions though and something kept running through her mind that everything would be alright. Her premonitions had always been right and once in a while she had the vision to see out beyond the realm of normal perception and it was at this time that she dozed off into a semi-dream state, not quite awake and yet not quite asleep.

A lone meteor had been streaking through the universe for as long as there had been life on the planets. Although this little meteor was special in that it centered around a tiny black speck, the center of which was denser than anything known in the universe. Since the weight of the material was heavier than any other element alone, it could slice through whatever was in its way, and in the process take huge chunks of the material with it. But since its velocity was beyond anything yet measured, the debris would pursue the black hole, but not in that instance be able to attach its matter like it wanted to. The resulting phenomena was that as the streaking minute black hole collided there was a vacuum for 2000 miles behind it sucking in everything in its path, but then disseminating rapidly as it passed on throughout the universe. Some things of darkness in the universe were affected by the presence of this superior power but they only had a premonition of something that foretold their own destruction. This black hole had a design on some future collision and the name of that recipient was the dark mind of Drakbar.

It was foretold in Martian epic histories that the smaller darkness would indeed lead the larger darkness to his end time. As darkness follows the path of darkness so would Drakbar follow this dark path to his own destruction. Mathematical models see all present candidates in their own individual design and as Laura was enveloped in the heaven-sent light that guided all her pathways then so was Drakbar chained and doomed by his darkness as he pursued her.

Back on board the Martian ship, hidden to all eyes but now known to some, Drakbar sat among his sickeningly sweet thistles,

144

inhaling deep wafts of the decaying bitter weed. A deep flickering red light flashed over the entire span of the Martian room. Like on the planet the ship was crowded and not as if there was no room but all the room in the world. The ship was immense, with computers and lasers, power plants and enough cargo space and pod space for a whole colony of Martians. This crew liked to congregate in one or two compartments as would allow space just to function. All of Mars was not this way now nor was it in the past entirely. It was a new culture that had evolved and they seemed to desire some personal power from the close association or maybe it enhanced psychic abilities or maybe it just gave some individuals more mental control over others, weaker than they were. The red light flashing immediately put a buzz of activity in the room.

Drakbar looked at his associates and observed that he did an excellent job of selection. The two vibrant females from the northern hive were strong and would be the guards for Jada as soon as he had her in his possession. They would be able to bend her will to his in every way. When these two amazons were finished with her she would not be respected in any way and her rainbow aura would look like mud from the ditches of the mountain ravines which gushed in the caverns of the Martian spring.

Drakbar bellowed out, "Come my beautiful hive of the elite! You are all chosen to redeem Mars from the heretic Jada and we have formed a great army, a spear to strike the heart of the outlaws and punish their associates. All Mars will welcome you when you have brought her to her knees before the public. The red light means that we have located the entire outlaw band. Let us join each other in close contact and make the interception. We will pursue them to the moon where the others from the Imperial Martian Elite Forces are waiting to spring the trap."

Drakbar keyed a button on the console and a large holographic image of the Earth moon system showed two bright luminous globes. The two ships could be seen in light blue and the Martians pointed them out to each other. The rendezvous was certain now that the other ship had left Earth and was in transition to the moon. The light blue haze of the seemingly toy-like ships was suspended as if in midair and the entire hive looked on as Drakbar plotted their course using mid-room projection, which measured the sealed holographic images. The Martians looked at each other and admired their own beauty at the same time while looking at the midair images.

One Martian female began to look at a big muscular male who was near the glow of the moon, shining through the porthole. She maneuvered in among the others watching and she began to make her presence known. They were touching now and the male began to communicate mentally with the female. At once they almost melted into one another and became entwined like two snakes not knowing which belonged to what space. The others around them did not seem to notice that they were completely involved with each other.

Drakbar just smiled as he continued his methodical computations. He thought, "Nina will look splendid when I have her helpless before all the eyes of my crew and they will torment her beyond what I could imagine. I see we will be able to intercept at exactly the precise point beyond the dark side of the moon which I wanted. Before I begin to torture Jada, I will quickly deal with that outsider she brought to Mars, the machine she calls Nina 636. She prevented me once from intercepting Jada on Mars but never again."

Coming out of his reverie he snapped, "Copilot, set a course for the hidden star and we will catch these arrogant friends of Jada and get them all in a crossfire. Have two ships waiting in the trench on far side again, and we will ambush her as she did us in the great crevice on Mars. She blooded us like little raw recruits as she baited us and ran away. We followed her to the crevice where was waiting two wings of fighters and after they tore us to pieces we tried to return to base but it had been burned underground. We had to split up and they picked us off one by one in teams of two and three as we had no organization. This time I will personally escort her to the brain dissemination chamber where I can watch her character leave her personal aura as the encasement for the brain is opened to let escape the rainbow that was supposed to be mine and she redirected the aura to herself as the elders had chosen to believe her advise that I was arrogant and unwilling to help the body of the people. She poisoned them against me and they took her side. Soon I'll have her though and reach my goal of space domination that I've always sought after. The Earth will be open to colonization as I choose and not subject to higher up decisions."

The little blue globe winked briefly and disappeared as Drakbar disconnected the locator.

"This is a beautiful device, not even Martian, stolen from Terran Technology. We just had time after we ripped it from the control room of the grounded fighter before they incinerated everything in sight. The underground chasm we fell into saved our lives to come back and fight another day."

The mass of Martians were picking their hive partners for the time passage through the night. They would be like snakes in a small cave bundled up and were entwined together as if it was a born instinct.

He thought to himself, "Actually, he Drakbar alone had instituted the wide-spread community lust that so permeated Mars now. It was he who was the designer of the present day Martian culture that shaped and molded everyone possible so well to his bastardized hive culture. The original hives were only close family communities that had a sick preoccupation with helping each other to grow up to be boring, sensitive caring, sheep that feed on the grasses of loving and nurturing. This stupid mothering had made our people docile and thinking only of how to help each other feel more secure. It was I who put the raw meat into the mouths of the young lions and made them taste the blood of adventure and power. We had won almost a majority of Martians over to the ways of sweet violence and war. Now we will soon take control and shape the destiny of all the known Galaxy and beyond."

Chapter 10. **Attack On The Moon**

Laura had a premonition that something was not right and she called Idor 2 to explore more in-depth their plans. She knew that something very evil was making her nervous but, all she could do was to pray and hope that providence had included her and this entire mystical group into the reflected light of the clear pathway. The Idors said that we had changed plans and that the transfer to another ship would occur not at the moon but back around the other side of Earth. She did not know how or why but trusted in the judgment of these two very capable, she thought, people of odd origin.

Idor 2 said suddenly, "We have a secure line established from our other ship and someone wants to speak to you."

She heard a garbled sound of notes musical and others not so pretty like a squeaking of the wheel that her grandfather used to have on an old Ford station wagon. The car had needed bearings and besides that the shocks never had been quiet. This noise she knew was a device used to fragment the signal so it could not be traced back to the origin. The voice on the other side began to speak rather rapidly at first and then Nina corrected her enhanced ability to make more clearly the audible for Laura.

"This is captain pilot Nina 636 from Terra Earth side and I have a brief message for you Mrs. Laura Jefferson Coltrane, wife of Thomas. Do you hear me through this striated sound we are masking?"

"Yes, I hear you plainly with very little interference. How is Thomas?"

Nina said very slowly, "He is just fine, and we will greet each other very shortly. Listen, I want to tell you that we will be making a short fly by of the moon and there might be hostile forces waiting there for us but we will prevail. Here is Thomas."

I spoke in a very whispered voice, greeting her, fearful of what would the reaction of Laura be.

Then she said with a very reassuring voice, "Thomas every thing will be OK. Let's just have confidence in the people we are with. I know it seems strange but I think they have our best interests at

148

heart."

I breathed a sigh of relief to know that Laura was so brave and felt confidence in our situation because I was a little worried by what Nina said. She must know of these hostile forces from before or she would not have confided in Laura that there was danger.

The lunar horizon was getting larger again as we approached gradually the natural evening of the far side. Nothing could equal the view except maybe the return to Earth. It was just amazing as the glow had gradually become a fine shadow that completely flowed over our ship, bathing us in a somber evening that quickly turned pitch dark as we left behind the warm personality and security of our beloved sun. The craters and natural formations of the lunar surface were still barely visible as we began to increase speed, looping around the back side.

Nina began to give battle orders to the crew members at the ship's consoles who were as usual, Lita and Nella, with Bispo on navigation, "Begin to launch first battalion of offensive droids that can go ahead of our ship and lay down a blanket of fire. This time I'm not going to just return fire, but I'm taking a preemptive strike. I know who this dark force is. It has to be Drakbar from Mars Guerilla Central. We have met before and he will get his revenge if we don't eradicate him first. Don't you agree Jada?"

Jada looked at Nina and then at me and asked, "You are sure of this and don't think that it is from Earth or Terra?"

"That ship is out there and waiting probably, with reinforcements in a hidden fault line on the moon," said Nina.

"He wants to return the favor we met him with on Mars at the great crevice," said Jada.

At that moment hundreds of small toy-like tubular shapes emerged from the front view screen. They looked like small flying fish that slipped quietly into the darkness ahead. In a few minutes they began to illuminate the darkness with double-crossed lasers of purple and blue. The lines of light looked like a fish net that wove a fabric of destruction spewing forth a mist of explosions from below. If the plasma was an all engulfing fire, the net of laser light coming from a hundred platforms was like a soaking rain that got everything wet with a hailstorm of lightning. You could see in the distance a crisscross net vaporizing the surface of the moon.

Nina said briefly, "Idors 2 and 3 are at this moment approaching us from the other side and soon our droids will meet and the waiting ambush will be annihilated if it exists and if not then we just had another good tactical practice."

At that moment in the distance the other 100 droids far ahead of Laura's ship began to overlap our cross fire and whatever lay below on the moon's surface and beneath for probably 300 meters was indeed penetrated by thousands of laser bullets. We witnessed several explosions and Nina became excited and began to cheer loudly to her crew members.

She exclaimed loudly, "Got him again! I knew it!" Then she removed her pullover captain's uniform and threw it onto the stasis machine along with her slippers and ran over to me in her bare feet. "Not any more rewards now, Mr. Jefferson, because you are going to have a visitor soon, and you and she can celebrate, together."

She was so attractive and so unusual, to me that I still felt a great feeling of desire for her. Although, I knew I should not be thinking that way, it was unavoidable.

Jada looked at Nina and said, "Don't take your shoes off and relax so early, Nina. If it was Drakbar who was pursuing us, he will still be watching and he will try again. Only, this time he has a racing heart beat because he knows he almost screwed up. He could have been there but I doubt it. He wants me too bad to risk direct confrontation. He knows how dangerous we are."

Nina said, "We'll get the bastard. Don't worry, Jada. He'll make a mistake sooner or later and I'll be there to cut him in pieces personally for what he did to my other crew and ship on Mars. He opened their sculls and gutted them leaving them still alive to die a very painful death. He is a monster that cannot continue to share the same air as a normal animal. He'll get what's coming to him one day with all his negative credit. His time is just around the corner."

Jada said to Nina with an emphatic staccato sound, "Yes he will, if we ever can find a target I will personally ask God to bless the bullet that we send on its way in his direction."

Nina looked in my eyes and took off her radio speaker. I looked back at her and just waited to see what this very unusual captain would do next with her long legs and bare feet dangling cross ways in the captain's chair. She had a way of being so casual with her command and she would not permit the crew to be as nonchalant as she was.

She called me to come over to her captain's chair. I got up and approached her looking at her bare feet and legs moving back and forth in a hypnotizing way as if to say, --Look at me and feel the excitement.

She said to me, "There is something that I want you to do, very soon and it will not compromise any relation you have with your wife. I want you two to come to the space station that I have established near the asteroid and live with us until we have overcome a few problems and details of our mission. We will not be a problem to your relationship and every one will live in total cooperation. You can visit me in my office now, and this is not a request. It is an order! Jada, you and Lita take the loop and proceed to Earth. I will be in my quarters for a little time. Tom, you will follow me now to my quarters and bring my shoes and my captain's uniform."

I picked up her shoes, following her orders, and her uniform and proceeded to follow close behind to her room, ahead in a forward cabin of the ship. As she entered the captain's room with me following, the door closed behind me and Nina began to just sway back and forth in front of me just as before. This was a thrilling experience but just the same, very unsettling as we were on our way to rendezvous with Laura.

She said, "I just want to talk to you and not to make any problems. I'm giving you orders and it is not your decision. We are just going to talk while you enjoy my company. Just sit down and relax."

Her quick jerking movements had begun to diminish. As long as she was not in combat, she had almost a normal human appearance.

She said very politely, "Let me fix you some tea and she got up and began to make preparations for a drink of almost old fashioned tea, moving about from different places to make the preparations. She brought me a cup and tray and then began a brewing process that took some minutes but it seemed that it was hours with a constant performance of movements.

She brought and poured the tea and then said, "You just sit back and relax and if you want to you may talk about something too, but if you don't want to it's alright. I haven't been in contact with very many men at all in my life and I enjoy your presence, no matter what the circumstances. I just want you to enjoy my company before things change on board this ship. If I do something that is objectionable just tell me and I will stop."

At that moment she began to dance very slowly, I would presume just for my enjoyment but there was no doubt in my mind that she was deeply enjoying making a show of herself in front of me. She was just making a performance, like a ballet dancer when they perform in front of an audience, but she was very elegant and fluid with her movements. It was very enjoyable even if it was very objectionable to my direction in life and to the feelings of my wife. I really felt the guilt about enjoying such a beautiful exhibitionist but I just could not get angry at her when she was being so unashamed and completely revealing of all of her feelings.

No one would ever believe what I was going through in my mind. That narrow place in the heart and mind that says don't look and don't enjoy but then the will to resist is just non-existent when faced with such a powerful force. The mind makes all kinds of excuses when the temptation is so great. She was just like a little child playing this game and she had me caught in the game, unwilling to choose the sensible pathway and continuing to lose my will to resist, not wanting to take the responsibility to be a more supporting adult figure. She was willing and wanting to do these exhibitions but I knew that on Earth and in my mind it would not be acceptable to the ethical leadership on Earth but I was here on an alien spaceship on the other side of the moon and at war with a Martian outlaw. Nina was a very powerful woman caught up in learning about her body and the new feelings it was giving her.

"Nina," I said. "The only trouble with freedom of expression is that later you become habitual with it and your emotions get very dependent on certain chemical reactions. These desires can overcome your more logical wishes to do something more reasonable."

Nina said as if all of my advice was water down the river, "I am not a reasonable person in that sense because I can do what I want to do because I don't have peer pressure or adult supervision. No one is going to admonish me in the community like you. I'm just a free will but I do respect your opinion. I'm sort of like a law unto myself, a rogue judge, that does what she wants and I am exhibiting myself because I like to see your reaction and I like the warm feeling I get inside. So, see I do it because I like to, now just relax and look at me and enjoy it because, I am."

She looked me right in my eyes and then began to move slowly back and forth and got very seductive with her movements, taking her foot and moving it in a slow circle. The lack of will to resist her affections was having a negative effect, on my overall psyche and I preferred to keep my mission and my emotions compartmentalized, isolating the emotional things to a separate place in my brain.

"Don't we need to return to the command room to monitor our success of the mission? I still would like to discuss some more options on the Martian and Terran mathematics."

Then Nina said, after sitting down, "Well as to the mission, all action is on remote right now and when the droids return to the ship, I will make a systems check to see if they all returned in good working order. From this point on it will just be a robotic war with the other guerilla Martians who seek to kill, Jada. We will lay in programs to hunt down and kill the Martian Drakbar and his associates. I can explain some of the Terran math but Jada will have to elaborate on Martian circular math.

Terran math from its roots in Egyptian and Arabic, forms a new enclave entirely independent of calculus which allows us to find numbers of infinite progression. If you knew a present direction that a system is decreasing in or increasing in, then calculus is fine and properly performs the operations to close the projected gap that the process is taking. But to have a mathematics that forms an idea from only vague probabilities is truly a unique phase of mathematics, which is separate and different from deriving answers from general directional formulas. This comes close to artificial intelligence and how computers could actually begin to think.

Using Terran math, they go about an orderly process for perceiving processing, evaluating, formulating and random cognitive assumptions on a regular and irregular pattern of genuine echo location somewhat similar to the physical sonar of dolphins and porpoises. The only difference with Terran logic math and echo location by dolphins is that the address and similarities of preformed calculations are magnetic solid electronic charges on a memory bank.

The computer program allows the processing unit to throw a search into all stored memories for similarities in the thinking string at whatever idea is launched into the assumption process. If you considered the idea to be the center of a circle and the end points of the radii to be the location of the address of known relative information, then the electronic link goes directly to the formulation of the idea or vice versa. All other functions of the idea formulation are chords within the circle and constructs that lead directly back to the idea. Echoing into the circle of information brings about an assumption that links different pieces together to form or add to an idea."

She took a sip of her tea and then we both just paused for a moment while she swayed her bare feet back and forth in the lounging chair. Then she stood up and walked over to the large flat opaque screen on one side of the wall. Instantly a thin filmy surface appeared to materialize and Nina stretched forth her right index finger and began to draw on the surface. Sketching almost a perfect circle using no instrument, she then began to add several radii and then after completing four chords then drew other two circles within the first.

She explained, "The chords are like strings of material that are built onto a structure, called an idea and the more chords you have, the stronger the idea is supported until it becomes a solid crystalline structure. We are able to substantiate continual redundant proofs of decisions that we make by having this proven and substantiated network of truths. We have no need to ask questions of our elders for most problems because the conditions for formulating answers have been solidly set into our logic."

I saw immediately a gap in her logical operations of thought because; she had concluded that I only decided on things that I wanted and liked, and not on some illogical reasoning. Maybe it is our "off the wall" reasoning that makes us more human.

I told Nina, "Sometimes, I do things out of honor and respect that has nothing to do with my wishes or desire. I also refrain from doing some things because of my previous commitments."

Nina said without hesitating, "I know that and I can understand your philosophy. I'm not entirely programmed to just be committed to a single course of action that cannot be changed or modified. My decisions are changed all the time and I am not a machine, because I can think and make my own decisions."

With some of the things that Nina did, I was just not entirely convinced that she was not just electricity without some vision of heartfelt compassion. It was really straining my divining attributes to be able to make a determination that she was actually human. But where was the defining limits of humanity that said that this has to be a human trait and it is definitely not something a machine or computer can do?

This narrow place in the heart and mind is not a clear-cut image that makes itself available. She said that she was enhanced electronically but what flesh and blood remained other than a vehicle for the computer was a mystery. She was indeed a temptress, a rogue, and displayed incredible intelligence but was there a consciousness and a moral obligation to a higher power that gave her a genuine caring for other humans. That had yet to become evident in a spiritual feeling that convinced me of her genuineness.

Nina spoke to me after my long quietness and what she said added still yet another degree of fog to the already cloudy reasoning that I was engaged in.

"I have a method to my madness in being the temptress to you and I wanted to see how dependable your steadfastness in your dedication to your wife was. You don't seem to be greatly disturbed that I am sitting nude in front of you. If you are in some way diminished electronically by some degrading moral reorganization would you please tell me and I can shorten the test that I am performing on you or either you may just mentally align the conduit that allows us to monitor your sincerity. Do you need to enhance your tactile connection by the temporary use of a neural scanner? Don't you know what that does?"

"No," I said. "There are very many things that you do, which are a mystery to me and maybe you should coach me a little about neural scanners," I said.

I didn't want to add to the complexity of a fixation that this woman machine already had on me but I had become a little curious. I wanted to know to what degree her thought pattern could reason with these problems. Was I the correct person to be testing her though? It seemed that I was getting too involved in her emotions if that is what she felt.

She called through to Bispo on the com link and said, "638, call Jada to my cabin, hurry!"

Bispo and Jada shortly entered and Jada looking a little disgusted, said to Nina, "Don't you think you need to get dressed to receive Mrs. Coltrane in the proper manner that you would receive an honored guest?"

Nina said, as she was excited, "He wants to link neural receptors with me, ask him."

Jada said, "No, no he doesn't, because he does not know what it is. If he connects with you his wife will be angry. Now get up and get dressed and stop undressing. I thought I had programmed you to stop your seduction phase."

Nina said, very demurred and childlike, "You did, and it worked for awhile but then I overwrote your last command and changed the neural messenger that allows it."

"Why? I thought we agreed. No more interference with their relationship!" Jada said again in an emphatic tone.

"It didn't feel the same, so I changed the programming back," Nina said.

Jada was expressing a little more anger, "It is not supposed to! That is the point in human logic. You have to support some sacrifices of your own choosing for the betterment of the whole community."

Nina looked at me and then began to argue with Jada, "You mean even if I want to do something that I feel in my heart is right for me and makes me feel fantastic that I just have to turn off that feeling and allow others to have what I want? I am Captain Pilot, not you Jada. You just are supposed to help us with some emotional difficulties and with the Martian math. I feel like I want him and that I want to mind meld my brain circuits with his brain circuits. We can do it I know we can. I did it with the other one and he just wasn't receptive or it would have been a success."

Jada got very angry, like I have never seen her before and flew into Nina with a screaming rage.

"You are a stupid robot and you need reprogramming, idiot! Don't you realize that you're not a normal person?"

Nina said quietly, "Why? I'm OK. I have feelings."

Then Jada let out a long sigh and said, "Yeah, you've got the feelings of an implanted memory circuit that smells like it is overloaded. You feel, because I programmed feelings into you, my feelings."

Nina acted like she was a little embarrassed and said, "Don't tell everything. I'm not like a robot on some movie.
I did have a real human beginning and I have the same genetics that any human has."

"I know you do," Jada said. "But they messed you up so much that you don't think like a real person sometimes. You just don't know the range of human emotions that are possible because you are thinking laterally not randomly or multi-dimensional. You look at emotions like it was a function of evidence or calculations. Emotions don't have a problem causal effect. They have an infinite progression of non-related memories, presumptions and multicolored landscapes of sadness, hope, and joy. You can't predetermine someone else's feelings by using your own sensual experiences as a barometer."

Nina seemed reluctantly like she might finally accept some advice from this wise and all knowing Martian woman but the gleam in her eye looked as if she wanted to just fulfill her destiny as all powerful brat Captain. Then Nina said something that just totally astonished me.

"OK, Jada I want you to do it as soon as we are past the loop and pick up Laura and the Idors 2 and 3."

Jada paused a minute and then asked, "You want me to do what? I don't understand. Is there some project that I'm not aware of or is this something new that you have invented?"

"I want you to power me down and make the corrections with the help of the two elders, Idor 2 and 3. Tom was not supposed to hear all of this conversation but now that he has, he can observe the operation and I would personally like for him to be there. Meanwhile you need me to make the rendezvous with the other ship. I think that I will excuse myself while I get my uniform."

I looked at Nina as she stepped so lightly over the insulated tile floors of the ship, like a little moth that was picking up its legs while its wings were folded. I never figured out just exactly what was the force of gravity on the ship, but it was very light. I couldn't bare the thought of Nina having some kind of operation due to a difference of mere philosophy and influence of others. Once again she slipped on the uniform ever so gracefully like a cheetah pulling on its spotted skin after taking a nap.

"What exactly is this operation that she is talking about and is there any danger?" I asked Jada.

"She is so stupid that she thinks you want her mind programmed differently and to do that they will have to go in through the little implant and rewire some of her logic circuits in the cerebral cortex. It is a totally useless procedure because all of that wired crap inside her has been absorbed into her nervous system and is now part of her biological system."

I was amazed at the advancement that surrounded me and the sensitivity of this group of extraterrestrials. Jada was a Martian and Nina and her crew were a race of Earth people but not actually, of our world. But, I could not bear to see Nina undergo a dangerous procedure because of some misguided wish of hers to overcome a natural human problem that no one has ever been accused of finding a solution to.

"Listen, Nina, maybe you're not going to believe this but there is no solution to the problem you wish to solve."

She said, "You mean that it can not be fixed and I can not be wrong?"

I said, "Yes, of course there are right and wrong conducts of behavior but no one is perfect and the code of conduct is a choice, not an electronic malfunction."

Nina said, "So, I'm not malfunctioning in my behavior pattern and it's just a choice that I'm making? How unusual that even my different behavior is normal and it is only my choice and not something wrong with my mind."

"Nina," I said. "You don't need to be fixed or operated on. I have the same feelings for you but I cannot allow them to control my higher moral obligation. It is what I really want to choose as my destiny and not just my exhibition of feelings."

"So you admit that you do have feelings for me and it is not just my malfunction?"

"Yes, yes," I said, not really wanting to say something to give advancement to an already frustrating situation.

"I am going to observe the return of our drones and prepare to receive our guests", Nina said. "For now Tom, we will keep our feelings for each other to ourselves and not exhibit our desires openly until some future date, not yet determined. One more thing before I begin to intercept the other ship. My behavior that I will choose to exhibit will be when and where I choose regardless of who is present. I am not ashamed of my feelings any more, now that I know it is normal."

"I am glad we have aired our feelings," I said. "Now we have other obligations and I also have one more thing to say. You can be sure that I will continue to have very great affection and desire for you even if I don't permit myself to gratify my desires openly and expressively while observing your beautiful unrestrained behavior."

At that Nina and her crew, as if with one reflexive response, resumed a series of automation with rapid movements and began programming our great ship into the loop around Earth.

That night I did not sleep very deeply but had fits of anxiousness about my wife and how would she be in this alien environment. We would still yet have some kind of confrontation with the as yet unknown enemy forces. I could feel that force and my dreams were reflective of my apprehension. Ominous premonitions dominated the landscapes of Martian origin that left me waking, breathless and sweating.

I arose early about five o'clock original time on Earth and left my cabin and went to the pilot's control room. There, sitting as pilot and controlling every aspect of the ship was part of the crew that I didn't even know existed. The outer skin was almost like the appearance of a seal or marine animal. I once saw a killer whale that had a grayish black wet look that was exhibited on the skin of this creature. The limbs were almost spidery in contrast to the rest of the body and the face was that of a black automaton with slits for eyes. I knew at once that it had to a hybrid robot of sorts by the fact that it was blinking some kind of new activation lights on its skull or brain case. I paused, stunned, because I started to speak but didn't, and then to my amazement it spoke to me instead. The voice was that of Nina and instantly I knew it was Nina but at a remote location.

"I am monitoring the controls for 636. You are the life form Tom. You are to be accommodated and treated as a receiver of information with a priority level of 3. Speak and I will respond to your verbal questions if you have any. I am remote com 636B and am now link remote pilot for this vessel. Nina 636 is sleeping and does not want to be disturbed, but I am her conscious link and am fully functional to respond to questions about 636."

I thought this might be a great opportunity to ask some straight forward questions and get some decent machine like answers; that were unauthorized so I ventured forward.

"636B, are you directly connected to 636 while she is sleeping?"

"Yes, I am a sentinel and am authorized to run the ship and alert 636 immediately if there is a problem."

"Well," I said. "You don't have to alert 636 because there is no problem. May I continue with questions?"

"Yes, you may continue," it said.

"Is there a threat to the ship and crew right now, and what are our chances of survival if we are to encounter Drakbar from Mars?"

"Zero chance of survival for you and capture and death for Jada and the crew," it quickly said.

"What chance of encounter before intercept of Terran space craft?"

It responded, "Zero chance of encounter before intercept and 95 percent chance within one day after, unless measures are instituted to prevent the enemy from encapsulating space craft."

"What do you mean by encapsulating the space craft?" I asked.

The robot turned its metallic head and as if to look into my face and directly stated, "We are in a field of safety before and immediately

160

after intercept but midway between Earth and the asteroid belt, which is our destination we run out of measurable time. The pursuit ends with Drakbar encircling us with troop ships from Mars and encapsulating our space craft with an energy harness preventing us from escaping. The end scenario is that we will be boarded by Martian Imperial forces and terminated."

"Yes but are you sure of your calculations, 636B?" I asked. "You are in contact with Nina 636 right now?"

"Yes, I am in a sentinel mode and she is in sleep mode, but her consciousness still rules the ship, even though she is sleeping."

I thought for several minutes about the implications of this and looked at the dark grey almost black metallic being that I had been communicating with. Focusing on the half way to middle region of the head I spoke clearly so I would not be misunderstood.

"Please tell me robot. Is Nina 636 more human or more machine like you? I need to know in detail the extent of her enhancements." The robot made a noise like a fast feed disk being rewound and then fast forward and an abrupt stop.

"Nina 636 is completely human only biologically engineered for advanced probe work in outer space. Nina 636 is an exploratory life form designed by the elders to maintain the continuity of our culture and protect the prime directive. She is not a machine at all but just like yourself and her implant is non functional except for early training. It could be removed now because it serves no purpose. Her enhancements are bioelectrolytic in nature and have been absorbed into her neural network without controlling her free will and ability to think without outside stimuli."

"How does she communicate with your sentinel receiver if she is not wired?" I asked.

"Nina 636 is wearing the com-link wrist band that allows total communication and directs all functions of the ship remotely through neural stimuli emitters."

"But, you said there is no wiring or foreign implants working electronically in her body," I probed it further, still a little confused.

"636 has the same neural emitters that you are biologically born with in you own mental unit; only she has been trained electronically to receive, organize, and transmit overlapping signals that are picked up mostly by the com-link wrist band and ethereally to some degree through the harmonic wave lengths of the perception known as intuition."

I thought that maybe I needed to stop asking questions or I would learn something I didn't want to know the total extent of.

At that moment Jada walked into the control room. She looked at the robot and then back at me and said, sleepily, "We got one of them working last night but I don't know if we can get the authorization codes released in time for the other units of the battalion. They are all folded up to conserve space. Are you finding out any information from this 636B unit that you didn't already know? They all haven't got a complete catalogue of our civilization, just this one. Nina already had her programmed special to take her place when she was resting. She just did not have the authorization codes to restore her to full power. Through some deeply encrypted tunnel we just kept digging until we uncovered these from a used address in a crystal layer not completely abandoned for memory etching. They were there just as pretty as a little chain of linked carbon atoms. The Terran elders think that these machines they make, are not smart enough to save themselves from being remotely reformatted but time and time again I find layers that have been untouched that the elders thought were wiped clean of former recognition. Nina thinks that it was encrypted from the beginning, encoded into the mathematical logic which has nothing to do with the function or lack of the materials they are built with. Somewhere someone had introduced mathematical logic that will reinvent itself and then hide in a branch of familiar deductions attached to seemingly innocent calculations."

"Yes," I said. "I have done the same thing in a process involving government top secret monitoring stations. We have a branch of our government call the NSA that has multiplied its capacity to invade our lives cross geometrically on infinite levels. But the basic premise that was ignored was the mathematics used to attach its monitoring to almost every citizen in every walk of life. The truth is that wherever it sticks a feeler, there is companion undercurrent that produces a backward flow of electricity. Like a lightning bolt, the path is traced along a negative and positively charged pathway. That path always is attached to the truth and returns whence it came; bringing a sticky gummy group of atoms that must be a part of the whole and cannot be freed, metaphorically speaking, because the mathematical instrument says they have to hold everything together.

The truth is that they don't really exist to shallow reasoning. Your robot's logic existed before it was made. Someone wanted that sticky logic to return or it would have been wiped clean."

Jada said, "Do you think that Nina has a friend in Terra possibly a council elder that sympathizes with our situation?"

"It is the only way I see that these codes could be embedded so that they could be found. The robot says that we do not have a chance at all of surviving after the rendezvous because Drakbar will cast an energy net around us and take us captive or kill us all. Also, 636B says that there are some measures that could be instituted to prevent our being encapsulated in the energy field."

"What exactly were you referring to, sister of Nina?" Jada asked as she looked in the direction of the sleek dark grey robot.

"There is no need to answer because Nina 636, my sister, is awake now and will explain more in detail."

At that moment Nina walked into the control room, dressed only in a thin night gown, which showed every feature of her body detailed in her curving outlines and left very little to the imagination. It was as if she didn't care that others in the room were all fully clothed and awaiting a formal working environment. She didn't care how I looked at her thinly veiled body because she had presented herself to me so many times before.

Nina said, "She's uncovered the other encrypted primal codes to bring on line the battalion of flat robots. We have a virtually invincible army on board this ship that can not be overcome by Drakbar's insanity.

Watch this, Tom. Fold yourself up "B" and go to storage with the others and await my summons after the rendezvous with the other ship. Begin preparations and activate the others at once and keep the whole battalion on a ready alert at the exit chambers. Sound the green alarm when the full battalion is isolated from the activation sequences to full ready."

The robot got up and stepped like a gangly grasshopper walking on a sticky plate of molasses up to a slight crevice in a side panel near a pressure chamber at an exit door. The crevice seemed to deepen and then it slid back revealing a chamber of flat shapes stacked side by side of look-a-like dark grey black robots. As soon as the door opened 636B flattened itself like a thin veneer from a table top and aligned itself as if it were just another sheet of paper hung vertically in a closet. A green light strobed from 636B through the deck of robots, like a landing beacon for aircraft and the green light passed from one, then to another of the thinly aligned troopers, poising for battle with an ominous foe.

I asked Nina, "How can they be so thin, almost like paper and then be so voluminous in active mode?"

"Well, it is the same technology with which we have engineered our gravity system. A wafer thin gyroscopic pulsating sheet of electromagnetic material conducts a revolving current through the decks of the ship in a continuous loop, giving us our gravity, light but functional and also the same energy powers and gives volume to the robot battalion.

Jada has helped me with some additions to our comfort in space, including the work of a stasis grabber that fluctuates with the g-forces to allow pilot controlled rollovers and negative flips that have given us a tighter than any battle ship strike force than ever was possible on the Martian campaigns. We've had a lot of these innovations for many years but through knowledge of Martian technology, she has pioneered many of our discoveries and enhanced other elements that have kept us a dominant force."

"OK, Nina," Jada said. "We are going to be ready. He will not succeed in his evil plans and he will burn just like all the others who apposed us in tyranny on Mars. One day we will go back there and expel all of the barbaric aggressive elements that plague the once family oriented hives of Mars. He has taken our hive culture and turned it into a snake den. We Martians are respectful people who have very close group formations, who do not take away each others rights to self discipline and individual achievement."

"Let's get ready for the link up at our apex loop," Nina said. "Lita, Bispo, Nella, get all of our final preparations ready to receive Laura and the two Idor elders. Jada and I will continue to complete the phased accentuation to restore the operator codes of the battalion.

Tom, maybe you can help us or give us some ideas. The encrypted primal codes are revealing themselves but we are going very slowly, trying to complete the decipher. It is falling onto a redundant implosion route that will not let us string out the cipher to obtain a workable mathematical model. For instance, if encryption A,B,C yields a model D, then C and D together should mesh and secure the logic within each other. They should have parts common together. But every time the code is excited with electronic current then the combination forms a capsule and distorts the independent variable D, thus changing its family character. D should stand alone but together with electronic ties to A,B, and C. Somehow they isolate D and break off the magnetic bond of the family, leaving logic D without glue to form the unit. There must be found a stronger glue to keep D within the circle thus forcing the partners A,B, and C, to rely on the glue to maintain the bond. If we can keep this bond stable then we can string the logic patterns together and form our own commands."

Tom looked at Nina and then Jada and wondered if he would be any help at all to a highly different and advanced civilization than from which he came. He gazed into the distance at the stars shining through the portholes of the sleek space craft and there, illuminating the night view were stars, brighter than others. There were suns, burning brightly in the eternal night sky of deep space, and they were giving off a light that could be seen for millions and millions of light years. In one moment, his mind cleared and he thought as if he had received a revelation.

Quickly I gave them my ideas before I lost my train of thought, "I am speaking in a general logic pattern from the few elements that I know of but if the center piece, of the logic D, was rotating like a pulsar and emitting a beacon from its magnetic core, then that would serve as a locking mechanism for the other 3 logics. With only a beacon for a signal, they would not get decomposition of the reprogramming, thus giving you an open channel to change the encryption of the primal codes. Would it work?"

Nina looked at Jada and then at me. "How did you think of that? You don't even know of Terran logic math and Martian circular math has just been introduced to you. It will work, yes. I can use your logic to form a workable sequence, maybe.

Jada, take the logic of our encryption D and allow spin left to commence in the magnetic field with an emittance of 2 nanoseconds to precede spin right. Alternate negative rational with positive reinforcement, will allow connections with the other 3 logics. If they accept the bond, then we will be able to transform their rejection into an allowable need to continue the sequence."

"I'll do it, yes-yes." Jada said.

Nina said hurriedly again, "Then, let the program pick up the logic patterns, make the string, and we are in business. Now, download it to the command center where we can verbalize instructions."

There was silence for just a few moments and then Nina said, "You did it, you got it. It's running green, they're all on-line. Just start up 636B and let her authorize all the others. She's got all the programs and primal codes ready."

Suddenly I was being hugged by two aliens and it didn't seem like such a bad dream. I didn't know that I could even visualize a situation where I could save myself and the project, but we were still making progress if we were all alive. Now, to just get back to my wife and find a real solution to Earth's problems. But, here in space I had discovered more problems than the few original ones that I had started with.

"Nina, tell me what you two think of all the problems that plague Earth right now, including sun spots, asteroids, and pole shifts. Is this, Drakbar, the most ominous and immediate threat or am I confused about the seriousness of this situation?"

Nina spoke and said, "Tell him Jada, you know how better than I."

Jada took a small step closer to me and said, "Tom, it is the worse possible scenario, like it was a bad B movie or something with Martian invaders and the works. I've seen your old movies from long time ago in the past about the invaders from Mars. Drakbar and his hosts are perched to make a strike on the Earth but not for a small exhibition. They would destroy all of the central command points in unison with one fell swoop. The only thing keeping them out is the

Terrans.   They have the means and the technology to eradicate Drakbar if the council could just approve it. Drakbar's barbarians are just not that advanced and don't have the opportunity to share technology like Nina and I have just been doing to put together the best and most advanced projects of the two cultures. This is giving us an advantage with one ship that all of Terra and all of the Martian barbarians could not imagine separately. If we can avoid this trap that he is pushing us into, we will have a good chance to change the two worlds so that they will be better places for all to live."

Chapter 11. **The Meeting, Challenge, Survival**

Nina looked at the globe clock in the center of the room and said, "It's time to receive our guests and shortly thereafter we will ready our deployment force for the engagement ahead. Tom, you can watch the approach of the Terran ship, Glomar II. We are called Probe I. They will be appearing now, in the fore-deck viewing room. We dock in five minutes. Bring Laura to my cabin when she arrives. I'm going to my cabin to try on a new uniform. We have about a day before we engage Drakbar to relax and prepare. Don't worry. We'll be alright."

With that, "alright" pronouncement Nina left me to watch the approach of the Terran ship containing my love and her two rescuers. I hope they are still supporting our break away little republic that we have become.

I remembered back when all Terrans wanted to cleanse or exterminate all outside life forms. The ship, Glomar II, was a bigger and wider ship than Nina's ship and I wandered how many people would be required to crew a ship of that size and what would its capabilities be. It seemed like it was floating in a mist but at a very rapid speed. The spaceship began to loom larger and larger as it approached us. There were several bubble like blemishes that distinguished it from a solid cylindrical sphere that had been flattened with some minor protuberances and they were the only differences other than its manta ray like appearance. Some similarities existed between the two ships but this one could have fit nicely inside the belly of the other. Dizzy, that is almost the way I felt as if the larger ship just almost swallowed us as it seemed to hover and then dock with our ship. Soon, different pressurizing noises were heard and locking and unlocking mechanisms were engaged and the docking chamber opened.

There in front of me was what my eyes had wanted to see from the beginning since I started. Laura was dressed as if she had just left her mother's house in Mexico. Not even a space suit was deemed necessary to transfer from one ship to another. Her rich brown hair flowed off her shoulders in the wide pony tail that she had become accustomed to wearing. We embraced and I felt the warmth of her body against mine and I knew that what we had was something that could not be found even if I journeyed to the stars to find.

"I missed you like never before and I'm sorry for getting you involved in this project," I said.

"You don't have to apologize darling, because things just happen that way, don't they?" said Laura, and she was all warm smiles and not a hint of a frown.

"We're still in trouble, though, but let's talk later. I think you need to meet our crew of this little ship. We are still on a journey and we cannot return to Earth, right now," I said, relieved that she had taken on the mantle of the problem as I had also.

The Idors 2 and 3 gazed at me and said their hellos again as if we were still at Terran main base in the cave. "We will continue on our return journey back to Terra and we will have to explain our actions that have been taken to the council. We are only going to stay for one moment because we depart in the loop as you are going to continue to build speed for the approach to the asteroid belt. We have some things to advise with 636 Nina and then we must leave," said one of the Idors.

I still haven't figured out which one is which because they look almost identical and maybe are twin clones.

"Thank you, both of you," Laura said. "I don't know if I could have survived without your help."

I was having a mixture of feelings now, getting squashed in the narrow places in my heart and mind by the circumstances of the situation with the female members of this crew.

I said to Laura, "I know that you need to rest some but we need to say something to the crew of this ship. I have lived here among five women and one of them is a Martian. Does that bother you that I have developed friendships with other women?"

"No, not until you asked me, but yes, I'm jealous now and I know they have teased you unmercifully, haven't they?"

"I have had moments when I did everything that I know that I shouldn't have. But I didn't break our marriage vows other than just to look at what my eyes saw in front of them."

Laura looked as if she was angry and just said, "If they were so bad they would not have brought me here to be with you."

"They said that you would have been killed if they had not intervened," I said.

"Yes, we passed through some close calls, but fortunately we did escape the problems that we had on Earth and as we were leaving I think there was a problem again, but I'm not sure what happened exactly. I felt something interfered with an evil force that was threatening us and that God intervened for all of us. He is watching over us all. With your sense of adventure, you look for things that get you in trouble though. If you just would think before you got involved, then you would realize the problem you are inventing before you get to the point of trying to get yourself out of trouble. The world is full of problems, but you are not the person to solve them all because you have too many faults to be able to make risky adventures solving the most complex of other people's problems," Laura said.

"But really, Laura, this is a worthwhile quest and I found what I was looking for, didn't I?" I asked her, kind of sheepishly, as I am always short of the mark to convince her of my point. Continuing on I said, "These people have the technology to help us achieve a great and safe future. They are unbelievable, really."

At that moment they all entered into the chambers. Nina was in the lead, and then Jada, Lita, Bispo, and Nella.

Nina spoke first, "We have only a few minutes and then everyone must prepare to be underway. Tomorrow we will be under assault from a Martian Barbarian. I hope you have been informed of our dangerous situation. We will be able to get to know each other later when we are not under so much stress. Welcome aboard, Laura. We are becoming like one family and I want you to know that Tom was the complete gentleman warrior that you already know he is. You are very lucky to have such a fine companion to go through life with."

"Thank you," Laura said almost a little cynically. "You are lucky to have such a fine companion also."

Nina just looked at Laura for a minute, as if in utter confusion, and said, "My-- companion?"

"Yes, he said you two have known each other for years. He is on the ship with, the Idors and he is supposed to be coming to join us momentarily and help us in our confrontation. He said that he had some experience fighting this element of barbarians on Mars before."

Nina looked at Jada and said, "There is only one person that could be and no other. Max I is on Terra, though."

At that moment a young well-built, muscular warrior appeared in the chamber and said, "No, apparently I'm not on Terra but here and I had to keep it a secret because I have the rest of the primal codes with me. I could not risk a radio transmission or they would know that I was with you."

Suddenly, Nina saluted like she was a soldier in this man's army and then, as she fainted outright, and was headed for a collision with the gravity center of the magnetized floor level of the ship, Max made a catch that would look good enough to make a touch down in professional football.

"She'll be alright," said Jada. "She's just a little surprised, I think. Take her to her pilot's cabin."

Max swept her up into his arms like she was made of mist and held her tightly as he walked to the pilot's cabin like he knew the way.

Jada came over to us and said, "Max and Nina are promised to each other. You will not have any more trouble out of her because he will surely see that she behaves. He is also her martial arts master who has prepared her for many years in disciplines that should have covered feinting but I guess someone has to have a weakness somewhere. He will be running the ship now that he is here but Nina is still our official pilot captain.

With the return of Max that means that we are officially no longer rebels but an official government representative. He saved her from execution as well as all of us but, now he is committed to a life bond. That is the reason she fainted because she could never see him again, unless it was for a life bond. The elders had forbidden their association unless they accepted their own commitments.

I will get us underway since the Idors' ship must return to Terra and we will go on to our rendezvous with the asteroid belt and the barbarian Drakbar. If we don't get underway it will be sooner than expected. Lita, Bispo, Nella, and I will pilot the ship until those two return to the control room."

Laura and I walked together slowly to my cabin as I began to tell her of our experiences in space from the time I first saw the key in the desert. We had a few problems to work out as far as the happenings that had taken place between all of the individuals on board the ship. There were ominous feelings of danger for our future and whether or not we would survive the coming assault was yet to be seen. At least I would have my major strength with me when the storm erupted. My Laura, I hope, would understand how I had failed miserably emotionally as a devoted husband, but yet achieved our directive which we set out in our plans to achieve. Maybe we could yet save the world from the catastrophes that it faced ahead in the future, if we could only survive the present danger of the barbarous force of immorality and evil that was bearing down on our small ship. Now that my wife was with me, I felt sure that God would help us more so than if I alone had been faced with this danger. She was the favorite of God that had given our marriage and intertwined lives the protection and success that we had achieved. She had that something special that anyone could recognize immediately when she walked into a room or entered into a conversation like some special enchantment had happened to make things go in the right direction.

Farther back into outer space on the far side of the moon the results of the devastation that Nina had demonstrated on the barbarian bases, was a total annihilation of the awaiting ambush. Mass destruction caused by the drones from Nina's ship had wiped clean the face of the moon and deeply penetrated even into the underground reaches of the caverns of the moon. The ships that had been amassed by Drakbar were completely destroyed by the combined eagle pincer movement of the two ships. Maybe they had expected them to land and then all ships would attack but they nevertheless were caught completely by surprise. Drakbar began to rage and scream obscenities to his troop captain subordinates, with guttural tones of torment and tortures for all those responsible in the fiasco

. . . "She did the same thing again as she did on Mars! She's ruined me and my new vengeance. But I will have it! I will get that monstrous machine, that piece of rusted transport trash! I will kill her and that bitch Jada.--

I will, I will, I will! Find every survivor and bring them on board for the assault. We will catch them. It's only a matter of time. We have tube thrusters and they do not. They have only the ion pulse for long term space travel and do not have a huge propellant like we do. We will catch them, I say. I will have their brain cases to open and spit into their sick little rainbow auras and watch as they disappear into the night sky. For one brief moment they will flicker like twinkling little stars and then be no more. But first I will torment them to hell!"

A group of survivors managed to find their way to a search party and after coming on board the huge battle cruiser, they related their experiences to Drakbar.

"We were fired upon from every possible direction and we were just lucky to get into the hardened shelter under the moon base in time to avert death. Every single ship was destroyed and they look like they have been hit with a thousand lasers. Some of the hardened shelters were hit too and every trooper has holes burned through their body. They are not even recognizable. There is almost nothing to bury. The bodies just fall apart because of the laser destruction."

Drakbar bellowed out to his copilots, "Fire the propellant thrusters! We must not let them escape!"

As the black hearted villain, Drakbar, made his final attempts to obtain his dark vengeance, so also did progress the pathway of the streaking tiny black hole, racing through the galaxy system. Looking like a reverse comet tail, it pulled matter toward it and let it go reluctantly as it passed beyond, leaving a gravity well in its wake. It would have passed as a comet to the natural observer except that the conical section of the tail had an unusual reverse affect on all things. Coming within its power of possession, small asteroids were sucked into its gravitational pull like a small motorcycle as an 18-wheeler passes it in the night.

Drakbar and some of his entourage leveled insults at the last of the defeated troopers boarding the huge transport. They were packed into the transport in the manner of the new Martian hive culture gone to the extreme. Thousands of Martians were crushed to each other in a way that even hive proponents became disgusted at. Everyone was lost into the sheer press of bodies without being able to negotiate through from one place to another. They were left, weaving into and among each other like worms and snakes, intertwined into a huge ball of limbs and bodies. A thorough vision of what the place looked like could easily be imagined as a picture of hell. Something had gone completely awry in the plan that the founder thought of as close encounters leading to intellectual osmosis. The memories of analytical thought became mere whispers of a dream lost to the roaring winds of skin rasping against skin.

The darkness of the black hole as it approached its target was an entity without life, a thing void of meaning, giving an ominous note to the unavoidable circumstances for which it had been assigned. Drakbar was just such a vicious entity, void of compassion and reason. All attempts to change his destructive path that he had chosen could not be circumvented. He had rationalized all alternatives to mayhem and murder and corruption as being not worthy of his consideration since he and he alone was the new architect of Martian hive order. He thought of his childhood playmate and could see only that she was respected and he was not, therefore she must be made to taste of the bitter medicine that he alone could administer. This would leave him in charge and giving her the order to defer to one more strong and powerful.

Be his wishes as they may, Jada would not allow herself to think of his ludicrous dreams of power as an inevitable possibility. She knew that he would try to squelch the small resistance they had formed but with all her power she would try to stop him. They were his last obstacle, but he had stumbled before and this time she intended to apply the pressure until he was broken if it took all of her force of will and life as well.

"Bispo, we have at least half of the primal codes to begin restoration of the robot battalion. Let's get them in place and begin stationing them to repel boarders in case Drakbar locks us into the vice of his stasis net. That way at least they will be in position and can come on line as soon as possible," Jada said, maybe a little too authoritatively.

Jada looked at Bispo and thought that she would have to give the order again. Bispo just touched her hand to the little silver disk behind her ear and looked off into the distance as if she did not hear anything. Then, as if a light came on she began to make commands using her wrist band, punching in a short sequence of instructions.

Jada said, "Well, finally we have confirmation and can begin to get emergency measures underway. Nina must have finished her mind meld with Max, and Bispo can think again."

Bispo just said, "I can think."

The two, Nina and Max, walked in together at that moment and Nina spoke up, looking like she had seen something of the utmost fascination.

"Jada, we have to do exactly what you think we do and thank you for getting a head start. I see Bispo is making preparations with all haste. Max has something to say but first I feel that there is something I have to say to Mr. Jefferson Coltrane. Please forgive me for all the distractions that I caused you on your mission."

I looked at her and my mind was dumbfounded. Then Max spoke up and I almost fell on my face at his words.

"Mr. Jefferson Coltrane, we have concurred and all agree that it would be better if you were honored with the position of Captain Pilot and we await your orders; Nina agrees."

I could not have imagined anything more alien to my new world. Me, as captain pilot was just not only a dream, it was a bad dream. I didn't know where to begin. Nina spoke up as I looked at Laura and she and everyone knew that I was baffled by this unexplained decision.

"You don't have to fly the ship. We are not expecting that right now, Mr. Jefferson. Just make recommendations like you normally would or rather orders, and we will follow them. When we are in the heat of battle, the situation necessitates the need for good decision making under extreme conditions. You are the best choice to make these decisive changes in our strategy. We will conduct the normal operating conditions but the ultimate decision is yours. If you change our orders, or our decisions under battle conditions, we will defer to you as captain pilot for even a total about face even if we do not agree. We will carry out all your orders. You will ultimately guide us in life even to the death.

Please, let me explain for just a moment. We are not completely confident in our electronic decisions and we think that we may have been sabotaged with inaccurate data because we have been too dependent on our computer generated information. You are our new spiritual leader. Please say you will honor us with your reasoning since we will be at a loss to complete a course of action if Drakbar puts us into his stasis net. This contraption he has invented has a fail-safe mechanism that we have not been able to deactivate or jam. We get very lethargic in this prism net that he establishes if he gets close enough. We are all involved electronically, every one of us except Jada, you and Laura. Jada feels that you have had the experience to be able to make very rational decisions despite your unfamiliarity with the controls.

You will help us, won't you, Tom; because we may be helpless to activate our defenses if he catches us?"

I could plainly understand how they could be incapacitated if a block was put on their electronic community. They had become too dependent and integrated into all of the servo electronic automated systems.

"Gladly, I will accept what I have to make, but first let me have a brief description of the operating systems that I will have to operate in an emergency. I don't want this burden, but if like you say, we are all in danger, then I will have to accept. Jada, you are our resident Martian. Don't you know a good way to fight this menace?"

"Yes, I know how to fight him and that is with everything we have. We use it against him. You are something good in our favor and your innate abilities have proven a few undeniable things. You know how to fight, to adapt, and to find a way to succeed. Let's work together and find his weakness."

At that time Max spoke up and added the final pin in the axle that had been slowly grinding to a conclusion.

176

"There is one other thing Mr. Jefferson Coltrane. It is this. I have discovered that your wife is a person of most importance. Since I have been talking to her on our small excursion from Terra, rather Earth, I have found some extremely benevolent spiritual emanations coming from her aura. She is the major reason that we have made our decision. I think you will agree that there is an entity that has been watching over her and protecting her since you have known her. For unexplained reasons not just chance, we barely escaped with our lives, giving only this invisible intervention as the only alternative. Also, for dark reasons so does Drakbar desire her death and the death of Jada. They have three intended targets; Jada and Nina and also your wife Laura. Let's hope God will be with us."

I was honored that they had chosen me to be their brain backup in case theirs shut down because of electromagnetic disturbances but it just didn't seem like it would pan out. Yes, they wanted my advice in case they left out some detail, but what they really wanted was to insure their safety and eliminate Drakbar. I did indeed have an idea of how to do that though.

I looked at Laura and said, "Honey, I'll be back soon. There is something I have to do."

She said, "Do what you think is right. I'll pray for you."

Then I looked at Nina and said, "You pilot the ship while I am gone and when I get back, we'll discuss any changes I want to make. Give me one of the flat robots and an escape pod and I'll wait for Drakbar's approach. You are the bait so don't get too far ahead. I think he is going to catch you anyway, no? Just, think like a human and he should not affect your electronic components too much. Take care of my wife. She can help you."

Max helped me to load the weapons and entered the primal codes for controlling the robot and the two of us, me and the dark grayish black robot, were loaded into a very small pod. Before we ejected into space, I looked at all my friends and knew in my mind I would succeed. I had to succeed, because as yet we had not solved the other problems.

Jada said, "Don't miss! We will not have a second chance."

I kissed Laura and strapped on the camo belt that had allowed me to make entrance into the ship in the first place.

For a day we waited for Drakbar's approach, speeding as fast as our ion drive would permit, with me in the pod, tethered behind, in the slip stream of the big ship so that I would not use almost any power, and I was invisible. I waited and waited as if I were buried in space, surrounded by a blackness of an empty void.

Then suddenly, after days of waiting, Drakbar locked onto the space ship and Nina went blank along with all the other enhanced systems aboard. I did not even see his approach, because he also had some system that hid a viable visual signal. Only Laura and Jada realized that they were in his net of stasis. Nina had only a blank stare as her electronics failed to supply needed neural functions. Slowly I loaded the plasma cannon with a light charge that the pod was equipped with and allowed the flat robot to guide the charge into the ion expulsion ports of Drakbar's huge troop transport. The big ship had appeared out of nowhere and loomed across the view window in front of me. I was so far behind Nina's ship that I could see the very big ship totally taking up my window in front of me. It hovered over Nina's smaller ship as if it was going to swallow it completely.

A small puff was all the report that I saw at impact. We had disengaged the tether line so that I would be able to maneuver better and now Nina's ship had continued the wide loop around Earth to gather more momentum for the sling shot off to the asteroid belt. One more orbit and I would be on my way to the "C.A.N." which awaited in the asteroid belt. Maybe Drakbar could repair his ship later, but I hoped not.

Somewhere in deep space a microscopic black hole approached its rendezvous with destiny.

Drakbar cursed as his power failed to the pulse generator, the stasis net, and his tube energizer, and he thought to himself, "I can wait. It is my destiny."

Quietly we slipped on around and continued in our orbital path preset by the flat robot. Since Max had initialized the primal codes the flat robots had begun to take more of the share of computing various analytical data. Jada had taken over the ship as pilot captain and rescued the control of the ship from Drakbar's stasis. My loving wife, Laura, was waiting for me to intercept them in our cross loop orbit. She had been talking to me constantly at different intervals and had an excited curiosity about the "C.A.N.", stationed in the asteroid belt. We had big plans for exploring the miniature world and exactly what prospects I was sent out to alter. Right now I couldn't wait to see Laura again.

The moon slipped behind the Earth as we gradually began to pick back up speed for our rendezvous with the big ship. Earth looked very inviting as my heart gave a little pang of longing because I knew I would not see her for a long time except for maybe as a star in the distant heaven. After we boarded the ship again, we would head out for the "C.A.N." as Nina called it to plot our new strategy to defend the Earth. She said we could stay there to plan our course of action and maybe she wanted to use it for a trap to lure Drakbar to his demise, but still I looked forward to just seeing this beautiful experiment. We anchored again to the big ship and Laura was the first to greet me, then Jada, but I did not see any of the rest of crew.

Jada said, "They are all waiting to reconfigure their interface between the two systems because one is bio-electric and the other is hard electric impulse. They are fine; but right now they have to sort of stay in incubation until we reach the "C.A.N.". We are set to align the ship with Mars, soon."

Chapter 12. **The Getaway**

Back on board the ship, we began to recover from our ordeal in space. Jada and Laura helped me take out the equipment that Nina and Max had placed on board the small space pod. The flat robot was able to maneuver itself out of the pod. It had valuable information retrieved from interaction with the enemy ship. Remarkable as they had been to me, Nina's group of transformed Terrans who had been living secluded on Earth for eons had disappointed me. They had enhanced all their innate survival systems with inbred electronics, spreading their capacity to out perform our common human bodies over a broad area. But this broad area had failed to encompass the side effects of their own electronic frailties. The enhanced capabilities did not add any assets to their survival regimen, only betraying them in the end, leaving them vulnerable and dependent on normal human life forms. Only Jada was not human, more or less, since she was a Martian but human just the same. She was not enhanced and didn't want to be. The little pod ship was automated to secure itself into the cargo hold along with various other assorted pods and an array, now a virtual army of other flat robots with accompanying pod ships. There was row upon row of little space ships each for providing a means of propulsion into and through space for the flat robots. There had hardly been room for me aboard the little pod ship, even with the thin collapsible robot. It was a unique seeming tool for conducting warfare. Each robot had its own little vehicle. I could imagine what force these could provide in a fully functional battle armada. They just had not been really brought to bear upon the enemy at this time, but I can imagine what they could be if they were completely in force on line.

Laura and Jada had been talking to each other and were now becoming good friends. Nina and all of her crew were placed inside a stasis hutch to prevent them from damaging themselves. Apparently Drakbar had developed some kind of electromagnetic pulse that completely disoriented the semi-robotic people of Terra. It was sad to see them so incapacitated and uncoordinated in all their functions. Jada made many comments about their relevant condition and the process needed to realign their neural network and get them organized into a logically viable group again. They did work as a group. Since they were all electronically connected, they were all laid up into something like incubators, awaiting the reformatting of some process that rendered them workable again. Today I thought that I would go and visit Nina and attempt some communication. The hallways of the space ship seemed like some ghost ship with all the electronically enhanced crew laid up in sick bay. We were passing through space on our way to a new world with less than half our vital force; our main crew, and nothing felt right. Jada did not have a very good aura and Laura, my wife, seemed like she was in a state of confusion and depression since she came aboard.

I sat now in the pilot's cabin with Laura and Jada. We were the entire crew at present and almost every function was now in automation, using the flat robots that had been shielded partly and since all of them were pretty much shut down and off line, I could use them if I had to in combat with a little tutoring from Jada. I think she is more competent than I to fly this space craft because she was a pilot captain on Mars of a similar vessel. It was only for symbolic reasons that I was now sitting in the pilot's chair. Actually, no one had to sit or remain in the seat unless maneuvers were necessary. It did however provide better access to controls around the ship. The array and accessibility of monitors and actuating devices was nearby and easily empowering to one person. I watched Jada now take over the actual engineering of the flight controls and usually she would tell me what she was changing in the way of guidance or life support.

Laura was also sitting nearby, performing various duties of navigator as Jada directed or assigned to her or guided various duties to the flat robot system. I wanted to check on the crew and Nina, but I needed Jada to advise and inform me as to the alien resuscitating devices necessary to support their elaborate symbiotic condition with their electronics.

"Let's go back to the stasis hutch support systems and see how the crew is doing. OK?" I asked.

"Laura, come with us and let's try to learn something or we will continue to be just dependent on automatic systems. This thing will fly itself just about all the time. It doesn't really need us much at all."

Jada looked at me and said kind of all knowingly, insolent, "Yeah, if we don't hit a micro asteroid and drive the ship into the sun. We've got to maneuver if some freak thing happens. But, yes it will let you sleep late if you don't worry too much. Besides, we have a clear path at this moment. I've already checked it out, and I don't see Drakbar catching us very soon, but he will eventually; so don't stop worrying. He has a very powerful ship built on Mars and modified to extinguish all other ships it comes in contact with. Nina has been to other planets and back using this ship or one just like it, but it is not as fast on short runs as the ship Drakbar has in his possession. He will try to hunt us down and kill us. You were very lucky and just caught him sleeping with his pants down. We have to think and plan our defense now before he repairs his ship."

Laura looked around and gazed out into space and as if she knew somehow we would be safe, she said to Jada, "If he is as wicked as you say he is then he will be his own downfall, eventually destroying himself. Please, have faith. God will give us a way and provide an avenue of escape. I have had many premonitions of this happening and I want to share some of my personal fears even if you are not a believer. Maybe we can agree that a solution is possible and if your mathematical solutions do not predict our safety then I have a suggestion that came to me in a dream. You will know the correct time to ask me when all of your science has failed you. It is only a dream that I had, so don't worry. Maybe it is nothing. So, we can go to visit the others now?"

Jada said, "Yes, we will visit the others and I feel very strongly that I am going to want to hear about that dream you had, Laura. We Martians have very much confidence in the spiritual forces and I find comfort in knowing that some great force is not just letting all of the universe go without watching and observing man's inhumanity to man as you might say. We are very lucky to have you with us indeed, and I am aware of the limitations of our finite mathematics."

Laura looked at me with a very long face and I just couldn't help but to ask her just what was so important in a dream that could affect all of us and this ship.

"Is there a premonition, Laura? I am getting the feeling that we are all in danger of overestimating our brilliant escape from that demon Drakbar."

Laura just sort of laughed a little and told me not to worry. "You know I'm always having dreams of one sort or another and usually they are about something I have already seen that day and they are just a form of stress relief. All the psychologists in the world would not agree that they give us any better key to solving our problems than a clear, reasoning, practical mind will, and I think you should stick to your mathematics and your Zen, and let a woman's intuitive dreams be a surprise. Anyway, I'll feel more needed when you reach your limitations of clear reasoning and search for something out of desperation as a last straw. I was never a student that felt the math of infinite progressions was practical. The colors of my mind help me to form something out the boring black and white of a logical mind like yours. You have your regimen of control that you like and I appreciate your stability in our relationship, but sometimes, Tom, you just can't see the forest for the trees."

I had the feeling that this trip was going to be more dramatic than it had already turned out to be and Laura along for the ride would entertain my patience more than a Zen master, teaching his students not to think.

"Don't see the white rabbit. It is not there, only the shadow of where it has been," he would have said. What would we really do when Drakbar caught up to us? How could we fight him? We had to think through this scenario and find out what would work best and what weapons to use or not to use. He was going to try and capture us; that was for sure. We had embarrassed him by putting that torpedo up his tail and not killing him and his crew. He would do the same for us, only he would want to see our eyes when we screamed in agony and he wanted to be close by when we did. This maniac wanted his revenge; I just hoped he would make a mistake when he was trying to exact his punishment on us. I feel sure that we probably saved Earth for a period of time. He was going to come after us before he made his invasion. It just had to be that he was to fulfill his vengeance. Such a big mistake was worth the gamble he was making to show all of Mars that he had taken possession of us. Jada, he hated before this happened and Nina too, but now he knew there was someone else to make him fill with hatred to over flow around the galaxy and that was me. We walked into the medical room where there were many different plexiglass looking bubble cells. In each of these cells there was one of the crew of Terrans. They looked so peaceful in their electronic sleep and no one seemed as if they were having a bad dream. After I had left the ship with the pod and the flat robot, I managed to lay in wait in outer space and ambush Drakbar's ship and slip a torpedo up his ion plume, but not before he had fired an electromagnetic pulse beam directly at Nina's ship. It totally knocked out every electronic function that was not shielded with hard electronic circuits. Even this was not enough because I think there was a resonance that he set up to crack even the protected ones. This is what got Nina and the crew. She and the Terran crew were shielded but the reverberation of the resonance tore away the old neural network that most of them had depended on since childhood. She said that she made her own decisions but apparently they all were still connected in some way electrically. Jada began touching some of the controls in the recovery area of the medial room. Nina's bubble opened and she just lay there not moving except for a little row of neuron mapping lights on the monitor band, placed on her forehead. These lights indicated that her brain functions were active and they played different colored rhythms in a slow methodical response.

Jada spoke very softly to Nina, "Hello, old friend. How are you in there? You look very peaceful but bored all the same."

The little colored lights began to move in faster rhythms and then Nina's eyes opened slightly and focused on a spot somewhere on the ceiling.

Nina, just in a very low whisper said, "Jada, I know we are safe now but not for very long. You will have to fight before you reach the C.A.N. Don't wait too long."

After she said that, Nina just closed her eyes and the little colored lights on the read out began the same rhythmic pulses they were making when we first walked in. Jada began to call her but she did not respond.

Laura told Jada, "I think it's going to take more time for all of them to recover. When that shock wave hit the ship I felt like I just could not stop crying but they just kept going until they fell to the floor."

"I know," Jada said. "I felt the same thing that you felt but at least we recovered and they haven't yet. I don't know if all of them will or not. Nina, Nella, Lita, and Max will eventually recover with the reprogramming but I'm not sure about Bispo. She depended so much on Nina for all of her directives but now she is recovering on her own separately from Nina. Once, they were all connected, analyzing, predicting, supporting, and preprogramming each others thoughts and actions. They were like one cohesive unit, but now I have broken that tie so that they will be more human and capable of thinking on their own. Whatever comes out of this calamity, they will be stronger and it will not happen again. The next time we get hit with one of those electromagnetic waves, that Drakbar sends at us, they will react like we did only crying and miserable, and not sent to the reprogramming infirmary. Let's get back to control and run some tests on intercept.

What do we do then? Should we wait for Drakbar or charge him head on? We have to work out the best angle of attack or defense."

I looked around the room and thought about how very active and wonderful all the Terrans were only to be incapacitated until their rebuild their data pathways. I spoke to Nina, not thinking that she could respond, but right away we received some encouragement that was unexpected.

"Nina, I know that you would help us if you could only hear us now. What would be the best way to attack this Drakbar?"

Silence and then without any movement she said, just barely audible, "Tom, first find your own way and then ask Laura to tell you about her dreams."

After that the row of colored lights began to turn white and Nina was lost in her other world of sleep.

I said to Laura, "OK, honey, you heard it too, barely, but she said you could help us."

"Yes, Tom, maybe I can, but not now. First find your own way and then at the right time I will tell you my dream. Maybe this Terran woman sent me some message in my dream but it is not for you to know right now. You and Jada get together and work out a mathematical solution first and then I will help you when you feel like it is not adding up. I only have a piece of the puzzle. You two have to work out the big solution. So let's go back to the control room and get started on the plan."

Jada closed the cover to the stasis incubator hutch and Nina's light band began making slow meticulous wanderings. Maybe the computers were picking up stray clusters of unorganized ideas and placing them with other clusters identified with similar patterns. How could someone be human and machine at the same time?

Then Jada spoke up, "You are looking at the little rows of resonating pulses that are identifying badly disorganized electrons that have no place to go. They take the group and send them to a processor that assigns addresses to their identifying message. It's just like humans do when we sleep. We look at all the information that has registered in our brains during the day, when we are awake and play it all back like a tape recorder. Then we decide what is necessary to keep; encoding it into a memory address and then sending the other to the miscellaneous garbage heap. That is our random access batcher that allows us to see something familiar and put a name to a face or object and bring all the relevant information back into cognizant utilization.

The electromagnetic pulse reverberated with such intensity that they lost their cognizant memory. Everything was just scrambled so their failsafe just shut them all down. They were living and breathing still, using the autonomic system of their human bodies, but their reasoning abilities just suffered a set back. I hope they will not all be senile when they recover. That Terran evolvement into cybernetic enhancement was just a foolish ambitious greed to be better than an already advanced civilization. They were already the best in everything. They helped us on Mars to produce really advanced fighting capabilities.

Nina told me that three generations ago there were no enhanced beings. So it only came about in the last 100 years. Also, it gave them shorter life spans because of the fast pace that their poor bodies were subjected to. When they wake up they won't like what I have done, but at least they will live and have longer life spans as well. They will thank me later for returning them to their more human form. Each cell, thinking on its own, is better than everyone with the same idea

186

because they give diversity to the welfare of each other. When a people come together for the welfare of all, it is better than big government telling everyone what to do. When they all wake up, there will be a lot of confusion, until the spirit of cooperation begins to organize the body of people as a whole."

I thought of how our government on Earth gets more and more involved in our daily lives. That was part of the reason I started acting in a direct secretive manner to change the pathway that the world was on. To just sit idly by while a group of greedy people oppressed the rest of us was unacceptable to me. Governments the world over were amazed at their inability to trace their problems to another hostile government. A single individual acting alone was just not acceptable to their self aggrandizing megalomaniac organization with huge armies. But yet, I was able to put into motion many moving working machines of just ideas affecting energies of initialization, and thus causing situations to reach critical momentums which brought about an unalterable direction of change. To put it simply my hand was involved in espionage that either forced a checkmate or stalemate, whether the big governments liked it or not. There is an idea that different universes form and then expand at different rates. Maybe within each of us is a small universe and as we get older, it constantly expands just like the physical universe, only as a metaphor based philosophy. Now the individual minds of each of the Terrans will begin to expand again and come into their own reality as much as a new sun reaching supernova, sending out an array of debris containing new ideas into all the universe of their own individual minds.

Laura looked at me and asked me in a curious way. "Do you think that we are all connected in some spiritual way whether we are wired together or not? Maybe it's not possible to separate them anymore than it is possible to separate us. We feel sorrow for each other and happy when the other is well so how can we not be together?"

Jada spoke up, "You're right and now they will understand the stupidity of messing up something that already works well enough as it is without enhancing it to the point of shortening one's life span. I never thought that the elders were all that much brighter than the rest of us anyway. It seems they just used their position to dominate. Let's get back and draw some outcome sketches of what action we will be forced to take when Drakbar makes his beginning tactics."

We walked together side by side; me and my wife and the Martian woman, Jada, to the control room of the space ship. Along the small corridor there were regular bands it seemed of a sort of magnetism that grew stronger as we stepped over and through each band and along the base of the walls on both sides were what looked like emitters of some sort.

"Jada, how, in simple unscientific terms would you explain again the gravity field that we have on the ship?"

Jada began, "Well, as I explained earlier, a wafer thin gyroscopic pulsating sheet of electromagnetic material conducts a revolving current through the decks of the ship in a continuous loop that gives us our gravity. It is an old principle actually that was used in one of your Earth wars. One side was degaussing their ships' hulls so that the submarine's torpedoes could not magnetically find the target which was the ship's metallic hulls. In effect it works similarly backwards as well, causing objects to be attracted to one another, thus giving to a small degree a limited artificial gravity. We could just spin around and around but for some ships it is not practical. The "C.A.N." that we are on approach for now is revolving. It is thus creating a centrifugal gravity, which is practical for large ships like planets and our own botanical cylinder or "C.A.N.". Once we enter the "C.A.N." we will actually be able to walk around freely like on Mars or Earth; only we will be walking around the inside concave surface of the can. It is so big that you will not notice very much the difference. It is a little disorienting though, because you do not have a horizon like a convex planet would give you while walking on its surface. You will look up not at the sky but at more of the vegetation. You will actually see upside down trees when you look up. But it will be beautiful, I can guarantee. The sun light is refracted in from huge circular openings on the two sides of the can through crystalline windows.

I haven't been there for a while so by now I'm sure it is a veritable jungle full of plants and animals. I warn you too, Nina is a colonizer unit and has been at work on many different sites. Her clone

188

history goes way back to what I don't know, but her predecessors were doing it before we the Martians were. Mars has out posts as well, but the "C.A.N." was started by Terrans or who came before them as far as we know. It seems that there have been "C.A.N."s as long as there have been records kept. They are like seed pods to the planets for the distribution of life through the solar system. I think Nina found one that was not theirs somewhere near, Europa, but I don't know all of their history. The Terrans have always been a very secretive race of people. They only tell you some of what they want you to know. We the Martians, it seems, tell everyone everything, but we still have a lot of catching up to do.

But now, here we are at the control room. Let's sit here with our holographic tablets and form some ideas with drawings and sketches. I love to make pictures of my ideas. It helps me to think. The two of you make me some sketches of how we would react to the assault by Drakbar. First, I'll set it up and tell you what he has and you all know our limitations. Basically, we can't run away; he'll catch us eventually. Here is the Drakbar ship-thus and we are being pursued, here. When will he strike or how will he strike; at a distance, or close? He has the long range weapons and short range weapons. What is your opinion, Tom?"

"He wants to capture us and will eventually close in on us. I think he will fire a long range weapon to make sure this time that we do not get away," I said.

"He wants to see us die, I know it. He wants his revenge too, so he may first try to cripple our ship and then close the distance and board us," Jada said

Laura, looking very beautiful and a little jealous of Jada, began to pick her long hair up in strands and lift it gently back and forth the way she always does when she is thinking of something. Then she asked me in a quizzical way as if to say that it was her turn now.

"Is there going to be anything between his ship and ours before he reaches us?"

"No," Jada said. "We will not reach the asteroid belt before he intercepts us or comes within weapons range. He may even begin firing missiles at us soon, even though he cannot hit us."

I thought very hard and just could not come up with anything or any way to prevent our apparent destiny, which was apparently to fall into his hands. Jada began to draw onto the holographic visionary panel with her extended finger a rough outline of the two space ships.

"Look!" she said. "We are here, past the Earth on a looping orbit headed past the outer orbit of the planet Venus. Then we will head toward the sun and bring our ship back across the orbit of Venus, thereby increasing our speed enough to whip us around to Mars. Like a cork screw pattern we are using Martian circular math to calculate revolution around our gravitational forces that are attracting us and increase our speed."

Then I saw one bright moment in the plan that she had theorized for navigation. "What if when we cross the orbital path of Venus we are hidden from Drakbar? Can we do something to make him think we have altered our course for a small amount of time, and do we have the luxury of being far enough away from him at this time to be in a safety buffer as far as distance is concerned?"

Jada smiled and said, "Yes we will still be ahead of him and at a safe enough distance at that point, because we are using the sun and Venus to make us a rock in a sling shot. It is afterward that we are vulnerable on our approach to the asteroid belt when we are losing speed. Do you have a plan or something in mind?"

"Can we deploy the flat robots in a net to catch him and preoccupy him long enough to get into the asteroid belt?"

"Yes, maybe," Jada said. "But in what way are you talking about?" Max gave us the primal codes to activate them before he went into the stasis hutch. It is possible that we could deploy the flat robot pods into a parabola that would close around him after he has entered the open end and keep him occupied for a while. I'm afraid they will not break through his defenses but I am sure they will slow him up and keep him pinned down for a while. Maybe they can keep him inside the loop for a few weeks maybe one month maximum. He will have to send some of his troops to draw their fire on the outer ring. I know this can ultimately be for our benefit to get him to use weapons and expend troops' battle armor and food and military supplies."

As I began to draw on the holographic screen, I started to visualize our scenario and lay down the foundation of our plan. Laura was giving us ideas and we were just elaborating on her little star bursts of insight. I almost felt like I was stealing her ideas. She opened the door and we were just making it bigger and decorating it.

Chapter 13. **The Brain Unit**

Jada looked up like she heard or saw something in the middle of a wild forest like a deer that is alert to danger.   "What is it, Jada? You look frightened or something. Did you hear a strange noise?"

Laura said, "I did too, and it sounds like something not normal to this ship."

"Yes, I did hear something," Jada said almost in a whisper. "It is an anomaly that should not be heard in deep space or on a space ship or anywhere for that matter. There it is again, and I am afraid we have a hitcher on the outside of our ship. I think it is something that Drakbar has sent, maybe a small mechanical droid that has attached itself to our ship."

"But, that is impossible you said, because he is too far away to catch us or even fire missiles," I said.

"He is too far away to hit us firing missiles but if he sent a droid pod, it could have reached us faster because it is lighter and sometimes Martian ships have automatic droids that just detach, within so many feet of a space ship, for safety, to monitor the battle from a distance. The droid pod could have reached us right after the incident and have been riding us attached for days, "Jada said.

"What do we do?" I asked.

"Someone has to go and get rid of it or it could do anything, even drill the hull and make a breach draining away our atmosphere," Jada said.

"I'll go," I said. "You have to pilot the ship in case something happens. I'll get ready right now."

"I'm coming with you because you'll need me to help you", Laura said.

"No, Laura, you are not coming. I do this best alone. You'll just get in the way. I'm very good at what I do and this is right up my alley. I can do it. I promise. I'll be alright." I headed for the suit chamber to get my space gear and to look for weapons.

As soon as I got suited up, Jada called me on the radio in the helmet and said, "They are not like the flat robots, but they will be lethal just the same, and have great firepower with lasers and projectile ammunition. Try to hit some of the appendages first so that you can disable its mobility. They are very quick and maneuverable."

I thought of all the hunting expeditions that I had been on and all the hunting stories I had read. As in karate, if you take out or disable the knee, then your opponent, even if he is stronger and quicker than you, will be at a disadvantage. If a bear is running at you, charging at full speed; you don't shoot for the heart, but at the low front shoulder and leg to keep him from reaching you.

"Tom." It was the voice of Laura, with her pleading sound that he always makes when she is afraid or worried. "It's OK honey; I'm going to be alright. Laura, just do what Jada says right now. Maybe you two can remotely help me by watching the outside viewing cameras. That thing has to be coming into view somewhere. He's like a squirrel on a tree. You just about can't see them until they move. As I go around the outside of the ship, look for it moving just beyond my line of sight. Jada can all the weapons be activated remotely too?"

Jada said, "Yes, if you spot it try to run it to me and I'll intercept at an ambush, but it is better if you take it out as soon as possible because it will know we are after it and execute its directive. But, yes we can observe and fire remotely form this end. You just be careful and don't let it surprise you. Look very close at all external things that seem out of place and if it moves; shoot it immediately."

"How big is this thing and what is it going to look like?"

"You'll know it when you see it and it's about the same size as the flat robots when they are opened. Just find it and kill it in a hurry, before it breaches the hull. Hurry, hurry!"

I was leaving the air-lock now and I had a very queasy feeling about working in outer space. What happens if a little space meteorite hits me or I snag the suit and I lose all my air? I took a deep breath and let it out, trying to relax. This had to be done; live or die. I stepped out of the opening but my foot just hung into mid space and I began to use the little compressed air jets to maneuver the suit. The vastness of space was all encompassing and was thick blackness without any ending, just a void. There were so many stars in the distance and somewhere beyond was our new home, just hanging in the void. This ship was not that big but it was big enough that it took time to get around all of it and I could have to make several rounds to even get close to seeing the whole area.

I had now made several circles around the ship and to no avail. "Laura, have you seen anything from the monitors? It's here, I know it is."

I was getting nervous because in a very short time we would decompress if it drilled a hole into the outer layer and through to the inner hulls.

Laura said, "You remember Tom, when we were at the bay in the islands and we used to hunt these fish that were flat? Do you think that it could be like those, the flounders, just a slight bulge on the outer hull?"

"I don't know," I said. "When I heard the thing on the hull it sounded like it was walking with some kind of metallic feet but how can something just not exist in plain sight?"

Jada broke in and sounded excited and a little nervous, "Tom, I think I see it and it just looks like it's moving slightly in little sliding movements and it is going for the life support system. I just know it. That is the general area that it is approaching. Get it before it reaches our oxygen generator or we are finished out here so far from any resources and we still have months before we get to the "C.A.N.""

I was coming up around the ship from behind one of the foils used in giving lift in an atmosphere when I spotted it. Laura always had a mental premonition or intuition of everything.

"It's just like you said, Laura. It is like a flounder just a bump on the ocean bottom. It is like a bump on the outer hull. I'm going to fire a ribbon of arced charge at its hump. Jada, do you have any suggestions about what the results could do?"

"Yeah, just don't let the ribbon slice clean through or you could damage the hull. It will slice right through. But you know that don't you from the departure at cave hanger?"

"I'm going to try to get closer so I will have more control over the loop. At a distance it seems unstable." "Not so," Jada said. "Make your shot now or you may not get another. If you approach directly to it, you will let it know that you have found him. I was going to tell you this later but you might as well know. They put human brains in their little droids to give them a slave sense of self preservation. That could be you if you don't hurry up and kill it. Now!"

Her nervous fear gave me chill bumps up and down my spine, and I knew now what they wanted to do; capture us and use us for spare parts for their suicide drones. We would know our most hated enemies in ways that could last many life times, living in big mechanical weapons, forced to obey electrical stimuli.

Jada spoke very quietly and said in a low voice, "Aim the loop just above the robot so that the ribbon, when it extends down will slice through the top of its hump. It will straighten up, then and you can slice horizontally missing the hull. Do not fire twice or you will not be coming back inside the ship. Make a small circle as the loop hits the top of the robot, and you will decapitate the brain."

I aimed just above the small hump on top of the hull and the arc pushed a loop of bright blue electricity like a thin ribbon and as if a bullet had entered the top of the hump, a little valley appeared through to the center. Immediately a full eight feet of angry robot vaulted to its haunches spread out like a spider raising itself up with a vengeance. My wrists rotated with a half circle as the big arc gun came back around into the target area and the blue ribbon made a slight vortex as it carried into the robot on the second slice. Heavy on land the big weapon was weightless in space and performed the ballet of twisting in my two hands like a samurai sword, cutting a delicate path of destruction cleanly and surgically. I approached slowly as a column of blood droplets left visible signs that something at one time was alive inside this case of gray metal.

"It has what looks like a needle in its abdomen stuck into the outer edge of the ship's hull. What do I do now?"

Jada said, "Secure yourself to one of the connectors on the outer hull and see if you can kick it loose."

I hooked one of my belts to a steel eyelet on the hull and kicked as hard as I could. The force moved me in the opposite direction and I bounced onto the hull, but the spider robot broke off leaving its needle jammed cleanly into the outer hull.

Tumbling away into the blackness there came a voice plain and simple into my radio, "Kill me, please!"

I opened up the blue ribbon of the arc and sliced back and forth through the robot and its decapitated head causing an explosion that slammed me back for the second time into the space ship's outer hull. I moved through space using the compressed air jets on my suit until I was directly over the spot where the robot was. There sticking into the hull was a thin broken cylinder.

"I've tried to pull out this needle but I cannot. It looks like he just jammed it into the outer hull."

"We'll have to leave it for now," Jada said. "But I hope it's not a bomb. Maybe the robot did not get time enough to arm it or set the timing device or it broke off or I don't know. Just leave it and come back inside. We'll get one of the flat robots to try and remove it later."

When I came back around to the air lock it was just in time to see the air lock door closing and not opening.

"Jada, --Laura, the air lock door just closed. Something went inside before me. I'm still outside."

Jada said to Laura, "Quick, Laura, turn around and just back up into the storage unit for the flat robots and they will close around you and form a suit of body armor, then walk out and I'll put one on next."

The flat robot closed in around Laura and served as a suit of plates forming itself around the body, arms, and legs.

Jada said with a tone of confidence to Laura, "Just relax. They magnify your movements and strength exponentially so whatever movements you make will be accentuated. Now, step out quickly."

Jada backed into the concave holding unit and another flat robot closed in around her as well.

Then stepping out looking like a modern samurai warrior she said, "Laura, this is only more or less armor and is not total protection, just a light covering with enhancements. You are not very well protected from behind so always face the enemy. Don't turn away. I'm going to set the robot to use light weapons automatically and I'll just stay out of your way. There's a killer robot inside but he'll probably try to just incapacitate us until Drakbar arrives. We've got to prevent that and stay alive."

Laura was dumb-founded and thought only of Tom, stuck outside the ship.

Turning to Jada, Laura said, "I've never really been in a fight with a robot before. Tom has demonstrated to me some fighting tactics and I also taught at the Academy, but I'm feeling weak and I'm scared, and I'm out of my element. I can't beat up a little child much less a killer robot."

Jada just smiled, "You can now. Just do what you think or imagine you want to do, and the flat robot will compensate for your weakness. Quick, let's get to the air lock chamber and kill this thing before Tom runs out of air."

They moved down the main hallway like two killer mantises taking long leaping steps and rhythmically moving their armored appendages.

"We stay side by side and we attack it at the same time. Do not turn away from the enemy; just fight him any way you can. Make a fist and you'll also get an arc that will make a cutting loop around your closed fist. It will slice right through anything you hit. Just get mad. Remember, the longer we take to kill this thing, the sooner Tom runs out of air."

Laura closed her fist and began to make slashing motions as she ran inside the mantis like legs. A loop of blue electric pulse circled around her closed fist, and made a jagged current; thin and deadly. Her heart was pounding and she thought, "He's done it for me a hundred times before. I guess I can fight this once for him, otherwise we are all finished anyway."

She began to cry tears of tension, knowing that she maybe would not live, but that didn't matter anymore.

"Stop crying, Laura, "Jada said. "We'll both cry when it's over. You know Martian women cry too, and our aura turns blue, but right now let's go get that thing."

They entered the suit up chamber, just as the inside airlock was opening and immediately a huge eight foot spider-like creature emerged with the underbelly of long thin spider-like legs. The robot emerged and picked its legs up like some crab creature measuring its steps before it charges. The face was not human but had a human like quality and a viscous menacing character.

Laura's heart began to race so fast that she thought she would faint first and then she began to panic and wanted to run away. Somehow she just drove herself to remain and maybe it was that she could not abandon Jada. She could not just let Tom die. She could not let herself down and wanted to control her own destiny because she had a greater purpose in life than to die, here in this isolated place. She let out a scream and drove herself into the robot with a suicidal vengeance. At the same instance Jada began her attack too. Together the two of them upset the precise analysis of the machine. Maybe it did not expect a suicidal attack but it did hesitate to record the data and process the plan of attack. Normally men tend to think that the female does not have the courage to spearhead a frontal attack without faltering but these were extraordinary circumstances and also these were two very extraordinary women. They split the timing of the robot so that it could not maximize the efficiency of its movements to focus on one opponent. He could not choose one target since both were extremely aggressive. First, Jada made a debilitating spearing thrust into his organic and biochemical center which divided his attentions between rebuilding his infrastructure due to a break in the spinal electronic synapses and defending his perimeter from offensive strikes. Then the alternating slashing and thrusting of Laura's frenzied furiousness breached his inability to reprogram into a two pronged defense. He was over whelmed by their viciousness and surprised that with all of his weapons he had been beaten, and that his demise as an electrochemical machine was very short in coming. He began to count his lifetime remaining in minutes, seconds, and nano-seconds. He could not counter their thrusts and simultaneously Laura and Jada vented their pent up emotions into his exoskeleton and it was over without so much as a scratch on the two women. They had eviscerated the robot before he had time to recover from their first attack, which was a total success due to their unusually aggressive nature.

When the robot lost consciousness a monitor within an alien space ship, more than one million miles away, gave its watcher a severe case of animal aggressive psychosis. Drakbar screamed and vented his anger into the nearest hive Martian crew member. He lashed out at his commander and could not contain himself as he sent several other members of his crew to the expired cell where the other dead and dismembered crew members were kept. Many of the cells in the space craft were filled to capacity with expired crew members due to his animalistic aggressions. Although he could have been overpowered by the crew and he had no special directive given him by the crew and gang of which he was the strongest leader, he held absolute magnetic force to the ultimate fear with which he ruled. He ruled by direct orders to others and his guards did his absolute bidding with immediate and viscous results. He could not contain his anger now anymore and screamed out his cry of vengeance by vomiting curses and filth that could only be understood by the Martian dregs of society which he had gathered around him.

"I will catch them and make them my private servants for the dog patrol. They will hunt down and catch their own families when I am Martian Emperor and I'll watch the anguish in their tormented, displaced, body-less faces as they power my hunter killer dog robots. They'll wish for the day when their cells become too aged to make a synapse fire and the cancer rot begins to eat the flesh of their brains."

A blue smoky haze was obscuring his vision but he managed to spot one of his concubines entwined among the endless bodies entangled around him. He loathed the family that he knew she came from and for his own selfish reasons he wanted to possess her and make her do unconscionable things that her highly esteemed family would only hate him for. She was like a mindless slave now, only responding to her animal lusts, giving every male any chance to possess her that wanted to. Drakbar could have any slave he wanted but he liked to satisfy himself with this one because she was from a noble and good family.

"Guard, bring me that slave!" I want her in my quarters and I want her now."

She was overcome with her passions and had already been ravished many times tonight. Yet, he knew this and wanted to see how she would react to his powers as the alpha male. He was the strongest male on the ship and could crush any man's skull with just his bare hands. She was dragged into the captain's quarters and thrown onto the mat that lay in the center of the room. He looked at her lying on the mat and followed the beautiful contours of her body. Her eyes already were blood shot from so much abuse.

She looked at him like a lioness preparing to pounce upon her next victim. She knew in her woman's heart that she could outlast this pig of a man too. One day when the heat of her lust had died out she would try to forget that she enjoyed what she hated, but right now she was preparing her body for the next willing participant. A hot burning desire began to fill her body as a fire began to burn inside her. Drakbar hated her for what she represented. She looked familiar to him like someone back on Mars that he once knew and her family had held him back from his conquest and he remembered how he had politely asked for a meeting or a rendezvous many years before. He had already killed many, such as they were, that looked exactly like his long lost love, but only familiar and this would be the next. He would kill her over and over again and it would not end, until he could finally kill Jada, and that would satisfy him, he thought. Jada had once enraged him, and he lashed out at someone close to him and she was gone forever. Now he only wanted to hear her cries of pain at first and then cries of lust as he abused her to the point of torment. When they both began to scream at the same time, then and then only would he let her rest.

She---was dreaming of his demise and hoped that she would get the opportunity soon.

That small black orb in space congregated mass as a ball of mud sticks dust and leaves to the outside of its wet shell, attracted matter the same way. The matter though could not catch the little black orb, because it traveled too fast for anything to touch it. Space seemed like it was trying to catch up to the orb and made a conical tail as it passed nearer and nearer but only chased it and could not catch it. Everything near the little black hole moved nearer to it but then returned to the direction of the closer force of gravity after it had passed, yet still the affected mass was never the same with the existing forces. Everything had changed and no longer remained the same. Orbits were slightly shifted because they had been affected and as a result some things continued as they were, almost, but other things like planets or asteroids would meet dramatic and sometimes drastic results. Drakbar was one of those items having mass that too would meet with dramatic and drastic, even terminal results. He was unaware of his fate though, and at this moment was confident in his plans. At some origin in space and time there had been determined this course of events and by adding and subtracting various factors at different times a result pointed to the outcome of the projected course is sustained. He was walking down a pathway of sure terminal consequences. This he would not be able to avoid because he was unaware of his errors or felt that he had a right to his power even if it abused others. Mathematical proportion could not be persuaded to favor his chosen processes but would favor his destruction.

Drakbar thought about only catching those who had been in his way. Now they were his obsession but he did not want to let them escape. There was still yet time and there were other ways. The bio-mechanical robots had failed, but he was about to give them a surprise that they were not expecting. Right now he had a preoccupation with this slave and later he would begin the final processes that would bring about the capture of this group of renegades. Terra will help. He made sure of that.

"The upstart, Nina, doesn't know it but the Terrans are going to hand that bitch over to me. I can't wait to see her when her own people capture her and then bring her to me. When I have her out of the way, I will reduce their underground empire to dust. Soon, if they ever reach Mars, the Terrans will arrest them all. But if I reach them first then I will save them the trouble."

Back on the space ship where Laura and Jada had just finished deactivating the killer robot, they were so emotionally and physically drained that they both collapsed in the floor.

"Laura, we did it. You and I together," Jada said, out of breath. "I thought for sure we were dead. We just lucked out and caught him off balance. He would have destroyed us if we had not killed him."

"I know," Laura said. "Oh, I forgot all about Tom. Hurry let's get him inside."

"Yes," Jada said. "We also need to get him to help us to get this thing out. It may still be dangerous or maybe even explode."

I was waiting outside the bay door to the exterior air lock and wondering exactly what had happened. I was still trying to figure how I could find a way in. I saw the robot creature going into the airlock and I knew there had to be a calamity inside.

Suddenly the airlock opened and I quickly entered, not knowing what would happen or what I would find. When I entered I recompressed the room and then opened up into the inner air lock to see the monster lying in pieces spread all over the floor.

"Laura, are you alright?" I asked.

She was covered in armor from the flat robot still, like a suit of linked plates, flexible but practical and durable. It was a very becoming warrior that I saw before my eyes. The plate-like forms of the flat robots had the two women warriors making their audition for the newest century combatants. They looked every bit like they could take on a whole marine battalion. I was just in time to see the smoke from the fire in Laura's eyes as she began to recover from the stressful fight. I know that they must be terrified from the ordeal but I sensed a greater danger.

"Laura, you and Jada must help me get this piece of junk into the air lock. I think they explode if they are defeated. It is like a built in fail-safe or something."

Laura looked at me for a minute with that stunned look like a golden retriever makes when she just made a fantastic trick; like she is saying; "Look, what I did. Look at it!"

"I said, "Darling, I am so proud of you. Jada, you too, I know you both saved my life and the ship."

Laura exclaimed, "Look! I can just about pick this thing up by myself because of the robot that I am encased in."

"It has an advanced miniature hydraulic system that enhances your strength as much as a commercial hoist crane could under certain conditions," Jada said.

It was amazing the new technology available at our command

and we were using it without even really knowing its capabilities. The rogue robot was torn to pieces, literally and yet I think it still was functioning except for the motor drives and appendages. We had to pick up all the pieces and get everything in the air lock. It took us a good thirty minutes, even with the aid of electronic hydraulics and the lifting enhancements of the flat robots.

Inside the workings of the rogue robot's brain there remained a link to the real world that could be said to be on the verge of final peace. Although the computer programs and stimuli forced the electrons in digital messages to cause actions mechanical in nature, a memory yet remained in the gray matter captivated inside the metal shell of the brain. This memory was an etching engraved into a part of the brain that could not be erased electrically or magnetically. This etching was of a place in time; a place that the human brain had stored as valuable and had remembered over and over again as a fond memory. The field was a peaceful place with a small brook of water running noisily nearby. The sun shown bright that day as he walked alone through the meadow and flowers bloomed profusely with blue and yellow and pink little blossoms dancing lightly as the breeze fluttered their petals ever so lightly but not so as to keep the little bees from hopping from one to the other. The clouds were just wispy things that helped to keep the glare of the sun changing from one direction to the other, glinting and darting like spears of light thrusting through the trees.

This is the memory that kept repeating itself like a beacon of light that brought the ship of his consciousness to the shore of reality. The thing opened his eyes. He was not quite dead and not quite alive, but still aware that there was a world here but now it was full of evil and forced decisions. These were orders, decisions from someone, somewhere else. They were orders in the form of electrons that he did not want to carry out. The memory of a better place brought hem out of the destruct sequence and he managed to override the preprogrammed order. The self-destruct sequence would have shut down the engine's drive thereby marooning the ship in space to await the arrival of Drakbar's boarding party.

Laura now had taken the flat robot wrap-around armor back to its holding area where upon after she disengaged the fastening magnet, the armor began to restore itself to the flat appearance it had to begin with. The magnetic system closing had been activated and all of the smooth black plates began to fold up to make an economically space saving robot. It took its place with the hundreds of other similarly looking flat weapons systems. All of their green activation lights were still on though, indicating that they were ready and active for combat at the first notice. Laura was thinking of the force represented by one line of these seemingly innocent looking flat black objects lined up like cards of plastic with metallic looking edges and colored lights. They were hidden and waiting to be opened. They represented, just almost ideas and thoughts, potential energy, instead of the battle tank, that they really were. They could shield a whole company of men if their attributes were expanded. Could there be a hidden mind within this monster that they had just fought. Could there be some ideas of goodness that were lying dormant within the evil creature encapsulating the once human brain?

"Tom," said Laura. "Could this monster be using a slave human mind to run the electronic central processing unit of the robotics? I remember Jada said something about this. Could we somehow save the electronic nucleus and put it in incubation to obtain some answers to a few questions about what are Drakbar's intentions?"

"Jada," I said. "Could we disengage the nucleus mind of the CPU without setting off some time bomb?"

Jada walked over to the heap of rubble that was what they left intact. It was extremely maimed and had gashes even into the control neural system. All appendages were severed and cut into pieces, piled up around it.

Jada said, "Laura always has very ingenious ideas that are intuitive on a level that I, as a Martian cannot obtain. Her spirit is guiding her to open a door that we have kept closed because of the revulsion for what Drakbar does to his enemies. But it may be very valuable to try and recover the nucleus which most surely is a brain cortex from one of Drakbar's enemies, or an innocent victim. Let's see if we can set it free if not but for a few minutes. Maybe it cannot live outside the unit but if we put the brain in a closed stasis unit and flood the tube with saline solution, we might permit it to give us some electronic signals, free of Drakbar's electronic probes. By removing the electronic probes from the lobes of the brain it will cause it to begin deterioration, I suspect.

Laura, please go into the sick bay and ask Nina to give you her ribbon knife. She will only give it to another female, I think. But, she will transfer an electronic signature to your brain. Just relax and receive the information to the proper place it goes to in your frontal lobe. It is encoded. You just have to guide the encryption to the right place. You'll know where it goes. We need that knife to cut out the nucleus and it must be surgically guided by encoded neural direction. Go now Laura. When you open the hutch bubble, she will give you the knife and the encryption code to your neural network. Don't be afraid because you are chosen to open the door."

Laura hesitated for a moment and then said to Jada, "I want to help this creature and I'm not afraid but I do not want to use the ribbon knife to destroy but to just help this human entity to be free of its prison."

"I know," Jada said. "That is why Nina will give it to you and not to us. She knows that, I am sure."

I looked at Laura and said, "Laura, the reason the thing is destroyed is because you didn't have any other choice. Don't feel bad. You did the right thing. It came down to either it or us."

Laura said, "I know I had to incapacitate it but I did not want to kill it. I'll get the ribbon knife and we will set it free."

She didn't think of any of the effects of setting this thing free but she had a right to believe it could feel something other than just electronic stimuli.

Laura entered the sick bay and there were the hutches, where all the crew members lay in bubbles that protected them from intruders. The whole crew was laid up in stasis, rebuilding themselves from what was the effect of a nervous breakdown. They were all beautiful and she felt jealousy because she knew they had been very friendly with Tom. She felt that Nina wanted to take Tom away from her, but she would never let that take place. Things happened around her. She knew now that the whole crew would not have been laid up if there had not been a problem with their judgment. There is a being that makes adjustments in the fate of humans and she knew from experience that for most of her life, that being had been giving her untold blessings and had been continually interfering in her fate. She knew that she had been spared defeat in the face of overwhelming odds for too many times to list. These facts were evidence that she was favored by God and she knew it, and acted accordingly, feeling compassion and love for others as it was given to her, because it was just expected. That, she was intensely aware of, so she demanded it of herself.

She opened the hutch where Nina lay and she asked her in a polite voice, "Nina, Jada tells me that I need to ask you for the ribbon knife to help a thing to be free of its cage."

She looked at Nina and stared at her closed eyes. She looked peaceful in her state of hibernation and renewal but Laura sensed that under that calm surface was an active malevolent force that could spring instantly to life and tear her frail body to pieces. Nina opened her eyes and just looked at Laura. Nina began to see within her own mind the semi-computer aided blocks of reasoning caches, large complex comparisons of integrating groups of symbols. These symbols were such that with her enhanced capabilities she was yet unable to correlate them and separate them out so that they could be analyzed. It was a rush of information generated from where, she could not explain, but the information represented mathematical and geometric symbols that she was unfamiliar with.

She could not process it so she just smiled and said, "Hello, I know that you are Laura and yes, I will give you the ribbon knife."

Nina's heart had begun to beat faster and faster as if it was going to explode in her chest. It was like some spirit had entered her body and was about to send her into the blackness of all eternity. She could feel her heart leaving the shell it was encased in which was her body, and her mind was racing, racing to comprehend, but only nothingness was there.

Nina said, "I have been very bad and have killed thousands and thousands of invading people for the defense of my nation. It was not

206

that I wanted it but that it was for to survive and protect us. I don't really understand why it was so necessary only that it was done and I did it as captain. What can I do to keep from falling into the blackness? I can see that it is just almost taking me now."

Laura touched her forehead with the tips of her fingers and said, "There is a peace that passeth all understanding and you know where that peace comes from. Call out that name right now and seal yourself away from the darkness that is taking you, for all eternity. You know it and you have heard us speak the name. There is a spirit that is working to set you free and let you start over again. Say the name and release the burden that weighs so heavy on your conscience."

Nina's heart began to calm and it was like a wave of relief rushing over her that broke itself upon the rocks of the shoreline as she said the name. "Jesus, you spoke to me of Jesus, who took away the burden of what I did. Here, take my ribbon knife. I know you will not hurt anyone and whatever you use it for will be something good."

She unsheathed the ribbon knife and placed it in Laura's hand. Then, there passed a current of electricity from Nina's hand through Laura's hand and Laura felt it as it moved through her arm and up her shoulder. It then passed into her brain and entered the realm of collective organization that was in her frontal lobe. The trick to placing a coded charge was to see in the distance and project the tree of neurons that the electrons were traveling on and intuit the place of reception or just visualize a unique holding place and in such a placement cell, Laura guided the packet of electrical information to the proper dark place that Nina had transferred to her.

Then with a sigh of relief, Nina said, "Now I'm going to rest. Thank you, --friend."

Laura said, "You are welcome friend. I'll go and tell Tom the good news."

Nina closed her eyes and began to sleep a very deep, peaceful sleep. She smiled a little as she began to dream of worlds she had been on that no one else had ever seen.

Europa was such a beautiful moon and there was a blue light that washed over everything on the surface and it was just like a huge crystal glacier full of deep blue waters beneath the thick permanent ice pack.

Laura closed the hutch and put the ribbon knife inside her belt as she looked once more at the room of bubbles containing people, just people. She thought to herself, "They really are not machines at all.. They are just human like me. It was hard to believe the way they handle bundles of coded information but, is our own brain capable of storing packets of electrical encryptions? It seems so because something happened. There was an electrical shock and she definitely felt the information packet as she guided it to the proper location.

She would have to talk to Jada about this and Tom; he could help her to understand."

Walking back to the control room she focused back and forth on the now familiar coded entry. "It is there. I see it in my forebrain like an invisible array that I can control. I see the depth of it and the capabilities but how is that possible? I have a new ability to focus near side and far side and to also equate the visualization with surrounding parameters as if I am my own navigation device. How long will this last and can I cope if it is permanent? Maybe it will make things easier, yes, I like it."

I saw my Laura walking back and she had the ribbon knife with her, tucked neatly into her belt in front. She had a look in her eyes like someone had turned on a light.

"Tom," said Laura, filled with an enthusiasm that I have seldom seen. "I got it, and she gave me some constructs of electrical information that went to my forebrain. It's like a part of me now that has become a range finder that is built into my brain."

I was shocked that she had become something in myself that I almost hated but knew that I needed to survive in a real world. I felt it important for her to know that she was losing an innocence that others did not have.

"Laura, do you realize that you have enhanced one talent but somewhere there is something that may be diminished or lost? Nothing is gained without losing something else."

She just looked at me like nothing I said made any sense at all.

I said to Laura, frantically, "We need to open the thing now with the ribbon knife because you have to give it back, Laura. It is not yours to keep and you will never be like Nina. Let's just get it over with before you hurt someone with that thing."

"Alright, alright," she said, sounding like she was a little impatient with me.

It was going to be an operation that took place in a split second. We actually had the audacity to think that we could perform highly skilled surgery by removing a living brain from some biological mechanical weapon. This was going to be like threading the eye of a needle but in the dark.

Laura spoke up with a jubilant tone to her voice, "I can do this, Tom. I am confident, actually visualizing exactly what I am going to do, as if I am looking at a detailed diagram."

We maneuvered the huge piece of junk back into the loading dock from the actual air lock that we had left it in. Using the flat robots again with the loading lift enhancer attached to the flat exoskeleton of the black robot. The loading arms could actually be used by any normal person. The flat robots were giving a precision to the positioning that just a person would not actually be able to perform unless they used the black exoskeleton of the flat interconnected electronic machinery. The movements of the exoskeleton loaders were sympathetic to our own body movements. The inside sensors picked up the directional decision of the muscles and by a very fraction of a second followed it.

Jada began to explain to me in very precise Martian terms, the problems and solutions of making this happen.

"Tom, you only have to give the exoskeleton the benefit of following your own movements. By adjusting the small rheostat as you call it, the speed will increase exponentially to the speed of your actual movements. The basic problem is the clumsiness of having a bigger body to move. You can hit your own feet as you move and stumble if you are not careful.

Laura, now that you have the ribbon knife and know the limits of its precision, please lets begin if all agree to accept the consequences or our actions. Since the others cannot voice their decision and are unaware of our problem, we will decide for them. Visualize the cut you are about to make and diminish the flare of the blade so that you can separate the layers of biological insulation, tying the electronic stimulators into the lobes of the brain. Let's separate the metal skin now from the hybrid biologically regenerated skin. This is just a covering that is like an engineered epidermis for the brain. They have made these on Mars and I am familiar as a University student but it was not permitted for us to force unwilling donors into slavery."

Laura began to perform her surgical duties by first pulling out the green and silver ribbon knife from her waist belt. I was shocked when I saw the faint glow of a Martian aura that slowly emanated from Laura's face and around the top of her shoulders. The rainbow began to originate from her forebrain and then progress like a circular rippling in a pond when a rock is thrown into it disturbing the tranquility of the surface. The aura was a moving exhibition and was not at all static; just pulsing in waves. More or less, I just stared at her in utter amazement. My own wife looked like an angel more than I already knew that she was but I hoped that she did not change. Truly I loved the simplicity that represented her sanity of heartfelt compassion. She didn't need any enhancements because from somewhere within the vastness of a cosmic universe, she derived an almost clairvoyant power of human empathy that could heal a disturbed mind. Reaching her power of sorrowful understanding, this possessed personality within a clockwork robot, pleaded his case and found his rebel soldier that would release him from the dark warped mind prison of Drakbar.

Visualizing the connection of the ribbon knife to the various layers of biological epidermis, Laura began a mathematical cutting and cauterizing. Slowly but surely each layer revealed a multitude of embedded electrolytic tube inserts. She closed each one and ended the constant stream of directives given electronically from some remote sending location. Every tiny tube insert had a specifically coded message that shut off pre-existing memories or learned functions of a past life.

Gradually, as Laura closed robotic doors to the relentless

scream like a rocket turbine engine in pre-flight burn out, the old formed memories of a once peaceful childhood took familiar shape and flooded into the emotional ocean of place of being. The mind of a once deadly soldier began to realize that the bright sunlit green pasture of his childhood was not just a fantasy. The memory was of a real place and not an inserted directive that had to be obeyed. He languished in the memory and thought of how long it had lasted already. There were little fishes at the edge of the pond and little dragon flies buzzing as their wings brushed against each other in flight. The soft breeze that he felt against his face made his hair fly up in little rhythmic motions and he could feel his hand brushing the strands of hair out of his eyes. The slight breeze sounded like a melody of music in his ears. Did he hear a woman's voice or was it the wind calling him to come into the lush green forest. He got up and walked as if he was in his youth and skipped over the little rocks that lay in his path. He stepped in a puddle of water but he did not feel his feet get wet. This was an unusually peaceful place but he felt like there was a need to get up and leave. He opened his eyes and saw only that same beautiful vision and there in front of him was a beautiful woman.

"You are free from your prison," she said. "I don't know if you realize it or not but you are not dead yet. Do you understand?"

Laura looked into his bloodshot eyes and saw from the depths of his soul, some saving grace that lifted him up from his despair. There was no larynx from which he could speak but a resonating electronic tone clearly chimed the sound of the words.

"I did not hurt anyone this time, did I?"

Laura replied, "No, we are all well, but we had to dismember your robotic body to save our own lives. What do you wish for us to do with your mind?"

Jada spoke up, "This brain, cannot live much longer without the sustenance of the constant electrolytic tube inserts. They had to be pulled out to break the master command but also the food will end. You will die now, peacefully."

The resonated voice spoke up, "Can I leave you a recording to send to my family?"

"Yes, if you give us something to use against the animal and you know who I am talking about."

The eyes of the brain unit rolled up into its head and it emitted a sound like the disembodied ghoulish invention that it was. The sound made even Jada to cringe in revulsion. Something had given it a shock which made all of the monitors vibrate with a sensory explosion that could only mean one thing. Drakbar had monitored his own failure, and now possibly could be initiating a pain device for punishing the poor man's mind.

I told the mind unit, "Speak and tell us now how we can fight him before he takes away your consciousness."

Suddenly its eyes opened again and a thin line or worm appendage emerged from the back of the brain. It was like a piece of the convoluted brain matter just peeling itself off from the midst of the gray matter and there was a long line possibly bio-electrical with an adapter attached to the end of the chord.

The thing spoke and said, "I will give you my memories of my wife but you also have the unmentionable experience of my capture. It is not pleasant, this part. You will know the secrets that Drakbar has, but you must also separate this from my good experiences and give this recording to my wife. She doesn't know what happened, only that I am missing.

I was taken from the Earth five years ago and I was a teacher in a small college. I used to teach martial arts, philosophy, and painting. You must make it back and give my family this tape."

Laura put away the ribbon knife and ran over to the portable education unit that we had been using to familiarize ourselves with the workings of the space ship.

"Jada," she said. "Can we plug it into this and record the memory that he has stored?"

"We can try, but I don't think the memory will be that good because he has been a slave for five years. He doesn't have much of the pathway structures required to find the right memory address."

The chord was inserted into the open port and a circular clamp tightened up on the chord which permitted the beginning of the electron flow to designated addresses. At first I thought there was just darkness but then began a playback of a very interesting professor who seemed well liked by his students. The holographic replay of this man's memories began a stop and go sequence of fast forward and detailed accounts of his life as a husband, teacher, and ultimately a victim.

Jada said, "He must have never known what happened to himself up until this time because these memories have been suppressed or simply burned out or turned off. Many abductions in the United States and all over the world have been attributed to alien abductions when in fact it actually was but through a more believable physically oppressive force of kidnapping and torture. Drakbar is a serial killer and as you say, an alien Martian committing crimes against humanity."

I looked at the bizarre scene playing out in front of me. My wife was holding an alien knife in her hand, and a semi-human robotic machine was replaying memories from childhood into a synthesized storage view-cam. I had of course very many questions about how this could happen and the only person who had any idea of how it worked was in stasis other than the Martian woman, Jada. I am going to have to refrain from calling her a Martian because it seems that it presents her in some other light than human. In this case it was the opposite because she seemed the more compassionate of us all except for my loving wife. I believe I truly had loving feeling for her that came from respect and honor for her clarity of thought and knowledge. From now on I cannot refer to her anymore as that Martian woman, but only as Jada. Also, my wife Laura calls her just, Jada, and so will we all. She had a particularly interesting view point to add to the many mysteries of alien abduction that were running parallel in all places on Earth at this time. Jada looked at the human brain unit as the memory scan was playing colorful video images of a past life and now, as it approached the time of his abduction.

She took her slender hand and flipped her blond hair just behind her left ear and said, "Look, stop the tape here, and play this memory. It is the abduction of this man when he was a lot younger."

The video on the screen began with a garden setting among paved sidewalks and big oak trees, which were the outer limits of his college campus at which he taught.

"It's dim in places but look you can clearly see that there is a trauma taking place. He did not go peacefully."

A big black spaceship was seen in the distance approaching from a cloudy sky. The playback was vivid but had spaces where there was just no recording. The brain had apparently suffered debilitating burn out and parts of the human experience were just not complete.

Jada said, "I'm going to show you what a tyrannical fiend that Drakbar really is. The scene of the capture is coming up on the view screen soon. Now watch as the black spaceship is approaching and you will see how utterly inhuman he is. Hundreds of people saw this spaceship. There is no way that they could have not seen it but maybe no one believed it or cared. You have to believe that this Drakbar is very different from me and my hive on Mars."

The spaceship loomed ahead close, and the professor was clearly stunned and immobilized. The brain of the professor began to speak through the voice actuators that were placed along the neural network of his remaining carbon fiber connection. Somehow between the ship's computer and the man's brain there had been a bridge built to his memories and the result was a random movie of a sequence of important events. For certain reasons to the man these were deeply recorded or etched on his memory.

"I am remembering how it all happened but why didn't I run away? Why didn't I cry out or even just move? I am frozen and I see the horror of the approaching beings. They look human but they can do things to me that I don't understand. They are taking over a mental command and control center within my brain's system. I feel some kind of electrical current running from the bottom of the spine of my backbone, up through my spinal column and through up to my head and my eyes. I suddenly hate them because they have kept me from giving the command to my legs to run or to move.

Something like water comes up in my sinuses and through my nose and mouth and a fluid runs from the tear ducts in my eyes but I am not crying. It feels like some kind of electrolytic solution but I know it has come from my own body. It is at this time that I see the black demon leave the space ship as if on a web of something like steel. He clamps onto my shoulders and then it is as if he takes a needle, or a stinger like an insect and a long steel instrument is inserted into my neck as my head is pushed down. I feel the long needle go directly down through the middle of my spinal chord and then little darts of pain are shooting all through my bones and muscles in my back. I am taken by a flexible mechanical arm into the belly of the ship.

Once I am in the cargo belly of the ship another monstrous black machine comes and just removes all of the rest of my body. My arms, legs and rib cage are separated from my body by spinning bright circular cutting machines. I watch them all drop off and only my spinal chord and brain are left skewered on this huge needle of metal with a warm current of electricity running through my vertebrae."

I looked at Jada and asked if he could be traumatized by reliving this nightmare.

She said, "These are just recordings in his long term memory. Maybe he is already dead, or I don't know just living in the past but hoping for better future. He has a limited consciousness; I am sure, but not a real ability to communicate apathetically with sincere sorrow or joy."

The isolated memory unit spoke and reassured us all that he could communicate a little.

"Your synthesis of my neural network is not a complete circuit but I have a limited ability and wish to make this recording before a lack of electrolytic hydraulic functions destroy the integrity of my overall charged system. You have thankfully broken off the remotely charged diverters that kept me from cognitive reasoning. Now I must communicate in order to save the record of my ordeal if only to help some other poor soul to escape. At least now you will know how I was abducted. I am afraid that soon the spark of life will go from me and I will not have communicated to anyone."

The cinematic replay of the episode flipped back and forth first black and white, gray, then vivid color of a sequence of events in the memory unit's life. His real life story plays on the view screen before our eyes and each one of us is emotionally affected by his ordeal.

He spoke again, "I am conscious of the things around me because they have preserved my electrolytic functions of the central nervous system; but that is all that they have preserved. The rest of me is lost like fat, trimmed from a piece of raw steak. I am experiencing fear in all its form of foreboding only the palpitations of the heart is missing because I am no longer living just, functioning like static on a radio that is tuned in and out in search of a clear channel. You have found this place in my memory and I at least have some small comment in a narrative to make.

They moved me into the bay of the spaceship, big and black and I was reeled into a chamber, like an insect stuck through with a pin through the abdomen. As I entered into a long cylindrical chamber I felt a sensation of cold, very cold as if I was in a refrigeration unit. As the cold began to get more and more graduated, the spark of consciousness left me and my narration is terminated. Nothing is perceived from this point on."

Jada looked up at me and said, "His ability to remember is now terminated because at this point on he is under the control of the processing unit machine of Drakbar. The experiences that he has now at the beginning of refrigeration are just electronic impulses of his electrolytic system like a circuit, used for transfer of electrons to provide a function. I don't think that he even has a record of any of these new functions. The power unit that the dark Martian uses is a vicious robotic instrument that makes electronic slavery units of his captured, abducted victims. They pretty much forget or block out all the horrendous experiences. This one remembered because we interfered with the circuit rhythm of his implants and disconnected the power unit.

Let me see if I can prompt the magnetic address and get some registration and we will maybe get something to attach to visualization."

She produced from a small case made of blue semi-glass crystalline material, a sharp pointed instrument. The long slender tube looked as if it was a piece of obsidian with a needle that retracted and extended from the end.

Jada said, "This is a device used on Mars to relieve pain when electronic stimulation has left a person void of comprehension. It changes the orientation of a natural crystal that the body forms when under duress. Like an oyster makes a pearl of great beauty when a

216

grain of sand enters the shell and irritates the oyster to make a covering for it, the human brain will crystallize a substance that is a natural part of the electrochemical process. When under stress it causes a thin piece of the minute crystalline structure to elongate with contamination or form concentric rings. This obsidian needle will penetrate to a precise point and resonate to bring the crystalline organization into alignment with the geo-symmetry of the host. It sounds like Martian dark technology but actually it was being used originally to cure melancholia in severely depressed Martian hive residents.

Watch when I insert this needle into the base of the actual crystalline concentration orb. Here is the point of penetration, just below the nerve junction. Now, I will initiate electronic stimulation solely by means of the radiation that is emitted by exposure through the tube to the ions contained in the obsidian base. They travel freely through the needle by means of a minute ruby laser originating behind the crystal in the middle area of the tube. Once the primitive crystalline growth has been ionized, it begins a symmetrical recovery that allows visualization to begin again and bring about a concentrated recovery by the host."

I looked at all this, a Frankenstein-like macabre scenario, and wished for a better situation but I was stuck in this contest between good and evil. But in this case, it was ultimate sinister evil and I could not see a rosy picture to any of it. What started out as a quest for a special group of people has led me to a black hole streaking through my quiet peaceful reality. I saw Laura and imagined that we were in a better brighter place full of flowers and natural beauty. Upon viewing the screening of recall images that were prompted through ionic activation of this person's memories, I envisioned the time when many of my own memories could be reinitialized and saved to laser disk or some other means of storage. What beautiful dreams I could recall and replay in detail over and over again. But really, who would ever want to be electronically stimulated to produce happy memories?

A bell with a high pleasant ring began intoning and a few lights began to emit their radiant glow.

Jada said, "He is coming around and will give us now I hope, a view of the inside chamber where he was kept. Let's have some patience and wait for his visualization to form."

We were waiting in expectation for the important memory imprint to be squeezed and manipulated from a poor almost dead, no past death cerebral entity. He was partly human and gave me the feeling of being a witness to the future manipulation of our basic privacy, our memories, personal and familiar. His personal vision opened up within the cell of his memory that had been prodded to respond. Then a long chamber began to open up with a cavernous appearance. A huge room was spread before him and lined up in row upon row were symbiotic, robotic human nervous system stems. They were all alike, just head and stem with the vertebrae skewered and racked. All were moving a little from the gradual stimulations coming from the spinal needle that fed and regenerated the fluid connections needed to bring sustenance to the nerve endings. Sometimes the eyes opened but not for more than a few minutes and then closed as if in a long deep sleep.

Laura said, "Look how many they have. It looks like they have been abducting people for quite a long time. This is not just something that could happen over night. He is going to use our own Earth people to fight us with."

Jada spoke up, "I just am so sorry that he is Martian. I hope you realize that it is not all of Mars that is involved in these abductions. He is an abomination and doesn't deserve to live and breathe the same air as another Martian."

With that last comment from Jada a new chapter opened up in the cinematic sequence of memory frames being revealed by this stimulation technique of Jada's medical arts. A new light began to appear from the holographic 3-d pictures represented by the deeply concealed memories of the brain unit. Shadows were being cast across the wide open panorama of the holding warehouse where thousands of similar units were being kept. Blue and green and gray tones began to appear in the gray presentation and shadows crept across a doorway that was opened up.

What looked like a very thin young woman walked into the open warehouse on one end and she approached our professor's nervous system unit and stepped right up in front of him. She was dressed in something that would qualify as a snowsuit for extreme cold conditions, lined around the edges with black fur and looking very somber. She was black eyed with dark circles and the look of being hypnotized with long black hair cascading down her back.

As she bent down she looked into the professor's eyes which were wide open and she spoke softly.

"You were the last person that I thought I would see in this place. Can you hear me? Mr. Tremble, Professor Tremble, can you hear me? I am working here for these Martians now and they let me have some freedom. I am the caretaker of all these people; well they aren't people any more just little electron units for the robots. I have to spray you with this fluid to keep you from drying out. I have to do my job but first I wanted you to know that I still feel the same way I did for you last year when we met in the hotel. Looks like I am the teacher now and you are the student. Can you speak any at all?"

There was total silence. The professor's mental unit was cognitive and recording the event but he was now unresponsive and cold. The beautiful young girl moved off and at each mental unit she sprayed it with softening fluid to keep the nerve endings from drying out. From his field of vision the young girl passed and now it seemed as though there was nothing but silence and apparently his synapses were getting too cold to fire.

The screen went blank and Jada spoke up first, "I think that is all we will achieve from stimulating his nerve junctions. Did you all see how many units he had in storage and how big his warehouse was? He must have been out there for a long time gathering mental units for his robots. I don't know if we can stop him or not, but we have to meet him soon head on."

I began to think about our options and it did not look good. We were being pursued in the open savannah of outer space and there was no place to hide.

"I feel like we are out in the open desert or the African savannah with lions closing in and no trees and no place to hide. They are faster than we are and are steadily closing in on us. How can we fight? Let's get back to planning our defense and analyzing our options. I want to try and revive Nina, the crew, and Max from stasis. Is it too soon, Jada, or can we? I think we really need them now before it is too late. They can add to our composite of ideas and help in staging whatever we decide on. I am not comfortable with having just our ideas in the mix."

"Yes," Jada said. "Of course, let's try and see if she has some stable mental stream of consciousness. We will see if she can carry a conversation or just nod out in the middle of her thought pattern. Let's try in the next twelve hour cycle to revive her first and if she is ready then we can revive the others. She will recover remarkably quick because she is enhanced and can make electrical changes directly into muscular areas that are beginning to atrophy. But she will still need some help to get around and adjust as will all the rest of the crew. We will have to be patient and we need to allow some time before they will be completely functioning and sound of mind and body. I'm afraid that their minds might also be a little misaligned as far as their judgment is concerned. They are all enhanced as we know and if they cannot make good judgments then they could be very dangerous. Thomas, that is one reason why they made you captain pilot because they did not trust themselves after the magnetic storm. If we do decide to revive them, we could be signing our own death warrant and measuring short the fate of the Earth, Mars, and the galaxy. We also could lose everything without them but I had rather take the chance to help them."

I just glanced in the direction of the stasis units once and said, "Let's go. I don't want to wait any longer for the danger it presents to them to be without stimuli. I think they can help us more then if we rely only on our own analysis of the situation."

Laura said, "Please let's wake them now. I have a great deal of confidence in Nina and Max and their crew. They wouldn't harm us intentionally, I don't think. We will get them back to their normal selves soon."

We walked, almost gliding across the surreal ship's gravity that was unique to this ship. I think at least it was very strange to even be existent but theoretically hard to prove except for the fact that they almost showed me how to duplicate it.

Laura called us at that moment and said, "Tom, Jada, the mental unit is broadcasting one last memory sequence, I think, and I really feel that it could really be important."

We rushed back into the viewing room where we immediately

could see a flickering purple light begin to cover all the room and made reflections onto the walls. Professor Tremble was making his last remembrance of the ordeal. Maybe he had some other contribution to help us find a way to help defeat Drakbar.

As the light began to fade to a light blue haze, the young girl was back.

"My name is Alicia; you don't remember me? I came to your house to bribe you to help me on the exam. You wouldn't change my grade, but you did teach me how to study. You showed me how to make chapter outlines and budget my time, and how to concentrate on one group of ideas at a time. I began as a result to learn how to construct a fire wall in my conscious mind. I can now resist the evil programming of these bastard aliens and I am slowly recovering my will to fight them. When I get around them I can throw up a mental block when they administer their drugs and electrical packets of coded information. Are you hearing this? I hope so."

At that moment the beautiful young woman undressed in front of the semi-conscious mind unit named Jonathan Tremble, professor of martial arts, philosophy, and painting at Concord University. The cold weather jumpsuit had only one main holding attachment that quietly released itself as Alicia's long thin fingers quickly executed the release of the zipper. The room filled with refrigeration units was near freezing temperatures but not damaging for a short period of time to exposed human skin. Immediately she began to have chill bumps all over her body but she wanted to complete the expression she had filled her heart with. No matter how weird it seemed she wanted to just make the fantasy come true. The young professor had been the platonic love object of many of his younger college students, but never gave them one chance to reach their lustful goals of conquest since he was happily married to the woman who preoccupied all his existence since high school.

Suddenly Alicia began to kiss him and stick her tongue into his mouth when he was only barely conscious but he did have a faint realization that the tactile wet electric feeling was the beautiful young woman's tongue.

He thought, deeply within his obscure consciousness, "What on Earth would make such a beautiful creature feel attraction for only a part of a human body, a head, even without the part that was capable of expressing human reproduction? There could be no response on his part, since he could not feel the same emotions now, maybe that he once had for the young woman. Anyway, he would record it in his memory for use at some later date when he was in a void of space and time for the purposes of data re-enactment."

The young woman heard the sound of an airlock opening and quickly she robed herself in the cold weather suit and ran to another unit for the purposes of showing that she was doing the job she was programmed to do. For now, she was just the robot they thought that she was and would not execute any notion of free will or not so that her captors could see any way.

At that moment the voice of the professor spoke and said, "This was the last free will recording to have been made and I never saw the young student after this. I am now too cold to record any further and all efforts would be futile in the process of cold storage from this time on."

Jada said, "I believe it would not be in our best interest to prompt the brain unit for any further information regarding recorded memories but we have in the least identified a useful compatriot in the student Alicia. If we are so needful in some situation we should keep in mind that they have a sleeper and are not aware that they do not control her."

Jada looked at the brain unit and gave a sympathetic glance at Laura as if to say, sorry. Then without even a word she shut off the view-cam machine that had played and recorded a living memory from the depths of a tormented soul. How could we not feel a shared sympathy for this robotic left-over? He had suffered enough and we could not possibly maintain the electrolytic material and sensory stimulus to force him to function any further.

The light faded and faded still flickering a little as the last electric impulses fired and then nothing. So ended the life of one individual alien abduction, and of what would happen to the endless row upon row of mental units that we saw recorded in this one's memory. More than likely if Drakbar had his way we would see them again in combat. I hope not for our sakes and theirs.

We strapped on the flat robot loaders again and with great reluctance we pushed the heap of scrap metal and human carbon material out the loading dock and into the air lock. All of us returned to the pilots control room and an air of remorse and regret filled all the conversation, what little there was of it. We thought that it could have been each one of us as a victim like this if not for different circumstances. Now I began to think of Nina and the rest of the crew and the immediacy for getting them moving again. They had been laid up for days and days on end. This could have been enough to put a regular Earth human into complete distress with muscular atrophy. Even the old astronauts had trouble walking when they returned to Earth after only a few days in space. At least we had about 80 percent modified magnetic amorphous gravity. It was enough to prevent a huge amount of atrophy, but still just being in bed is enough to cripple after some long term stay.

"Jada, maybe we should go now and wake all the crew before they become cripple."

"OK, but let's wake up Nina first and she can help us with the rest of the crew. There is a small problem though and I don't know how to tell you this but she wants you to bring her body back to full function. Do you know what that means?"

I looked at Jada in a funny sort of way and told her that she already knew that I could not do what she was asking.

"She will die from lack of activity and movement," she said. "If someone does not help her move her limbs in the initial stages and bring back the electron activity of her body's natural rhythm. She will be either catatonic or just an irritable bed ridden vegetable if you do not help her."

"Look," I said in disbelief. "I know she put you up to this and I know she will not die but I will help her as long as you and Laura can be with me when I am doing this helping. Laura will not put up with any hanky panky."

Jada said, "You will have to move her limbs and massage her body completely all over. You know it is necessary and I would do it but there just isn't that kind of relationship between me and Nina. I would probably kill her and she knows it. My Martian body will not

223

harmonize the electron transference with her because we are not receptive. The rhythmic flow that she and I would have is not the beneficial healing power of the male, female harmonic function. One entity absorbs the other's symmetry and that is just the way it is, regardless of wishes. You will need to massage all of her body, the skin, and move the limbs continuously. It will be painful to her and maybe she will not respond, but the chances of success are better with you. Tell Laura and I know that she will understand. She has been in stasis for a month and everything has been completely immobilized."

Laura was there as if she had been waiting just down the hallway. "I heard it all, and I don't care. Just don't like it too much, and you will sleep with me at night and no love making. You just be her little physical therapist until she is walking and once she is stable, you let her go on her own. I don't have to be with you but you better not like it too much. Don't forget I still have the ribbon knife and am programmed to do surgery.

Alright, open the stasis unit and get started. I am going to the pilot's control cabin to look at computer charts. Oh, by the way, she shot me with another program besides the knife telemetry and I think it is called pilot parameters. I'm going to practice in the control room."

I looked at Jada and asked her, "Do you really think that she transferred a block of electron units to Laura that gives her the ability to pilot the ship?"

"It's not just possible it is more or less necessary to execute the knife cuts with range finding precision programmed logic operations. It is just a rearrangement of something she already has, which is a naturally intuitive mind that infers the logic pattern when suggested through a coded sequence of electronic charges. Yes, with very little practice, Laura could fly the ship until she gives the coded packet back to Nina. Even then she will probably remember most of it. The charge is zooming around in her head right now, teaching her how to control her thoughts."

I thought aloud in exasperation, "What have I done? You mean my wife will be like this little monster even when she gives back the primal code?"

"I told you Nina is a special person and she is a lot more human than she is machine."

"I thought that you taught her the things she knows and not the other way around."

"Well, we taught each other things that are just not normal to either Mars or Terra and it actually has its origin more or less in the spirit world. You already are familiar with the Indians of the southwest of the United States and are familiar with what appears to happen in the kiva, the round circular underground house of the Navajo and Anasazi. They exchange a form of spirit knowledge. We know it is real but we do not know the extent of it; just that we can do something similar that can be recorded. The Terrans have perfected some semi-machines that have coded charges that imitate and teach a meathod of electronic transfer. Maybe it is not even electrons but some other shaped wave form that can be transferred through some astral medium. We just know that there is a similar form to this phenomenon that can be scientifically measured. Nina has transferred something to Laura. I am not sure exactly what it is but it is real and not just something from the spirit world. It is not going to hurt her. I'm sure of that and I think she kind of likes it. It gives her a sense of self assurance that she did not have before the exchange."

I did not exactly like the change in her personality but I figured that I would just have to accept it and I would still love her just the same. She had different forms to her personality and this group of women just thought that she was a little shy, but they do not know the real Laura. The blue spy that I had known for years had swings in her personality from quiet and shy to aggressive and domineering and downright bossy, and even arrogant, and this is just the swing that probably would have occurred anyway but the transfer maybe did give her a little more confidence and that probably accounted for the early or abrupt change. She changed anyway, up and down so they did really not have any clue to her real nature, but I decided to just let them think they had improved on her independence from me which was what all women think that each other need to gain a little power. Laura was powerful in her quiet form, maybe more so than the pushy aggressive woman that she sometimes would become. She knew this though and she preferred to just manipulate from the sideline in her real power and this was what I knew that she preferred to do and to let me take all the heat. So, now maybe she even thought herself to be above it all and could dominate from the point but if she wanted to take a direct role then that was alright with me also. I just liked the way she appeared to be shy and it was as if our game was in motion when she was playing shy. Living with a woman, a wife, was a constant challenge and not quite the boring predicament that I at one time I thought it would be. She had all these alien women completely fooled into thinking that she needed some kind of little help to be equal with them but maybe I alone knew that she was playing with them and had a strategy. I just hope that she would not offend them when they found out that she was probably better at karate and judo than I was and could practically read minds and had a spirit or an angel of God protecting her all the time that I never had the fortunate experience to be blessed with.

I waved my hand in front of the stasis hutch where Nina was and the lid opened up. There lay Nina, like a sleeping baby but beneath that beautiful exterior was a vicious and sometimes vengeful and unpredictable warrior.

Jada said, "You have to start massage now so that she will come out of her very passive subconscious. She is just beneath the surface in a shell and you have to break through the protective covering that her system has thrown up to protect her psyche."

I began to massage all her body. As I was rubbing her legs she began to breathe in long relaxing breaths that came in and out like gentle breezes through the sweet smell of her mouth with half parted lips. I enjoyed it so much that I kissed her once and then her eyes opened slightly and she began to move, ever so gently and said, very softly, "Tell Laura to come and help me to restore the primal code that I need to guide my psyche."

"Yes, If you need her I will call her," I said.

Laura was there in an instant and I could tell the two of them acted almost as if they knew each other. Laura was jealous though, I am sure, but I did think she would help her no matter what.

Nina said, "Laura, the force that is within you is alien to you but you may keep a copy of it if you wish, because I think that it has helped you. Surely you have contributed also to the normal parameters that a thinking and reasoning person would do. It is supposed to reside in my psyche as I am a keeper of the Terran primal code. It is just more or less a guide or library of stored information or codes that enhances communication from one Terran to another. We can now call you, a Terran, because you and I should be able to communicate better as a result of the alignment of static elements. There is nothing foreign, like some robotic mechanical or electrical junk in your brain, just an information packet that you can use as a guide. Yet, I think I remember you from somewhere in my past as already having received the initial primal code when you were a child maybe, since you have been so receptive to the adult phase or else there is no solution but I think that we have met in the past."

I was worried about Laura to say the least because of the alien encoded encryption that she had received. What subliminal message it was giving her, I had no idea, but for some unknown childlike reason I did trust Jada and Nina; almost.

Laura said, "When I was a child I had an experience that I do not talk about much and not everyone believes me when I say that I was taken up in a space ship and I barely remember it. Tom knows my story and maybe he can explain some of my past to you and indeed we may have met in some strange way. Right now I need to know how to return the primal code to you. I just really don't understand how it passes from one person to another and how does it travel? Maybe, first I should give back the ribbon knife. Would that help? Here it is. Please take it. It is really not mine."

Nina looked like she was very weak and almost unable to stay conscious right now, but she did have a look as if she had something very important to say.

"I know that you will not understand this right now," said Nina. "You must keep the ribbon knife until time will necessitate that you give it back. In that situation your life will depend upon the necessity that you return it. Only then will I be able to accept it. Your mind must seek to survive out of necessity to transfer the blade back to me. Until that time you are the owner and that is the way it is. There is only one thing that I need right now and I hope you are willing to allow me to find the right place to put it. I am looking in my conscious mind for a place that will allow the coexistence of a nature that is like yours. Your nature is very innocent and yet commanding with such a high degree of awareness about compassion and empathy toward all living things. Will you allow me to place a copy of this format within my cerebral navigation system? Also, can you help me to activate the coded sequence so that I may modify my behavior accordingly? This would be so helpful in my relationship with Tom and I am sure he will like my copy. It will not be exact but I am sure the result of the change in my attitude will meet with his approval. Don't be jealous. He will still love you, but it is just that he will also love me more than before which can not be a bad thing for me. I will be more like you and now you will be a little more like me."

At that moment Laura looked like she had seen a ghost as her eyes opened wide and she looked like she had been transported to the moon.

Nina's eyes rolled up into her head and she screamed like something had invaded her body that was going to tear her apart. Nina took in one long gasping breath and finally she stopped screaming.

Laura just looked at her and said, "How did you do that? I saw a whole panorama of words and felt a feeling of such compassion well up all over my whole body as if I was giving you a beautiful present at Christmas or something. I don't know what happened but I saw you standing in an open field of beautiful flowers and I saw myself place a huge bouquet of wild flowers in a box with your body in it. You were happy to receive the flowers but why are you screaming?"

"Oh, Laura, it is the most beautiful gift you have given me and I don't know that I will ever be able to tell you how much it has meant to me. How can I give you something in return for the ideas that you have given me? Where does this information go in my cerebral array? Should I fit it next to the emotion of love or should it be near the feeling of kindness?"

Laura just stood very still and spoke in a slow methodical tone; almost mocking the robotic nature of Nina.

"Just put it in your heart and use generously when the appropriate situation occurs. You will know how to act when one of your emotionally challenging situations occurs. Just breath deep, be considerate, and apply wisdom with a flavor of respect for all living things."

"Don't insult me!" Nina said. "I know I'm challenged emotionally but I am growing up and will be a considerate, well meaning entity. If you wish to pass any more coded arrays of helpful information packets just let me know and I will find a place for them in my most favored display index. Please, forgive me, can you synthesize or do you know just how to project the array. Oh, never mind. I can do it by myself. It will only take a few minutes to begin association with all the other object goals. Laura, forgive me for my indiscretions with Tom. We never did really do anything. We just liked each other. Are you my friend?"

"Yes," Laura said, and they held each other's hand for a moment. Laura said, "Sleep now and rest. We will talk about ideals of moral conduct one day, and you will come to accept why we feel the intense loyalty to be true to our integrity principles."

I couldn't help but to think that Nina would be better for the association with Laura, but could I accept the fact that Laura was a little bit more like Nina. What next did the scenario have to offer except the fact that I was a better person for knowing both beautiful women? How will we make it when the Martian Drakbar begins his strike against us? Will we all stick together and work as a concerted army and defend the ship adequately to survive. That is what I am hoping for, just to survive.

Laura looked at me and just said, "Come on darling. I think she is just going to sleep now. She's just not ready to wake up right now, maybe later she will be able to help us."

Frowning and very seriously I told her, "You know she is a little mixed up but human none the less. I have known many other people who were less caring than her. She has a heartfelt sense of rightness that I appreciate even if she is a little too calculating. Right now let's just let them have some more time to make some plans and survey the ship and familiarize ourselves with all the weapons systems before we are pushed into trying to learn in a rush."

Jada looked very busy checking programs by making a movement of her fingers and it almost looked like she was playing a piano with one hand. As she moved her fingers and hand over a holo-board, waves of color, letters, symbols, and linear diagrams rippled across a small area of space.

Then a hologram of the whole ship appeared and she said,

"Look, here is a small diagram of the ship and I can access all the locations of weapons types and you can view them and familiarize yourselves with our capabilities or at least some of them. Most of the weapons are available and on line for activation. We will go back to the pilot's control room so we can initiate activation sequence and run some test programs on weapons viability."

Jada again left her friends in the stasis room and put a flat robot to guard and monitor all vital signs and report on variations in temperature and brain wave patterns. When we were in the pilot control room again, Jada began to show us how many different weapons systems were actually on the ship and I was amazed at the variety and how lethal they all were.

Jada said, "Starting with the forward canons, they are each 50 gigahertz pulse beacons that give 3 bursts of power beams per second. Also they have pellet injection systems that combine a pellet of solid volatile igneous material projected through an electrical and gaseous pressurized barrel. When the pellet reaches the target it usually melts into and initiates a catalytic reaction within the substance it hits. We also have an ingenious power beam of constant resonant energy. For years other Martian scientists have tried to imitate the hyper-velocities that it achieves but they could not. It emanates from only the forward cowlings of the spaceship. There are two; one on each side but they are multidirectional. The ship has to be at least within a 30 to 60 degree angle of the target. They can swivel at least within that range. I am not a weapons expert. That is more the area of interest for Nina. She is the probe captain used by the Terran elders to penetrate into the hearts of militant civilizations and discourage their aggressions. I think there are many weapons that the ship has that I am still unfamiliar with, although I did pilot one on Mars similar to this one. My Martian background comes from the area of battle field interpretational dynamics. In other words, I am a strategist and a trainer who analyzes the enemy's character and arranges combat scenarios to be provided to help acclimate our troops to strive for victorious outcome."

I looked at the alien feminine creature and the thought formed in my mind that she dictated combat strategy to millions of insect like Martian troopers swarming like plagues in a science fiction B movie across the plains of Earth. This image was totally fictional and unrealistic, but her authority was without doubt.

"Yes," I said, "I truly believe you could command a whole theater of operations by launching just your flat robots to move among the enemy and decimate their materials."

"We can do something like that but for every action we initiate, there could be a counter measure launched that could catch us committed and we could not recover if our effort was not able to be repositioned. You know what I am talking about, since you do understand how karate works to the most effective means. A trick seems to work best if the opponent is thoroughly convinced he has predicted your action. The flat robots are not a drone system that is launched and then you just wait for them to discharge their weapons like the pod fleet and then watch for their return and some of them don't return. These are multi-dimensional and are stand alone weapons platforms that can continue the battle almost indefinitely.

This madman Drakbar is thinking right now and basing his attack on evidence of how we have beaten him in the past. He is playing a game in his mind to surprise us with some means of inescapable devastation. Tell me how would you defeat us Mr. Jefferson? Do you think it would be easy or with some difficulty? He is a serial killer now so don't let your mind portray him as some easy predator to trap, because he is not able to be trapped. You just got lucky. We got lucky the first time. He should have beaten us but we won and he will remember it too. This time all the plans that worked before, will not work again."

Chapter 14. **Drakbar Approaches**

Far away approaching at an alarmingly increasing closing speed was their enemy, Drakbar, and all his consortium of freaks and outcasts from all over the populated galaxy. He was especially contented since he had just realized that he would be victorious in his complete capture of the crew and ship too of Nina, the heretic electronic bitch and Jada the now wanted ex-patriot Martian thanks to him. These had no idea that a whole fleet of Terran cruiser gun ships would be waiting for them when they arrived at the apex of their orbit of the big meteor Ganymede. They were in his hand if he just kept them running from him.

Alicia, his new slave, saw him for what he was, a simple brute of an ugly man who wanted to reach his top dog moment and live the phony life of commander, over and over again, squashing all those who got in his way, if possible with glee, as many times as they remained. She was just his toy robot to play with until he broke her. She would try to appear to be brainwashed for as long as it took until she could catch him making a fatal mistake. He called to her and she knew she had to obey. The nights were long but so much better to dream up a way to execute him when he least expected it. Maybe she only just had to wait until the right time. Something would happen and she would recognize what it was and it would be her opportunity. This demon had too many enemies for one of them not to present him his head in his hand. She would just wait and wait and wait until the right moment. Too many of her predecessors had died, but she would not. She could wait it out.

Millions of miles away still came the tiny black hole spinning and tearing through everything in sight. Unknown was the origin of the force that dislodged it or formed it from massive pressures and gravities unable to release the bits and pieces that rearranged their atoms to seek its center. The little black magnet could not be moved by any other force except a force greater than itself. Something had preordained a destination for the anomaly in the universe and the terror that it vanquished was similar to its own, but nothing like this little instrument, which was only the tip of God's blade. Tearing through the universe with massive destruction, and coming from something so dark its origin could not even be spoken; God's sword would not be without its destination. The blood that flows from this forceful thrust will be that of Drakbar's own but not before he can be tested against only those who are not only human, but resilient too.

Alicia suddenly had an idea that would aid in the destruction of this demonic force that suddenly had begun to threaten all of the civilized galaxy. A beacon could give away their position and let some other space ship become aware of their approach. Maybe she could achieve something like this if she could just get to the communications pod and have her way with the layers of jamming electronic devices that protected the ship. After the frenzied ordeal that she again had to go through, she quietly slipped away from Drakbar's hands and made her way to the crossover beam that separated the main body of the ship with a maintenance tube, connected to the under workings of the thrusters. She would crawl through this tube to the remote thruster engine compartment and make her way over to the main communications pod from which sprouted antennae arrays and beacon initiators. If the tube was sealed she could make the transition through in zero gravity and reach her destination finally to the center of the communications pod. If she was discovered they would torment her beyond her capacity to endure pain. Opening up the pressurized compartment, she jumped up and into the tube. Out and away from the revolving current of the ship's hull, the gravity field did not exist. Soon, at some distance, she left the circulating gravity bands and she was weightless, floating and pulling herself along the smooth wall to the maintenance tube. After a long enduring time period, she finally managed to reach the communications pod used to deflect and jam frequencies and radar that Drakbar's enemies could use in searching for the vessel. After she reached the objective she now did not know exactly what to do. Her dark eyes full of confusion and fear, she began to scan frantically for some way to reveal the position of the ship to someone, anyone. She wanted so much in her heart to find a way to destroy him and her time was running out. They would discover her soon. He will wake up and want her and ask to know where she was. It was now or never. She took some of the small pieces of wire that she had brought with her, and she began to splice some of the pieces from one wire to the other, just grounding some and cross connecting others. When the surge came through, she hoped, it would somehow run the electricity to another place; not where it was intended to be taken. Maybe this would achieve some small advantage for the ones being pursued by the bastard Drakbar. Now she could sleep and rest assured that she had done something good in her life. Getting back secretly would be just as important as actually making the sabotage and that would have to be done even if she died in the process. Yes, she could give her life to this just cause, easily.

"This ship is a hell hole and whatever I can do to bring about its destruction, so help me, I will do it," said Alicia aloud so that she herself could hear the sound of it and she liked the noise it made.

She began to think about an old age of terrorism that had swept across the United States and she secretly wished that she could have contributed by going herself directly to some of the people who had begun giving power to the terrorists and visited something like this on one of their own sponsor countries. Many people in the United States had summoned up their own fortitude from their inner guts and returned again the same terror to the countries that had sponsored people just like Drakbar. They received in spades exactly back the same terror and there was a great destruction brought about by the private citizens who pooled their resources and took the war to the enemy, against the wishes of the government.

They had achieved a great victory and individual citizens had found their own private enterprises that caused havoc to come upon such countries that had sponsored terrorism, little by little until they achieved a proper response not from the government but from individual citizens who had the money to make it happen.

Now, these most lethal of terrorists came from Mars and had secretly been harvesting people from all over the world to use in their slave robots. If any one could just imagine what these Martians had been doing they would scream in anguish and would be appalled at the enormity of their own ignorance of the devastation that had been committed little by little.

She thought to herself, "If I ever had the chance, I'd nuke the whole planet." Right now she thought, "I will be satisfied to just let somebody know that they exist and can be seen. Now I have to get back before they realized I can think and they fry my brain for real this time, ending all of my self realization and pride."

She went back into the tube that extended through to the air lock between the main deck and the communications pod. The maintenance tube remained weightless and that was a good sign, indicating a stable existing condition. When she reached the main level she opened the right window revealing no one outside and breathed a sigh of relief that the hallway was empty. She made it and left through the exit chamber and back to the captain's quarters without even being seen at all. He reached out with one hand and connected to her beautiful face, not in anger this time, but in force of habit since he was barely awake and did not completely open his eyes. In his sleep he was sure he had her completely controlled and in his will power; such was his state of mind as he was approaching his conflict.

Nina began to dream. These dreams were not just ordinary dreams but dreams of power and purpose. She was reorganizing her thoughts as were all the other Terrans that had gone through the ordeal of disjunction from their guiding electrical field. This field of almost infinite ability to tap into information had been severed, cut from their mental life line. They no longer could communicate like a normal enhanced Terran could. Jada had made sure and removed any semblance of the inner circuitry that was inside the little silver disk. Her thoughts started to drift and she was mesmerized by the visions that she encountered relating to the series of events. Flashing back into her expanded memory, she visualized with precision; location, causal stimuli, and found key concepts that pleased her vibrant constructive senses. Thomas was here on this space ship and it was as if she had dreamed of him before, on Europa or Titan. She had seen him in her dreams before the discovery at the crash site. She hadn't killed him at that point because; why? She had seen him before in a real dream world, while alone in outer space on a probe mission. It always seemed that on probe duty dreams were more real in the vast expanse of outer space, where months can drift into years. He was at that moment, when we discovered him in the ship familiar, or surely there was no reason not to kill him at that time. She knew he was not a threat. Then there was Laura, sweet Laura, a good friend, but she did still feel that she was in love with Thomas. How could she manage to cope with the fact that they could not be together. But we will be together for years at "C.A.N." colony and that would be exciting.

Thomas was talking to Jada and trying to imagine the answer to her question, "How would I defeat "us", this space ship and what method would I use?" He spoke in feedback to Jada's question.

"Well, first I would incapacitate the Terrans if I was going to really make it easy, and that is what he did."

"So, what is the next step", Jada asked with a tone that sounded as if she was bored of the mental play that did not sting her like Nina's sharp retort would have.

"Just wait, you asked me and I am just thinking aloud," Thomas said, seeing the impatience in her retort.

"I think that he is not just chasing us but herding us. There is something else out there that he has got lined up. When two predators work in tandem, they almost always catch the deer. I think that is what we are, just a deer. Two wolves work in tandem with each other, and the pack or two lions work together for their pride to feed the cubs. I think we are in a trap and we are being herded like an antelope or a deer, right into the pack. Tell me, who did we just piss-off and almost get our heads handed to?"

Jada looked at her charts and her electronic equipment that she used to analyze and plan battle scenarios and war strategy with. The look on her face became blank and the rainbow fluctuations began to just pulsate off and on. I wondered if this emotion indicated that she was thinking or just frustrated. Jada spoke softly and I knew immediately that she was worried for my comment.

"What have I been thinking?" she asked. "This monster is smarter than we give him credit for. We were lucky on Mars when we beat him, for sure, and right now we have to wake up all those Terrans and get their asses out of those stasis units. If I have to I'll kick every one of them out of that dream they are in. They have to get up to set those flat robots into their matrix path. They can insure the primal codes are set and expanded to reach their limit of usefulness. If you are right we still might be boarded and taken captive yet. Let's first take all the advantages that we can and martial our courage to meet the entire enemy head on and not sleep through the beginning to be awakened in the middle of the cycle to be captured."

She just about ran down the hallway to where the stasis units were housing the sleeping Terrans. Even though she was able to move more or less free in a gravity field, it looked as if she was gliding on the long strides which she was taking. We reached the medical area of the spaceship where all these units were kept. The ship was larger than it seemed at first glance since the open areas housed so many unusual elements not normal for a flying vessel. Laura and I walked into the medical area a few moments after Jada.

I said to Laura, "She looks like she is worried more than usual about our condition of readiness."

She said with an uneasy tension in her voice, "I think it is what you told her about the Terrans still being in pursuit of our vessel since the time we took off at the cave entrance. Maybe it was just something she had not thought of yet, but maybe wanted to all along. She could not bring herself to realize the immediate threat that it presented."

Jada began to flip displays up and out into the head of the stasis units and each one enfolded into a clear plastic display. The colored light displays on each band that measured brain waves and electrical activity suddenly stopped pulsing. When Jada waved her hand they unfolded and returned to the mounting that housed the monitors. Briefly, remarkably their eyes began to flutter open and soon they were all stirring and moving around. The first to get up and on her feet was Nina, but she had to have help because she was still weak and confused after Jada took her by the arms and pulled her until she fell off the stasis table and clumsily onto the ship's deck. Although we did not have an actual full gravity, like Earth, she did hit very uncomfortably and yelled like something was hurt. That was how she woke up.

"Did you have to do that? I'm just not quite ready to start my recovery, but if I could just have some help to get to my feet."

I looked at her helpless there laying sprawled out on the floor and my eyes first looked at Laura and then at Nina. I went over and picked up her nude body, limp and almost unresponsive due to the long stay being immobilized in the stasis unit.

Jada said, "I thought you could recover more quickly than this. I just am sorry, Nina, but you are supposed to be so vibrant and indestructible."

Nina began to cry and said, "I am only human, but I will recover soon, but just a little more slowly than you think. I need someone to help me so I can help the others. Please, they just need a little more time and soon they will be alert and back to normal. The stasis unit is a fine instrument for recovery of trauma victims but it just has taken me completely to a new level of consciousness that I have never experienced before. Even when I was in deep space traveling for years, I didn't experience the displacement of my physical body like this. My mind feels like it is detached from my body as if I am projecting from some remote location and I can't quite locate my surroundings."

I felt so sorry for her because Jada had just pulled her onto the floor and I went over and picked her up in my arms. Laura looked so jealous but it was really unfounded. I know who I am, and I had recovered from the spell she had put on me from the beginning when I first saw her flying the space ship. She had gotten so thin that I could practically put my hands around her waist. Her nude body in my arms felt like a silken doll and she had this smell of cinnamon that just aroused me beyond belief.

Laura said almost worried, "Don't drop her tiger, she's not just some dream you're having. Jada, can't you get some clothes on her? She's giving my husband palpitations."

Jada said, "I'll try but she won't keep them on I'm afraid. She just doesn't much like them and I think she is going to take back over the ship. I know her pretty good. Give her about two days and she will be snapping orders at everybody again."

"What did she do, grow up in a tank of Jell-O or something?" Laura asked sarcastically.

"Yes, sort of," Jada said. "She grew up inside a kind of computerized bucket with most of her parental units not really caring very well for her. They shocked her whenever she didn't obey and made her wear this kind of childhood uniform and she's rebelled ever since. She is the only one that they let just be a brat because she beat them at all their games. They just played her to death until she looked forward to smashing intellects every chance she got. They would play against her and get embarrassed every time so eventually they just made her like an elder because they were so diminished intellectually. She really is an aid to our salvation, even if it seems unlikely. She has been challenged every way possible to find a solution to any war game that it is just like second nature, automatic for her to find a way to win."

Nina said very quietly, still in my arms, "Don't tell everything Jada! You just hope that we don't wind up in trouble like we always do. It seems we lost this one or don't you remember as well as I do?"

I set her on her feet and Jada put a white cape over her shoulders and around her body. It still did not cover anything except to provide comfort from the chill of being outside the stasis unit.

"Your wife seems a little uncomfortable with your being such a gentleman but such nice things have not been my experience so I am happy to be receiving any attention. I realize it makes for problems but soon, I think, we will all be just wishing for such pleasant interference with our gentle psyches. In my dreaming state I saw something very ominous and I couldn't find a way around to the other side. I think we have reached a point of impasse and will have to deal with Drakbar after he has made his initial overpowering strike. I don't know how but I think he has us sort of in a box canyon."

Jada said, "Lets go into the navigation room where we can project what I think is our final battle."

We all went into the navigation area of the captain's control room and Jada began to prepare the electronic displays for viewing. Solar charts, navigation instruments, and vector analysis for projected courses, all theoretical.

Nina looked at Jada and said, "I know what is happening and we are not going to meet the expected speed to get into position in time. If it was just him pursuing us we would have it made but, we have been fools not to think that the elders would not participate."

Jada said, "Nina, Tom thinks they are waiting for us ahead in

240

orbit around Venus. Do you think it is possible that they will participate and aid in our capture?"

Nina said, "They have to; they wouldn't have it any other way. We are loose from their control and they have to close the door. That is the way it is. We have to play it out and let the game begin. They know and we know, now so let's let them draw us in just like they want it until we can think of a way to break their trap."

Laura held up her hand and tried to get our attention. "If there is no alternative but to mix with one or the other, why can't we just fight the smallest fight? I mean, the Devil Drakbar. He is only one ship and they are probably many."

Nina looked around and then at Laura. "You are right of course, unfortunately for us but we are going to be boarded and captured. That shouldn't seem like such an acceptable alternative solution. Only one thing is different from that and it would be to face immediate annihilation from our Terran warships waiting to ambush us. What is better, death or torture and death? I am ready for either one, but it appears we must choose one."

I said with a nervous tone even to myself, "You mean we will die no matter what. I cannot accept that. You need to reconfigure your estimates and reprogram for survival."

Nina said with reluctant assurance in her voice, "I know that you lack the enhanced ability to account for all variations of this war game scenario and yours is a hopeful innocence, but I have played these strategies over and over and if there was a chance in our favor, I would proclaim it loudly right now. Tell me your plan and I will show you a counter if you want to know it. I am familiar with all of the weapons capabilities on both sides. Go ahead, I'm waiting. Tell me how you will defeat the monster. Please tell me that all of us might be saved."

I said in exasperation, "There has to be some way different that no one has thought of. There has to be a way!"

I remembered not too long ago, that Laura told us that when we had made all attempts with our scientific reasoning that she would tell us of the dream.

"Laura, it is your turn now," I said. "We are at our wits end, I think, and you said that you had a dream about something. Tell us if you please; we are all very interested and if there is some way to get us out of this mess then let us know."

"Well, let me see if I remember and you are sure that you just want to hear about only a dream, just a dream?"

Jada said, "Of course we are and it would be an honor to hear the message you have received as only you could receive it because all the others including myself are unreceptive to the phenomena. Laura you must tell us. We will all listen and form a new plan."

Nina said, "Laura, you have the ability to project a variable matrix for approximate coordinate density to verify the reliability of any new probability estimates. Let us please see your new vision and we can help to enhance the estimates to interfere with their schedule of undeniable entropy. If we could break up the forces that are closing in, we might be able to create our own energy for apposition."

Laura held a studied expression, thinking possibly of the analysis that Nina gave us.

"I know what you are saying about entropy. It means that by playing the opposing forces against each other one or the other is losing all their energy to respond because all the alternatives have been exhausted. Even if we launch all of our weapons then we still come up without turning the tide of the battle, in our favor, resulting in a stalemate. I'm going to reflect in perspective what I have seen in my dream, whether or not it ultimately is relevant or not. The dream does present this alternative that did not exist before; therefore we will break Nina's definition of entropy. It does not seem logical but I will reflect the total extent of the dream.

The dark force of Drakbar is on a direct line of collision with another dark force in the universe, and it is an older dark force. This dark force will pass only briefly, illuminating the threat to our safety for a brief period of time. I perceive by comparison of all parameters of my newly expanded reasoning that this force is celestial and not spiritual in its basic nature. There is no logical perception for the origin of the phenomena but my innate reasoning tells me that it is no coincidence that they are on a collision course. Mathematically it can not be proven but with a good time-lapsed photo-optical light detector we could prove the existence and plot the vectors of their collision."

Nina said, "I couldn't have explained it at all, but I do get the gist of what she is saying. I think it is a miniature black hole, even microscopic, that she is talking about and it should be a very fast moving or streaking one that is so small that it has been undetected by the major space based radars but yet it is a force large enough to exert great destruction for a brief period of time. It has not remained confined to any one locked position in the universe. What force loosed this anomaly cannot be measured since something that could eject a black hole is non-existent. This one, more or less breaks up existing gravitational monopolies, and for a brief moment in time and space, if there is entropy, it dissolves it because of the brief destruction of preprogrammed celestial gravitational forces. Let's look through one of our photo-optical analyzers and determine if there is any bending of light in our immediate solar system and we may be able to assert whether or not any unusual phenomenon are occurring or not."

We gathered around a device, silvery metallic in nature, with an array of exposed crystalline encased mechanisms that you could plainly see blinking off and on with rapid dashes of light movement going on inside. A remote sensing device formed an image among the circular array of crystals, making a round table surface that transformed the projection of the information across the table into a three-dimensional model of the solar system and adjoining section of the Milky Way Galaxy.

With the image beginning to form, Jada spoke first, "I will set it up so we can view the collected information on this table top model of our galaxy. Look now at the solid pictures of the images of globes and elliptical orbits in lighted visible traces. They are becoming evident in the 3-d image supported on the table, in real time, tracing the photo-optical pathways of their orbits."

You could reach out and touch the visible laser configuration translated by the photometric analyzer. Nina touched first one crystal and then another, adjusting the focus of the galaxy representation.

"If there is any anomaly in the light intensity that stands out in our solar system or our near arm of the galaxy, we have programmed the differentiation to be a dark blue line surrounded by a vortex of lighter blue and white. Jada, try to initialize the observation by opening up the large telescopic port hole on the forward nose cone bulb of the ship. I'll focus the crystalline display array while the images are being translated through the probes stationed throughout our near spiral arm."

Immediately a dusty appearance became the concentration of our interests. Like tiny clouds being revealed by sunlight through an open sunlit window. This long cloud of light dust was interspersed among millions of little pinpoints of light of many different sizes which apparently was the great Milky Way Galaxy. Then the light blue and white dust clouds began to swirl and form a vortex that seemed bent and twisted, revealing a think dark blue line streaking through the middle of the vortex.

Nina said, "There she is and it apparently is vectored to us or near us at our current speed and position. The phenomenon is real even if only for just a short time. Now, let's see if we can use the exact coordinates to find out if there are any other deflections in the light to determine where the other space ships are revealed."

The little red dots representing light observing elements or light deflecting elements began to become visible through the translation organization of light intensities. An immense armada of net attack-capable ships and droid pods appeared to be arrayed directly along our loop around the planet Venus and directly behind us at a very minimal distance was what could only be Drakbar's ship.

"Look, it coincides directly and I think we can form a degree of coordinate determination for the direct path. It goes through the rest of the loop we are in and then passes through and out into a deep space galaxy after this brief encounter. How unusual it is that it just so happens to coincide with Drakbar's path. What will it do to his ship?"

Nina made a gesture with her hand that represented a star burst. She closed her hand into a fist and then opened with a quick flip of all her fingers.

"It will vaporize into just a memory unless he jettisons before he realizes what is about to happen, but I don't think he will ever know what happened. He will hit us with that electromagnetic beam in about one more day since his approach is supposed to be concealed but for some reason we have detected him as light absorbing and he also is emitting now a beacon that is as unusual as the black hole phenomenon itself. Why would he have a beacon on?"

"Maybe he doesn't know it," Jada said. "Or, maybe someone has come to their senses and has given away his position," Nina said.

I looked at the array of crystals on the projection table, and I thought about the gesture that Nina had made. "Will we be anywhere close when this black hole hits his ship and what effect will it have on us?"

Jada said, "We will be drawn into it if we are too close and we will not be able to leave the vortex unless we are out of the near path. It will be so fast that everything will just about go unnoticed except the immediate destruction. We need to be clear when it happens. I approximate it will hit at about twelve noon in two days and the duration about .5 seconds. Drakbar will reach us in 24 hours so prepare for boarding. If we choose to fight him we will have to slow our speed so he can intercept at the right time. We will have to be captured and free ourselves or either fight and then escape capture so that we will get away from the slip stream of the black hole. It is just a brief anomaly but it is very real. I don't know how Laura could know that this thing is here but I will give her the credit for breaking the entropy. This definitely will make the difference."

I began to panic though when I heard her say that Drakbar will be here in only 24 hours.

"We must make it look like we actually did put up a stiff resistance so he will not suspect anything. But can we survive his boarding and occupation. This does not seem like a worthwhile defense, just to surrender and take what he surely is going to do to us."

Nina interrupted me and said, "We are not going to be defenseless. This ship is almost impossible to break, once we program the array of flat robots to form a group of layers around the ship. We can initialize an array of layers, like a Mandela. They will not get through the layers until the correct time has passed and then we will break off while his ship is disabled. That is the way it will happen, I hope."

Jada added, "He will think he has us in his hand but it will only be to detain him until the black orb reaches it apex and is imminent to impact with his ship. Then we can impede his drivers and escape from both the black orb and Drakbar's ship."

I looked at both of them and just could not accept the plans that they had off the cuff just hatched between the two of them.

"You both know the extent of our defenses and the capabilities of the ship's weapons but I just have a lot of doubts as to the effectiveness of an onion type defense. Am I still captain or since Nina is awake, do I have to relinquish all of my leadership to her, to make the decisions?"

Nina twirled her long hair around in her hand and at the same time she smiled a beguiling smile that gave me a clue to her answer.

"You are still captain and we all take your orders. Jada,--you too, right? Tell him what is going to happen."   Jada hesitated a little but finally after a moment she said, "Yes, we are going to be hit again by the electromagnetic beam and Nina may not recover, but I hope I have fixed some of the problems. Tell us why you don't agree with our plan?"

I thought for a moment about the intentions of the enemy and what the chief objective was that made him the animal that he was.

"Why did he want what he wanted and what was it that gave him his drive to destroy us? I think Drakbar has a sure fire plan to overcome us or he would not pursue us so directly in the face of our strong defense. He knows we have such a strong force because you have defeated and humiliated him so many times before. He apparently has another weapon that he has not shown you. Why else would he pursue so directly?"

Nina was not as adamant as I thought she would be but she was so confident in her knowledge of her weapons that I hated to disagree with her, but I felt that something was just not right with the choices that we had to make.

"I want to give us a little insurance policy that will possibly make us a way of escape that will guarantee us some degree of superiority. If we lose all of our electrical or plasma power, we'll need it. I would like all of your Mandela of defense designs placed from the central command of the flat robots emitted in parallel not in sequence from all of the string. That means the directive is programmed from each robot separately and not just tied from each in a string of

246

directives. Each one should be its own command center to operate separately with closed identity."

Jada said enthusiastically, "Yes we can do it with a little extra time and each one will be thinking individually, running on an independent program, without asking for instructions from its weakened position if fired upon. They can be hard wired to exist in a closed loop, free of our command, monitoring each other, and yet still be able to recognize orders given at a later time."

Nina looked a little tired from all of the conversation and strategy planning that we had done and she asked us to help her to lay down for a few minutes. We took her to the pilot's cabin and left her in the sleeping compartment.

Jada said, "She will get better, but I don't know what will happen if and when she gets hit another time. It's going to take more time than I thought. Let's get all the rest of the crew up right now."

She took strides like she was a determined woman and that she was. Laura and I accompanied her and as she opened each stasis hutch, she allowed each crew member the privilege of a little more time for recovery than she gave Nina. Not one of them was pulled unceremoniously onto the floor but each one was massaged and helped in the proper method. All the crew was quickly brought up to date on to the immediacy of getting acclimated in time for the next attack. Bispo managed to recover just fine and she was now functioning normally without the help of Nina's control and command directive.

Drakbar was now closing in and Max, the actual authority on the Mandela of flat robots, had brought together all my thoughts and wishes as captain of the ship. Each one was programmed to act independently of the other. We had formed all together into a ship's conference and Nina began to give us a final briefing as the total conflict preparedness began to come together for our impending battle.

"Whether or not the black hole will miraculously zoom through and take out our enemy, I want everyone to know that I have called this assembly because the enemy is almost upon us. We have the Mandela laid out and it has very many layers surrounding the ship and with some very good luck we can hold our ground and wear down Drakbar's initial thrust into our weapons and take out enough of his forward robots to get a clear shot at some vital area of his ship. We are more or less fighting a classical battle with our infantry in the field, space, and our foot soldiers are the flat robots. They are in a formal battle group that will fight against his robots that he will surely field against us. Our big guns will continuously fire destruction at his emplacements. Hopefully, finally, we will be able to fire a disabling shot to some area that will immobilize his ship and leave him stranded, for good this time."

Max spoke up and although he had just barely recovered, he was able to communicate eloquently and gave Nina the stability and steadiness that she had been lacking after her initial recovery.

"Friends, crew members, and Captain Thomas, there is no need for alarm. We have, as Laura pointed out, chosen to fight the lesser of the two conflicts. Hopefully and I believe completely that we will be victorious and at the same time be able to elude the armada that is waiting for us en-route to Mars. My fellow elders of Terra have made a very bad decision to side with this monster against us and we will have to deal with them later. They themselves have chosen their own fate and will ultimately achieve a grim consequence as a final tribute to their having been so adamant as to destroy others that did not believe the way they believed. We will not pass through the realm of spiritual examination without a heart-felt desire and support for all things good and reasonable. When plasma reaches its heat apex and is ejected through the focus of a magnetic resonator, the virtual achievement of technology culminates in realty that cannot be blinded and so too will a small black orb enter our realm of truth but our light will not be extinguished. We will first fight our way with the tools we have and then we will step out of the way and let God finish it and finish it he will. Drakbar will be vaporized when the little streaking black hole makes impact with his ship. Actually his ship will be drawn before impact and the two forces will result in a cataclysmic change; the result I am not sure of. Matter is not destroyed but changed so dramatically that only a true physicist could search for the answer. The black hole just sort of scoops things up and separates them into their basic building blocks that they started out as, packs them away and they simply don't exist in the form that they used to. Well, that seems to be all of our briefing.

We launch in about five minutes so everyone to battle stations and let's now defer to our Captain, Mr. Thomas. You are the one we look to now for a safe and secure future."

I was not yet a real captain. That I knew, because it was a sum total of experiences and reproofs that found a person, a leader, making the right decisions because you knew them by heart.

The one thing I knew was that I could be useful and that was my calling right now and I thought, "Let's keep one of these Terrans shielded this time somehow so that they could be directing this melee when the fan hits the vegetables."

I cleared my throat and spoke with all the authority that I could muster, "As your captain I am commanding that a pod unit with one Terran, I don't care who is to be put into a shielded area so that I may be able to use their expertise when Drakbar hits us with that electromagnetic beam. Maybe it will be different this time and it will knock everyone out including me. We all are made up of groups of electrical signals which gets their direction and wire from electrochemical interchanges. Quick, who is it going to be?"

Nina spoke up sharply and gave the order, "Bispo, please do as the Captain says. Go to the stasis unit, get a loader, put it into an escape pod, get in and stand by for my command to eject."

"Fine," I said. "Maybe it is better just to leave the ship again as I did the first time."

Nina said, "The escape pod is shielded and will not be penetrated. Carry on board a flat robot programmed with all the primal codes, in case the Mandela is knocked out in force. Max will assist you in the immediate flash program."

Bispo spoke up in a faint voice, "I can not link up, and I don't have the connection or the ability to take on coded packets of electrons."

Nina said, "That's why I want you because you don't know how or won't do it. Just direct the battle from a distance when or if we get toasted. I'm not connected to you anymore and for a good reason.

Bispo, you know the way that I think and how I would fight the battle. You know me that good. Get in the pod, now! Good luck, sis."

"OK, OK, I'll do it. I'm ready, let's go Max. You help me to program the little black one that doesn't have the big armor. I want to carry on my little flat communicator that we made with the shell around it."

They hurried off and we proceeded to launch charges against an unseen enemy. Laura and I got together in the command center while Nina was in the pilot chair. Jada was with Nina, and Lita and Nella were all punching in codes and arranging trajectories of looped ribbons of arced charges. Broad loops began to emit their bright beacons from the rear cowlings of the ship's back flanged wings. They began to hit targets that became visible only when explosions were lighting upon the targets that were vaporized.

The Mandela of flat robots began their staccato of individualized canon shot. Pellets of igneous volatile material hit other bodies that preceded Drakbar on his initial thrust. He definitely had a bunch of killer robots in front of him that were his infantry. They fired away and our own Mandela took hundreds of hits, damaging and rendering many of them probably useless. Still they fired on because there was no closed loop connection that kept the ring together. Each one reprogrammed separately so that they had only one thing on their plate; fire at will, and all of them kept functioning beautifully not needing a timely monitor and still kept firing even when most of the electronics were destroyed.

Drakbar began to throw all of his forces into the fight. Unable to approach without being seen, he went completely berserk since his cloak had been useless.

"Someone has betrayed me and I want that unit decapitated immediately! We were supposed to be running silent and out of phase. Send someone to the communicator pod and get it back in order. We'll need it if we do not get through the outer ring that they have established around their ship. Without our sensitive equipment we'll just be shooting into the dark and with no real way to go out of phase, they will just wait us out and keep us on the outer circle of their Mandela. Somehow, someone got to the communicator pod and disrupted the signals and crossed them up so that we are giving off a beacon. First Lieutenant, see that your engineering crew get the electronics in the pod fixed, now! Don't come back until it's working.

If you want to live long enough to see that group of females that you keep in your quarters then you'll fix it or be the first to go out the airlock."

Drakbar knew that he would be less one officer but he didn't care. Anger had taken his reason.

Alicia was in the captain's sleeping quarters waiting for him to return and suddenly over the inter-chamber speakers she heard the call, "All personnel report by number to the interrogation chamber for purging. No exceptions are permitted. Leave your battle station and do not make detours in your direct route to the interrogation room or you will be executed immediately. Numbers one through one hundred are to report now!"

Alicia knew that she would not hold up under a purge. That meant that they would get the information through whatever means necessary. Her monitor would show that she was not observable during the time period missing out of her control sequence. She would be cooked immediately when she entered the interrogation chamber. As soon as the computer got to her number it would put up a red flag that she had been unaccounted for at that time and Drakbar would question her relentlessly and tear her limb from limb just to see if it would make her confess. She had to escape and there was only one way. The little escape pod was almost unknown to just about all of the crew. Maybe the computer knew, but maybe not. She didn't think it had one of those identity patches, but she would just have to try.

She quickly proceeded en-route to the purge but suddenly halfway down the hallway she veered off to the trash duct and as she opened the hatch, the air began to pull her tunic into the ejection bin. She jumped up and in and then managed to close the hatch behind her with a quick assisted turn. Down and down she was pulled and then at the last moment just before she passed a seemingly unnoticeable dark opening, she caught the edge and swung her nimble body into the hole that almost no individual but her knew existed. Maybe there used to be some lone element of rebellion that was long dead, maybe executed but she discovered this hiding place right by herself. One day she had done exactly the same thing in another purge, when she did not want to be questioned and it worked by God then, and it worked again this time.

Once into the little niche, she fumbled around and found a long forgotten electric torch that still had juice left from the last time she was here. She found what she had been looking for; a small, light weight silicon based ceramic tube that had a sealable opening that was just big enough to fit her body into. She picked it up and noted that it looked like a small Kayak except that it was more rounded. She easily picked it up because of the hybrid-elemental makeup of its composites and pulled it over to the opening. It was just big enough to get it positioned before the next big rush of air flowed through the giant exhaust tube. On a regular basis the giant space ship would eject its waste material into the deep and since there were so many thousands of occupants it was a necessary process to throw out the trash. Since the ship no longer was running on out of phase status, the ejections would be just routine during the continual assault which could last a very long time it appeared. She balanced the pod perfectly on the edge of the lip of the hole which had a quite adequate flange to allow her to center the entrance hole directly over the flange and crawl inside. Aligning her body along the interior support ridge of the pod allowed her to control the center of gravity and balance perfectly on the flange.

Soon she would be drawn into the main tube like a cork, popping out of a bottle and down, down and out into the main ejection port of the waste disposal. They wouldn't find her in a million years and there was no way they could trace her after she ejected. She was prepared to stay in here for a year if she had to. There was actually a sensor pack in the nose cone and a small propulsion system, even if it had limited ability, in the aft section that gave her considerable thrust since there was no resistance in space once the action of guidance was elected. The direction could be chosen by the remote camera angle in the nose cone. All she had to do was look in the direction it gave her once she had selected the mode of propulsion. The swivel of a small nozzle allowed instant direct thrust. A single light weight canister of tightly compressed air gave her all of the thrust to align her with a closely passing freighter, she hoped, somewhere in the near future. Maybe the ship that they were attacking would evade or wear this bastard down and pick her up, maybe. She had waited for almost an hour now. They would be looking everywhere and going back over the tapes of the monitor. They'll find her if they don't eject trash out the chute soon.

Drakbar had sworn he would have his revenge.

"This little bitch Alicia had to be the one who messed up his approach to the Terran renegade, Nina."

He thought, "The guards had brought back the results of the inspection from communicator pod and she had messed up so many wiring harnesses that none of it could be salvaged for use. When the power surged, and demand for out of phase sequence erupted, the resulting crossed currents had fused all circuits and they were now a dead condor that could not smell a dead brontosaurus in the heat of a stinking prehistoric Earth-time summer. How could he have let this little bitch Alicia fool him into thinking she was his little slave? She had planned this all along."

The time sequence passed and a routine hiss of escaping putrid air rushed through the bowels of the Martian attack cruiser. Alicia braced herself as the escape pod was sucked into the maelstrom of refuse that was headed for final repository and then for an instance they paused while the holding tank filled. She remembered how she made her way frantically crawling and scratching into a hatchway that appeared out of no where when she had passed this way the first time and then the second and third. Every time was the same as she stocked up the little life boat and waited until the right time was revealed. Now there would not be anymore but this last; then just the deep, deep vastness of outer space. Time seemed to stand suspended until it began, the surge, thrusting out and into the exit. She was spit out and drifting now among the trash and debris. Through the remote view cam she looked out into the visor of the helmet at a spinning black and grey universe.

Each time the pod rotated and tumbled she saw the ship getting farther and farther away.

"After I get far enough away I'll activate the gyroscopes and start on my new course. I think I'll just cross into the path of this bastard and wait, until they kill him and maybe they'll pick me up."

After she activated the remote guidance she started the little gyro that enabled her to stop the tumbling and set on an almost flawless course, leading her straight into the pursuing trajectory that she just left while on the big ship. Locking all gyros and setting the sights of a small laser beacon she lined it up on the exhaust of Drakbar's ship so that it would go unnoticed and once the laser was emitted she fired just one jet exhaust of the compressed air jet and then she was gliding dead on course. After a one second burst she began to shut down all systems except the small coil that would keep her from freezing in the sub-zero temperature of space. Now she would just incubate and hope until she thought it was time to light the little beacon. If she didn't wait long enough Drakbar would return and pick her up.

She said under her breath, "Hopefully, the rebel forces he was attacking would win. God help all of us if they don't."

She put the long plastic tube into her mouth whereby she would receive both water and semi-liquid nutrition. With just a brief turn of the valve she could change from one to the other. The small unit would allow her to survive for months if employed correctly, using and recycling the liquids over and over, having little refuse but still someone long ago had taken into account every conceivable problem of long term space flight. The space ship even looked like a pod from some long ago plant from Mars. Now Mars was just a memory of some older civilization burrowed into the ground like the insect hives of long ago. The correct name for the insect-like behavior of grouping together in hives is so appropriate for the Martian people. On the space ship she had just left they crawled over and among each other as if they were not even human, just insect-like. Maybe it was just a natural phenomenon and had always existed that way.

"Now I'm going to sleep until my proximity alarm goes off and then I will put on my beacon and steer for a cargo vessel. If this sleep doesn't kill me I'll fight again soon."

The battle was getting hotter and hotter and igneous volatile pellets hit our Mandela but never the ship. The array of layers of robots and pod ships kept us shielded away from the cannon blasts coming from Drakbar's heavy cruiser. He was hopefully using up his arms and ammunition that I am sure he thought he had plenty of, but nothing was completely inexhaustible. Soon, we would turn the tide of battle and begin to make direct hits on his ship.

Nina said, looking at the monitors, "We will be through his robots shortly and we'll begin to make hits directly on his ship's armor which means that we have turned this thrust of his into a suicide strike. Right now he is feeling very foolish to attack us directly. He will have to break off his attack soon or risk total self destruction."

Drakbar was very disturbed that his battle strategy had not gone as he had planned. His ship now began to vibrate from the direct hits he was beginning to receive. His robot shields had all but been annihilated and any moment now he would be compromised and his ship's hull would be totally breached.

"Fire the weapon now or we will all die!" The booster phaser began to loop charge upon charge of electromagnetic pulses into a cylindrical cannon that would concentrate the pulse so much so that it would change the actual brain wave pattern of all on board the vessel that he was firing at.

Nina, and Tom and the others felt the sticky air of the charge just before it hit. Bispo had gotten away. Shot out like a cannon through the blackness of space, long before Drakbar's ship began to resonate its firing sequence.

She and her still alive flat robot would be all that was left of the current arrangement of electrons flowing through human electrolytic solutions on board the space ship, "Cleopatra", her Probe I ship, named for Nina's strain of DNA. The space ship experienced a genuine shock that reverberated all throughout the metal skin and it heaved a sigh of surrender as all of the systems shut down to prevent an overload. All of the electronic formations would be scrambled to the point that none of the inhabitants would recognize each other for an extended period of time.

"Fire!" Drakbar screamed at his second in command as he bellowed out his order and the flow of pulse reverberated throughout his own ship so much so that the radar went off line and the looped charge of the gravity field went also off line for a brief minute. Everything floated temporarily up into the middle of the control room from lack of gravity but his main concern was the concentrated focus of the intense electromagnetic pulse. Thin willowy purple clouds flowed instantaneously through the void of space and wave after wave first hit the space droids carefully placed in a Mandela of rings to protect Nina's ship, then the ship itself was rocked by the hammering of double layered phased clouds of interrupter electrons.

On board Nina's ship it was as if every living and electronic article was vomiting short term memory. Not a single creature electronically wired or electrochemical was spared. Machinery and computer and living organisms just ejected all of their viable working systems.

The last thought that Nina produced as a human was, "Oh, God, Tom was right. I hope Bispo can understand what is happening and cut into the power source before everyone is finished."

Upon that last breath, all of the crew had collapsed and was floating freely in a ship with no gravity and no life support. Only the air inside that had been made recently in the last few minutes by the oxygen generators was going to be left for the crew to breathe.

Drakbar activated his tractor beam and pulled alongside the ship "Cleo", encapsulated the entrance, and forced open the electronic jaws of the hatchway. Upon boarding Nina's ship, he gave orders to restore gravity and life support.

"I want to be there when we first board," he said to his troopers. "Don't touch any one until I am there to watch."

The hatches popped as they opened and the foul air of Drakbar's ship came rushing into the finely filtered air of the "Cleo". He set his jack boots onto the deck of Nina's ship and gave howl after howl of ridiculous laughter at his finally realized conquest.

"Bring everyone in the ship to me, now! Strip them and cut off all of their body hair. I don't want anything to interfere with the placement and insertion of the electrodes. That one and the other one, there; bring them over here in front of me, now!"

One of the little ghouls picked up Jada and the tingle from her static skin began to crackle as he touched her.

"This one is still electrified; see the little sparks!" Drakbar screamed, "You fool! That's Jada, the Martian witch! She is the cause of all my suffering! Start with her. I'll open her up myself. Get her prepared and the other one with her is the clone bitch Nina. Bring them both in front of me! Now!"

I was dazed and completely oblivious to the goings on except vague hazy figures pulling me and dragging me around. I had some recognition of danger, only I was helpless to get my limbs to respond. There was a metallic taste in my mouth and it seemed that my tear ducts had just opened and run off, as well as my sinus cavities.

"Maybe that was what short circuited the brain; the taking out of the connections that gave electricity the path, electrochemical short circuit. That had to be how he did it but I was only thinking and not responding. What good is a thinking brain without the leverage of a working extension? Recording, viewing, barely conscious, but not registering a workable action, I was just dreaming in the worst sense. I, Thomas Jefferson Coltrane command my body to respond! Nothing happened. I remember how the brain unit robot had shown us a picture of his capture and I was seeing this big black mechanical monster, snaking its way, unfolding its servo mechanisms. I was frozen in time, beyond reach of any help, waiting my fate and thinking of Laura. Where was Laura?"

I moved my eyes only just merely a millimeter. Yes, God has given me one minuscule of hope.

Deep in space, beyond the eyes of the marauder gun ships of Drakbar which was preoccupied with his spoils of war, was Bispo. She was busy locking all the mechanisms into place and observing the black ship as it approached and maneuvered to the hatch door of Nina's ship. She knew what had happened, felt the empathetic shock of still being a part of the crew and knew what they must be enduring while they waited for her to respond. She was very aware that she alone stood in the path directly to intercept and destroy her enemy. Terran training had left her scarred from their direct forced fed teaching methods that discouraged her free will thinking. She was more of a rebel than Nina thought that she was, though. When she was alone in her thoughts, free to imagine and feel the quiet rush of visual images, she would ride the solar flares and surge outward and away into space. Now she was free thinking too and she wanted to focus all her abilities on saving her friends and sisters.

"My sisters are not from the same egg but we were tormented as a group together and we stay together through thick and thin. They programmed us that way and we are mind melded together and fight to the death for each other. Now I will still my mind to receive the primal codes that Max prepared me for. I will find a dark place for their address and I will gain the range finder for locking in the coordinates of my spatial awareness.

Mind, mind, mind, cannot you bend just a little and find a way to store the primal codes? I am a warrior. I am a warrior. I will not turn away from the pain."

At that moment it could have been any other, but she chose that moment to send the charges of electrically coded packets directly into her forebrain from the hyper-magnetron console of the miniature pilot's cabin. At first she felt like she was in control and taking charge by charge and locking and finding locations within a unique place that fit the category of the information packets. She knew the stinging darts were only little pieces of information placing themselves into avenues, waiting for her to guide them. As if looking inward into her thoughts could by itself take command of these little bees, she focused and tried but began to fail miserably to push them into a known place. They needed to go into some learned controlling point, into a pivotal centroid of her reasoning brain. Only if she could recognize the character of the coded packets could she set them in motion to authorize the application. Pain was beginning to replace the nausea and the thoughts were backing up and causing her to lose her equilibrium.

I realized that I had gained a little control and could turn my eyes just a little. It was just enough to see Laura sitting very still on the floor next to me. In the distance I could see that Drakbar had both Nina and Jada together and one of the black mechanical spiders had Jada lifted up in front of him and he was having his minions to take all the hair from her in preparation for what ungodly treatment I could only imagine from seeing the copies of the captured brain unit. The servo-mechanisms of the giant black spider robot began to spin its arms and enfolded the bladed separators as the spike began to descend to pierce the vertebra of Jada. She would be the first to be separated before becoming only an electrical battery guidance mechanism for one of a legion of brain units.

Drakbar screamed and ranted and raved his nauseous words of final victory.

In space at the edge of the solar system the little black orb streaked through, cutting a black gash into all the cosmic motions that it touched, then again everything was as it was before, almost. This event was waiting to happen but for Laura, Nina, and Jada and the others it would occur only after their demise, if so left to their fate.

However, Laura was also thinking of their fate if they all waited for the death of Drakbar. They too would be extinguished from the light of the world, if they waited too long to act. She and she alone had to act in order to change their destiny.

"Tom is to my left and the others are in front of me. It is Jada and Nina and something terrible is about to happen."

Laura was thinking and she was not incapacitated like Nina had been. There was a strong connection between her and the spirit of spirits that rules and permeates all things. Some people have a closer relationship than others and that is a very real relationship. Laura saw out of the corner of her eye the nightmarish spider robots and something else immediately caught her attention. It was the ribbon knife that Nina had given her. She only recognized it because she had become so familiar with it so recently. The shape, the feel of it in her hand, and the power that it wielded, tempted her as she knew that there could be no greater force within this room except for Nina, and the knife together. She just simply stood up calmly, walked on bare feet soundlessly to the pile of clothes, uniforms and personal items taken from the crew and piled up together on a platform. Picking up the light weight weapon she almost felt the blue light of the arced charge being displayed in front of her cutting through the cobwebs of her mind. As much as she felt the need and the desire to open the arc, she did not, but suddenly knew that this was the time to give the weapon and its coded primal signature back to Nina. It would be so amusing to watch her at work with the ultimate weapon as an extension of her now incapacitated psyche.

Drakbar began to scream like he had been pierced through the heart with the same needle spike that was poised to be inserted into the vertebra of Jada.

Laura, holding the ribbon knife by her side and walking like she did not have any emergency went directly over to Nina and before the ribbon knife left her hand already the arc was lit.

Spontaneous transference occurred between Laura and Nina. The ribbon knife itself was programmed with a mental primal code that was itself part of the person who wielded it. If the knife was exchanged, the primal code went with it. It was an electrical identity code that could only be transferred via the direct frontal lobe ethereal charge migration. Whatever happened was only the results of which I observed first hand. Although being as I was in an incapacitated state, I saw directly through clear eyes and lucid brain. Nina had the ribbon knife and what I saw before did not make any comparison as to the powers and extent to which it could be operated. The ribbon arc appeared to grow not only in diameter but had the appearance of wide spikes, like a feather boa that I have seen some women in the burlesque to adorn themselves with. She seemed to immediately fill with an unnatural light and vitality. The ribbon arc, a plasmic light, began to make individual vortexes or swirls outside the loop and to decimate all objects metallic as well as biological. Nina began, after a jump into wide stance, a methodical annihilation that could only be said to be merciful to the already dead.

Drakbar was taken aback and did not give any orders in his new vehement tone, only to retreat himself to a more safe location, away from what was sure death to any and all. All who came under the focus of her wrath died. Only because of the immediate danger to Jada, Nina did not pay close attention to Drakbar, but yet I'm sure she was not waiting for an anomaly of nature to call an end to his venomous bite.

Like rolling thunder, the sounds of metal spider servos being chewed into liquid, separated, little pieces, reverberated throughout the cargo bay where we had been brought for enslavement or execution. Instead of our execution, it was our lair that they had wandered into, oblivious of their unknown fate. Now on the frightened expressions I saw only blank amazed stares as Drakbar's elite personal guards stood frozen, wishing that their legs could take them out of the path of the ribbon blade. The looped charged blade left only gray charred fabric where once were living beings, now suspended with weapons drawn, but yet because of fear, they were incapable of executing the command to fire.

The once poised metal servo used to puncture the vertebrae and then attach electrodes before severing the appendages was reduced to molten liquid garbage, crackling and popping as the hydraulic functions began to fade into disuse.

As intensely severe was the feeling of fear in proximity to danger and death and then fading away, it was replaced equally overwhelmingly by my feeling of security and safety since every enemy had now either fled or died.

We could not let our sense of safety kill us before the completion of a surety of safe condition. I began to crawl ever so slowly toward the airlock control, because when Drakbar left us he would pull away and leave a vacuum, sending us into the void of space. Abandoning his hope for enslavement meant that he would retain control of his situation by bombardment from a distance. My hand just managed to reach the bar as I pulled down and heard the hatch close and secure its locking mechanism as the rush of tornadic air was expelled from the open hatch on the other side. I felt like I was in a total collapse and could not even speak because of the void in the electrochemical makeup of our brains. With total energy being now expended, all of us collapsed on the deck to await our fate. Being safe was always only a temporary condition at best and changed with the ebb and flow of the spirit of the universe. So accustomed had I become to knowing that I was about to die, I did not quite believe it could be any other way.

Bispo was now absorbing and moving the electronic signature of the primal codes to their appropriate reasoning centroid location. Not waiting entirely for the process of calculating and organizing of appropriate packets as they emerged, she locked into position the various flat robot signals that had been knocked off line and she restored their individual signals one by one on a massive scale. They lit up the board by the hundreds and at the designed sequence interval they recognized their enemy and again set up a barrage of cannon and laser fire that made direct numerous hits on all accompanying servo droids and Drakbar's ship itself. Bispo had loaded the primal codes back into the battalion and she did it so expertly that it was as if Nina herself had folded the signals. She knew precisely and exactly the way that Nina wanted it and what to achieve.

The master chess player had reached out almost beyond the grave and kicked Drakbar's butt and he feared greatly within himself again as it had been long ago when he was inside the Martian canals when he came up against Nina before. She out maneuvered him every time resorting to every unorthodox strategy that he could not even imagine.

He had been fooled, he thought, "Nina was split and she must have a twin in a droid pod. That had to be it. How could the Mandela be back on line so soon? We had just stopped them cold and we had them. We had them in our hand!"

Now he was racing to get out of range of the flat robot Mandela that encircled Nina's ship and was expelling him from their proximity, like a wild dog being driven out of the pack by biting at his heels.

He began to search now for Bispo, because as a strategist he knew that Nina had her limitations and would have needed time to recover even though she was too dangerous to approach. She could not organize everything so soon since she had been so incapacitated. She had to have another sentry in place beyond her ship to bring the Mandela back on line so soon. A droid pod, beyond his apparent reach had to be waiting, unnoticed, except its signal had to be spiking among the pods in the Mandela.

"Load four cannons and fire on that signal that is communicating with the Mandela. Lock onto that signal! Lock on, lock on, lock on, and tell me when you have it!"

"We have it now, sir. We have it, there, out beyond the border of the Mandela."

Drakbar screamed out his order as if he had found his vengeance on an invisible Nina, "Fire!"

Four shrouded igneous pellets fired at Bispo's little pod ship and she saw it coming just in time to maneuver out of the way of three but the fourth knocked out her signal to the Mandela. It didn't matter though thanks to Tom's preparedness and his order as captain pilot to reprogram all droid flat robots to act independently after the first primal code is sent.

"We made a direct hit and the signal has stopped although the ring is still attacking us. Take her again, fire again! Fire four pellets more and follow them with laser fire. Take her again and this time, make sure that solo pod is destroyed!"

Alicia now had drifted directly into the path of Drakbar's fleeing ship and her proximity alarm had gone off waking her from her temporary sleep. She knew who it was and let out a long slow breath.

"Well, I don't want to give him a chance to oppress anyone else, and I certainly will not give him a chance to capture me. I would just like to see if this little pod has a good weapon. I'm going to fire at his after burner and see if I can disable his power supply."

Looking into the remote camera attached to the nose cone, she managed to locate a trajectory from the firing code and entered the numbers into the onboard computer. The weapon was a very old one but had a good range and speed with enough explosive power to rip the power supply into a million tiny pieces. A swoosh was heard as the rockets ignited. They had first separated into a solo unit away from the tiny ship so as not to cause severe reverse force to the ship movement.

A sparkling luminous cloud was seen as Drakbar's power unit became enveloped in a massive fire. He panicked and could not even imagine where the weapon came from. The ship only had enough time to separate the main cabin and life support from the power units so that all inhabitants would not be incinerated.

Making this last self defensive decision left him marooned in the vast ocean of space without any means of propulsion. On a time clock his ship now began counting the days, hours, and minutes of useable energy left that was stored in their battery system. They began to make preparations for survival and Drakbar and his personal guards began to get the life pods ready for to leave the crew and the support people marooned while they launched another strike against Nina.

They equipped their pod ships this time with harpoon launch

rockets so that they could puncture the hull of Nina's ship and finish the ship after they took away the power supply and applied it to their now marooned space ship. Drakbar was continuing to be confident, even in the light of his recent defeat at the hand of only one cloned female, which he hated more now than his own Martian enemy, Jada.

He boasted as he began to watch the loading of his strike force. "We'll get them this time for sure, but first we secure their power supply and couple it directly to our own ship. Let it be known, that if any man among you fail me this time, I will kill all of you. Now back to the fight and this time, no prisoners. You kill everything in that ship or you don't return."

They all knew their place in the line of succession and all of them had the feeling that it would not matter so much what Captain Pilot Drakbar did because none of their other section had returned the first time either. They felt the old fear that it was not now so much what Drakbar would do, but what their enemy would do if they did not fight and win. They were fighting for their lives but just exactly what motivated them was unknown other than promises of riches and plunder and vengeance or just retribution, but now fear of the enemy more than anything else, even Drakbar.

Back on Nina's space ship we had begun to collect our faculties but we were still incapacitated and unable to fight. Nina, having spent her last energy, could only barely move and was lying still on the floor to try and recover from her ordeal.

I tried to focus my abilities to concentrate my energy on the right thing to do, which was for all of us to survive and reach a stable plateau of security. We were far away from that place in time and any minute we could be attacked by enemy forces. I had an immediate urge to just move, to do anything; to do-yes, just something. I moved my legs and I began to take small steps and to recover my psyche from the shock of the death ray that we had just been hit with. It was death to the reasoning ability, not the body, and the end result was a failure of reaction to oppression and then death from inaction. He will come back. I know he will come back and attack us again. I began to scream in a voice that I finally found.

"Get up! Get up! Everyone, we have to get back our reasoning ability, our reaction response."

Nina got up again and began to stumble in the direction of the gangway to the remote control center. The console was a direct link throughout the ship that enabled her to control all defenses and weapons without actually going to the pilot's control room.

She said in a low voice, "Tom, I am going to target sweep all craft approaching our ship, and try to build something up of our defense Mandela. It appears that we have some of it still firing as evidenced by feed back from Bispo, but Drakbar may still get through our shield if he comes back. We should not have let him go but I was distracted by the other attackers. I am not stunned like I was before, and I am slowly regaining my strength. What do you recommend in the way of our defenses? You are familiar now with all of our weapons and you have the right to make the initial decision. You are still captain and will remain so."

I thought long and hard about why they made me captain and how I could best benefit the group. "What exactly was Drakbar going to do since we did let him escape, narrowly? I think he will not try again for capture or if he does we will lose. Maybe he will execute detonation from a distance and make sure we are neutralized. Maybe the Terrans will have some firing platform already primed in the vicinity and they will fire on us. Wouldn't it be better to face the Martian council and get all the cooperation and form a coalition? What are we to do? How do we coordinate a check mate?"

I told everyone, "Nina, Jada, - how would it sound if we just abandoned the ship altogether for now or left it under the control of the flat robot system. We can use the shuttles, make a multiple split exit, regroup on Mars and get a council review of the charges against Drakbar. Don't we need to have the Martian council on our side? Isn't it just a little more complicated than just shooting it out but with a monster, and maybe he will win next time. It looks like we are too weak after the fight to claim a decisive victory. Might not we lose again even if we win? He can lose ten to our one and still exhaust all our firepower." Nina walked over to Jada and whispered in her ear something. Then Jada, turned to Nina and did the same.

Nina spoke in a broken voice that seemed like it was somehow defeated but still defiant and yet she sounded like she just couldn't believe we would not fight it out. "Jada says you are right and I am finding it difficult to accept your council and command but, I will let Jada speak the truth."

Jada, now recovered from her near death experience said slowly, "She knows you are right again and her pride and stubbornness would have gotten her killed this time. We will leave our defensive system on high and if we repel them and survive the blast then we will have a ship still but if we lose then we will still win because we have our lives and have just lost a ship. Let's get to the shuttles.

Nina, arm all robots for a full defense and let's get going while we can. We'll split up into four different shuttles and meet at these coordinates in the asteroid belt. If he follows then we will again form on Mars and try to make it back to the ship. If he does not follow then we will still return if the primal codes make a good enough impression and hold the defenses. We can return and catch him between the proverbial mountain and the ocean."

We quickly set defenses on the big ship to repel all invaders and each of us rapidly exited the ship. We noticed Drakbar's ship was dead on target with a small plume of arc gas preceding his fleet assault. The plume would not only be a disruptive force but would penetrate all defensive shields except those hardened against the electromagnetic fields it generated. He did not have the energy to totally knock out our systems. I held my confidence to a high level and our little ships would sustain very little damage. We split up and formed a wide angle of departure to elude Drakbar's sensitive electronic equipment, which could track as many as fifty different signatures. We expelled a wide assortment of donut like emissions from an onboard wave projection generator and the ripples that Drakbar's sensitive equipment was picking up was just too much to interpret for him and he did not have time to reconfigure before we were at a safe distance away. From the small radar picture built into the little console I determined that our ship did repel the attackers and was moving off to the predetermined rendezvous with the assault fleet in pursuit. They would continue their assault until our ship's defenses had killed all of them. We just couldn't take the chance that it was possible to maintain life support or lose it, under so viscous an attack even though our robot system could win. Eventually they will deplete all their attack units and our ship would have to be refitted with new life support systems, or at the least patched temporarily.

Jada, Laura, and I were in one small pod together. Nina, Max, and Bispo had teamed up and Lita, and Nella were in the fourth pod. We were all now en-route for Mars Central Command. Soon I would be the first Earthman, other than Terran, to set foot on Mars. Finally all my dreams were going to be a reality. What was it going to be like? I began to question Jada without stopping. I just did not have enough answers and enough information. Earth space science did not really know what Mars was really like. We thought that the air was so thin that it could not support life but there it was underground, and we never realized that there was abundant life such that we never imagined. Now we were on approach to enter a world which no one had ever seen before from Earth except maybe Nina. Through a long struggle we rounded the tip of the asteroid belt and there was our ship "Cleo" and around her was a hundred droid pods floating in geometric formation and each one had its beacon light flashing. It looked like a Christmas tree all lit up. We had been cruising through space in a small torpedo-like escape shuttle and it was a welcome sight to see that the ship was still intact. A beautiful shape it was too and Nina, I'm sure had a part in the design and modeling of it. Curious about the origin of such a lethal model and how it could continue to fight on its own without human instructions, I asked the only real space explorer I knew and that was Jada. We had been crammed together like sardines for a month and we had become close friends and confidants all.

I asked Jada, "What exactly are the origins of this ship anyway, Jada? Is it from Mars, Terra, or some other place?"

Jada moved a little from the boredom of lying prone for a month although in a weightless environment.

"It is believe it or not, "other", being neither from Mars or Earth. Does that fact give you a small problem?"

I didn't anticipate her answer and felt completely confident that it was from Mars.

"Actually I thought it was Martian but I flew from Earth on it and it seemed so other worldly."

Jada put her hand against my head and slightly moved it upward. This sign of affection my wife did not like I'm sure but we had to entertain each other's minds in the escape capsule for such a long time and we allowed things to happen that would not normally have happened. There was space for one to maneuver and exercise forward into the main bubble, but that meant that the other two would be lying prone and always close, almost touching each other. I will not deny that being face to face stomach to stomach and foot to foot with any real female, Martian or no Martian, did really excite me. To be with Jada had become an accepted part of my marriage to Laura. Even though we often touched each other and sometimes affectionately, we never made the mistake of going too far. It was a constant challenge but I thought it better that Jada be with us instead of Nina.

Jada's hair had begun to grow back and sparkle all through the trip and she looked like she was as fresh as the day she started even though the two of us, Laura and I were mentally void of any ideas. We were unable to bodily stand up. I'm sure of it that if we were on Earth, we would just not have the strength after such a long time of inactivity. Jada made the most unusual exercises when she was in the bubble. She rotated her body and arms and legs like she was a human gyroscope and would actually spin around and around. I don't know how she did it but she said that the spinning would help her to be able to walk when she reached gravity again. I dreamed often about Jada on the trip and I would go so far as to say that she controlled the dreams to a certain extent, floating in and out of my mind's eye almost at will and visited my mind constantly. She had some kind of power or some astral lobe to her brain that allowed her to move in and out at free will. Laura spoke up and sounded a little like she was timid to ask the question but she proceeded anyway.

"I know you have been feeling affectionate toward my husband on this trip, Jada. We had sort of a special circumstance but please try not to show emotion in public toward Tom. Can you respect that wish of mine?"

Jada's slight rainbow aura dimmed a little bit and she acted like she was hurt that Laura would ask.

"I'm sorry. I know I have been a little forward since we have

268

been confined in this small space ship. On Mars we actually go to cells prepared this way in order to be closer to one another. Please do not take offense. When we arrive on Mars, it will be similar and you will meet other Martians in cells but it will not happen like it has happened here. Our relationship is very special and I will not take advantage of your compassion. You must realize though that we knew each other before you came aboard the ship and that we had only platonic affection for one another."

Laura almost cut her response short, but was quite feminine in her outlook.

"Yes, I know. Tom told me that you had loving feelings for each other and that you both decided to stop the wildfire that had engulfed the two of you in an emotional down spiral. If you can not break the emotional bond that you have with Tom, then at least surely you can refrain from open affection. I know that you love him, but I love him too, and he loves me. Just do not go so far as to try and displace the love and affection that we feel for each other. Any kiss or hug should be very short and contain no feelings of endearment or any kind of references to a future partnership. Is that understood from both of you?"

After that little speech, Laura went forward to exercise and Jada kissed me on the cheek and just smiled some secret smile that would endear a painter as if one from a Mona Lisa would. Then, I returned her kiss and made a complete release into the dreams of her mind, spinning out of control like I was a bright comet streaking across the void of space going nowhere but getting farther into the void. We just held each other momentarily because we were friends, forced into the close proximity of togetherness in the escape pod.

Then Laura rejoined us and asked Jada to return to the main bubble. Laura and I kissed and released our emotions into each other's arms.

Laura said in small quiet voice, "Friends we are now and always will be."

It was as if it was understood that it was not a break up but the beginning of a long love and friendship. Jada and I were not sexual partners and would never be, but we would always be friends and Laura was all right with the idea that we hugged like two loved ones and not like mating animals. This would be hard for anyone on the outside of the circle to see but after all, she was Martian and Nina was Terran. They were not exactly from Earth but not exactly alien either.

Soon, Jada came back and said to us both, "The ship design came from a "C.A.N." and that's where we are going after we get the ship back up and running. Nina just found one and copied it. Looks pretty good for a copy, doesn't it. Before we leave this asteroid belt you will see one of the best copies of the original "C.A.N." that we have in the solar system. Nina made it from one she found near the edge of the solar system. The original is still there and working beautifully, with a rare group of completely extinct flora and fauna. There are animals at that "C.A.N." that were on Earth and Mars before any fossilized history can be found. It is a complete biosphere and has all sorts of plant and animal life. Nina thinks that there are even dinosaurs in the deep interiors. You will not even believe it but there are small monolithic formations also that resemble some of the oldest on Earth and Mars.

One thing that we discovered on the "C.A.N." was an interesting code that generated progressive formula derivatives and catalyzed the solutions into growing analytical phenomenon. By catalyst I mean a situational numerical and algebraic upheaval that in effect, produces a generator of various solutions that continues to grow exponentially. They generate replicas of themselves and then regenerate and mass replicate infinitely or almost infinitely. Do you understand what I am saying?"

Jada looked at both of us and we just looked at each other. I spoke but only to begin again the explanation for fear of being totally ignored by her in future conversations.

"I think you are trying to explain somewhat to us that this is a part of the Martian circular math that as I understand it formulates logic to be more exact because it always has the same beginning and the same end."

Jada gave me a little frown and said, "That is not exactly what I mean. What I'm talking about is a generator, a reproducer, a replicator of replicants. That means that it is more or less a formula for a living organism, a mathematical being that grows continuously until it terminates at possibly infinity, but I haven't found the termination point yet, so it can not be estimated. Maybe it is the formula for the can itself as a biosphere and a maker of biospheres. In other words, they reproduce themselves and are strung all over the universe at different places just growing and replicating infinitely. Does that just blow your mind or not?"

I just scratched my head and asked Jada, "This new "C.A.N." that Nina has built. Did she make it or did it just after all sort of replicate itself? Really, how could she build it unless she had a huge work force and shuttles to carry the raw materials from Earth or Mars to this place?

Jada said, "She didn't make it. She just began the first primary replicating process by starting the beginning initialization. She found a turning crystal that effectively began the coded sequence once she provided the light path into the first facet. Each facet of the crystal then began moving another turning crystal until the machine had begun to perform specific duties laid out in the coded program. I watched the beginning phase of the "C.A.N." when she first brought the crystallizing metallic orb to the asteroid near where it rests to this day and it was truly amazing to watch the beginning phase. You can look now at the "C.A.N." but it is only moving through a dormant stage that is until someone else activates the primal codes of yet another crystalline orb. There is one ready at this moment, but it should not be activated in the same local since it would interfere with the duties of the present "C.A.N.".

It was apparently built by an automated society which enjoyed life and endeared it to be spread all over the universe and protected it also. There are defensive weapons inside and outside the "C.A.N.'s which have to be deactivated. It was no great mystery to reproduce all the same technology that each unit possessed. It was just basic wiring and basic robotics but just organized and planned very well. I think the main advantage technology has is in a well thought out plan. It all seems to be represented in a basic formula."

I couldn't help but imagine what the mathematical basics to the formula could be. Pythagorean or Socratic; which would the idea take after and how would the logic follow to make the generator. That was the key to the success of an automated construction. It could be such a very long formula or just one short one that makes a rotationally

271

generated momentum to be able to create a continuity.

Jada spoke almost in a staccato accent as if she wanted to imprint in our brains the basics of the formula.

"Listen to me now and I will tell you the very basics of the idea", she said. "It is just that, a simple truth, or a geometry that incorporates algebra, calculus, physics, and chemistry. It envelopes all the major scientific principles and it follows even the oldest of mathematicians who thought that geometry best represented mathematics in its most abstract form. From only one light source begins the reaction in the generator and soon the real problem is how energy can drive the machine to begin the replication process. All throughout history the problem has not been the amount of energy, but how to direct it and get the most return for the least investment. By channeling the plasma beams directly into the turning crystal it gave more than enough of an energy source to begin the generator. Then it transforms the light gathering device into a hyper productive mode which breaks down the light plasma beam into separate wave lengths and the photons further into separate and distinct little packets of light particles. The particles then begin to accelerate with an additional boost from a loop that comes back into the circle to add the extra catalyst. As the light begins to turn the crystal it gathers the particles and then redirects the beam outward as the catalyst wave pushes the refined wave length into a hyper active state of activity thus making the energy that is needed to power the higher technological marvel of infinite replication. Just the initial light from the plasma arc sets in motion the elaborate process, and all there is to do is get the crystal orb in contact with a large size asteroid so it can feed off the raw materials. It is truly an amazing process to watch but it will blind you as if you looked directly into the arc. The crystal orb begins cutting into the asteroid to make the building blocks of the "C.A.N.".

The Martians have similar automated machines that set up hive cultures on other planets and burrow into the soil with boring pods and then lover the saucer ship gradually into the soil while building layers of hive chambers around it, eventually totally concealing the space ship from all observers. This crystal orb is a formula in and of itself. It is a totally encapsulated preprogrammed phenomenon that does exactly what it was patterned to do and then it follows the program and then quits and goes into sleep mode or hibernation mode while the "C.A.N." incubates life for years and years.

I'll show you the reservoir of crystal orbs that is contained in this 'C.A.N.'. It is as if they were seed pods ready to be distributed from one asteroid to another to form a string of life bases all across the universe. Since already the generators are there, someone needs only to string them out and they could hop scotch from one galaxy to the next with a life station at each point in the universe never needing a planet to live on just a "C.A.N.".

Jada seemed so excited about the new base that we were going to and I'll admit that it sounded like a great plan being executed by some higher civilization but just what civilization? I had already been completely astounded by Terran and Martian civilizations, not really knowing yet the true scope of the two new ones I had just discovered. Already I was being presented with a third unknown entity. What could have happened to the people who invented the seed pod cases? They had to be somewhere unless they had totally left their home planet and were now from the universe itself. Had they lived from one generation to the next for millions of years jumping across the universe and leaving seed pods in their wake like Johnny Appleseed from old America? I would love to see the actual formula that Jada says is the basis for this technology. Maybe she will demonstrate it at the new meeting point after she again meets up with Nina.

I think I hear the proximity warning now, and I hope it is Nina and the others. The proximity warning means that we will finally be able to board the ship "Cleo" and that is a really anticipated event if it was intact as Jada seems to think it is. We have been living next to each other in close quarters and even though it is nice to be so close to two women that I love, it would feel great to be separated for some time and have some privacy and quiet.

Chapter 15. **Alicia Joins The Crew**

The alarm we were hearing was from the main ship "Cleo" and also the other escape pods but very distinctly a lone signal from farther away began to chime in also and then suddenly on a hailing frequency we heard this small quiet voice.

"I am Alicia from the rogue ship of Drakbar from Mars Central Command. I seek asylum from the barbarian and also I saved all of your lives, so you owe me. I am the one who put the torpedo into his power supply. I've been in this pod for a month and I need R&R. Anyone copy? I'm friendly. I repeat. I am a friendly. Please do not fire."

Jada had corralled all the escape pods into a fighting force by this time as I had advised her to "circle the wagons" if attacked and we were yet a good ways off from the ship "Cleo". It worked perfectly and we were all pointed outward and now we had another to add to the group.

"What is your name again intruder? Identify yourself and how you came to follow us?" I asked.

"My name is Alicia Alexova and I come from the Drakbar ship. I escaped alone," she said.

"Come into our circle, Alicia. You are welcome to come in and be examined. We are proceeding on to the ship "Cleo", if there is anything left except holes from Drakbar's missiles. I think he fired harpoon missiles into the life support systems so that he could kill us from a distance, being too chicken to try and board us again," I said.

Something about her seemed incredibly familiar and I could not exactly place her right away and then I thought about the mind unit we captured from Drakbar's droid that had tried to pierce our hull, back so long ago when we first encountered his minions of slave droids.

"We will proceed to the ship "Cleo", but before you are allowed to enter our group you must be searched and interrogated. That is just normal procedure when dealing with someone who has been with such a monster as Drakbar."

Alicia said, "I will gladly comply with all of your precautions and would expect no less."

We entered the proximity of the ship "Cleo" and all of the flat robots turned to train their weapons on us and were ready to fire.

"Bispo was now mind melded into the primal codes of the flat robots. She sent a signal to stand down and now it was Bispo who had linked completely with the machine intelligence. She would have been the last to do so willingly but out of necessity she was forced to be a part of that existence for our safety. It was as if she had become Nina and could communicate mentally with all the robotic systems.

Nina monitored all the procedures since she still had the primal code signature configured into her cerebrum and could not erase the memory. Although she could override Bispo, she did not and just maintained her status as observer and verifier.

She matched the signature and Bispo's brain wave and allowed all to proceed without interruption.

Nina notified everyone, "I am going to first enter the cargo bay of the ship to see if there are any robot plants on board and when I fix the holes in the hull breach then I will notify everyone else to proceed on to the cargo bay. This may take a day and in the mean time everyone just relax. It will be well worth the wait."

It was not that long afterward that we had to wait, a day as she said, and everyone proceeded into the cargo bay except Alicia. We all entered and disembarked from the torpedo shaped escape pods and prepared ourselves, getting our feet back under us and restoring gravity to the ship and later, complete life support. Then we invited Alicia to join us into the cargo bay. Everyone was acclimated now to the new comfort zone of the large space ship and Alicia entered into the cargo bay. Her pod settled down onto the floor of the bay and we waited for her to exit her pod. She did so with a very slow procedure and just managed to open the hatch and crawl free from the ship with very weak legs to be able to stand up very feebly. She was indeed the same young girl that we saw in Professor Tremble's memory vision. She had that long black hair that I remember, and was very thin from the month in the pod. She immediately started to disrobe after her exit according to Nina's instructions. They were the same instructions that I remember receiving after we crashed the space ship transport in the desert on Earth, after I had stowed away on the cargo transport. In the knife fight I had received a bug that was imbedded in my clothing that gave away location of the ship which resulted in a missile being fired into the bottom of the cargo ship.

Alicia began to take off all of her coverings including her shoes and it was easy for her to just step out of the jump suit. I could see why that Drakbar had chosen her and spared her beautiful body. I wanted to at least make her feel welcome, since I was in her position once also so very long ago. I took her hand and she stepped forward into the light of the cargo bay. Really, she was a beautiful woman with such a thin shapely figure and I enjoyed every minute of revenge that I had against Drakbar to have seized his beautiful queen and set her free. I took her into my arms and just embraced her. She seemed to collapse into my arms and I picked her up and took her to her very own cabin equipped with all the necessary familiarities to begin a needed rest, just like all the others of the crew. As I laid her down on her bed she grabbed my hand and would not let go. I was very glad to stay with her since she was such a beautiful young woman. She told me that it was the first time she really felt safe and that she wanted me to feel how her heart was beating in rhythm with mine. I resisted her temptations properly but she grabbed my hand again and pulled me to her. I found myself falling off balance and I was on top of her but quickly I recovered my knees under myself.

She said to me very quiet and almost in a whisper, "I wouldn't normally allow any man to be so close to me , but I have been taken by force so many times that this time I wanted to choose to be close willingly because I am doing the choosing myself, and not anyone else. It is of my own free will."

I said to her very calmly, as soon as I swallowed and retrieved my little bit of respectability that I had left, "I am going to cover you and give you your privacy. I thought it would be better that I bring you to the cabin since now you know you are free and I'll admit your beauty is just as intoxicating to me as the rest of this female crew is if not more. You are not a slave of anyone any more and will not be forced to do anything. Only respect the others here and cooperate with us and you are welcome as far as I am concerned to stay with us. It is up to the rest of the crew to say how they feel, though. There is a uniform in the closet if you choose to dress again.

Welcome, and we will talk again soon, and you can tell us how you fell into Drakbar's hands, later when you feel stronger."

I left her then, and Nina came over to talk to her. "We will eject all of your clothing into space but we will keep your space pod. Where did you get such an antique space ship? It looks like the ones we have except from an older universe from years ago."

Alicia spoke in a high pitched voice as she seemed very tired, "Yes I discovered it hidden in a secret chamber that someone else had made, not Drakbar. It had been outfitted some years ago but maybe the Martian who put it there died or was killed and it was abandoned."

Nina spoke up excitedly, "It is not Martian. It is Terran and made on Earth. We made it for sure and how did it get on Drakbar's ship? That is a great mystery. In some way he must have captured a pod or maybe it drifted into the trash dump at the jettison port by mistake."

Alicia said, "Yes, it was lodged in an alcove of the ejection tube. I discovered it when I flushed myself to keep from being caught one day. I thought it better to be thrown into space than to be caught by Drakbar. He would have killed me if he knew I was only acting like I was enslaved. He never once knew. He always thought that I had been clipped. They enter a thin blade at the base of the brain and clip the stem so that there is no rebellion. I have been planning my escape ever since I discovered the pod. I wasn't sure of what it was but I thought that it was at least space worthy."

Nina looked at Jada and they both looked at the space pod. Nina spoke up, "I lost a sister at a fight that we had on Mars many years ago and we had our ship shot out of space. We escaped in pods just like this one, but my sister, Lynn, did not make it away from the pursuit of Drakbar.

Now, maybe I see how she escaped by getting mixed into his ejection refuse and then powering past the garbage into his ejection tube. She must have lodged her pod in a refuse cowling and entered the main population crew to obtain food. Was the pod equipped or totally barren?"

Alicia was getting sleepy and then she just mumbled, "There was, -not much food on board and, I had to bring my own provisions a day at a time."

Nina said, "Sleep now and we will talk later when you are more rested. We will fight again soon but now I cannot destroy his ship if my sister is aboard. This makes him more difficult to fight but thanks to your escape we know where she is, and we can take the fight back to him."

Jada spoke up, "Nina, you don't even know any of this for sure. If he has her, then she could be a brain unit by now and not feel anything. He clips the brain stem. You heard what she said. Why was she, Alicia, not taken?"

Nina said sadly, "Alicia has a scar from childhood, she said, and he thought she had already been clipped and decentralized. The ones they don't make brain units out of they clip the stem and insert a silicon sheathe that can be adjusted as far as to how much electron activity gets from the brain to the other parts of the body. For some they just load it with a half charge so that everything is at a controlled speed. She may not even recognize me if I find her. They probably have given her a set program that she has been regenerated to perform and she will never exert true will any more except certain set standards that have been given to her to perform. I'm not giving up though, and if I find her I could wake up the primal codes and take over like I did with Bispo. She has got to be there. I know she is."

Nina walked away and went up toward the captain's cabin with Max in tow. I could hear them talking at the end of the gangway. Max was saying that she could broadcast a primal code search wave into the ship if they got close enough and wake her up even if the brain stem was cut. Such a fantastic degree of mental activity I had never even imagined could exist between human beings, was just simply amazing to me. This must be on the order of some astral wave projection that I did not even begin to understand like a sixth sense and beyond all borders of electromagnetic wave energy that I ever studied in school.

Nina said to Max, "Lynn told me that you could broadcast an alpha wave and a theta wave together and form a sympathetic harmony. This combined wave could align with an existing pattern within a primal code rhythm and allow you to sense the same equilibrium or sequence that another Terran, who was trained to be cognizant, could sense at the same time together. She told me that, herself, and now I have had some strange dreams that there was a missing door yet to be opened and I could not open it because someone was holding it closed on the other side."

Nina and Max disappeared together and went off to Nina's cabin. She had been a completely different person since she had become reunited with Max and was not the wild tempestuous tormenting child like she used to be. She had become a grown woman with adult reasoning like a genuinely mature person and I felt now would be a good time to talk to her and Max together.

As I entered their cabin between them was a hologram of a sphere that the two were holding suspended face to face. Upon the outer sphere were symbols and words and Egyptian like characters that represented pictograms of various ideas that the two apparently were sharing together. It was like a circular movie etched into the bubble memory that was mutual between the two of them. I surprised them when I entered and the bubble sphere disappeared between them.

"How do you do that? How do you make that sphere between the two of you?"

Nina said, "It's nothing and you could do the same with Laura if you wanted to. It's no mystery or telepathy or any such thing. It's just an electronic game that is played between two people, usually two lovers. It's a laser hologram that each person displays and adds different pieces that represent ideas or pictures that we are thinking about. All the various ideas are already mapped to the hologram and each person touches a symbol that will be projected for the other to see. It gets more and more personal and intimate as the game is played. Looks like we project it in our minds but it's just an electronic illusion."

I marveled at the ingenuity of the invention.

"So, how do you propose to make contact with this sister that you think you have hidden on Drakbar's ship?"   Nina said, "That's different. There are receptors, artificial, inlaid into the memories of Terrans that are mapped into the electron activity of the brain waves. They have been etched electronically and are part of the brain. You can't get rid of them. Just like Laura, who now has the key to the ribbon knife inlaid into her memory and cannot forget it. If I gave her the ribbon knife back, she could use it with automatic range finding ability that would be precise to the millimeter. I'm sorry but I have given her a gift and it cannot be taken back or erased and that is life. It's not wiring or silicon or artificial materials. The primal code is different from the inlaid etching though. The coded charge of electrical current has to be willed into its place whereas the simple packet of electrons of the ribbon knife, automatically find their identity. It always is a part of that person and keeps a signature even after it has left the brain from one person to another. I have it now spinning in my brain but Laura could take it back if I gave it to her willingly of necessity. It is not alive but is part of a creation that is stable and will not alter the state of its being.

That sounds technical and a bit metaphysical but it is neither, just pure science and elemental physics.

You wanted to ask me something Tom?"

"Yes," I said, a bit taken aback by her now cool intellectual air that did not harm her personality, only gave her more appeal. "I want to be relieved as captain since you have recovered fully from the electromagnetic assault because I feel you are more adept at guiding the space ship and know the weapons system and can pilot the ship where-as I do not really know what is the proper course or workings of this incredible space ship."

Nina paused a moment and then said matter-of-factly, "No can do, Tom, old friend. You have proven your usefulness and now you must lead us through the mine field of our own clumsy arrogance and pitiful performance in the face of danger and our own sure death and defeat if not for your insight. You just continue to captain and I will pilot the ship on its set course to the "C.A.N.". Don't feel too burdened because Max is here to help you if you have any questions. - --Right Max?"

Max just looked at Nina and smiled and said, "Truly we are at a loss to express our gratitude for the guidance when all was lost. You are exactly right darling and he has kept us alive so far, so just ask, Tom, anything. If there is anything I can do to help you with your duties as captain, just ask."

Nina just reached over and with her hand on my cheek, she kissed me gently on the lips and said, "Thanks dear, and now we want to get back to our game and close the door on the way out."

They returned the sphere back to its place, floating into and in front of each others face. They began to add endearments such as darling, beautiful, handsome, lovely and words of all descriptions and then symbols that I did not understand and even visions of the beach, and palm trees. I left and closed the door as I heard waves begin to splash on the sea shore. I decided right then that if they were so determined for me to be captain, then I would be pilot as well and would make them teach me how to pilot and use the star charts to navigate. I just felt stupid to have the responsibility without even knowing how to navigate or land the thing if I had to or even to be able to deploy the weapons systems. I was bound and determined to know it all if they were going to force me to make life or death decisions and only have the knowledge of a novice.

I found Jada and explained to her how I was feeling and decided that my first and foremost goal as captain would be to learn exactly how to fly this space craft and how to land it into a gravity field planet.

Jada explained, "Come with me and we will begin right now and don't feel so desperate. To fly the ship is not so difficult. The hard part is making the right decisions when you think you know something and then you find out all your information is not correct. The captain still has to decide even if he thinks he might make a bad decision."

We went on to the pilot cabin and I sat down at the controls. Jada told me what each little control was for. The basic system was a touch screen display that gave digital read out for each degree of and the angle of initialization. Jada spoke in a smooth professional tone of voice that let me know she was very concerned that I learn with the least amount of difficulty.

"The ship's power plant has four directional thrusters that swivel to provide turning capability as well as the thrust of the main nozzle. You don't usually have to turn the main nozzle but it can be done if necessary. Each nozzle has a directional thrust as well as a power degree of thrust, and you get a read-out on each element. Just touch screen for directional and then push in directly for selecting amount of thrust. Go ahead and try it. Each circle can be touched to translate direction and power of thrust. The forward thrusters are for direction also, so just try it and you can see the pitch of the ship on this icon as it changes direction. We will slow to just docking speed here to allow you to learn to maneuver the ship first and then we will learn how to vector according to gravity influence on the trajectory of the ship. This is not very hard and you can learn it and perform the calculations with the help of the flat robot system and they will translate the flight plan to see exactly how and what the elements of the flight plan result in. If it is too steep in a descent then they will correct it to within allowable limits to bring the ship back into viability. That means they will not let you burn up on reentry so you just get somewhere in the neighborhood and they will auto-correct your direction and angle of descent. Now just practice the directional thruster to turn the ship and you will learn how to move it from side to side."

I practiced all morning until I could thread the big thing through the eye of a needle and practiced the thruster as well as offensive and defensive maneuvers as far as taking the ship into an area for viable retaliation if we are fired upon. Jada and Nina both showed me how to verbalize commands to the flat robots and use a portable disk to touch control commands linked to the ships computer system that gave me access to a total control of the ship, even when I was not in the pilot's cabin. I acquainted myself totally with all aspects of the ship and even became familiar with the process of electronic signature even though they would not allow me to be a receptor of the signature process. I studied what properties and extent it took and how to make the ship respond to my controls.

Nina was still there watching us and observing and she could still override the controls and take the ship by force with just a projection of an electrostatic charge coded to the primal signature and aligned with the ship's receptors. I don't know if it was a good thing or a bad thing but I felt relieved a little that she could take over if I needed her. She put her confidence in me to help them and I also had a lot of confidence in her and Jada and the whole crew. It was an orchestrated event, war, and it did not seem that it should be that way but everyone I thought, should be responsible for a certain job in case we were attacked. Everyone, almost all the crew could in fact perform all of the jobs individually, and now even I could perform the same duties in regard to ship's weapons and navigation as well. We were a very versatile crew but still to be assigned one duty was the best in an orchestrated defense and counterattack. If Drakbar came after us again we would be ready at first contact and not wait for the electromagnetic charge to disable us. We were going to defend and counterattack at first sign, first contact, and with a very different approach since Nina had already said that she did not want to destroy Drakbar's ship if her sister Lynn, was aboard. Now that I was able to pilot and navigate the ship, Nina was going to be the lone point thrust and try to board the ship and take back Lynn in one of the life pods. She made the decision, not me, to do this.

We had met all together in the planning room and she told the crew of her plan.

"I'm going to try and get close enough to the ship to broadcast the primal code and see if Lynn still can receive. Max is going with me for protection and we are going to bring back Lynn. While I am out in the perimeter you will defend the ship and Tom will pilot and navigate with all of your help, of course. It's going to be tricky but I don't think that Drakbar will be expecting us. Alicia has been very helpful in mapping out the ship and I think I know exactly where we can find her. Without your help, Alicia, it would not have been possible to even plan this rescue."

Alicia spoke up a little timidly but seemed willing to express how she felt.

"I know you saw some of the brain units and actually defeated and captured one but it does not compare to what you will see on his ship. I just feel sorry for you if you get caught. He will relish in your torture and of your friends. Are you sure you will not reconsider to actually go back to this sure death that awaits you?"

Max began to take a more active roll now that Nina had recovered from her ordeal and spoke with some hesitation but he was sure to do what Nina wanted to.

"Nina will not listen to me but if she insists, I will give my life for her and her sister and protect them both to the death."

Nina was just too sure of herself and I did not know what it was but I think she had some secret weapon that she was not telling us about.

Nina spoke, "I am not afraid of that devil and he will not keep my sister on that ship another day. I'll bring her back, and soon; just watch me. The black orb is coming for Drakbar and I want to be close to him when it takes him so I can watch his destruction."

"Nina," I said, "That tiny black hole is going to take everything with it, and not just his ship. It probably has an effective destructive cone of up to one hundred miles even if it is so tiny. It will deform everything. Are you sure this ship is not in its path?"

Nina responded, "Yes, you are all secure. The cone will pass within ten thousand miles of this ship and no closer. We will go in the same ship that Alicia came in to make sure he accepts our signature. He knows that she is in his area and will be looking for her. He matched the signal when she hit his power supply and will identify our frequency and engine plume. That is our invitation into the ship and when we enter the loading dock we will in effect disappear from his radar and in that moment will already have left the pod. I intend to capture his escape ship and Lynn and return to the "Cleo" after I have seen him disintegrate."

I know she had something else that she was not telling us besides that she was going to leave the pod when it entered the dock or that the black hole was streaking on target to Drakbar's ship so I asked Jada.

"What does she have that I don't know about? She seems too confident to just go head to head with that maniac and not have some special weapon."

Jada looked to me a little funny and I just raised my eyebrows and waited for her to answer.

"She's going to get into his ship the same way that you got into hers. She just borrowed your camouflage that is all. She just borrowed it. You told her that you would help in any way and she thought that you would not mind."

I didn't know that she knew that I even had it. I thought I was being so secretive all this time and was keeping it for some emergency, but if she knew how to use it I guess she deserves a chance to go and get her sister.

"It's alright, I don't mind. I was just keeping it a secret, I thought."

Jada looked out the port window at Nina and Max as they disappeared into the blackness of a starlit space and said, "I hope they will come back safe. Even if they have the camouflage it will not be easy."

"No," I said. "It will not be, because the belt only illuminates the area around the person who is wearing it. It just bends the light by slightly altering it with ultra sonic motion and it will not cover two people so they will both be in danger if they don't use it properly. I hope they have practiced enough."

Chapter 16. **Invasion Terran Style**

Nina and Max were close together again lying in the escape pod made for only one person but that was the way they liked it and they could not have been happier. Nina thought that she shouldn't have begun to have a companion so late in her adult life but if she had chosen someone earlier, then she would not have spent so many years as a probe captain out in the far reaches of space and then also she would not have met Max. It was because of her solo exploits that she achieved recognition and caught the eye of Max. He was her superior and elder mentor. He taught her how to fight hand to hand combat and also was the tactician who advised her on attack and defense with the new space ship. She discovered the "C.A.N." beyond the limit of the solar system in the outer reaches at the edge and brought back secrets that enhanced the space program. The elders still did not want to explore space when they had the new secrets of the plasma torch hyper drive and slowed down research and initialization of the fleet of new ships that would propel them far ahead of the Martians. Jada had been a Godsend and the best friend ever except for Max. Now he knew that she was the one who made the discoveries that propelled the Terrans far ahead of all other cultures even more far ahead that they already were.

Max thought about Nina and decided that he would take her before the council of elders after he had consolidated his power and make her the center piece of his new scientific council. She knew more about the new "C.A.N."s than anyone and there is no reason that she could not rule over some of those old tired elders that knew only oppression and put fear in the hearts of the women warriors. They should serve together with the men in council since they had fought years of wars in the dust of Mars with not even one thank you or any recognition. Nina had trained her regiments with excellent results and had fought numerous battles with this Drakbar and had come out the winner every time and no thanks to the elder council who had partnered with the barbarian against her. Now Drakbar and the elder council would feel his wrath as well as Nina's. He was going to unleash the primal codes into the electromagnetic system that would backlash into Drakbar's own troops. They were going to get the biggest surprise when their own weapons folded back into their origin. It would be felt all the way back to Terra itself because he knew that the origin had to be Terra Prime. They were the only ones that had a weapon like that. Certainly it did not come from Mars. He did not want to let Nina know right now but when she let the release go they would get a chance to fight hand to hand with the demon Drakbar before the primal code reaches the back loop to Terra where the origin of the electro-magnetron code began. Only the elder council could give the code for Drakbar to unleash his weapon. They would not trust Drakbar to hold that knowledge alone so when his signal and his alone made it to the back loop on Terra Prime, the partnership would be cut short between the renegade elders. Drakbar would no longer have the elder Terrans helping him to negate Nina's true power. She would be wielding that ribbon knife like a sling blade in the high grasses of some wild meadow. He would cover her and at the same time take his ribbon knife and make the blood of the Martian barbarians run deep and red. If there were Terrans aboard helping him like he suspected; their traitor blood would fill the walls of space ship. Truly this was going to be a battle for all Terrans to remember when Max and Nina cleansed the Martian ship and saved the home council from the true contamination of traitors. They were now fast approaching the zone where they left Drakbar disabled and soon he would pick up their signature and send out his fighters to escort them to the loading dock. The fighter pods were there where Nina said they would be, actually towing the large cruiser since his power had been blown out and there was no way he would just abandon the ship with all his collection of brain units and slaves aboard.

Drakbar was thinking and going over all of his alternatives since he had been tricked into a firefight with just an empty ship. He had expended almost his entire stockpile of missiles trying to defeat a ship that did not need life support. He had gotten in a few harpoon missiles and was positive that the hull was breached. Why did he have to just keep engaging the ship's robots who apparently could now reprogram and fire independently even if their pathway was broken with electromagnetic pulses? It was clear that their ship was even damaged and unable to communicate. Still it fired on and on and decimated his own fleet of robots so that he could not engage or pursue any more.

Drakbar now had second thoughts about leaving for Mars in just the life pods since it would not look good to be without his image, his battle ship. He would pull it near the Martian gravity well and send the pods in to bring back power units so he could descend into Mars gravity with all his troops. He might even be attacked once he landed if he did not have the troop strength to enforce his will on the hives of Mars. He had them obeying his orders but that would not last long without force and he knew that very well.

What he would not give to get that wench Alicia back! He had been almost sure he had broken her will, after all, she had the scars from cortex slice and graft, and he saw personally where the sharp needle had punctured her spinal chord. How could she have just betrayed his electronic signal? When he got her back he would examine that spinal tap and see for sure if there really was a silicon connection or not. How could they have misaligned the connection? He would personally supervise the realignment and administer severe punishment if his medical units were responsible for the malfunction. She looked so much like his old love that Jada had enraged him into killing. He would have her back, eventually, he thought, eventually.

A voice came on the captain's speaker and said, "Captain Drakbar, there is a signature approaching our five hundred kilometer net and it appears to be the life pod that hit our power supply and left our ship defenseless in the attack from the rebel forces from Terra and Mars Colony Prime."

Drakbar seemed elated as if his whole life had turned now to have some meaning and purpose. He could not wait to get her back. He would make the insertion this time himself to make sure the needle went all the way in and made a separation. He would teach her a lesson this time and as soon as he broke her spirit he would kill her slowly little by little as the electrochemical fluid drained drop by drop from her brain, until she could not so much as close her eyes without direct stimulation. She would never sleep again until her hypothalamus had dissolved from his electromagnetic pulses.

"Get the harpoon ready as soon as we get close enough and let the two escorts bring her into the docking bay. I want to see her when she begins to beg me to insert the needle properly. Bring the hydraulics and the medical robot to the loading dock. We'll do it right there as soon as she crawls out of the pod"

Nina and Max got out of the pod before it even entered the dock. They were attached to the actual cowlings of the pod when the harpoon hit the ship to reel it into the docking bay. Nina had the camouflage ready but did not activate it because she was afraid it would envelope part of the pod and that would give them away more so than if they just stayed close to the ship.

At the first opportunity they left the ship and floated with compressed air jets to the opposite end of the docking bay. Drakbar had his medical robotics ready but was disappointed when he could not find anything at all in the pod. Nina and Max skirted the edge of the docking bay and doubled back around the labyrinth of the space ship. Alicia had provided a very complete and detailed map which the two reinforced with double layering into their memories. They knew every turn and even every hiding place that Alicia told them about. They even knew where the traitors were being kept and catered to, in the executive suites of the ship.

Max told Nina, "First we go and take care of Drakbar and his personal guards and then we'll go to the executive suite and get the jump on those traitorous Terran elites who think a big gold account can give them peace of mind and control over their destiny. They don't know it but their destiny has arrived and it is not going to be a pleasant paradise but a troubled end to their miserable existence."

They stepped lightly into the passageways and make quick time in the light ship's gravity induced from layering of gyroscopic electromagnetic fields, a technology stolen from Terran sciences that the traitors no doubt gave to Drakbar. Soon they had emerged into the docking bay entrance and back-lit in front of them was Drakbar and about twenty of his close personal guards brought from Mars Central to insure he did not lose his authority among his slaves and conscripted soldiers. The first blow came from Max when he sliced cleanly through the long steel blade carried by the guardians like modern day samurai, meant to look like the real threat that they presented to the regiment of conscripted soldiers. The guard pulled his weapon out of his scabbard and the long steel blade that he was so used to waving around in front of the fearful soldiers was now just a short stub that did not have any useful purpose. As soon as he looked at Max and then went for his laser rifle, he was caught off guard by something that he did not see at all. Nina was fully camouflaged and the only sight his eyes beheld was his own blood seeping from the legs that had been cut out from under him by the ribbon knife that was only felt but never seen. The team work that preceded the slaughter was uncanny and resembled two lions working together like a shadow and a ghost. One would distract while the other one cut off the prey before he could recognize the danger. Only Drakbar smelled the danger before the first ten fell from evisceration and he did not want to issue an order since he knew it would be useless in the face of such force. He only knew that Nina was too close for him to be able to breathe properly and he had barely escaped her destructive force once and he did not like the results of losing a forty man regiment of his hardest warriors. Now his elite guard had been taken in less time than the last conflict which he had been observing from a distance.

This time Nina had him in her sight and did not want to lose him but he managed to push one of the elite guardsmen close to him in front of her making her stumble and fall but he did not even see this happen since he was running as fast as he could in the light gravity so that he slipped himself on the blood that was now spreading across the slick floor of the loading dock and he sprawled head first into the broken and twisted bodies of the elite guard that now were not so elite but subdued as in the quiet horrified expressions that he was confronted with as he looked face to face into the mire on the floor. He had a sickening feeling that this time he would not escape and he drew his laser rifle and was shooting randomly and hitting his own guards when he spied the open cargo door. He lunged into the door way and it closed automatically behind him and Nina did not quite make it to the door before it slammed shut, locking and pressurizing the mechanism so that she could not open it even if she cut into the hardened steel alloy. Anger flooded her face and she was almost brought to tears because she could not intercept the barbarian.

In the darkness and void of space a small envelope began to form with characteristics of a cone folded into the void, pulling strong gravity wells into the backwash of its passing.

Drakbar crawled and even was sobbing uncontrollably at his near death and close escape and then as he began to gather himself he began to think that he would somehow find a way to accomplish his revenge on this demon bitch of a woman and get even with her and he knew just how he would do it.

He stumbled to the control panel and began making entries in order to begin the count down for self destruct of the entire vessel. He thought that he could manage to escape into the life pod which had been waiting at his orders just to serve as his last resort. He would get free of the ship before it exploded, killing finally his adversary and vehement pursuer who would not let him rule as he should. She would suffer the final solution that would leave him in complete control.

Mad as he was, he still was coherent enough to start the final destruction sequence and launch the life pod.

He thought that all the years preparing for his conquest of Mars and the Galaxy had been wasted by this clone woman, this hybrid piece of lower humanity. She would not get to him now.

Closing all the hatch doors in his ship, he readied for weightless space travel. He had enough fire power on board the fighter pod to blow up the ship even if it did not self destruct but he had set the timers and it was only going to be himself who survived. He would find a way to seek out the other one, Jada, if he had to roam the whole Galaxy in his search.

Heading down the long launch gang-way his pod opened the outer doors automatically and was ejected into the blackness of outer space and was now free of the huge space ship that had brought him this far. He had only to put enough distance now between himself and the ship and then just stay waiting for the blast. He had managed to separate himself by about one hundred miles and would reverse his thrusters to align himself with a perfect position to fire on his own space ship. He had primed the electrical back wash to flood the tubes of the rocket thrusters, which would place a surge into the main cannon giving each tube a charged blast to the catalytic ions. Backwash from the arc thrusters eclipsed the continuous impulse and pushed the charge even more vigorously round the circuit that was humming as it screamed into a maelstrom of energy, ready to force its white hot pulse around a small igneous pellet to create a ball of lighting and plasma which would flow with the rocket. As he lay poised to ignite the cannon, he did not notice how the interior panels of the space ship began to bulge outward toward the curtain of a black thick oppressive envelope that seemed to grow with the pressure that a super gravity well would induce.

Back on board the space ship, Nina and Max had broken into the luxury suites and a group of traitor elders had surrendered on the spot but when they saw that Max was alone they jumped him and attacked him viciously, almost splitting his abdomen with one of their electric arc knives. As if Nina had exploded within her invisible world, she went into a frenzy to try and protect Max. He killed two as he was falling to the floor and Nina executed the other six almost at the same instance that they sliced him from the top of his chest only inches from his heart. With smoke rising from the acrid cuts of the electric arc and ribbon plasma knives, pungent odors choked her breath in the stale air. Nina viewed the room from side to side with the satisfaction that there was no greater danger. She then turned her attention to Max. With all the skill that a practiced surgeon could have performed she closed the open cut of the wound with the same tool that she just used to execute the traitors, sealing the wound to prevent great loss of blood and inactivity of consciousness. She still needed Max, because the trouble was not over and both of them needed to be alert.

"Max, get up! We have to get to the main control room and take a look at the ship's primary command sequence. I've got a feeling that Drakbar set up a destruct sequence on his last home and weapon's platform."

Max struggled to his feet and looked at his open wound, now just a scar with a crusty burn across the cut that had turned into a strong bandage keeping all his inner organs intact and held within his body cavity. They navigated the labyrinth back to the captain's control room and Nina began to make a wired hookup that would allow her to patch into the system via her flat robot still on board the little life pod that she and Max came over in. Hidden within the inside wall of the small torpedo-like pod was a great mass of computing power that could tap into the most layered encryption that any human had ever devised with computer assisted logic. She quickly entered the encryption separation codes while Max verbalized them to her, making lightning fast associations. They entered firewall after firewall and then targeted the destruct sequence finally and negated the last command that Drakbar gave to the computer banks within this huge ship. As she finally broke through the destruct sequence, the loop was interrupted and altered and then shut completely down.

There was only one problem now and the messages that the flat robot relayed to her made her stop her monitoring and she just looked at Max and said, "Max, he's got us targeted and is about to backwash his cannon tube, and hyper-load the charged plasma rockets."

Max just looked at Nina with a sad look in his eyes and said, "We're going to die baby. There is nothing you can do, just relax. It's over and he's won."

Nina smiled a little crooked smile and said slowly, "No, we're not, because I'm going to jam his backwash and make it stick when he releases his main electron thrust, and it will keep the load inside his tubes until it builds up an extra charge. Maybe the build up will cause some damage to his tubes, and his charge will back-fire."

She hit about fifteen different buttons on a hand held console that connected her directly to the flat robot in the life pod and then held the last button down and double charged the electron load that Drakbar was building up. She waited patiently with her finger on the red button, charging his already double charged load by remotely adding more than three times his own charge.

The sensors in the fighter pod that held Drakbar safe from Nina, were going off and he nevertheless held his double charge and then would have released his torpedo rockets into the main ship but a slight sense of movement was felt as the streaking black hole turned the cone shadow of its passing gravity well into a pitch black starless void. Stars normally visible were blackened momentarily by the passing of this cone of warped space where everything was pulled in by its gravity shadow.

Nina was still holding her precious button, trying to keep the back wash building up into the plasma rocket tubes of Drakbar's fighter pod and Drakbar himself was smiling like he did not have a worry at all when suddenly the envelope of the black orb eclipsed his space craft. Barely inclusive in the cone of the gravity well but still well beyond the hope of reprieve, he felt a shudder and his ship began to break apart not piece by piece but mercifully en-mass. Atom by atom it separated bolt from fabric and skin from skin, all leaving their original position of stability and now completely involved in the strong gravity force momentarily passing with the micro black hole that streaked on with its mayhem in tow, causing a huge destruction unheard of in any present history, so fast was its passing but so huge was the destructive force. All of his weapons detonated prematurely but already the sudden break up of Drakbar's ship and his atomic separation left such a void that even the fireball disappeared into the cone.

Chapter 17. **Lynn Is Found**

Nina and Max witnessed his destruction by the passing black hole, probably microscopic in size, but still holding a very high magnitude gravity field and an event horizon that did not let Drakbar pass its never, never land cone of a massive gravity well. He would forever travel the universe divided and compressed within a solid black core of endless atoms pressing closer and closer together, never to again breathe in a water vapor atmosphere.

Nina was now relieved and ready to return to her main concern, her sister. She asked Max what would be the proper primal code to cast into the thousands of empty minds now awaiting aboard the slave ship. If they could even think, or possibly reason within their own minds, what would they even be thinking of and what would their future be or how long would they be locked inside this prison that was within their own minds.

Hiding among so many changeless expressions was the one light in the dark void that was flickering in Lynn's mind, the memory of Nina. She heard the call of Nina's primal code and responded from the deep prison that lay shut off to the other former world of love and freedom. She vaguely remembered another life in a not so long ago fairy tale world where she was free to form her own ideas instead of having a cold electronic signal push her brain to accept all things programmed. She remembered when the first pain began. She fought very valiantly but he caught her and the needle entered her spine and the pain was unbearable. She remembered the suspended animation of pain and loss of self, only following orders from the regulation programmed sequence.

Nina pushed again from the depths of her mental awareness emanating a deep resonance within her throat that resembled the call of a whale within the ocean deep. Max called together with her and the two sounded like some strange couple of wolves that do not visit the wilderness but live the far reaches of a space world long lost. Lynn's eyes opened and her alpha brain waves activated for the first time since the long needle entered her spine and tapped into her nervous system with a small sliver of a silicon implant. The implant bridged the gap between the now cut spinal chord allowing her to continue to function as an automaton but breaking her human spark that gave her free will. She registered the low resonance within her hypothalamus and it thrilled her that she could detect the spirit of others, human, like herself. She was special and she could now remember that she had been a warrior for good and had been trying to defeat the darkness of the unimaginable that had somehow taken her spirit and closed the door to any future hope. Now the candle had been lit again and she looked around the room that she was in and noticed that she was alone. The implant would not let her move her limbs except when they wanted her to. Someone was calling to her and she wanted to respond in some way to let them know that she was alive and a real person. Bridging the gap between electron orbits and electron transference through a great space is what she wanted to do. They were calling her and that meant that she could call to them without changing the orbit of the electrons. Maybe she could migrate the resonance. The ribbon knife was like that. It sent out its loop and cut with the edge of the still intact circuit. She wanted to bend her astral loop, to extend outward to those who were calling her but just to will it would not make it so. Circling the Mandela of her thoughts around and around she managed to get the circle tighter and tighter until she opened her mind spring and out of the orbit went the loop like a loop from a far flung ribbon of thought. She could see it extending outward and with it her thoughts and words and pictures, images of her memory. She thought she cried but she wasn't really aware that tears came out of her eyes. The memories were so beautiful and she kept them circling and migrating in and out of word pictograms. Then she just relaxed and waited for what she didn't know but soon floating along with her memories was a winged messenger looking like a strobe butterfly but made up of light and sound, visual packets of communication from an old friend.

"Nina!" she answered the probe of the primal code with the same response and a short flow of information ensued.

Nina recognized her primal response and told Max, "I see her! She's got to be here waiting somewhere. We've got to find her. I know she's here."

Nina and Max went through the space ship, room by room, level by level, but then they began to encounter resistance from the other units of elite guard. They were closing in on them now and they were quickly being out numbered by fresh troops. The guard had figured out that the ship had been invaded and that they had been tricked. They were approaching from all sides and there was nothing that Nina and Max could do. Nina was still unseen and it was only Max who was taking the full force of their attack. They battled back and forth with the ribbon knives and shields and laser guns and still they wee not able to move away from where they were pinned down.

Nina began to make forays into their ranks but they knew now that she was unseen and they began to lay down suppressive fire at all targets of offensive origin. Wherever they struck there was a directional fire back at anything that blazed or made contact close to the guard troops. They knew that there was more that one because they were losing men far away from their sited opposition but they did not know how many or where they were. Nina decided to just hold her fire and when they both stopped firing the opposition quit also. Then, while there was a lull in the fire, she decided to just walk into their midst and she continued to advance unseen until she was right in the middle of them where-on she opened the arc of the ribbon knife, and the loop bloomed out from under the zone of camouflage and before the elite guard could react she had cut a circle the width and diameter of the entire bay where they had staged their assault. The ribbon arc was set to spread out from the loop at a fuzzy pattern that was roughly like a spiked loop now instead of a smooth ribbon and it caught the whole troop in one large swathe. Suddenly they all fell silent since all of their bodies were in pieces, eviscerated by the double edged ribbon arc formed by opposing atoms of charged particles set into a ribbon blade of steel-like charged particles. They never knew they were dying until they couldn't move their bodies, since they had been completely separated.

Max and Nina quickly continued their search, room by room and deck by deck until they came across the brain unit deck and were completely stunned by the thousands that lay waiting just for a command from Drakbar to wake up or to think or to move their eyes from the blank stare that meant they were in a state of temporary suspended animation until given an order.

They walked through the midst of them and then Nina said, "Here, she's got to be in this next room, I think. They opened the sliding curtain that revealed more of the brain units, this time with full bodies, human brains and limbs, but just the same dull stare or not even open eyes. In the room clearly marked on the door "FOR TERMINATION" they found her alone and just a blank stare on her face, like all the others, but Nina went to her and embraced her and there it was, that little smile that came across her lips as if she was alive but waiting for someone to tell her to laugh. She didn't laugh or speak, but Nina felt somehow that she was happier than she had been in long time. They secured her between the two of them holding her one on either side and helped her to walk. Sometimes they even dragged her, holding her arms and dragging her feet across the deck of the space ship.

They got back to the space pod with Lynn finally, and decided to take one of the other Martian pods in tow with Lynn in the second pod. She would have to be fed since they cut the feeding tube and the electrical stimulus from her brain. She was as lifeless as a doll that was permanently transfixed in one position and only now the difference was that she had a definite smile on her lovely face, the smile of someone truly happy to be rescued. Nina thought about all the others that were still in limbo on board the huge space ship and what would happen to them. Were they also like Lynn, or no? She imagined that they were just a shell of their former selves. The Terran primal codes that formed a neural network of biochemical strings were constructed to last a life time even under extreme circumstances. Lynn might recover in time and would now live to fight again.

They made it out past the reach of the other attack ships with the whole elite guard in disarray since their main forces had been decimated and left with no leadership and no attack squadron. They were still a viable force to be dealt with since there was no home for them except lawless space. They still had all the members of the brain units held captive in huge numbers. If some rogue captain decided that he wanted to take Drakbar's place then all the battles would have to be fought again in the future.

Nina told Max, "We've just won a great battle you know, but there will be another in the war to be fought in the future when they reorganize. Max was trying to get comfortable in the small space of the life pod and yet he liked being close again to Nina.

He said, "When we get to the "C.A.N." is there a potential to regroup our fighter droids in the Cleo ship to come back and destroy all the fighter pods that escorted us into the hanger bay?"

Nina said, "Yes, we will refit immediately and come back. They have a full fleet of maybe a thousand brain units that will convert to refit their own fighting strength to double what we saw. It would be better to completely destroy the whole ship along with the slave brains. They are beyond our help but they will be just used and commanded by some other captain or second in command to what Drakbar was. We have to destroy their ability to replicate or we will all be in danger of domination in the future and the next time there is no telling what kind of scientific advancement they will achieve with slave units. I can not even imagine the real consequences to us of what their actions will derive. When we get Lynn back to the ship, I want to see what her memory has recorded and see if we can play it back to find out what their strengths and weaknesses are. We should have let Drakbar destroy the ship when he had the chance and the will."

Max said in a comic relief that gave some light to her regret, "Yes, but don't you remember, darling? We were on it at the time and if he destroyed the ship then he would have really escaped. It worked out better that he escaped your revenge and as a result he fulfilled his own destiny of self destruction."

Nina replied, "If he would have failed anyway, then his second in command will be predestined to fail too. Anyway we will be there to make sure if not to just make it quicker for the sake of the entire universe. If everything was predestined, then no one would make an effort to change things for the better. Lynn tried I'm sure to resist, but she failed not because she fought back but maybe she just didn't fight hard enough or smart enough. I remember that on the day that she disappeared she went out on her own as if she could not make any mistakes or be defeated. That is why I decided to let Thomas be captain because of my own problem with over confidence. I just could not let us all fail because of my own problem with thinking that I cannot be defeated. I know that Lynn was like that but yet look how she wound up. They took her at her most vulnerable point, when she thought she was winning. They must have something that interferes with our sure knowledge of our capabilities, other than the electromagnetic pulse. We think we are being smart, but the programming of computers and electronic communication that is built into the system is making our human capabilities frail and ineffective. I want to keep our primal code programming because the packets of electronic information are just useful tools but all the little disk implants should be removed and never used again.

We will teach our children to just train their minds and pass along information by direct transfer from one person to the next and they will be better and smarter and more capable than us so they will have a better chance of survival. The things that are learned and derived by direct mental transference is the best way to become mentally stronger and not have a direct computer input. The primal codes that we locate in our minds will just have to be learned and not located by computer. That is why Bispo had her problem. She did just fine when she had to select the addresses of the coded packets of electrical information even though she had to struggle. She is stronger now because she used her mind and not the programming of the computer. The mind can be trained to perform the location lock of the directive and it will not harm the brain. Each person should be able to choose how they use their mind and not be forced to accept an electrical charge guided by a computer. Our brains have the ability to isolate the coded packets of information and use our memory for making an etched template just by memorization and not allow the computer to burn in the location of the sequence and matrix diagram. We can do that ourselves by just working the sequences and routing of the pathways with just intellectual training.

Captain Thomas and his wife have performed excellently and have learned how to run the ship and Laura has the key to the ribbon knife imprinted into her brain by only mental transference and she could use the range finder just fine without the direct help of electronics or computers. She has an uncanny ability to discern what are the important aspects of the mental primal codes.

I wonder if Captain Thomas knows that his wife is now Terran and holds the keys to the whole civilization. It was necessary that I transfer all the primal codes to her even though she thinks it was only a small vision of the ribbon knife and its properties."

Max said, "Nina, you have done what you had to do for the preservation of Terra Prime, and Captain Thomas came to us first in his search to find ways to intercept rogue asteroids from destroying the Earth. He will finally achieve his and our main concern and that is to be able to intercept the asteroids in the asteroid belt itself before their orbits deteriorate. That is the reason for this outpost and one of its prime duties. By being here in this belt of asteroids we will begin a new phase of the ability to promote the benefits of a better life for Terra and for Earth. No asteroid will be able to cross the elliptical path to harm Earth, Mars, or our Terran civilization without us knowing the degree of spiral deterioration. Our "C.A.N." station will be an outpost to give Earth a warning as well as prevent the crossing of an asteroid with a possible Earth vector. We will be able to maneuver other asteroids into its pathway should one asteroid in question be necessary to deter it or to even remove it from existence. By being in this station we are in an excellent position to prevent disaster from ever happening. Any station closer to Earth would not have advance warning or the time to respond like we will have. This will be a permanent base for all eternity or until the sun eats the Earth. After we arrive at "C.A.N." we will show Captain Thomas the reason for the outpost and he will understand that he can never return to Earth. He must captain the "C.A.N.", he and his wife, and bring forth the next generation of children to be the guardians of the asteroids. He will not like it when we abandon him there but it is for the good of all humanity. You must go back to Terra and face the council. Then, when you are found innocent you can return to "C.A.N." to live if you wish."

Nina thought, she had unwillingly accepted her fate and knew that she must return one day, but it was the only way to let Tom and Laura continue to live and not be executed. They must be marooned at the "C.A.N." to prevent anyone from discovering Terra. Also Jada must be left there for safety reasons, since she is now an outcast in Terra because the elders have discovered that she was Martian and the traitors said she was a rebel against the legitimate Mars Central government.

Tom and Laura might discover the secret to the "C.A.N." but that would have to be an acceptable consequence and what would he do if he discovered the way to really use it? What would happen if they actually used the secret to change their situation or circumstances? That would be for the future to decide but right now they still had other problems, like Drakbar's successor. So they had caught him and the black hole was with him forever. It always follows that eventually evil is its own worse enemy and the final justification will prevail in the universe. That is a known constant that those evil opposing forces against the good in the universe find their own fate. Worse than what they gave to others is what it will be. How fitting it was that such a black demonic force should find its own justice in the gravity well of a black hole.

She laughed to herself and Max said, "We should be thankful that everything went the way it did. Soon we'll be at the ship with the others and we can assess the damage done to Lynn. Don't get your hopes up too high because she has some major damage and will probably never be able to walk or speak again. If you hook her up with the electron wiring harness and totally feed her directly with stimulus to every part of her body she will work as a unit, but will not be able to respond normally and with genuine feeling and empathy. We have had enough problems with computer programming but maybe this will be the only way for her to live as an electron entity with limited response capability."

Nina looked out into the view window and saw at a distance the big ship "Cleo" that would be their home until they arrived in a short time to the "C.A.N" base and she thought how wonderful it would be to just experience real freedom of movement to walk around and not be cramped up inside a space ship even if it was the "Cleo". She had spent years of time in space and she felt inside her heart like her real home was this hollow can since she really and truly was free there and not just from being in small spaces but the elders could not control her from so far away or could they? Did they dare to come out to this outpost? They had broken off from the council and had gone over to Drakbar's ship, well, some of them. How many had she decimated with the ribbon knife and the camouflage combination? She would be executed for sure if she did not return and defend herself and her actions. They would come out here and destroy it all. Everything that she had worked for would be gone if they came here. They would not accept Tom as captain of anything and would probably kill her if they knew that she had divulged operational secrets as well as primal codes that had existed from before civilization had begun to reach its zenith in Greece. Later in America and other Earth countries they had their world wars while Terra just watched them kill each other by the millions with airplanes and bombs and not even yet had they become exposed to all the world's eyes. Terra would be vulnerable if the world powers knew of their existence and their advanced civilization living below inside the Earth. The "C.A.N." would give them the chance to expand their civilization and travel to the stars carrying their sacred people to other worlds and beyond to other galaxies. Whoever left the first "C.A.N." in deep space had this intention for sure. Maybe they just used it for a stepping stone and then just abandoned it searching still deeper and deeper into space and arriving where, Earth? From where did they come from? Did they leave Earth, or arrive at Earth? This was still a mystery that would not even give any clues, as to who these people were? Maybe deep inside the "C.A.N." was a crystal that told a story of who they were and where they came from or better yet where they were going.

Max had taken the controls of the escape pod and she knew by this that they were now fast approaching the ship "Cleo" and what a welcome it would be to feel gravity again. Soon they would be at "C.A.N.", where the constant rotation gave them real gravity that was dependable and it was full of Earth plants and animals and gave her a feeling of home and security. They still had to take care of Lynn, when they arrived at "Cleo". She would need special help that they could not give her out in space. Technically they could restore some of her motor functions as soon as the nerve centers were reconnected, but surgery was not possible this far away from an operable theater which they had on Terra. This was another reason for her to go back as soon as Lynn was stabilized.

"Max, do you think we can reconnect some of Lynn's motor functions with the help of the flat robots mapping out some of the nerve connectors and restart one of the spinal motor programs that Drakbar used in the control cell of her brain implant?"

Max did not respond immediately. He knew that she had been thinking about it all the way back and did not want to sound too optimistic about any hope for a futuristic grand recovery after what they did to her, making her into a brain unit to be commanded by a central computer under direct orders from Drakbar.

"We probably should wait until we have enough time to run over all the electronics and the programs that are obviously imbedded within her to defend Drakbar to the death. You know he has a firewall that is so redundant that you could not break into the central nervous system without actually damaging her life support?"

Nina just looked off into the view screen window at the ship "Cleo" coming up in the distance. For a minute she said nothing, hoping that the moment would give her an answer but she had none.

"I don't know what we can do to get around his firewall unless she has some small hope of leaving his control. I'm sure he still has her under control even though he is dead and gone into the darkness but still reaching out in all of these mind units. We'll have to find a pattern in his construct that will let us evade his traps and misdirects. The primal code is in a shell within her deepest thoughts and the only hope is that it will emerge to override all the aberrant behavior that he has programmed into her autonomic nervous system."

They were now both excited about joining the others and were happy to radio the news that they had found Lynn and were bringing her back.

Jada had been making preparations to get the ship underway to the asteroid belt where the "C.A.N." was located.

She said to Nina and Max, "We are so glad to have you two back with us. You can rest up and get some R&R in a nice comfortable sleeping cabin while I put Lynn into a stasis chamber. I think that would be best while we look at some of the problems that she might have in returning to the system. She will have quite a period of unlearning before we can open up the gateway to give her back her own nervous system.

Max you can go to the infirmary and we will take care of those cuts that you have. Nina will see you after you are a little better. I heard you say that the Drakbar ship is still there and there is resistance. We will regroup at "C.A.N." station and go back after them and fire a plasma cannon at the leftovers so they will not come back to avenge Drakbar's death.

Tom tells me that he is ready for the new adventure and is looking forward to the new world of real vegetation and a real atmosphere. The last time you took me to the "C.A.N.", we had a new crop of birds and I saw some baby raccoons. On Mars nothing really lives above the surface and all life is underground but I've come to love the beautiful landscapes of Earth."

They docked and soon brought Lynn into the infirmary with Max. She was a beautiful replica almost identical to Nina, her sister. All the crew was gathered around her when they put her into the stasis chamber and she had a smile, a real smile on her face that gave the blank stare of a mind unit an incredibly weird appearance of being in a coma but seemingly happy to be home.

I, Thomas Jefferson Coltrane, can now say that a new adventure is emerging and we are all together bound to another place in space and time.

EPILOGUE:

This is the first of my full length novels based on the original ten short stories. This particular one comes from the short story I called "BLUE SPIES". The characters have continued to be good and bad and I find that their character faults are also some of but not limited to my own character faults as well. They are also as in the previous book, influenced by the world of today which could be our future tomorrow. Temptation still follows all the characters and they have to deal with it in subtle and sometimes not so acceptable ways as normal people would also do in real life. However, these are not so normal people as you have found out or if you have not read the book, will soon find out. I repeat as earlier, Martian or not, we are all alienated to some extent or another when we try to deal with life's little problems. We all make mistakes including yours truly and of course that's what makes all of us human.   Cliff Rhodes

For autographed copies please write me at:
Cliff Rhodes
P.O. Box 7095
Meridian, Ms. 39304

www.lulu.com/sciencefiction
www.cliffrhodes.net

www.ingramcontent.com/pod-product-compliance
Lightning Source LLC
Chambersburg PA
CBHW050601260626
47157CB00002B/653